Silver's TROUBLE

SILVER BROTHERS SECURITIES

LACEY SILKS

MYLIT
PUBLISHING

"Life is what happens to you while you're busy making other plans." ~ John Lennon

"I don't want to remember that life and the pain. I don't want to be sad anymore. This life, with you, is much better. " She took my hand and snuggled in closer. Somewhere deep inside I agreed. This life, with her, was much better.
~ Julian Silver, Silver's Trouble

I originally wrote Layers Off in 2014. When I reread the story in 2021, I found a great need for improvement. Once the ball was rolling, the novel developed into something I didn't expect. The fresh plot, a new point of view, deeper connections and storylines, finally completed the story.

If you've never read this emotionally charged and page turning romantic suspense, I hope the tension, conflicts and character motivations satisfy your every craving. The Silver family has wrapped its talons around my heart and has helped me through the most difficult times of my life. I expect them to take you on that same adventure filled with love, laughter, and plenty of smut.

His job was to keep her pure and protected. And he failed in every way.

Trouble was Kendra's middle name, and it sang to my every fantasy as a man.
But as her guardian, I made a promise to her parents.
My goddaughter was forbidden and untouchable until I stopped resisting the temptation.

Her job was to keep a low profile. And she failed in every way.

Julian Silver was my father's best friend and the sweetest eye candy a girl could imagine. But a cruel twist of fate made him my hot, irresistible, and unattainable guardian. His bright eyes, sizzling body, and experience made for a tempting combination.
He may have called me Trouble, but I preferred Temptress and I planned to live up to my name.

Silver's Trouble is the fifth novel in the *Silver Brothers Securities Family Saga*. Can be read as a standalone novel, however, the author recommends beginning with *Silver's Rebel, Book 2*.
Intended for mature audiences.

Chapter 1

Julian

Trouble was Katherine's middle name, and it followed her like a puppy follows its mama's lead. The first time I babysat, I learned that chaos flowed through that girl's blood. I was only eighteen, and she choked on a Lego just before her baptism. My Lego. Jake and Ashley would have killed me if anything had happened to their baby girl, but I saved little Katherine because the hero complex coursed through my blood. It turns out that's not such a bad thing when you're a bodyguard. And Jake and Ashley never found out. They also never found out about the sock she flushed down the toilet. I spent half a day unclogging the throne. Or the time she fell in the pool because maintenance left the gate unlocked.

Like I said, they would have killed me. Over the years, Katherine grew, and I eased Ashley and Jake's busy schedules by babysitting. I walked through the park with a stroller while Jake completed his political whatever-Ph.D. alongside his wife, studying somewhere on the bench. I graduated from NYU and did what all the Silvers do best: built relationships. Plus schooling. Lots of fucking schooling because that's what it took to be a good private investigator. And tonight, all that prestige earned me a late night emergency phone call from my best friends.

I scanned my card at the front entrance and hurried down the long hall to my corner office, where the night security guard was waiting by the door.

"They're inside."

"Good. Inform me immediately if anyone buzzes downstairs."

"Yes, sir."

I pushed the door open. Jake and Ashley launched from the couch toward me, Jake in a pair of sweatpants and Ash in leggings and Jake's sweatshirt. The power couple from D.C. were on their way to another Congressional nomination and a win, and they looked like someone had dragged them through the trenches.

"What's going on?" I asked. "Is Katherine okay?"

Ash shook her head, crying, while their fifteen-year-old daughter sat behind my office desk, looking out the window into the night. The sky was clear, and the moon outlined Manhattan's beautiful horizon, but if I had to bet, my goddaughter wasn't paying attention to the city skyline. I glanced over at her. She was picking at the skin near one nail, and she looked like an absolute mess. Her plaid skirt was shorter than I remembered. She must have hemmed it, and Ashley must have freaked. But the spunky girl I'd known since birth seemed off.

"No. Nothing's okay. Nothing."

I passed her a tissue. "Start at the beginning."

"It's Katherine," she whispered. "She's in trouble."

Katherine drew her thumb to her mouth and chewed on her nail, staring at where Lady Liberty's flame lightened the night. Her lifeless posture combined with that stare gave me the shivers.

"Why is she in her school clothes?"

"We found her four hours after school was out, in our back-yard. It had rained, and she was soaked and didn't want to change."

"Are those blood stains?"

I hurried to the corner basket and picked up a white plush blanket, a gift from Stefanie. The psychiatrist gave my office a facelift last Christmas—and gave me a blowjob the next morning. I draped the blanket over her shoulders, and Katherine looked up. My body turned numb when I saw her features. Her long, tangled brown hair stuck to her face and neck.

"She's been asking for you. She says you're the only one who can help."

I picked her up off of my chair. A pack of bubblegum fell out of her pocket as I carried her to the other couch. Once there, she lay in a fetal position, shaking.

"Hey, Kay. You're safe now. Whatever happened, we'll fix it." I turned to her parents. "Did anyone hurt her?" The words barely passed through my throat.

"I… I don't know. I don't think so." Ashley's tiny sob broke my heart in half.

"I can make things right. No matter what it is, we can make everything right."

Katherine twisted my way in slow motion and looked up at me. The spirit I recalled in her saucer-shaped eyes had vanished.

My heart picked up speed. Jake's desperate glance over at his daughter punched me in the gut.

"What the fuck happened?"

"I need to speak to you privately." Jake stood up.

It was that serious.

"All right. Come with me. Ash, we won't be long, and you're safe. You're both safe. I promise you that."

"I know." She smoothed her hand over Katherine's arm, whispering softly, "I'm sorry."

Jake followed me through the revolving bookcase. I poured us both a scotch and handed him a glass.

"What's going on?"

"We've already spoken to Fred and Jacob. All the Silvers are on board with the plan. I called you earlier, but you weren't available."

I left the office early today for a date with Stefanie. Jake called, I answered, and thereby guaranteed myself a pair of blue balls.

"I had a date." I waved my hand. "It doesn't matter. What plan are you talking about?"

"Julian, you're her godfather. You've taken care of her since she was in diapers."

"I love her like my own."

"That's why I know we've made the right decision."

He handed me an envelope I hadn't noticed him holding. "In case something happens, this is a key to a safe deposit box. You'll find the instructions with documents. Tristan and James are setting up the operation for tomorrow, and I hope you agree…to this. We both hope you agree to this because we need you to become Katherine's guardian. Temporarily, of course."

Where the fuck did that come from, and why hadn't I woken up yet?

Blood drained from my face, and I set my glass aside. I knew the Moores were in the middle of a Congressional fight, but I had not not realized they were in trouble. "What the fuck happened?"

"We need to disappear for a little while."

"You're going into witness protection?" I guessed.

"Yes, but we can't take Katherine."

"What? Why?"

"The profile of a couple with a teenage daughter will draw

everyone we need to avoid. It won't be possible to give her a normal life, or as close to normal as we'd like."

"The Federal Witness Protection program deals with this every day. I'm sure they can handle Katherine."

"But you're the only one we trust to give her what witness protection won't: a life. A normal life."

"What about New Zealand? She was born there."

"But her life is here."

"What life, if she's in hiding? You haven't thought this through, Jake. I'm a single man without kids for a reason." Work was my life, and dating was an extra-curricular activity I enjoyed mostly in bed. Or against the wall.

He shook his head. "It's the only way to keep her safe. Your father and brother are already prepping for tomorrow." He lowered another thick manila envelope to the table. I refilled my glass and emptied it in one painful but extremely satisfying swig.

"What's happening tomorrow? And what happened to Katherine?"

"There was an accident at the school, so she can't go back. She'll have a private tutor from now on, and we'll keep in touch. Maybe not immediately, but soon. She'll stay with you, close to your parents. She loves your family, and I know you love her too. We should be back by summer." He said it like they were going on a vacation.

"Jake, I don't even have a kid. I don't have a wife or a girl-friend. How am I going to explain having a teenager?"

"The great thing about you, Julian, is you know how to adapt. And you're a good best friend and a great godfather. If everything goes according to plan, it won't be long before we're back. The FBI will find the evidence against Donaldson, and we'll be in the clear."

"Congressman Donaldson?"

"The one and only." He gripped my shoulder like the deal

we'd made to take guardianship of my best friend's daughter, all in secrecy, was final.

Wasn't it?

She was my goddaughter, and I'd vowed to protect her when her parents couldn't. The answer to that promise was simple, and Jake must have seen it in my eyes because, along with my hero complex, flowed a tsunami of courage.

"Thank you. I knew you'd come through."

"I didn't say yes."

"Your eyes did, and that's enough."

He handed me the other envelope with a thick stack of papers, marked *Kendra*, he'd been holding under his arm until now. How many of those did they have?

"Who's Kendra?"

"Ashley liked the name as a new one for Katherine. For now."

"And does your daughter know it?"

"Obviously not. We're not paying you the big bucks to do all the work, Julian. She'll need a psychiatrist, and I know you know a good one."

I couldn't get Stefanie involved in this. The reason we worked was because we were free of drama.

"Jake, I know we've been friends for a long time, but—"

"But there's no one else who can do this job better than you, and I trust no one else. You're her godfather, and it's only for a few months, Julian. After you hear the plan for tomorrow, you'll agree you're the best thing for Katherine. She already knows you, and she's comfortable with you."

"What's happening tomorrow again?"

"It's in the envelope. We have to find a place to clean up and hide out for the night, but if we're alive come morning, I'll see you then."

He turned around and went back to my office. I set my glass on the counter and hurried behind him to where Ashley was sitting beside her daughter. Katherine lay curled in a fetal position. I'd never seen the bubbly girl so frail.

"She fell asleep," Ashley whispered. "I gave her my Xanax."

"You gave her what?" I stopped mid-step. "Ash, those are addictive. I'm not sure a fifteen-year-old should take Xanax."

She turned to Jake and anchored her gaze to his. "Didn't you explain what happened?"

"I had no time for that part," he replied.

"What part?"

"We have to leave and hide before tomorrow."

"Okay, just give me a sec to catch up."

I pulled out the papers from Jake's envelope and flipped through the pages. "Oh, crap."

"You see our problem?"

I saw their problem, but I couldn't see a way out of my predicament even if I tried. No matter the choice, there'd be trouble. Lots of trouble.

"Where are you guys going tonight?" I asked. "Where are you staying?"

He pulled his fingers through his hair. "There's a contract on our lives. Donaldson hired a hitman... His name is Martinez, but that's all we know. I'm not even sure whether the security out there is sufficient." He nodded toward my office door. "I don't know where to take my wife and my kid to keep them safe."

I lowered my hand to his shoulder and gave enough pressure so he could sit beside his wife and daughter.

"You're already where you need to be. You can take Tristan's bedroom by his office. There's a shower there, too. I'm sure he won't mind. I'll move Katherine to my bed when she wakes up." God, what sounded so innocent at the time would become one of my dirtiest fantasies. Had I known the trap I was setting for myself, I would have never agreed to the arrangement.

I pointed to the stack of papers from my father. "Looks like

I have some reading to do before morning. There's food in the staff room; I wouldn't risk ordering out. Don't make any contact. Turn off your cell phones. In fact, hand them in right now."

"We already gave them to Tristan."

"Good. Well, maybe we should have started with that."

I wanted to explain the task they'd asked of me would be hard; pretty much impossible. But Silvers were great at the impossible, and I couldn't let my friends down. I'd hide Katherine in my house, and… yeah… impossible.

Fuck.

I didn't know it then, but I wasn't ready for the trouble my best friends were handing me. I was totally out of my mind, thinking Katherine could stay with me.

Then again, I hadn't been ready when Ash and Jake came over to my penthouse when Katherine was four. That emergency evening of babysitting ended with little Kay applying makeup to my face. The smeared lipstick stains over my bathroom counter weren't as appreciated. Katherine washed them off with my toothbrush. Dipped into the toilet.

"Wait a minute. What about her godmother?" I asked. "What was her name—Jodi? The one from your mother's side, Ash?" I waved my finger in the air like it was a wand and I could make Jodi appear out of thin air.

"Jodi passed away from cancer three years ago."

"Shit."

Ashley lowered her cold and shaky hand over mine. I could ask my parents, but Emma was only eight, and they had their hands full. Besides, I wasn't about to cop out. That wasn't in my blood.

"Julian, we wouldn't ask you to do this if we didn't have to."

Ashley's raw voice and pleading eyes broke through the thick wall around my heart. I covered her hand with mine and gave her a comforting smile. Katherine had definitely inherited her mother's beautiful eyes.

"I already said I'll do it," I whispered. "I'll do whatever you need me to. It's what families do, and we've been a family for a long time."

"Thank you," she sobbed, slobbering into another tissue.

I stood up and loosened the top button on my shirt.

"You two know where to find Tristan's office, and I'll have Greg show you the private quarters. He's waiting out in the hall with your security, which I assure you you don't need in this building. We've got plenty."

"Thank you, Julian." Jake handed me one more envelope. How many of those did he have?

"What's this?" I asked.

"Details about tomorrow's plan."

I scanned the papers all the way to the end, where my father and uncle had signed off on an agreement with Jake's crazy plan. We were taking a private train ride across the mountains, and tomorrow, we'd throw off the search for the Congress members and their daughter with a single flick of a switch.

"You've got to be fucking kidding me."

"It has to be real, Julian."

"You're dying?"

"Best way to stay out of the way is from six feet under. Katherine can't come with us. She needs a normal life, and you can give that to her."

They had no clue what they were asking, but the point was they'd asked, and I couldn't say no.

Ashley and Jake left for their room, and I moved Katherine to my room and my bed. I removed her shoes, coat, and sweater and tucked her in before settling back at my desk. I read over the plan my father and uncle had put together more than a dozen times that night. It was an ambitious plan with too many holes and moving parts, and it nurtured my insomnia until the morning.

I watched Katherine sleep that night, completely clueless it would be the first of many nights I'd spend with this girl. And not a single one of them would be easy, because Trouble was her middle name.

Chapter 2

Kendra

They called me a troublemaker, but that was only half right. I avoided trouble like the plague, but it followed me like a curse. My family blamed me for every broken glass and minor mishap, but if climbing out a second-story window and down a tree twisted my mother's panties, then let them twist. I might have stepped on the peonies in her front garden on the way down as well, but a party awaited. In a world where the label on your clothes and the size of your wallet defined your teenage status, the least one could do was show up. And I wanted to show up, but from now on, I couldn't. Starting today, Julian Silver would keep me jailed in his house.

I crossed my arms over my chest, and a memory of exploding brain matter flashed through my mind. I shuddered, shook it off, and stared out the train's window at the passing yellow fields of wheat. They stretched far off into the distance and glowed in the setting sun. Wheat was a lot nicer to look at than blood. The scenery had mesmerized me for three hours and helped me forget the mess I'd created. We'd reach the mountains and long tunnels by nightfall. We'd left Silver Securities at five in the morning, and I was craving a smoke. I

11

hadn't had a cigarette since Julian caught me lighting one up in his office bathroom last night. He tossed it and dragged me straight back to bed. They all thought I went to sleep, but I didn't. How could I, after what I'd done?

We sat in the upper train lounge where the glass rooftop and sidewalls opened to a panoramic view of the plains.

"Psst," I heard from across the seat, and lifted my head to meet Julian's stare. His brother was sitting next to him, dressed in the same slacks of a different shade of beige and some sporty polo shirt. They scrolled through their phones while air-conditioning tossed their fluffy hair. From what I'd been told, the women in their lives liked the messy look. Okay, nobody told me: I eavesdropped. Polo shirts and ironed slacks weren't my thing, but the Silver brothers' secret confessions by a bottle of scotch at late-night family function hours were priceless.

"What?" I barked.

"Want to go get some ice cream from the back cart?" Julian wiggled his brows. What the hell was wrong with him?

"Wouldn't that be breaking protocol?"

"Given you've broken all the protocols, troublemaker, ice cream won't hurt us."

"Yippee. Ice cream. This family escape is so much fun."

"Cut the sarcasm, Katherine. You want ice cream or not?"

What I really wanted was a cigarette. A nice, long puff to take the edge off the fact there was a contract out on my family and they were sending me to be imprisoned with my godfather.

"Is that a Glock 19 mid-range?" I pointed to the piece in his holster.

"It is."

"Fifty bucks says I can aim it better than you. Long range."

"Fifty bucks says I'll chop your little fingers off before you can get your hand on my gun."

"Fair. You're possessive. Just like with the dentist." I had no intentions of backing down, though.

"This is going to be a nightmare." He slouched in his chair. "Listen," he started, and I held back the eye roll. "I know you don't want to do this, but it shouldn't be long before life can go back to normal again." His gaze skidded to his brother, who had set his phone aside.

Tristan shifted in his seat, switching the leg he crossed over the knee.

"My house has a theater and a games room. Think of this as a nice getaway from your old folks."

"You mean old like you?"

"Me? Thirty-three is not old."

"Okay." This time I did roll my eyes, and Tristan snickered.

"What I'm trying to say is that if you stay with me, you remain invisible."

I popped my bubblegum. "Words every teenager wants to hear."

"I'll keep you safe, Kay, and you won't really have to hide."

"You don't have a pool."

"I have a hot tub."

Tristan elbowed his brother in the ribs.

"What? I do have one. And a sauna. So stop pouting and come get some ice cream with me. I'm not as boring as some orthodontists would like to believe."

He stood up and reached for my hand, pulling me off my seat.

"The dentist thinks you're boring?" I did a double take.

"No, the orthodontist does. But it's not her, it's me. Kissing someone who can't stop staring at your teeth gets weird after a while."

"Sounds like you two have a lot in common," I snickered.

"What?"

"Conversations that aren't interesting."

We stood in the middle aisle, swaying back and forth with the train's momentum.

"What do you know about dating, anyway?"

"For one, I wouldn't take a dentist to a museum. Her life is boring enough as it is. See, I know more about dating than you think. I'm not five, Julian."

"I can see that." He grunted.

"And if we're going to do this babysitting thing, I have rules."

His brow lifted, and I cleared my throat.

"Number one, no curfew. Number two, no going into my room. Number three, no touching my diary."

He gripped the seat side, steadying his stance. His jawline tensed and his forehead creased. At least, I thought it did, because Julian was good at this stone-face impression of a grumpy cat.

"I'm glad we cleared that up because I only have one rule," he said.

"One?" I looked up.

He nodded, lowered his gaze to mine, and I swallowed hard.

"You have no rules."

No rules?

"You mean as in, I have no rules and can do anything I want, or I can't make any rules at all?"

"Which one do you think?"

Right. Something told me Julian Silver would keep the reins tighter than my old security guards. It was a good thing I knew how to adapt.

I shot a glance at the back cart. "I'll tell you what. Let me make this babysitting thing easy on ya. I'll bring the ice cream, and you relax."

"You don't need me to go with you?"

I curled my ponytail around my finger, because guys got confused by the gesture.

"I'm not eight, Julian. I can handle ice cream."

What I really needed was a cigarette: a nice, long puff of nicotine to settle the anxiety in my chest. I could take another Xanax, but the addictive pills had already done a number on me a year ago. My mother just didn't know it.

Julian's brows furrowed, and he checked his watch.

"All right. A vanilla-chocolate swirl for me."

It worked every time.

"One vanilla-chocolate swirl coming up." I grinned and reached out my palm. "I don't think ice cream's free."

He regarded me for two-point-three seconds, and I added an innocent shrug. "It was your idea."

He frowned and handed me a crisp fifty. "All right, kid. I've got this one."

Kid?

Jesus, this would be easy. He wiggled his brows, and my mouth lifted into a slow curve.

They never learn.

"See you soon." I popped my bubblegum, let go of the hair from around my finger, and spun on my heel. I'd milk this crap for as long as possible.

I hurried down the hallway as I overheard Tristan whisper, "You're so gonna fail at this. She went the wrong way."

Once downstairs, I ran. I pushed my feet to the floor as hard as I could until I found a bathroom four cars down. If I locked the door, I'd gain fifteen, maybe seventeen seconds for a nice, long drag. It would take more than a cigarette to come to terms with the fact I was about to lose my parents and gain one of Manhattan's most eligible bachelors as a guardian.

I have a bodyguard for a guardian. Wonderful.

I locked the bathroom door, clicked on the fan, and fumbled for my cigarette and lighter. My hands shook, and I tightened my fists. Maybe this brief break I'd get from my parents was a blessing, and Julian was a good godfather. A pretty fun one, too. He sometimes dropped me off at school on his motorcycle. Heads turned and girls squealed. At least, that's what I'd seen and heard as I hopped on and secured my helmet. He sported a darker stubble during the week, but shaved on the weekends for his boring doctor dates. I knew that because he spent most weekends at my parents' pool, drinking scotch with my father. Eavesdropping was my thing.

I finally found my cigarettes, removed one from the packet, and lit it, inhaling long and hard. The first hit of nicotine hit my lungs. I let out a cough and quickly took another drag. Julian would kill me and the sooner I figured out when I could sneak out, the better.

I already knew he slept on guard. He also stuttered when he was nervous and had that notorious look of mischief. I liked that best about him. I bet the doctors weren't as good in bed as they were at their jobs if none of them stuck around. He needed someone fun, but also, someone who knew him. It obviously wasn't the orthodontist.

The nicotine eased the tension around my neck, and I leaned back against the wall. If I could just forget yesterday… An image of splattered blood flashed through my mind. Suddenly, a hard knock on the door sounded like a gunshot in my ears, startling me.

"Ahh!" I screamed.

"Kay? Are you okay? Are you smoking in there?"

The train car hit an uneven track, and I shut my eyes, "Noh, argh…" I coughed into my sleeve.

"Open the door, Kay. I can smell it out here. Your parents are going to kill you."

"Which is exactly why this door should remain closed."

"Open the door," Julian warned. The door handle wiggled, and the lock clicked next. I dropped my cigarette in the trash and exhaled the smoke before he broke through.

"What the hell are you doing?"

"I'm on my way to get ice cream."

His jawline tensed because we both knew I wasn't.

"You screamed. Why did you scream like that?"

"Like what?"

"Like someone was about to kill you?" He looked me over. "You don't remember, do you?"

"Shut up," I whispered. "I don't want to remember. I close my eyes and there's blood and brain matter and more blood. So no, I don't want to remember."

"Is that why you smoke? To take the edge off?"

I chewed on my fingernail, waiting for the lecture. Julian sighed and braced his hands on his hips.

"You're not the only one who doesn't want to be here, you know?"

"What? Are you missing out on a date? It's not like you can't get another one."

"Something tells me I'll be missing out on more than a date," he mumbled.

I so wished for another smoke.

"Which one is it this time? The dentist or the OB? I know it's not the nurse from the night shift—"

"How do you know?"

He towered above me, and I leaned in until his shadow covered my face. I looked up. "You took the dentist to the summer Silver brunch, the OB came to Thanksgiving, and the nurse showed before the OB pulled away in her Mini Cooper. Mini Cooper, Julian."

He inhaled with control and wiggled his nose, sniffing the air. "What's wrong with a Mini Cooper?"

The train swung around a curve.

"He's into a therapist now." Tristan braced against the wall, and Julian threw him a dirty look.

"I haven't met the therapist," I said.

"I didn't know you smoked." Julian removed the lighter from my hand. "But I get it. You're upset."

"You won't tell my parents, will you?" I stepped outside the bathroom, and Julian shut the door with such force that I jumped.

"You know what? It doesn't even matter if you do, because they're going into witness protection."

"But it does matter, Kay. You're young, and your life is just beginning. You just have to get through the next few months."

"What life? No dating, no boyfriend, no school, no friends. You...you'll get to continue as you were, and everyone else... They'll think I'm dead, Julian. How is that fair? All of my friends will grieve."

"That's only three people, Kay."

I shoved my fist into his hard chest, and he gripped my wrist.

"You're an asshole, you know that? That's why the gyno canceled her last date."

The train slowed around a curve, tilting, and I fell into Julian's firm hold. He released his grip on my wrist, and I looked up at his grumpy face.

"You'll attend school online," he scoffed.

"Why does school matter, anyway? I'm about to die, aren't I?"

"Technically." Tristan kept his stance wide and steady on the train cart, looking around for something.

"It's not *technically*. On paper only." Julian set me straight, fixed his polo shirt, and spun me back to our car. "And temporary. Now let's go back to our seats."

The train lights flickered. The car turned dark for a moment, and before the lead lights in the floor illuminated the cabin with a soft glow, I realized the grave mistake I'd made. I turned around and bumped into Julian's hard chest.

"I've got you." He held the sides of my arms to steady my stance.

"What's that smell?" he asked.

"I made a mistake. My cigarette…in the bathroom garbage."

He whipped around and went into what I could only describe as Julian mode. Smoke billowed out the door.

"Quick, get an extinguisher."

Tristan lunged to the floor and grabbed a fire extinguisher from a compartment I didn't know existed. He threw it over my head at Julian. "Stop the fire before our location is compromised."

I covered my face with my sleeve.

"What the hell did you spray in there, Kay?"

"Hand sanitizer. I left my hand sanitizer on the sink. That's all."

He opened the bathroom door and pulled on the extinguisher handle. White foam spewed out, covering the smoke and fire. A high-pitched sound pierced my ears as the screeching brakes halted the train's momentum, raising goosebumps on my arms. Julian dropped the fire extinguisher, and I flew forward, right into his arms. He gripped a handle overhead, supporting both his weight and mine as the force pushed us together. Tristan crushed in behind me, squeezing me into Julian and forming a Silver sandwich with me in the middle. I'd eavesdropped on that one too.

"Change of plans," he said.

"What change of plans?" My head whipped up to Tristan.

He exchanged a look with Julian, who grabbed my hand and pulled me toward the exit. The train door opened, and the three of us hopped off. Bright orange fire billowed out of the panoramic lounge where we'd left my parents.

"Oh, my God."

Tristan grabbed my hand. "Let's go, Kay. We need to get out of here."

"They found us? Oh, my God—they found us because of the fire. It's my fault they found us."

An explosion blasted from the front of the train and through the tunnel. Julian slammed his body into mine, forcing us into a nook. My ankle smashed against the wall. I must have screamed, but I couldn't hear my voice through the blast. Hot wind blew, and the ground shook. I opened my eyes and peeked over his shoulders at the rushing thick smoke.

My parents!

Julian grabbed me under my arm before I screamed again, removed me from the nook, and swung me over his shoulder like a sack of potatoes. I lifted my head and watched the fire spread through the train cars in the tunnel while Julian rushed me out of the darkness. He set me on the ground. The brothers supported me underneath each armpit. I hopped on one foot over a steep bank into yellowing bushes, but landed on a bunch of rocks, losing my footing. I pulled the brothers to the ground, and we tumbled down the hill. Rocks and brush thorns scratched along my arms and legs. My foot hit someone's jaw, and an elbow connected with my ribcage. I wanted to hurl, but we finally came to a rolling stop, with me on top of Julian.

"You all right, kid?" he asked.

I blinked rapidly, trying to process what had happened. I didn't know it then, but it would take years for the shock to settle.

The brothers rented a car and drove us back home to Julian's house on Long Island in silence. Marge Silver, his mother, had left steaming food on the counter, but I had no appetite.

"You can switch rooms tomorrow if you'd like. You can choose whichever one you like." Julian showed me to a perfectly staged room, with white and black pillows, crisp covers, and not a wrinkle in sight. He turned on the lamp at the bedside and opened the bathroom door.

"Thanks," I said.

"That's the bathroom and the second entrance to a library."

He pointed them out like I didn't know every nook of this house from the days we'd played hide and seek. He was trying to be nice. I got it, but the train blast had stripped my emotion.

"Julian?" I stopped him before he left. "Are they dead?"

"You need to get some rest, Kay. Tomorrow's a new day, and… We'll get through this, okay?"

I gave a clipped nod, and he sat on the bed beside me.

"Your hands are freezing." He closed his large hands around mine, gently massaged them, then drew them up and blew a warm breath of air. "Kay?"

"Yeah."

"I'm sorry."

"For what?"

"Everything. It can't be easy being a congressman and congresswoman's daughter."

"It wasn't easy. I didn't think they'd die; and now they're gone." I had no tears left inside of me. I had nothing.

"I'm sorry," he whispered and pulled in my stiff body for a hug "Good night, Kay."

"Good night."

He tucked me in that night the same way he had when my parents flew out of town for work, and I never thought I'd miss my mother's tuck more. But this wasn't my bed, and it wasn't my home. It never would be.

I tossed and turned well past midnight, listening to every sound and crack in the new but familiar house. What if they found us? What if they knew we had escaped? What if they found Julian's house? Who were *they*, anyway? I finally pulled the covers aside and tiptoed to Julian's bedroom, where he was snoring. I slipped underneath the covers at the foot of his bed without waking him, and I fell asleep.

Chapter 3

Julian

six months later

Kendra's scream tore through the house like a hurricane. I let go of the coffee mug and it crashed on the floor.

"I'm coming!"

I raced up the stairs two at a time and into my bedroom, where I found her curled in my bed, sobbing and shaking. I lifted her off the sheets and cradled her in my arms. She snuggled against my chest, muffling her whimpers.

"Wipe the blood. You need to wipe the blood. It's everywhere."

"There's no blood, Kay."

"It splattered on the floor."

"It's okay, Kay. I've got you."

I held her against me, swaying back and forth until her tears stopped. Her long hair stuck to her neck and chest. Kendra's nightmares had recurred every night since the first night we'd come home. She snuck into my bed because she couldn't fall asleep, and finally, I just let her use my bed. I set up a mattress by the wall for myself. I tried using one of the guest bedrooms, the couch, and even the hammock outside, but she always ended up beside me for the night. Kay couldn't be alone, and this was the only way I could help.

I brushed her hair out of her face. "All better?"

She snuggled harder into my chest.

"I had a dream where I was someone else." She exhaled, letting go of the night terrors. "I had a different life. I went out to the movies and walked around the park. I... I wasn't an orphan anymore, and I wasn't afraid."

I wished I could explain she was stuck in circumstances beyond her control, and that one day, life would go back to normal. Except I didn't know when that day would be.

"That sounds nice, Kay," I said.

"But is it?" She pulled away and looked up. "Is it a real life if all I can do is dream about it?"

The sight of her flushed cheeks and swollen eyes broke my heart in half.

"You're right. It's not. That's why I've asked my father and Tristan to reevaluate your case for a threat."

She sat up straight and adjusted her t-shirt. "What does that mean?"

"It means maybe things can change. Move forward."

"Can I have friends?"

"Ahem... We can work on getting you some new friends. No old ones, because... Well, someone could still recognize you."

She wiped her cheeks, slid off my bed, and shuffled her feet toward the bathroom.

"I'm... I'm a basket case, aren't I?"

I followed her to my washroom. She'd left her toothbrush in my cup on day two. Every time I moved it to the washroom beside her room, it found its way back here, so I stopped moving it.

"You're not a basket case."

She turned on the tap, moistened the brush, and added toothpaste. "Of course I am. I barely passed algebra."

"We can find a new tutor for September."

"That's not my point, Julian. I thought I'd be back home by now, and now... Now my life is a mess. I'm gonna be stuck here for the summer, aren't I?"

The plan my father and uncle had made for Kendra's case had gone AWOL. Well, half-AWOL. We needed evidence of self-defense, and we couldn't find it. Bottom line was, Kendra would stay with me for a while. Also, Kendra hated her new name.

"You're not stuck."

"Then what do you call it?"

"Adapted?"

She rolled her eyes. "Summer's just around the corner, and you don't even have a pool."

"You can swim at Wilma and Fred's."

"Don't you get it? It's not about swimming. I don't want to swim, I just want to *live*, and it feels like I'll never be free. Six months, Julian. I've been stuck here for six months. That's one hundred and eighty-three days. If my parents are dead, why would anyone want to go after me?"

Donaldson had a million reasons to put a hit on Kendra if he knew she was alive.

She put the toothbrush in her mouth and brushed her teeth with quick, hard strokes, her elbow flying like a violin bow. The first three weeks of her grief had been the hardest. I could barely leave her alone for five minutes, but we'd made progress since then. I worked from home, organized her doctor visits, and called one Silver meeting after another to change Kendra's trajectory. Her faked 'death' on the train had bought us some time, and hopefully her new identity would keep her safe until Donaldson was behind bars.

"The therapist said—"

She removed the toothbrush from her mouth. "I'm not going back to therapy."

"Kay—"

"Over my dead body, you hear me? I get it. I'm stuck here. I have no life. How long is this gonna last? Two more months? Six? A year? It's not like I have a choice."

She stared at me, but I had no answer. Unfortunately, the choice wasn't up to me. Her parents' directives had been clear: keep her locked in the house.

I shuddered. I'd never had a kid, nor a teenager, but I imagined keeping them behind closed doors was no answer to any solution.

"You don't even know, do you?"

"Kay, it's complicated."

"Maybe it's time to make it less complicated." She shut the bathroom door in my face and locked it.

"Kay." I knocked on the door. "Kay, open the door. I don't want you to feel you're in a prison."

I heard her open the drawer and fumble with something.

"Kay?"

"Privacy! Want to know how to live with a teenager? Then give her privacy."

I punched my fist through the air and used another bathroom to get ready for the day. An incoming message dinged on my phone from Stefanie.

Stefanie: Looking forward to tonight

Shit. I'd forgotten about the date. Dating with Kendra in the house wasn't as simple as it used to be. I no longer brought women back home because fucking without making noise was impossible. Hotel rooms might not have been as personal, but much better than having a teenager listening to my groans on the other side of the wall.

Julian: Me too

I went downstairs, cleaned up the broken mug and poured

myself a fresh cup of coffee just as Kendra sauntered into the kitchen.

"What the hell did you do?" I covered my mouth with my hand and set the coffee aside.

She stood in the doorframe, outlined like a perfect picture of desperation. Chunky strands replaced her long hair, all different lengths, and the sheer pain in her eyes broke my heart.

"It looks that bad?"

"Wh…why would you chop off your hair like that, Kay?"

She drew in a long sniffle, then blew her nose into a tissue she had scrunched in her hand.

"Because there's nothing else left of the old me in here." She pressed her fist to her sternum. "I don't even have my name, and I want to… I want to go to the movies or sh…shopping. So…so no one can recognize me." She was stuttering. Kendra never stuttered. "I don't want to draw attention, but now everyone will look at me because I look like a freak."

She pointed to the attempted pixie cut and broke down, shuffling her feet to the kitchen. I took her into my arms and wrapped my arms around her and held her until the sobs stopped.

"Can you fix it? You can fix anything, Julian. Can you fix this?"

I let her go and removed the ingredients from the fridge.

"I can't, but I know someone who can. I'll call her after breakfast to come over and…fix it."

She drew her arms close to her body. She'd chopped her long locks in uneven lengths, and I hoped Grace Wagner could work some magic.

"You know what? Grace actually owns a private salon. Like for celebrities. I'll drive you there myself."

Kendra perked. "Wait—you mean, I will actually go out? To the city?"

I gave a slow, measured nod.

"I'll have to come with you, but I think it's safe enough to arrange a haircut. You need a life, Kay. And you need new friends. I don't know how to do that…you know…get you new friends. It's been a while since I've had to make friends."

Her smile grew the widest I'd seen in months. She jumped up, threw her arms around my neck, and wrapped her legs around my waist. I lowered her to the floor, her petite frame brushing against every part of my body that needed a lay, and suddenly felt awkward, which reminded me to call Stefanie.

I lowered Kendra to the floor, texted Grace, and received an immediate reply.

"One o'clock appointment."

"Ahh," she screamed, dramatically stamping her feet in one spot and then spinning in a circle. I laughed out loud, watching her sing a tune I didn't recognize and dance around the kitchen. It was a much nicer sight than watching her crumble.

Kendra's knees bounced on our way to Grace's salon. We parked in the back and used the employee entrance, with no one spotting us.

"Oh." Grace covered her mouth when she saw Kendra.

"That bad?" Kendra asked.

"Nothing I can't fix. I've been wondering when you two would show up." She looked straight at me.

"You have?"

Grace glanced over at Kendra and lowered her voice. "You'd think a bodyguard would know changing appearance can keep someone in hiding safe."

"I know. It's been…"

Between the nightmares, homeschooling, my work, and becoming a parent of a teenager, I'd slipped. I shouldn't have waited six months to do this. "Forget it. Thank you, Grace. I truly appreciate it. How long do you need? Half an hour?"

"Well, you're obviously not a woman. Four hours minimum."

"For a haircut?"

"No, but Kendra deserves to be pampered." She shrugged. Kendra's head flew from Grace to me with a big smile, and she tiptoed on the spot. "So, that's what we'll do. Facial, manicure, pedicure, a mud-bath, light massage, and then the cut. It's not like she's busy, is she?"

"I'm not."

I sighed, glancing over at the stretching grin on Kendra's face. The last time I'd seen her this hyped was just before we got on the park carousel when she was eight. "All right. Let's pamper the girl." I set my watch. "I'll be back in three hours."

"Four hours," Grace corrected.

"Four."

"Can I use the washroom? I was so excited I forgot to pee at home."

"First door on your left. I'll be right in."

Kendra went inside, and Grace touched my arm.

"Don't worry, Julian. You may feel you're alone in this, but you're not. The family's been working hard on integrating Kendra back into society as your niece."

My brows furrowed. I'd discussed Kendra's progress, or lack thereof, with doctors and family daily. She was free to go between my house and my parents' adjacent property, where she used the pool, but the space around the cove wasn't enough for a teenager. She had no friends, and I was certain the lack of social life would eventually catch up to her.

"Wait—how do you know this?"

She rolled her eyes. "I own a salon, Julian. People talk."

"What people? No one's supposed to talk about Kendra. No one's supposed to know she's alive. I promised her father—"

Her grip on my arm tightened. "Except she *is* alive and likely feels invisible. Today is a good first step. You did well.

And by people, I meant family. I did Wilma's hair last week when she came in with your Aunt Teresa."

I let out a shaky breath and smiled. "Thank you for your help, Grace."

"You're welcome. I'll see you soon."

I went back to my car and dialed Stefanie's private number.

"Hey, how's it going?"

"Not too good. Kendra cut her hair. Actually, she chopped it. Grace is fixing it, but I'm calling you about the thing we talked about last week."

"She's not my patient, Julian."

"I know, but would you meet up with her? Just for a walk in the park, or something, to see if she qualifies."

"Your niece should see her own doctor."

"Whom she doesn't trust? The same one she won't open up to?"

I heard her sigh over the receiver. "All right, but I'm at work right now."

"Are you free after work?"

"I am."

"I'll text you the details. See you soon."

I stayed in the car, lay back in the seat, and closed my eyes. Kendra's nightly terrors and my disturbed sleep were catching up to me. Watching her body twist during her nightmares was pure agony and sometimes, I wished she could forget the past. I wished she could concentrate on her future. A hard knock on the car window startled me, and I reached for my gun.

"Open up. It's me, silly."

Kendra's eyes flashed open wide, and her smile stretched from ear to ear on the other side of the window.

I pulled open the door and stepped out of the car. "Is that makeup?" I asked, and Grace shook her head.

"Girls my age wear makeup." Kendra pulled her coat together.

"It's nice. You look good. I like it."

Her smile broadened. "Really? Like…you like it enough to let me go to a shopping mall?"

"Baby steps, Kay."

"That's the point, Julian. I'm not a baby anymore, and I'm tired of taking baby steps, whatever that means."

"You may not be ready for a shopping spree, but we are going out to dinner."

"We are? Today? Where to?"

"It's a surprise. Hop in."

Kendra threw her arms around Grace's neck and I was pretty sure my heart skipped a beat. Kendra ran around the car to the passenger's side, and Grace handed me a bag. "I gave her some product to take home—you know, because she said she can't go shopping."

"Thank you, Grace."

"And you're welcome to come anytime you'd like, Kay. I mean that."

"Thank you. Hey, Grace?"

"Yeah?"

"I'm not good at this parenting thing. Or talking to a teenage girl thing. Is it okay if she calls you sometimes?"

"Of course. And for what it's worth, you're doing great."

Kendra buckled in and I pulled away. As I drove, I listened to Kendra tell me all about her experience at Grace's salon until I pulled up to the cemetery and she shut up.

"I… I didn't know you were going to take me here."

"You haven't been to your parents' graves yet."

"I haven't been to my grave, either."

"I think it will help with the grief and help you move on."

She sat motionless, and I wondered whether I'd made a mistake. The silence buzzed in my ears, and I waited for what seemed like hours for her to say something.

"Okay, Julian. I trust you. Let's do this."

We walked to the gravesite hand in hand. Kendra's grip tightened as we stepped in front of the gravestone.

"You okay?"

"I'm not sure. It feels weird seeing my name…there."

"With time, you'll be able to come here and chat with them."

"It's not the same," she whispered with a shudder.

"What are you thinking about?"

"The train. The accident. All those times I told my mother how much I hated her, instead of telling her I loved her." She pulled in a sniffle. "Every time I see the sun rise, I remember our beach walks. When I smell coffee, I can see my father sitting by the kitchen counter, and when you pop in the frozen croissants, I can see my mother making a fresh batch."

"I'm sorry, Kay. I wish I could do more to help—"

"How do I forget, Julian? How do I forget so I don't have to remember all this pain? How do I forget what I've done so I don't have to feel this void in my chest? I'm tired, Julian. The nightmares exhaust me. They're on a loop, and I ride that stupid train and can never get to the destination. I'm not sure it will ever stop hurting here." She pressed her fist to her heart, and my chest tightened. "I'm an orphan, Julian. An orphan with horrible memories and no social life."

This was the most Kendra had said to me since I took over her guardianship.

"You're not an orphan, Kay. You have me and I've got you, so there. Not an orphan. And I have an idea how to help you, but I'm not sure if it's the right way to go."

"How?" she asked.

"The therapist I'm dating is a hypnotherapist. She said she can ease the disturbing memories and nightmares."

"Like help me forget the accident?"

"Not forget them—suppress them, and make life easier for you. You could go to the movies or shopping without fear. Make new friends, and—"

"I'll do it."

"There are risks."

"It's not like they can bury me again."

I sighed. "Kay, there are people in this world capable of more harm than murder."

"Is that who I'm hiding from?"

I tipped my head once and pointed to Kendra's old name on the gravestone. "You're safe for as long as they believe the writing."

"What if they recognize me?"

"Even I couldn't recognize you with this hair, but we'll take precautions. The contact lenses help too, but most importantly, no one suspects you're alive. It's exactly what we wanted."

She stared at the gravestone for another forty minutes, standing still, like the angel statue three rows over. Kendra took a deep breath, released it, and turned on her heel to face me.

"I'll do it. Whatever it takes to suppress these memories, I'll do it. Hypnotize me."

Chapter 4

Kendra

one year later

$\mathcal{J}$ulian cleared his throat. I lowered my book and looked up at the set of keys he was dangling in front of my face.

"What's that for?"

"You have your driver's permit now, so I thought we could go for a ride." He grinned.

"Me? Drive?"

"That's the next step after a permit, isn't it?"

"Well, yes, but I don't even have a car."

"Driving is a life skill, whether or not you have a car. Get dressed and come to the front. I'll pull out in front of the garage."

I swung my legs off the window seat and jumped into his arms. "Oh, my God!" Julian set me down, and reality hit me. "I'm going to kill us both."

"You won't."

"You should wear a life jacket."

"It's a car, Kay, not a boat."

"Still, wear something. Preferably something fluffy. You know, to protect yourself, because if I crash and kill you, I'll have no one left."

His breath hitched, and he stared at me until I wondered whether I had spinach from my morning omelet stuck between my teeth.

"You'll be fine. I'm an excellent teacher. Come on, get dressed."

I hurried upstairs, put my hair in a braid, and changed into a comfortable pair of leggings, but when I stepped outside, a new predicament hit me.

"There's water on the ground, Julian."

"That's usually what happens after it rains."

"It's slippery. I'm going to total your car."

"Then it's a good thing you're not driving my car."

I followed him to the side driveway where someone had parked a pearl white Jaguar with a red bow on its hood.

"Happy early birthday," he said.

"My birthday's in six months."

"I thought you could use it earlier—you know, go for a drive. I don't know."

"Julian, I don't go anywhere."

"Which is exactly why you need a car. Look, I'm not telling you to drive on a highway. Just the neighborhood. And again, it's a life skill."

I didn't need life skills when I had Julian. Since the accident, he'd become my best friend, drove me to therapy, answered all the questions I asked and never lied. But he wouldn't be mine forever, and he was right—driving was a life skill. I removed the keys from his hand with a grin.

"Let's go, if you dare."

It turned out I was a skillful driver: like riding a bike. Julian had lowered the convertible's roof, and warm wind blew through my hair. We cruised around the neighborhood before taking the shoreline drive to Oyster Cove Park. I parked along the beach, taking up two parking spots, backed out, and straightened the car into its place.

"You've driven before. You must have," he said.

I scrunched my shoulders against my neck. "If I have, I don't remember."

There was a lot I no longer remembered from a year ago, like why we went on that damn train trip in the first place, but I tried not to focus on things out of my control and create my story. After my third hypnosis session, the nightmares stopped. A session later, I couldn't recall the terrors, just that I'd had them.

"You did awesome, Kay. Come on, there's something I want to show you."

We walked along the beach end and turned inside the park, where a horse and carriage carousel pinned the park's center. As it spun, kids cheered over the music. The twinkling lights, laughter, and the smell of popcorn, hot dogs and fried oysters brought back nostalgia, and I stopped.

"You remember this place?" he asked.

"I think so. Sort of, but from long ago."

Julian sat on a bench and stretched out his legs. I sat by his side and glanced his way.

"I used to take you for walks around this park in a carriage while your parents studied. Then when they ran for office, we'd make a special trip out here for hot dogs. You topped them with triple the sauerkraut."

"Ew, gross."

He laughed, prompting my chuckle, but then his expression fell serious.

"Your parents loved you very much, Kay. You had a good upbringing and a good life. What I'm trying to say is, the things you don't remember don't make you who you are. *You* make you, and you're growing up to be a smart and beautiful young woman. I'm very proud of you."

I felt my cheeks heat and my heart warm. My belly swirled and my insides flipped before settling. I took Julian's hand in mine. "I have a good life now too, with you, so thank you for taking care of me."

A flush of red dusted his cheek.

"I mean, come on. You bought me a frickin' car. You entertain my wildest requests—"

"Ordering pizza at two in the morning is not wild."

"But flying out to Key West and then driving up along Florida Keys to ease my anxiety is."

"You had a nightmare," he whispered.

"And I no longer have them, thanks to you."

"So you don't wish you could remember more?"

"Not at all." I squeezed his hand. "I have everything I need."

He leaned in with a whisper, his warm breath curling down my neck. "I'm glad to hear that, but you know what I need?"

"What?" My airway constricted.

"Sauerkraut hot dogs." He pointed across the park to a vendor.

Sauerkraut hot dogs?

I licked my lips.

"Come on, Kay. I bet you'll love it."

He pulled me up off the bench, and I let go of his hand. We walked across the park and ordered two hotdogs, topping them with the pickled cabbage. I took my first bite and my eyes flew open.

"Wait, wait. I need more sauerkraut."

Julian belted out a laugh. "Told you so."

I scooped more onto the hot dog until the taste reminded me of something I loved in my past. The happy feeling wrapped around me like a blanket.

"You know what this reminds me of? Being happy. That's all. I just want to be happy." I stuffed the last piece of hot dog in my mouth and washed it down with root beer.

He placed his hands on my shoulders. "I'll make sure you are happy, Kay."

"Because you made a promise to my parents?"

"That, and because I care for you."

I leaned into his side and against his muscular arm. "Thank you for the car. I didn't expect it."

"That was the point of the surprise. Also, I've been thinking about what you said last week. Let's screen a few of your friends from online school and see if they can come over. Do a movie night or a bonfire by the lake."

"You're serious?"

"There's no threat, Kay. We've kept low key for a year, and with ongoing precautions, I think we can integrate you back into life. You'll be an adult in a year and a half, choosing schools and a future."

"Except I have no clue what I want to do."

"Well, whatever you decide, you'll have my full support. I promise."

"Pedophile." a male voice called out from behind us and we both turned around, clearly confused.

"Yeah, I'm talking to you." He pointed a finger at Julian.

"Shut the fuck up. You don't know what you're talking about."

"I see what I see, and he's looking at you like... well, gross."

"We are none of your business." I swept my arm for him to go away, while Julian stood up and paced around the bench. His calculated, confident pace toward the guy near the swings gave me the shivers. He towered over the blond dude with shoulder length hair who couldn't be over twenty-one.

"Get the fuck away from here, punk," he said.

"It's too late. I already called the cops."

"What?"

Julian spun on his heel and strode my way.

"Take the keys and drive to my parents. Not our house, you understand?"

I blinked rapidly. The tightness around my eyes brought on a headache.

"You'll be fine, Kay. You can drive."

"I don't have a license."

"Then drive well, because you can't be here when the police arrive." I glanced back at the fuck turd. "We don't know who we can trust."

"All right, all right. I can do it,"

"I know you can. I'll join the family after I deal with the police and this fuck turd."

He kissed me on my forehead and turned me toward the car.

"Wait, where is she going?" he asked. "I called the cops."

I glanced back over my shoulder to Julian's stomping legs and determined walk. He was fuming, but looked pretty hot from the distance.

"They'll get here and give you a ticket for false accusation and wasting force resources. After that, I'll sue you for personal defamation. By the way, she's my niece, you fuck turd."

I don't know what happened afterward, but I hurried to the car and drove back to Wilma and Fred's. The two Rottweiler puppies ran around the yard, wagging their tails, and Emma squealed in the middle of them both.

"I see you caved in." I hugged Wilma.

"Did you drive that car here?" Fred asked.

"We ran into trouble at the park. A guy called Julian a pedophile and called the police."

"What?" Wilma took me into her arms again. "Oh, honey, I'm so sorry."

"It's not that big of a deal. Julian's my guardian and a good friend. I see how someone could misinterpret that."

A frown etched into the side of Fred's mouth. "He'll take care of it, I'm sure."

Julian showed up an hour later and simply told me he'd

handled the situation and I had nothing to worry about, so I didn't.

We stayed with his parents until the evening. His aunt and uncle joined, along with his cousins and their girlfriends. My evening of laugher and charades was nice until Stefanie arrived. Julian's girlfriend, whom he never referred to as a girlfriend, wrapped her arms around his neck and kissed him hard on the lips. He pulled away from her in discomfort, and I looked away when Stefanie caught me staring. Julian never favored public displays of affection. He handed her a wineglass and whispered something in his ear. She laughed and pulled her finger down along his arm, while he bent down and kissed her shoulder.

I continued my treatment with Stefanie every two months, but it was weird seeing them together at a family function.

I grabbed Hunter by the elbow and pulled him aside. Although Julian's cousin didn't work for Silver Securities, he'd already guaranteed himself a job at the family-run investigating and protective services company.

"How serious is this thing between Julian and Stef?"

"You're the one who lives with him. You should know." He shrugged.

"I can't know because he never brings her home, and he doesn't exactly tell me when he goes out on dates."

"Why do you care?"

"I don't know. I just don't want him hurt or used."

"They've been together longer than Gabe and Joanne, and James and Tiffany."

I rolled my eyes. "Tiff's such a gold digger."

"Yeah, but she also gives ass whenever James wants."

"Gross. So you think that's why Julian's with Stef? For sex?"

"Three years is a long time at his age. If he felt more, he wouldn't be sneaking around with her."

"How do you know he's sneaking around?"

"Has he ever brought her home?"

"No."

"That should tell you how serious or not they are. Aren't you a little too young to think about sex?"

He tipped his bottle of beer and sighed, like he was quenching a week-long thirst.

"You're six months older than me, Hunter, and I know you're not a virgin, so stop being a hypocrite."

"Who's a hypocrite?" Hunter's mother, Teresa, walked up, and I greeted her with a kiss on each cheek.

"Hunter."

"She's kidding, Mom."

"I hope so, because I'd like to think I raised my boys better than that."

"How was Mr. Silver's heart surgery?" I asked.

"No complications. He should be released in a few days. Hunter, I thought you updated the family on your father's progress."

"I haven't had a chance, Mom." He then turned my way. "Dad's doing well, Kay."

"That's great to hear. Please send him my best wishes."

"Thank you. I'm gonna go make my rounds." Teresa gave me a kiss on the cheek and went to refill her glass with wine.

"See you later, Mom." Hunter waved, but then Grace Wagner drew my attention to the rocks. She was wearing a very revealing and sexy dress and headed our way.

Hunter stilled and stared as she sauntered down the lawn in her high heels, staying on the front of her feet until the walk on the grass became uncomfortable and she removed her Louboutin heels. He watched as she took off one pump, then the other. His lip curled and his grin spread as she paced bare foot. Though she was walking toward us both, Grace seemed focused on Hunter.

"Hey, you two."

"Nice to see you again, Grace." We exchanged a quick hug.

Hunter stiffened at the exchange.

"Are you coming to the spa for some R & R soon?" she asked. Grace had been nice enough to book me in for some spa time every few months, and she never charged me a penny. She was a role model, and one day, I hoped to be half as successful a woman as she was.

"Of course. I was thinking of taking Emma for her birthday next month."

"Oh, I've got that set up already, so you're all booked in."

"Sounds awesome."

She turned toward Hunter and twirled her hair around her finger. Apparently I wasn't the only one with sleek moves.

"Hunter, I was wondering whether you have some time tomorrow. I need help with the boat. The engine's making weird sounds."

"Yeah, I'll drop by. Just tell the ladies not to stare so much this time."

"Stare at what?" I asked.

"Grace's neighbors like watching me do maintenance work on her car."

"You fix her cars?" I asked.

"It was just an oil change."

"Hunter's very handy." Grace tracked her hand over the muscled part of his arm.

"Grace," someone called out from the bonfire. "Grace, come look at this."

"Sounds like I'm needed elsewhere. I'll see you tomorrow."

"Yeah, see you tomorrow."

I waited until she left and punched Hunter on the same arm where Grace's hand had been.

"No!"

"Shut up. Nobody knows."

"You and Grace? I thought you two hated each other. I

believe you said you were sworn enemies at some point. How long has this been going on?"

"A while, and I swear to God if you say anything about Grace, I will tell Julian you have a crush on him."

"You'd be lying."

"Would I?"

While I would never deny Julian was hot, I didn't have a crush on him. He was my best friend and the one person by my side after my parents' deaths.

"I can't believe you've got a Mrs. Robinson situation on your hands."

"No offense, but older women know what they want."

"Isn't she family?"

He shook his head. "She's a Wagner."

"You're a Silver."

"But my mother's not related to Grace's, like Julian's and Tristan's. That's the difference."

"Still family."

"Grace is a fantasy come true. That's what she is. OI once dreamed of an older womean have experience and Grace… Grace is all about all the experience I need to be a man. breaking me in, but now I have more experience and a desire to satisfy my partner in every way. Besides, a strong independent woman is sexy, no matter what age."

He grinned like he had life figured out. He didn't, because I'd heard the gossip at Grace's salon and things didn't sound this peachy.

"Wow. That's a lot to take in."

"It's awesome. Think about it—a partner with a few years of extra experience, someone who knows what they want from life and has it figured out, makes my life ten times easier."

"How is school?" I asked.

"Can I tell you a secret?"

I leaned in, even though there was no one around.

"I quit."

"You quit school?"

He nodded. "I figured life experience is much better. Nobody knows, so if you squeal, I'll know it was you."

I pulled my fingers over my lips like a zipper, and he smiled. "Good."

"Can I ask you something you'll keep to yourself?" I asked.

He stepped back, like he knew. A warm gust of wind blew by, flipping his shoulder-length wavy hair. Hunter belonged on the beach in California, not in New York. Perhaps he was right; life experience had its benefits. But Grace was only eleven years older than Hunter. Julian had eighteen on me.

"All right." I released a tight breath and shut my eyes. "Do you think Julian's too old for someone like me?"

He coughed out his beer. "So I was right?"

"I don't know. Maybe it's a crush, but how should I know? It's not like I remember dating or… Jesus, I don't even know if I'm a virgin. I'm sure you know about my hypnosis sessions."

He cleared his throat.

"Don't worry, Hunter. I know the truth."

I knew some of it, at least. I had quickly figured I was a case at Silver Securities, and Julian confirmed it. The hypnosis might have altered my memories, but Julian never lied.

"If you're curious, my recommendation would be to see a doctor. Get examined and get your answer. But if you want my opinion, I don't think you'd forget it, and you're still young, so I vote virgin. Not that it's any of my business."

"Was Grace your first?"

He allowed a crinkle of a smile. "I don't kiss and tell, Kay. And need I remind you, Julian has a girlfriend?"

"You mean a fuck friend? That's all they do when they go out on dates. You know, he's never brought her home before."

"I wouldn't worry about it. You still have time, and the

world is filled with plenty of Julians. You just haven't met yours yet."

Maybe he was right. In the past year, I'd mourned and grieved. I'd stayed home, fought demons, and healed. I'd had no chance to meet my Julian.

We returned home late that evening. I showered first while Julian put away all the leftovers his parents had packed. As I lay in our bed and listened to the running shower, I took the chance and tiptoed to the bathroom. I pushed open the door enough to see him underneath the stream. The mirror's reflection fogged, and I stepped further in. Water streamed over his sculpted back and taut ass. Illicit thoughts consumed me. Dirty ones I wouldn't dare admit, because if Julian discovered my growing ache, he'd throw me out of the house.

He tilted his head back, bringing his face underneath the stream. My mouth opened wider with each inch of his turn until he was facing me and I stared, wide-eyed. His semi-hard dick rested at the side of his thigh. It was huge and absolutely stunning. I backed out of the bathroom before he opened his eyes and returned to our bed. I slipped underneath the sheets and fantasized about stepping naked into Julian's shower. He stayed in my mind until I fell asleep and dreamed about him as my lover.

Chapter 5

Julian

$\mathcal{L}$ights flickered and music blasted at Club Forever. Scar Wagner's strip club drew a crowd of wild women who spent wilder cash stuffing bills inside men's G-strings. We sat behind a glass wall, watching them scream through the act change. More importantly, we watched how many returned from what Scar liked to call the Hall of Doom.

Club Forever shared an area in the building with the business Brad and Chad Hartley ran on the other side of the wall. Guess what kind of business? A by-invitation-only strip club in the building's basement.

The brothel catered to the men with all sexual flavors, and since it was by invitation only, getting in was impossible. No client complaints and no leads. The handful of girls who returned never talked about what they saw. While the clients came with a personal invitation, the women who came to Club Forever had been preyed on for years. But we had no proof.

"There, that one." Tristan pointed. "She has a card in her pocket."

"That's one of our staff." Scar smiled broadly.

"Sorry."

"Listen, I've got this. I've known Brad since high school. His father may be shady, but Brad doesn't have the balls to break laws."

"I know what I heard." Gabe focused on the hall's entryway. We had a bouncer standing at the door, then another one halfway through the hall where the properties met. Every girl leaving had her ID checked and recorded. I couldn't believe his father had just given him a club, but Jeffrey Hartley was capable of much more than forming a brothel.

"Let's err on the side of caution and assume he's shady. Scar?" Gabe pointed through the glass. "Who's the guy in the black top hat?"

He wasn't difficult to spot and must have just come in, now carving a path toward the wall. He focused on a booth, removed his hat, and stood next to a guy with shoulder-length beach hair.

"That's the fuck turd," I said.

"What?"

"The guy who called the cops on me and fled."

"Why did he do that?"

"He saw me with Kay at the park and called me a pedophile. Cops traced the call to a Jace Donato, and I'm gonna fucking break his face."

I stepped away from the window, but James grabbed my arm. "Hold on there, cuz. Let's see if we can identify your fuck turd's friend."

The new guy in the trench coat, a long mustache, and a unibrow, sat in the booth across from Jace.

"We may not have the time. Look. They're dealing." Tristan hitched his chin their way as the new guy passed Jace a stack of cash.

"Which means they won't be here long."

Jace slid something across the table in return.

"Scar, you've got drugs at your club," I said.

"Okay, okay. Go get your fuck turd."

"I'm coming with you. I'll grab the other guy."

I took the stairs with Gabe. We squeezed through the crowd of intoxicated, horny women who mistook us for the next act. One pulled on my shirt and another gyrated against my leg.

I could only imagine the laughter from the group of men I called family and my closest friends on the other side of the one-way window. We walked up to Jace alone in his booth.

"Remember me?" I took the seat next to him, pushing him aside.

Jace squinted through his bloodshot eyes and dilated pupils. He swayed in his seat and definitely didn't remember me, at least not while stoned. "Who was your friend?"

"Who? Martinez?"

"Martinez what?"

"He just goes by Martinez. We just met. Nasty guy." He stroked his throat and recoiled.

The name rang in my ears as I recognized the name of the hitman Donaldson had hired to kill the Moores.

"What did he pay you for?" I asked.

"I got him some Molly. That's all. It's for his boss and their girls. That's what he said."

The dreamy look faded from his face.

"Hey, I remember you." He pointed. "You're the pedophile."

My swift punch took him out. He slumped in his seat with a nosebleed.

"What the fuck did you do that for?" Gabe asked.

"We got all the information he was going to give."

"That's as much bullshit as I ever heard, Julian. I'm gonna go look for Martinez. Maybe you should go find your temper?"

Gabe left, and I rolled my eyes. What could I say—when the guy called me a pedo, it hurt. Kendra was my best friend's daughter, and the defamation left a bitter taste in my mouth.

Jace groaned in his seat and opened his eyes, and I grabbed

him by the front of his shirt. "Where did Martinez go? How did he contact you?"

He opened his eyes wider and concentrated on my face. A spark of recognition twinkled in his doped eyes.

"Your girl was pretty. I'd fuck her too."

This time, I punched hard enough to knock him out for a while longer. The bone gave into my knuckles. Blood dripped from his nose, but he'd thank me for the rhinoplasty later. He needed it. I removed the fuck turd from the booth and draped him over my shoulder.

Truth was, Kendra had grown into a beautiful young woman, and I'd experienced the trouble her body attracted firsthand when she stepped inside my shower, naked.

It appeared she'd had too many champagne glasses last month on New Year's Eve, a few days after her seventeenth birthday. The image of her pink pointy nipples, perky breasts, semi-shaved pussy, and her fucking gorgeously toned body stayed with me during the nights. From that day, no matter how hard I tried to preserve the image of her innocence, I couldn't, and like a pervert gave into my hand's pleasure instead. I masturbated to the fetish ever since, dreaming about succumbing to her temptation.

That night, I helped her out of the shower. Her soft, dry body against my soaked and hard need tested my control. I towered over her and put her to bed, and once she fell asleep, I jerked off to get rid of my appetite.

Jace winced as I carried him out into the cold. Snow drifted to the ground, and the first frost nipped at my skin. Goose-bumps scattered over my arms, and I quickly realized I'd left my jacket upstairs. Jace groaned, and I set him down in the snow against the wall.

I checked his ID while he semi-consciously mumbled some shit I couldn't understand. Hopefully, I hadn't given him a concussion.

"Jace Donato from Oyster Cove on Long Island." The fuck turd lived in my neighborhood, but on the other side of the cove. "Where do you get your Molly, Jace?"

He opened his eyes as if he'd heard the magic words.

"Here and there. Everywhere."

He fell in and out of consciousness, slumping. I lifted him up, grabbed him by his arm, and guided him to my car. I buckled him in and drove to the hospital, where I left him with a nurse in the ER.

"Never show your face to the club again, you hear me?" I told him, but I doubted he'd remember tonight in his stoned state. I went back to my car, and my phone rang with Gabe's number.

"Martinez works for the Hartleys. He's Jeff's new go-to guy."

"Martinez is the name of the hitman Donaldson hired to kill the Moores," I told him.

"Kendra's parents?"

"Yeah. This feels too close. See if we can get more information on the guy."

"Well, Martinez replaced Donaldson's old guy. He's been scouting the streets already."

"How are they getting these girls to agree?"

"My guess is a combination of drugs, blackmail, and violence. Joanne will try to get in on the inside, but we'll need a few days to prepare." Gabe's wife was itching for her first case, but I didn't agree Martinez should be it.

"Tell Joanne to be careful. If Jack and Ashley's legislation passes postmortem, it will cut Donaldson's funding. Their network will fail on its own."

"Kendra would be proud. You should tell her. Let's regroup at the office."

He hung up, and I checked in with the nurse. Jace would be fine. They'd clean him up before they sent him on his way.

I slid in behind the wheel and my thoughts returned to the night Kendra had stepped inside my shower. Was the fuck turd right to call me a pedophile? If not, then why couldn't I forget about her skin covered with faint tan-lines around her nipples and hips? The last time I listened to her masturbate under our shared sheets and cover of darkness, I came.

I hadn't told Stef about my sleeping arrangement with Kendra. It wasn't anyone's business if my bed gave her the safety she sought. I'd switched to sleeping on the couch when I couldn't trust myself next to her. I'd been sleeping there more often.

Stefanie went away for the weekend to a conference and left me with a stiff cock. Hoping cold air could knock some sense into my head, I decided on a dip in the hot tub. Instead, I found Kendra sitting in the garage. She fumbled with her fingers and stared at the motorcycle.

"What are you doing here?" I asked.

She shrugged. "I dunno."

"What's I dunno?" I chuckled.

"I'm bored, and if you really want to know, I'm horny and can't sleep."

I coughed into my hand. While I shared her sentiment, I didn't think I should share it with her.

"You want to ride it?" I pointed to the motorcycle while she looked at my dick.

"Looks dangerous."

She pulled her hand over the leather seat, and I walked over to the bike.

"You rode on the back to high school. I picked you up sometimes, too."

"It sounds like one of those memories I wish I still had. The ladies must have gone crazy to see you pull up on the bike."

"Your little friends called me a GILF back then. It got even more awkward when their mothers stared like a bunch of…. Well, horny women."

"I'm not so little anymore," she said, and stared at me. Her nipples poked through the sweater and she caught my lowered gaze with a smirk. No, she definitely wasn't little anymore.

"Is that why I stare at you? Because I'm horny?" she asked.

"No, that's not what I'm saying. Why *do* you stare?" My voice cracked.

"Because you're a GILF." She winked.

"Godfather I'd like to fuck?" I whispered.

"Godfather, guardian. Whatever floats your boat. The motorcycle is definitely sexy. You look hot. No wonder the therapist digs it. How's that going?"

Had she just dodged the fact she hinted she'd like to fuck me?

I poured myself a shot of tequila I kept in the garage and swung it back, telling myself it was to warm myself up, hoping it would ease the sudden testosterone flowing through my veins.

"She's away, and I'll be fighting insomnia for the rest of the night," I said.

"How come you never bring her to our house?"

She shifted. The loose sweater twisted around her perky breasts, and if I had to bet, I'd say she wasn't wearing a bra. This time, I didn't hide my stare. I simply couldn't.

"Wait here. We're going for a ride." I ran up the stairs and splashed cold water over my face before changing into a pair of slacks and a sweater. I hurried back downstairs, secured the helmet over her head, and gave her one of the leather jackets I'd kept from my teens. Her eyes grew wide as she slid her arms into the vintage sleeves, pleased.

I rolled the bike out of the garage, slid to the back, and waited for her to mount in front of me. She leaned forward and reached for the handles. She glanced back, and her eyes crinkled with a smile. "You sure I can do this?"

"Don't worry, I'm right behind you. But you already look natural on the bike."

She grinned, and I checked her stance from behind. Her petite body hid within my frame as my front and her behind molded into one. Her soft curves gave into my hold. My experienced muscles dominated her soft flesh. She shifted forward, and her ass slid over my erection. I nearly lost it right then, just like that night she'd touched herself.

God, if she weren't my best friend's daughter and my foster kid—

The thought forced me backwards.

"What's wrong?" She turned around with her lower lip out.

"We can't, Kay."

"Can't what?"

"You can't rub against me like that."

Her gaze lowered. "You obviously like it. I thought you wanted me to ride in front, but you seem to prefer me from behind."

"Shit, Kay. Stop it."

"I'm kidding, Julian. Jesus, you need to relax. If you want, I can find a rub and tug for you."

"Kay!"

"All right. I'm done. Sorry. I know my ass is hot and irresistible."

She wiggled her behind against my dick and turned on the ignition.

"Am I getting it right?"

"So far. Your rear break is under your right foot and the lever under your right hand is the front break. Twist the throttle under your right hand to accelerate or slow down. Left foot controls the shifter and that's your clutch lever. Nervous?"

"Nah-ah. I've seen you do this dozens of times and it feels familiar. I think I've got it."

I let it go and concentrated on the ride, but as expected, she was a natural. It had snowed all day, and fresh powder covered the city. We rode through the winter wonderland along the shoreline, past the park and the twinkling lights. Kendra maneuvered like a professional, and I had to assume her father had taught her how to ride a bike. Half an hour later we returned home.

She hopped off the bike in the driveway and removed her helmet, her cheeks flushed and hair wild.

"I knew you'd be fine," I said.

"How?"

"Because you could obviously drive a car. I think your parents omitted telling me a few things."

"So I can ride a bike." She shrugged and wiggled her brows. "I bet ya I can do a lot of other things you wouldn't expect."

Her sultry tone forced me back a step. "It's late. You should go to bed."

"What about you?"

"I'm going to soak in the tub a little. We should definitely book your driver's test. I think you're ready."

"Sounds good. Thanks for the ride, Julian, and thanks for tonight."

"My pleasure."

Her focus lowered to below my belt, throwing me off. I knew I didn't have a hard-on, but I reached to my crotch and checked. I was right, but Kendra smiled like she planned on watching me touch myself. She turned on her heel and went to her room with a grin of pure satisfaction.

What the hell?

I checked my email, changed into my swim shorts, poured myself a drink, grabbed a towel, and went outside. By the time

I reached the hot tub, foam was bubbling over its top and I barely saw Kendra's head.

"What the hell did you do?" I asked.

"I thought you were soaking in the tub," she said. "As in the one at home. And I can't really sleep either, so I wanted to soak out here."

"I meant the bubbles, Kay. What did you pour in there?"

"Pomegranate-eucalyptus essential oils with a mint-infused bath bomb. I didn't know it was a soapy one."

I could either waste time explaining how those weren't for the hot tub either, or I could enjoy the relaxing aroma while it lasted. I chose the latter and climbed into the suds, sitting across from her. The night was dark but clear with stars, with a touch of much-needed crisp air. I took in a lungful, and the eucalyptus cleared my nasal passage. Out in the bay, a boat crossed the dark waters. Kendra shifted, drawing my attention. Her head floated on a cluster of bubbles, and laughter charged out of my chest.

"You know, I remember you in your first pair of swimming wings and a float. I used to drink scotch by your father's pool while you dove for hoops."

But my smile faded when I saw her eyes turn into large saucers and her lips part.

"Why with the somber face? What's the matter?"

"Sometimes I wish you didn't talk about me like I'm a kid. I'm not a kid anymore, Julian."

"I'm sorry, Kay. I meant no harm. Truly. Truth is, you're part of my life, and I'm part of yours."

She stared at me, her eyes wide and freckles popping as her cheeks flushed with heat.

"I'm your godfather. I'm meant to take care of you."

She bit her lower lip, and I wondered whether she'd heard me. "There's something I need to tell you, Julian."

"What is it?"

She cleared her throat. "I didn't know you were coming here, and I thought I'd be alone."

"We've already established that."

"What I'm trying to tell you is that I'm naked."

I stilled. Her little disclosure held the power to draw all my blood south, like my imagination of what lay underneath the bubbles hadn't done enough to my dick.

"Say what?"

"I don't have a bathing suit, which you obviously can't see because of the bubbles, but I thought you were staying in the house."

I stood up. "Okay, I'm leaving."

"Don't leave. I enjoy talking to you. Just pretend you don't know I'm naked."

"But I do know, Kay."

"No, I'm not. I'm wearing a bathing suit."

"Are you?"

"No, I'm not. See what I mean? You don't even know the difference."

"Kay—"

"I'll stand if you stand," she blurted as fast as she could, and I lowered myself back to my seat.

Naked.

The thought drew the picture for me, and just that fast, the bubbles between us no longer mattered.

"Just relax, Julian, will you? I'm not going to bite. Unless you want me to. Kidding. Just kidding." She laughed.

She might not bite, but if she continued teasing me, I might fucking choke someone. Or something. My dick would be the first victim.

"It's not like you haven't seen a naked woman before. I know you've seen and fucked plenty."

"Kay, I'm warning you."

"What I'm trying to say is that we're family."

"I believe that makes it worse," I grunted.

"So we're not family?"

That didn't help either.

"Change the subject, Kay. Please, for the love of my hard dick, change the subject."

"You have a hard-on?"

Fuck.

"Did I say that out loud? Jesus, Kay. I mean, I shouldn't. I'm sorry—"

"I'm not. It's kind of hot, you know, to think I turn you on."

"Except you shouldn't turn me on."

"Why not? You're a man. I'm practically a woman. It would actually be weird if you didn't get wood. I'd be offended."

I settled in the tub and listened to her chat about her friend's opinions on mutual attraction, morning wood, masturbation, virginity, and Kay feeling like she was losing out on one of the most wonderful experiences of a lifetime. According to her friend's stories, she was the only one without experience. Her chatty mouth wouldn't stop, and it was nice to forget about work for a change.

"You'll have years to have sex, Kay. And it's not always all that it's hyped up to be."

She gasped and covered her mouth with her hand. "You've had bad sex?"

"Well, no. It doesn't happen to me."

She rolled her eyes. "Of course, it doesn't happen to Adonis."

"Adonis?" I laughed.

"You know—beautiful and fertile. That's you and don't say no, because I've seen your cock and it is all that."

"Kay! When did you see me? Like that?"

"I was half asleep and walked in on you showering. It was a long time ago. I never mentioned it because I didn't want to embarrass you like I'm obviously doing right now."

I sighed. "It's all right. We live in the same house. Things like that are bound to happen."

"We also sleep in the same bed. What other things are bound to happen?"

"Kay—"

"I'm warning you." She mocked my voice, and I splashed the suds her way. She laughed, retaliating with a wave to my face. The suds moved around the hot tub enough that most swept over the edge, and Kay's breasts bopped free on the surface.

I couldn't pretend I didn't see them any longer, and I stepped out.

"Everything okay, Julian?"

Crisp air nipped against the layer of my skin. I grabbed my towel and stretched it out between us. "It's getting late, Kay. We better get inside."

She stepped out, and I wrapped it around her.

I slept on the downstairs couch that night. It would be the first one of many nights I excused myself from our bed.

Chapter 6

Kendra

 jogged the usual route down the shoreline, past Julian's parents' and the Jacobs', Julian's next-door neighbors, and made my way back down the street. Summer's wind blew against my face with the beautiful scent of the first day of freedom. And I intended to make every day count. Cami and Megan from online school, along with a few others, were coming over to celebrate our year-end by the pool. One more year and I'd finish, except I didn't know what to do after high school. I used to know, but the further my memories from before the train accident faded, the less I remembered.

Julian had the pool installed last summer: a gift for my seventeenth birthday. He surprised me with the plans for Christmas when we returned from an annual family vacation in New Zealand. He had a way of helping me forget about the pain and the grief. It never went away, but if I tried hard, I could numb it. Still, I'd never take another train ride to Canada again.

"Hey, need a ride?" I halted my jog as a Mustang convertible pulled up by my side. I glanced sideways and picked up my pace.

"Hey, Blondie, I'm talking to you," the guy called out. I

recognized his eyes, but didn't remember from where, and I doubted he knew me. Julian had a rule about screening anyone I talked to. My new extension from Grace gave me a new look, so he couldn't have known me. Yet here he was. An outsider.

"No, thanks. I enjoy running. It's good for you."

He rolled his car along my jog. "I guarantee you can find pleasure in easier activities. And if you can't, I can." He wiggled his brows, and I couldn't hold in the laugh.

Creepy… but hot.

"I'm Jace. You from around here? Feels like we've met before," he said.

I stopped, and he pressed harder on the brake.

He looked familiar. His bright eyes and sun-bleached hair fluttered in the wind, and all the things Julian had taught me flew out of my mind.

The screening rules, not talking to strangers—which I obviously broke—no talking about my life or giving anyone my name… Oh yeah, and the one to not tell anyone where I lived. All of it, gone with the toss of some hair.

Poof.

The wind tossed his hair to the side again, and I totally got why the longer strands looked so hot on the Silver brothers.

"Yes, I'm from around here, hence, why I don't need a ride."

"Hence?" He chuckled and revved the engine, looking out into the distance before turning my way again. He leaned back in the seat, extending his muscled arms. They weren't as large as Julian's, but impressive enough.

"Come on, Blondie, let me give you a ride. Even if it's a short one. I promise I'm the good guy."

"Which is exactly what the bad guy would say. Thanks, but I don't do rides with strangers."

"Maybe we shouldn't be strangers."

I tossed him the side-eye.

"You don't give up, do you?" I folded my arms in front of

me, and his sly smile grew. "Come by my house later. If you're brave enough. I'm having a party."

It was more like a small gathering with a handful of friends, but *party* sounded so much cooler. I'd never needed to be something more than just me until now.

"What do you mean, brave enough?"

"My bodyguard will screen and frisk you. He's my godfather and very protective."

Jace drummed his fingers on the steering wheel. "How well does he screen?"

"Imagine you're passing airport security and a sniffer dog sits beside you. He's that sniffer dog."

His brows furrowed for a moment, but then he grinned. "All right. You sold me, Blondie. I'll come to the party."

"My name is Kendra."

Poof.

"Blondie suits you better." He added gas to the engine, lightly rolling the sports car back and forth. "I'm Jace. See you this afternoon."

Jace reached into a compartment under the dashboard.

"Maybe it's better you sneak this in for us." He flicked a pouch with a handful of white pills my way. I caught it in both hands and tried not to act like it burned me.

"Next gate?" He pointed to the driveway's entrance, and I nodded.

He winked, gave me a silly thumbs up, and pulled away. Jesus, why didn't his personality match the face and the body?

My hands started shaking, and I fumbled with the pouch. After a quick look, I recognized the set of emoji pills as ecstasy. Julian would flip if he knew I'd invited Jace to my house. I turned around and jogged back to Wilma and Fred's. I ran along their driveway and hid the bag underneath a rock before making my way around their house and to the back door. Julian would kill me if he found pills on me. Right after he killed Jace. Worse yet, I'd be forced back to online school for my senior year, and I couldn't go back to being alone. I had friends now.

"Good morning." I hopped up on the breakfast stool beside Julian's eight-year-old sister. "How's it going, Ems?"

"I'm making lemonade for my lemonade stand. Mama needs money." She shimmied her shoulders back and forth, and Wilma's eyes grew wide.

"Emma Rose Silver, where did you hear that?"

My chuckle burst out. I might have said the phrase in front of Emma last week, but truth was, I wanted independence, which meant I needed a job.

The little girl's gaze skidded my way.

"I'm sorry. It's my fault," I said. "Julian is teaching me how to drive, and I was hoping to get to get some work experience, but Julian said I don't need a job, and then I was trying to figure out what I want to do and how to make money—"

Wilma lowered her tea to the counter. "Julian hasn't told you?"

"Told me what?"

"Wilma," Fred cleared his throat. "It's not our place."

"She's seventeen and responsible. It's time she knows." Wilma turned my way. "But it's not my place to say anything either."

"Say anything about what?"

Wilma clasped her hands together and glanced at Fred.

"I know, I know…"

We all turned toward Emma.

"You don't need a lemonade stand, Kay. She's talking about your inheritance. Money, dinero, l'argent."

"What?"

Wilma crossed her arms over her chest. "How do you know about this, Emma?"

"People talk around small kids because they don't think

we're there. That's how I know. Want to try my lemonade, Kay?"

She poured me a glass without waiting for my reply.

"I have an inheritance?"

"It's big. Millions."

"Emma." Wilma and Fred accosted their daughter at the same time.

"What? I told you people talk, and she asked. You wouldn't want me to lie, would you?"

Wilma sighed, and Fred poured himself a cup of tea. He stepped past me, gently gripping my shoulder. "You should talk to Julian."

"Thank you."

Fred sat by the window, and I turned to Julian's little sister. "Are you coming to my pool party, Ems?"

"I can't. Horseback riding lessons today and swimming at five in the morning. Maybe next time?"

"Sure. I'll see ya' later. Thanks for the lemonade."

I kissed Mrs. Silver on her cheek and left through the back door, crossing their backyard to Julian's house. The new pool sparkled in the sun. Julian had surprised me with the plans on my seventeenth birthday. I worked with a designer, and we added a little sparkle to the concrete patio slabs. The sleek wooden furniture, secluded cabanas, and a pristine landscape of decorative trees and roses turned his bachelor pad into a getaway.

A splash near the pool's end drew my attention to where Julian was finishing his morning laps. He lifted out of the pool like the Adonis I liked to call him and stepped underneath the outdoor shower stream. The summer tan went well with water. Lots of water, splashing over his arms and abs, then down his muscled thighs. His shorts clung to the thick curve underneath. Julian was definitely more beautiful than Jace. More manly. Maybe boys like Jace grew up to be men like Julian?

I hurried to the pool house change room, shed my joggers, and quickly showered. I had little time and many decisions to make before this afternoon's party, and Julian could help.

I changed into my first bathing suit option for the night—glittering sequins crossed over my nipples and down into v-cut. I spun in front of the mirror and stepped out as Julian finished the green smoothie from the juice bar. He gaped and coughed through his drink.

"What do you think?" I asked.

"Is that sparkly dental floss?"

"I'm serious, Julian. It's for my party."

His gaze shifted sideways, avoiding me. "Unless you plan to borrow my shorts and shirt, that's a no."

"Okay, wait here. I have another one."

"Kay, look over there." He pointed to a lounge chair with a box topped with a red bow.

"That's for me?"

"Happy end of the school year. Grace picked it out. Hope you like it. I… I have to go. The chef should be here soon."

He walked backward, tripping over his feet, but he recovered with an awkward arm swing.

"You hired a chef? Julian, I said it's a small gathering."

"HenceWhich isHence why I hired one chef instead of two. Now, excuse me."

He turned on his heel and hurried inside, awkwardly stomping over a decorative flamingo.

I changed into my swimwear from Grace's. The cover-up tied the bikini into a complete outfit. I checked last-minute details with Julian's hired security and snuck Jace onto the guest list. By five o'clock, the pool party was in full swing. Music blasted, and the summer cinnamon-and-spice theme filled the yard. Enormous balloons, fluffy seats, and sparkling lights brought the indoors outside. The fire pit glowed, and I handed my friends virgin mimosas. Julian stood by the barbecue, watching Olivier's burgers. And me.

"I heard Julian Silver was real, but I never believed it," Cami sighed. All six of my friends stared at him like he was our evening's entertainment, appetizer, and main course.

"One of the most eligible bachelors in New York," Meghan said.

"How do you get a hunky bodyguard as a roommate?" Cami elbowed me in the ribcage.

"He's not my bodyguard. He's my guardian."

"He's not your uncle."

"No, but he's my godfather."

"So, not blood related at all?"

"You're gross."

"At least, he's loaded."

"It's not about the money, Cam." We all, clearly, had trust funds, Cami included. Mine just came from dead parents. I hadn't had time to ask Julian about my inheritance, because I wouldn't know what to do with it anyway. "What we need is someone our age to play with, so it's a good thing I invited someone to the party."

Cami took a step back. "If he passed Julian's screening, he's a nerd."

"He's not being screened," I said. "And there's nothing wrong with nerds. Although, he's not a nerd. I snuck him on the guest list."

"Julian will spot him and kick him out the moment he does."

"Don't worry. I know what I'm doing." I removed the cover-up from my shoulders, revealing one of the smaller bikinis from Grace. It was modest, but it had a beautiful cutout over my ass, and I had a nice ass. The fabric dropped. I spun in a circle, and Julian disappeared inside.

"Perfectly timed, Kendra. I think your boy is here."

I turned around and saw Jace. He was standing by a cabana,

taking in my body. His mouth curved upward as he scanned me over and, just like that, I felt naked. I crouched to the ground and picked up the cover-up, scrunching it into my chest as he strolled my way.

"You came." My voice trembled.

"You invited."

"Ahem, no trouble at the gate?"

He came to a fast halt in front of me.

"I'll leave you two alone." Cami stepped away before I could stop her.

"Where is this uncle you warned me about? I want to see what I'm up against." Jace skewered me with his hot gaze. We were attracting attention and it wouldn't take long before Julian found us.

"He's inside. We should take a walk." I took his hand before he objected, and most importantly, before Julian returned. We walked around the decorative bushes and into the rose garden, where he pulled me down to the first bench we found.

"You need to relax, Blondie."

"It's Kendra."

"Kendra's even more beautiful." He pulled out a plastic pouch from his back pocket and removed a smiling emoji pill from within, similar to the ones I'd hidden earlier.

"You've got a lot of those."

"As many as you want. Open your mouth and stick out your tongue. We're gonna have some fun."

"My friends call me Kay."

"Stick out your tongue, Kay. We're about to become very good friends."

I hesitated.

"It's ecstasy. Trust me, you'll feel great. You've got family and friends all around."

It was one pill. That was all. And Jace was cute, fun and, if I had to admit it, his dangerous vibe appealed to my senses. I lowered the throw over my knees and removed the pill from his fingers, ignoring all the warning bells ringing in my head.

"You open up," I whispered.

He stuck out his tongue with a smirk. Shivers ran down my arms. I placed the pill on the tip of his tongue and leaned in for a long, deep kiss. He snaked his hands around my waist and to the back, skimming up my spine. I swept the pill off his tongue on the first stroke just as a voice cleared behind us.

"Get your hands off of her!"

I jumped up and away from Jace, swallowing the evidence, the pill passing through my throat like a golf ball. Jace dragged his fingers down my thigh, like he was testing Julian's patience.

"I said, get your hands off of her."

Next thing I knew, Jace was flying into a bush of thorny roses. He let out a painful groan, but stood up.

"What the fuck are you doing here?"

"Aha—now I know where I recognize you from, Blondie."

"You know each other?" I asked.

"It's the fuck turd. The guy who called me a pedophile."

That wasn't him, was it?

"You broke my nose." Jace pointed at Julian, who grabbed his hand and threw another punch. Jace flew back into the rose bushes again.

"Oh, my God." I covered my mouth and pictured Jace a year younger, with even longer hair, and definitely a different nose.

Julian went in for another swing, but I grabbed his arm. "Stop it, Julian! Look what you've done. He's injured."

"He'll live. Get the fuck up and get out of here before I call the cops. You never step a foot on this property again, you hear?"

Jace shot up to his feet and walked through the roses and thorns, scraped and bloodied, without a shadow of pain, like a hero. He leaned into me and left a quick kiss on my lips, with another pill on my tongue, whispering, "You're welcome. I'll see you later, Blondie."

I swallowed again. This time, the pill plummeted to the bottom of my stomach and echoed back with an ominous sound of trouble. Shivers scattered over my skin. "See you."

He tugged at the bathing suit on my back and gave me a dangerous smile.

I turned around as Jace left, and Julian's attention flew from him to me. My bikini top slid down my body, exposing me, but my hands felt too heavy to lift and cover up. The world went in and out of focus.

"Everybody, out. Now!" I heard Julian scream. He pulled his shirt off. The fairy lights from above shone over his abs. I stared at the path of perfection until he approached and pulled his shirt over my head. It hung around me like a dress, smelling of barbecue and man.

Julian lifted me into his arms. My vision blurred, and the surrounding sounds faded. The party cleared, and I couldn't understand why until my body spasmed in Julian's hold, and I couldn't think at all. He ran upstairs and into his bedroom, setting me on my side on his bed. My dry mouth filled with white foam.

"I want to puke." I looked up, my hooded eyes begging for help. He lifted me and ran to the washroom where he set me by the toilet.

I emptied my stomach and heaved until I had nothing left inside of me. Julian held back my hair and supported me underneath my arms, as I had no strength left. The sound of running water, and the smell of lavender and eucalyptus, lifted me from a daze.

His stained shirt came off my body, and my bikini bottoms were next. Julian looked away and set me in the bath. I submerged beneath the bubbles with only my face above the water.

"What happened to the party?" I asked, and he turned to face me. My head felt heavy and my memory fuzzy.

"It got cut short when Jace gave you drugs. Where do you know him from?" he asked.

"The park." My eyelids felt heavy, and I closed my eyes. "When he called the police on you."

"That was a year ago. Did you see him recently? Did you invite him?"

I nodded. The disappointment in Julian's eyes broke my heart in half.

"He's trouble, Kay. He hangs out with bad people. The same people who were after your parents. You need to stay away from him."

Jace wasn't trouble. *I* was the trouble—because I'd invited him.

"I'm sorry," I pouted, and Julian's expression softened.

"Why would you invite someone with drugs?"

I drew a path with my finger through the bubbles, popping the larger ones.

"I didn't know he had drugs," I lied. "He was nice. He kissed me deeply, with tongue, and he made me feel things I haven't felt before."

Julian stilled. "What kinds of things?"

"The kinds of things you don't tell your godparents about." I bit my lip, and he looked away. I didn't want him looking away. I wanted him looking at me the same way he looked at the dentist and the nurse. I was a woman with needs.

"They were naughty thoughts," I whispered, bringing Julian's attention back to me. "Like, I imagined his fingers inside me. His dick, too. I wondered how thick he'd be."

Julian coughed into a towel. "What the hell, Kay? I... I didn't know you think like that. It must be the drugs. Do you feel lightheaded?"

"It's not the drugs, Julian. Truth is, I would like to know what it feels like to have a man's fingers inside me."

"Shit, Kay. I think the drugs—"

"It's not the drugs. I'm horny because I'm this broken virgin princess trapped in a castle…" I trailed off, waving my hand. "Okay, maybe it's a bit of the drugs."

"Listen to me carefully, Kay. A guy like Jace wants one thing, and that's getting inside your panties."

"That's exactly what I'm talking about. I'm almost eighteen. I can't stay a virgin forever."

"No, no. You're not hearing me."

I grabbed Julian's hand to show him what I meant and pressed it to my breast. His mouth opened and eyes bulged as he stared at his palm over my boob and my nipple poking through the bubbles and between his fingers.

"You…you can do better than a bad boy like Jace," he whispered.

"I don't need better, Julian. I've got you." I guided his hand from my breast to the belly button ring and down to my pussy, but he yanked his hand away before reaching my apex.

"I… I can't, Kay. You're… You're Kay, and you're drugged." He rose and passed me a towel. "Cover up. Let's get you to bed, and I'll bring you some tea. We'll chat about drugs tomorrow."

I didn't want to chat. I wanted Julian's hands on my skin again: calloused and experienced, arousing and titillating. A yearning stirred deep in my belly. I knew I'd wanted his touch before, but I didn't realize how much that need had grown. Now that he was standing in front of the tub with a towel stretched out, looking away, I realized I wanted that touch badly. Very badly.

When I didn't move, he lifted me from the tub, wrapped me in the towel, and carried me to my room and the bed where I never slept.

"I'm sorry, Kay. I shouldn't have allowed this. You're incapacitated."

He pulled the covers to my neck, wrapped me like a burrito until I couldn't move, and left.

The sound of running water jolted me awake, and I pulled the sheets away. I tiptoed to his room, where I dropped the towel and slipped into one of his t-shirts. I snuck into his bed and underneath the covers, where I pretended to be asleep. He returned from the shower and sighed hard, but went around to his side and turned off the light. I waited until his first snore and then slid my hand between my legs. My fingers ached and my pussy throbbed. They might not have felt as good as his would have, but they were enough to ease my burning need for the man who was sleeping three feet away.

Chapter 7

Julian

$\mathcal{I}$ quickly learned little Kay wasn't so little anymore, and her teenage hormones were driving me up the wall. One minute, we were kicking the ball in the yard, and the next, she tackled me, straddling my hips and exerting all her feminine power over my body. I had no fucking clue how to react. Kendra was fun and thoughtful. She helped redecorate Emma's room and made sure my favorite pair of slippers were always waiting at the bedside. But the times she wanted to go shopping for fluffy things, sexy things, and things her experienced teenage friends promised would bring her pleasure, I felt helpless to stop her. I drew the line at the sex shop Kendra casually drove by when practicing for her driver's license. Her friends promised the Pleasure V-Bunny 8000 could do better than any man.

I doubted it, but then again, I'd never viewed sexual accessories as competition. But I couldn't picture those same accessories in Kendra's hands; the same hands that used to bake cookies but now had manicured nails and trouble dialing for take out.

The same little girl who used to jump into my bed because

she had nightmares now sauntered in her black negligee toward me like a temptress. I set my coffee mug on the kitchen counter and stood still, fearing I was having one of those dreams about Kendra I didn't like to admit I had. Her perky breasts lifted the sheer fabric, her pink nipples much prettier than in my dreams, which meant the moment had to be real.

"What the hell are you wearing?" I grabbed the nearest kitchen cloth and threw it her way. She didn't catch it on purpose and twirled in a circle instead. The transparent fabric showed off her ass and the lace G-string cutting between her cheeks, which made me want to search down its path.

"You like it?" She spun in a circle.

Fuck me.

I swallowed hard. "Cover yourself, Kay."

"For what it's worth, I didn't know you were home."

"It's seven in the morning. I'm on my way to work, like every morning." I sipped on my coffee. Thankfully, she was standing behind the kitchen island, which covered her from the midriff down. But her nearly exposed breasts were still a problem for my hardening dick. Why the fuck was this happening to me?

"I bought it as a Halloween costume, but it's a little risqué, even for me. Do you think Jace will like it?"

I nearly choked on the coffee. I still couldn't believe she was seeing the fuck turd. He hadn't shown his face since the day I kicked him out four months ago, and I hated him even more.

"You're seeing Jace tonight?" I grunted, set the cup down and backed away as she approached. I kept walking all the way to the family room where the couch stopped me.

I looked around the room. Something was off.

"I changed the sitting area arrangement," she said.

"Again?"

"We gained half a foot of space near the fireplace." She

stepped closer, her pink nipples making her negligee worth every penny.

I extended my arm out front to stop her, like I held Skywalker power.

"Kay, stop right there. We don't need more space in this house. What we need is to give you something else to do. What you need is a hobby—and not to parade naked around our house."

"Nobody's forcing you to look, Julian, but I do need an opinion."

She was a walking, breathing contradiction.

"Besides, I don't want to watch another movie or play arcades. I'm pretty sure I'm ready for the good stuff, and it's Jace's and my four-week anniversary, so it's time he pops my cherry. I don't want to be eighteen and a virgin, and that's coming up quickly."

Sometimes I worried her eighteenth birthday wouldn't be here quickly enough. At least, I wouldn't feel like a pervert who looked at her like she was made for me, and only me.

"What the hell, Kay? Why would you say that? Why would you want that?"

"Why wouldn't I want it? Most girls my age have lost it ten times over, and Jace is nice."

"You're a virgin?"

Not that I ever thought she wasn't. Truthfully, I hadn't thought about it because if I knew someone had touched her while she was under my guardianship, I'd kill them. And hearing her confirm her innocence made me want to protect her that much harder.

"Any advice for a first timer?" she chirped.

Oh, my God! This conversation wasn't actually happening, was it?

"Don't do it," I whispered.

"What?"

"Don't do it, Kay. He's not the guy."

"If he's not the guy, then who is?"

Me.

"Definitely not Jace."

"How do you know?" Her hip tilted outward.

"Do you love him?"

"Ahem, well, I'm not sure. He hasn't said it, and—"

"There. That's why you shouldn't do it. When you do it for the first time, it should be with someone you love, without a doubt."

"Is that how it was for you?"

No.

"Yes, that's how it was for me," I lied. There was no point explaining my situation of screwing my professor at university. I never even told Professor Ingram she was my first. She probably knew and diligently taught me all the ways to find pleasure in giving pleasure. She taught me to worship a pussy. Kendra's pure pussy needed proper worship, and definitely not from someone like Jace. And why the fuck was I even thinking about her pussy?

"Oh, that smile on your face. What was her name?" She startled me out of thought.

"Michelle."

Professor Michelle Ingram.

"You really were in love, weren't you?"

"Yeah, you could say that," I lied again. "Which is why you should take that thing you're wearing—"

"A negligée."

"Take off your negligée. And don't put it back on until it's for a man who deserves it. Jace is not that man."

"I'm gonna stay a virgin forever." She released a strangled breath, but then perked up again. "How old were you when you lost your virginity?"

"Eighteen." This lie itched the tip of my nose.

"Wow. Were you a loser, like me?"

"No. I was busy with school. So busy, in fact, that the moment I went down on Professor Ingram, I guaranteed myself an A all the way through my Master's." I bit back a grin.

"You ate professor pussy for grades?"

This conversation turned so wrong, so fast. My dick got hard at I thought back to my younger years, when all I wanted was an experience from someone more experienced. And now, somewhere deep inside, all the earned years of pleasure nudged me. Professor Ingram had taught me well, and I had a lot to share. I had a lot I'd never share, and looking at Kendra, with her pursed lips and naïve eyes, the urge to contribute to her experience grew.

"Was she good?" Kendra brought me out of my daze.

"Let's just say I wasn't Professor Ingram's only special student. She went for the good-looking ones, because she knew she could get every fucking single one of us. But this isn't about me and my pussy eating—"

"I imagined what it's like. You know—a man's lips down there."

"Kendra—"

"I can't talk to Jace about it. I barely know him."

"Exactly my point—why you shouldn't be sleeping with him."

"I'd rather learn these things from someone I trust. Someone with experience, and my peers certainly don't qualify. Cami thought she couldn't get pregnant while on her period until she did."

"Cami's pregnant?"

"No. She took a morning-after pill."

If I was visibly shaking, she didn't let on. I pulled my gaze away from her and fixed my tie, looking in the hall mirror.

"You see? That's what I'm talking about, Kay. Sex at your age, you just don't know enough. You—"

"There's always the internet, but I've read an article that says porn does not show real life. And that's what I want. Real life."

I hid behind the counter so I wouldn't have to see her protruding nipples, and she wouldn't have to see my hard wood. My comfortable morning had turned into a throbbing ache in my balls.

"Jace is certainly someone who won't show you real life. He'll cloud it with tiny white pills."

"That was a one-time thing. Things don't have to be that hard."

"Sometimes, real life is even harder than you think. Harder than you ever, ever realized..." I started, but stopped when I saw her backside's reflection in the mirror. She slumped into a chair and covered herself with a blanket. I paced toward her.

"All right. What do you want to know, Kay? What questions do you have?"

"Does it hurt?"

I froze, completely not ready for that one. I watched her mouth slowly lift into a curve.

"Are you fucking with me, Kay?"

"I'm almost eighteen, Julian, yet you still see me as an innocent girl. I may be a virgin, but that's by choice, because I'm saving myself for the right man. And you're correct. That man is not Jace. But *I* decide who deserves me. It also doesn't mean I'm stupid. My friends blabber about sex enough. Sounds like they don't know what they're doing most of the time, but I've eavesdropped on enough conversations between you, your brother, and your cousin to know what men like. I have more experience than you think."

I stepped into the wall's shadow.

"So, does it hurt?" she asked again. "I just want to check with someone experienced."

I sighed. "If the guy's doing it right, it shouldn't hurt." I grabbed my car keys from the drawer and turned into the foyer.

"Have you had a virgin before?" she asked.

I turned around. She was standing in the doorway, in her see-through negligée, still like a picture, her perfectly ripened body framed in the streaming sun. If I could have a painting, I'd like one of her, like that.

My throat lurched with a hard swallow. "I don't kiss and tell."

"Which means, yes. You would have said no if you hadn't."

My hands found the safety of my pockets, and I realized I was getting hard.

Fuck. Not now.

I drew on my memories of Kay's puke on my shirt, dirty diapers and obnoxious tantrums, hoping to pull all that blood collecting in my groin north. It wasn't working.

"Anything else, Kay? I know you're growing up and have questions—"

"Growing up?" She snickered. "You know, my friends call you a GILF. If you don't remember, that's a *godfather I'd like to fuck*. If my friends fantasize about you, why can't I? We're not related."

"The fact we're not blood related doesn't change the fact I helped with your diapers."

"Maybe now you can help with my panties."

Fucking hell.

I turned on my heel, but stopped when I heard her approach. I whipped my body around. She walked up to me, until I could only see her face. That was easier than looking at her naked body, except now her heat and scent overpowered my other senses.

"You may be older than me, Julian, but I know what men like. There are plenty who prey on girls like me, and who love to—"

"I'm not like that." My face burned, yet my dick strained as more blood pumped through my veins. I would never hurt her.

"I'm happy to give myself to Jace. He's decent and patient, and we can take our time teaching each other all the things you already know."

She drew her finger down my chest. She had a way of getting to me, and this was it. I gripped her wrist. "If Jace fucking touches you, I'll have him prosecuted for statutory rape.

I caught the twisted smile on her face. "Kay–"

"No need to warn me. I'm a big girl, Julian."

I removed my hold from her wrist.

"I have to go to work, and you'd better not be wearing this when I get home."

"Yes, sir," she snickered. "But I'm not canceling my date with Jace."

Fuck.

I hurried to my Tesla and left for work with a hard dick. If it weren't for the meeting at Silver Securities, I'd jack off. I gripped the steering wheel so hard the entire way, my knuckles were still white when I joined my partners at the conference table. Thankfully, my hard-on was gone, but the next four hours stretched into infinity.

We had an update from the company lawyers, closed old contracts and secured fresh ones. The one file haunting our family remained open, and it involved Kendra. Rumors about Kay were spreading, and the fact her current boyfriend had befriended the mafia's go-to boy meant trouble wasn't far behind.

"What's the matter with you?" Tristan threw a ball of scrunched paper my way. "I tell you we found Donaldson's contact, and you have nothing to say? Don't you know what this means?"

"It means it will take you many more years to take down the organization than you thought, which also means Kendra's stuck with me and in danger. Maybe it's better she has no fucking clue who she is."

"Nobody even knows she's alive."

"For now," I grunted, "but you know Kendra. She likes attention, and she attracts trouble."

Our cousin James leaned back in his chair and threw a ball of paper of his own at Tristan. "Donaldson's contact is your old father-in-law. I could have told you that."

My brother stood up from the chair and braced himself on the conference table. "Hartley wasn't my father-in-law, and need I remind you, I'm aware of Jeff Hartley's abilities more than any of you. If the new intelligence is correct, they've grown to a secret club for the elite. They control the sex traf- ficking market and cater to the perverse and untouchable— government officials, law enforcement, royalty, doctors, lawyers. If you have money, Infinity has the girl. The Hartleys will back Donaldson at election time again and will secure prime real estate to traffic the girls. Nobody talks about it in the open, but the women who survive and live to tell tales often wish they'd died. Most who talk get murdered. It's the largest crime ring in the country."

"Why aren't we on this?" I asked. "How do we stop them?"

"We are on this, but paperwork and legislation take time."

"I fucking hate red tape. This is exactly what Ash and Jack fought, and look what happened to them. And look what happened to Kendra. She lost both parents. Fuck legislation." The words slithered along the bitter trail on my tongue.

"How is Kay?" Tristan asked.

"Growing up." I slouched in the chair. I threw the crumpled paper into the corner trash, missing both times. "I didn't know they turned into women this quick. She'll be eighteen over Christmas."

"In Colorado. We should throw her a birthday party."

"I don't think she wants a birthday party. She wants different things only Jace can give her."

"She's growing up, Julian. Maybe it's time to let her go? And don't you have a therapist to worry about?"

"I promised Kendra's father I'd take care of her if anything happened."

"And you have."

Right.

"What if I feel my taking care of her includes beating the shit out of Jace some more? The guy's bad news. He's trouble."

"Wouldn't have anything to do with the fact you've fantasized about getting inside Kendra's panties for months, and the little prick gets to call dibs?"

"Fuck you. It's not like that with Kendra. He's wrong for her."

"And who's right?"

I refused to give them the obvious answer I heard in my mind: It was me. *I* was right for her. It was my responsibility to protect her, and Jace not getting inside her panties was part of that.

I stood up. "I say we collect information on this organization. Names, contacts, and ways inside. If they're as tight as these papers show, it will take time to infiltrate Infinity. Now, excuse me. I have a date this afternoon."

"You're still fucking the therapist?"

I shrugged. "Stefanie's smart, sexy, independent, and experienced. She knows what I like and vice versa. Why change what works?"

The words sure didn't convince me, and I didn't give a fuck if they convinced my brother and cousins. Though my evening date wasn't up for hours, I left the meeting in haste.

Kendra was lounging by the pool, video-calling some friends, surfing the net, and a minute before I left to pick Stefanie up for our dinner at the Marina, she reminded me she had a date with Jace.

"Don't worry. We're going out for dinner. I really appreciate our talk this morning, and I'll take things slowly with Jace. I'll let him court me."

"Court you? Yeah, I guess courting is good as long as it doesn't lead him… Well, we already talked about this. Just don't rush, okay? You make sure the guy is right."

She gave a single nod. "Like you. I decided I want someone who likes pussy. What is it you guys call it? MTP care?"

"That's not what I said, Kay."

"It's exactly what you said. Remember Professor Ingram? I bet you excel at mouth to pussy care."

She had the nerve to lock her gaze with mine, accentuating the last part of her query.

"It feels inappropriate for you to tease me this way, Kay. I… I promised your father to protect you. I'm your guardian."

She worked up a cocky grin and sauntered toward me. Her breasts swayed freely underneath her tank top.

"Well, when I get myself off, I picture you as my hot guardian whose brains I want to fuck."

"Kay—"

"I picture your hard cock inside my tight pussy, because that's what does it for me. And my imagination is so good." She closed her eyes and tilted her neck sideways. I stared down at her neckline and the exposed part of her cleavage. Her top barely covered her nipples, holding my attention on the fabric hugging her breasts. Fucking Jace would stare at them all night.

When I didn't reply, she looked up and fluttered her lashes.

"You leaving already?" she asked, oh, so innocently, yet I

could see a plan forming in her eyes. Everything Kendra said she'd pictured, she'd do tonight. With Jace.

I turned on my heel and headed straight for the garage. She followed me. "Have a great time, and tell that fuck turd if he touches you, I will chop off his dick." I waved and jumped inside my Bentley.

I picked up Stefanie, but changed to pick up our order at the Marina, opting to stay in for the night.

"Where are we going?" she asked.

"I thought we could go home. My home. We can light the fire in the back."

"It's raining."

"Then we can snuggle by the indoor fireplace under a blanket. It will be the perfect evening." I leaned in and kissed her.

"Sounds perfect." She smiled against my mouth. I couldn't wait for her lips to curve around my cock. "I've never been to your house."

"No? Well, then maybe it's time you come more often. Spend the night?"

"That sounds nice. But I didn't bring my pajamas."

"You won't need any."

I put the car in gear and drove back home, and the scene we encountered nearly gave me a heart attack. The temperature rose inside me with every breath as I stared at Jace on top of Kendra, on top of the family room couch, pushing his hand underneath her tank top.

"What the hell are you doing?" The tension vibrated from my chest with a glass-shattering growl. They both jumped up and off the couch, adjusting their clothes.

"I thought you were going out."

Kendra hurried to button up her shirt and fixed her skirt. I could see her barely-there panties from the hall.

"I changed my mind, and it looks like it's a good thing I did."

"So you can stop me from having sex? Again? Face it, Julian, it's going to happen whether you like it or not."

"I know it will happen, but not tonight. Not in my house. And not with the fuck turd."

"What?"

"Get the fuck out Jace, before I give you another nose job." I pointed at the door, and the boy hurried to put on his pants, fumbling halfway through. He left in his junkyard Mustang, and I shut the door.

"I hate you!" Kendra screamed, stomping upstairs.

Stefanie stood in the hallway with her arms laced over her chest. "Should I leave?"

"No. Wait here. I'll deal with this, and we can continue our date in a moment, I promise. Please make yourself comfortable."

I poured Stefanie a glass of wine and walked upstairs. I knocked on Kendra's bedroom door, but she wasn't there. I lowered my shoulders and went to my bedroom, where she was sitting on our bed. I walked up to her and stood at the bedside, and her legs swung over. I parted her knees and stepped in closer, lifting her chin. Her eyes filled with tears as I brought her in for an embrace.

"Did he touch you?" I asked, and she shook her head.

"Good. But you wanted him to touch you? And you lied to me tonight."

She nodded. "You can't keep me a virgin forever."

"I'm not trying to keep you a virgin, Kay."

"So stop trying." She lowered her hand to my pants and curved her palm over my erection. "Julian, you're hard."

I knew I was fucking hard the moment I saw her in that plunging neckline and short hem, no bra, and likely a thread for panties.

"You're very hard." She looked up, and I looked down. She bit her lip and my cock twitched. The force of her heat rose along with her scent. The light note of a whimper raised my need to a new height, and my arousal punched hard through my jeans, straining and begging for release. I shut my eyes. The image of her small hand wrapping around my hard dick and removing the pressure flashed in my mind. When I lowered my gaze and saw her brush her hand over my erection, I gave into the pressure.

"Oh, my God, Julian."

Oh, this was embarrassing. So fucking embarrassing.

"Did you just come in your pants?"

I lowered my mouth to her ear and whispered what I knew she'd wanted to hear for a long time. "You see what you do to me, Kay? The thought of you makes me come. You're wicked in the most fucking appetizing way. That's just one reason Jace doesn't deserve you. He doesn't see what I see, and he can't have what I can't have."

"Why?" she breathed. "Why don't you want to touch me?"

"I made a promise to your father. He was my best friend, Kay. And I'm twice your age."

Her brows scrunched, and she gripped both of my arms, pulling me down to the bed and over her body.

"My father wasn't being explicit in his request, but let me be. I believe *taking care of me* means taking care of *all* of me. It includes my body and my needs. All of my needs, Julian, which you ruined today when you so rudely interrupted my date. Jace was supposed to satisfy me, and now… Now I'm throbbing for you."

Her warm breath curled around my face. If I hadn't come earlier, I would have now. On a normal day, her being here, on my bed, wouldn't be crazy, but her small body now pinned underneath me on the same bed we shared every night felt different. It felt wrong…and right. Her deep breaths lifted her chest just shy of the hem where I knew pink nipples lurked underneath.

I gripped her by the wrist and dragged her off the bed, but she resisted.

"It's time you sleep in your room, Kay."

"No. I'm staying in my bed."

"This isn't your bed."

"Then I'm staying in your bed." She ripped her hand from mine, and I backed away, slightly confused at the girl's power.

"Fine. Have it your way. But you'll be sleeping here alone."

I left Kendra in my bed and quickly showered. By the time I finished, she was lying curled underneath the sheets. I pulled an additional blanket over her body and went downstairs to see Stefanie, who was on her third glass of wine.

"Sorry about that. Kendra can be a handful."

She slid her hand over my chest. "She's a teenage girl. Maybe she needs an outlet?"

"Like sex?" I asked.

"No, like going back to something that's familiar to her. Like shooting."

"She could remember what happened to her."

"She could also find pleasure in something that comforted her in the past. She was a pre-Olympic candidate. Maybe remembering something that brings her joy wouldn't be so bad?"

"I'll think about it. What I really need right now—"

I paused as she reached for the towel. She grasped the edge, and it slid to the floor. Stef grasped my straining dick in her hand. "I'm not a seventeen-year-old girl. I know exactly what you need, Julian."

She slid to her knees and lowered her lips over my crown. I shut my eyes. Kendra's pouty lips flashed through my mind. I fucked Stefanie's mouth and pussy plenty that night. Once on the couch, twice against the wall, on the staircase from the back and by the fireplace, erasing the image of Kendra's tight virgin pussy and Jace's flea-infested dick from memory. I fucked Stefanie until all those images washed away on one wave of ecstasy after another. She fell asleep in my guest bedroom and left for work with a smile on her face in the early morning.

I showered again and put on a pot of coffee, waiting for my horny Trouble to walk down the stairs in her in fluffy pink slippers, tank top, and a robe.

Chapter 8

Kendra

The smell of life and redemption dragged me out of bed. I threw on my robe and followed the coffee aroma downstairs, hoping Ms. More Please had left. Julian made her come eighty bazillion times last night. He thrusted, and she moaned. He pushed harder, and she screamed louder. I was sure he'd run out of energy and would sleep in this morning, but Julian was sitting by the counter, sipping on black boost juice like an Adonis, the morning-after fuck glow complementing his grin.

"You're a hypocrite, Julian." I poured myself a cup of coffee and took the seat next to him.

His brow lifted. "Do tell?"

He sipped on his coffee like he wasn't the biggest jerk in the world.

"I heard you the other night with Stefanie," I blurted. "You told me to wait with Jace, but you fucked her behind my back."

"What? It wasn't behind your back. I'm—"

"Fine—I saw you fucking her against the wall. Also eating her out on a staircase and doing all that MTP care you told me about. Did you do that on purpose? Did you *want* to make me jealous? I have officially seen things that cannot be unseen."

Like his fine dick slamming into Stefanie's pussy. Like his mouth between her thighs and his fingers in her ass. Just the thought made me tingle.

"You saw us?"

I slid off the stool, strode to the staircase, and sat on the third step. "I watched you."

"What?"

I pointed up to the second floor railing. "The skylight falls right on the staircase, and when there's a full moon, you don't need light to see."

"You saw me—"

"Four nights ago, I saw everything I wanted Jace to do. Well, I'm not sure about the fingers in the ass thing yet, but judging by the noises Stef made, it must have felt good."

He winced like he was in pain. Well, so was I, when I had to rub one out in bed later that night. On my own, thinking about all the *ohs* and *ahs* I wasn't making.

"Shit, Kay. I'm sorry."

Was he? He must have known I would hear him.

"Well, I'm not. I finally know what I'm missing, and that's a lot of orgasms. But it sounded like Stef enjoyed it. I'm not much smaller than the therapist, and Jace is quite a bit smaller than you, so I'll be fine. I can take him—"

"Stop it, Kay. You don't know what you're saying."

"But I do know. I saw what you did to her, and I want that to be me. I want to orgasm with closed eyes and curled toes. Jace better fucking step up tonight."

"What?"

"I've been thinking about it, Julian. I get it. You're too protective of me, so it's better to pop this cherry sooner than later. Face it; we both know I can't be a virgin forever. I'm getting to that age where it's embarrassing to stay a virgin, so... What if I lose it to someone you trust?"

I bit my lip, wondering whether he'd take the bait.

"Like who? Jace? Because I *don't* trust him, so he's out."

"No. I mean you."

"Me?" He waited, and I waited, likely a fraction too long. "It's not happening, Kay."

I frowned and stamped my foot. If Julian had the balls to fuck a woman in the same house where I lived, he'd better find the balls to listen to me talking about losing my virginity. I'd make him listen until his ears bled because I was on a mission to be a woman. I wanted Julian, and I wanted him badly. I wanted him to be as willing as Jace—but most of all, I wanted him to be the guy who could show me the way to... Well, oblivion was a good starting place.

"You know what you're doing. You can show me everything you showed Stef. And you could teach me, Julian. *You*, instead of Jace."

"No, no. You've got it wrong. I can't... And you can't do what Stef and I... Well, at least, not the first time. I mean, we can't do... Jesus... Your first time needs to be gentle and special. For fuck's sake, it needs to be with someone who cares for you. A lot." He pulled on his hair and rubbed the back of his neck.

"Exactly. And who cares for me most in this world? Who is it, Julian?"

"Why the fuck are we even talking about this?" He frowned. "You're setting me up."

"I'm stating the obvious. You and I make a perfect match. I have a pussy and you have a dick. We already live together, and no matter how many times you pull the godfather card, we're not related. You buy my tampons, and I pretend not to see you walk out naked after the shower. I pretend not to hear you whack yourself off in our bed, and I wait until you're snoring to touch myself."

"Kay, I'm warning you—"

"Think of me as an art piece. A fresh canvas no one has

explored or touched. You can show me the right way to fuck and to make love."

"Kay, you're pushing me…"

"And if I push too hard? What are you going to do, Julian? Punish me? Because when you talk dirty in your sleep, I like that too. I miss you in our bed, Julian. I really do."

He'd slept on the couch downstairs the past few days, and I'd missed him. I craved his closeness.

He set his coffee aside and threw his hands up in the air. "You're unbelievable."

"No." I uncrossed my legs, fully aware of how the robe slipped and exposed the black sheer panties he loved. "You do not know how unbelievable I can be, and one day soon, you'll wish it were you between my legs, deep in my pussy, claiming what's yours already. You're hard just thinking about it." I pointed to his dick.

Julian stood up from his chair with discomfort and shamelessly closed in on where I sat, pressing his erection against my knee. He was larger up close, thicker and inviting. My mouth watered at the offer.

"If you want someone who knows what he's doing, that's not Jace," he said.

I rubbed my knee over his length, stroking one way, then the other, but he didn't budge. I looked up as he shut his eyes and gritted between his teeth. "At this moment, I'm not sure whether it's any other man either, but I also know you're my best friend's daughter, and you're forbidden." He stepped away. "At least, for now. No matter how much we each secretly masturbate."

He watched me as I swallowed past my unshed tears.

Did he just admit to thinking about me as a woman?

I'd been trying to show him I was a woman for the past year and a half. I'd thought nothing worked, and I was crazy to think he would ever think of me as more than a little girl.

"You whack yourself off thinking about me?" I asked.

Julian stepped closer again and brushed the back of his hand over my neck and up to my chin, tilting my mouth at that perfect angle. He lowered until his lips hovered over mine.

"I dream about you, yes—but obviously, our relationship is complicated. I owe you a guardianship, your parents a promise, and you're…you're just a child."

I reached for his hand, removed it from my chin, and casually slid it underneath my robe, then tank top, and placed it over my breast. He shut his eyes and wanted to pull away, but I held his hand over me.

"Kay, please."

I added a little pressure, letting him have a squeeze and feel before I let go.

"Three weeks, Julian. I'm turning eighteen over Christmas."

He waited before he slid his palm slowly over my nipple, letting it graze between his fingers as he pulled away. Pure arousal stirred between my legs.

"Even if I wanted to, I couldn't do this to you, Kay. I could never take you."

I looked up. "Why? Jace wants me. God, the pleasures he promises me."

"You need to stop mentioning the fuck turd and pleasure in the same conversation. Forget him. I won't say it again."

"I live in the same house with every woman's wet dream, and I have to get myself off fantasizing because he sees me as a girl. The man I trust and want rejects me—"

"It's because I see you as my daughter, Kay."

I slid off the chair and faced him, body to body. "Say that to me when your face is between my legs."

"Kay! You can't say things like that to me."

"Why not? Does talking about my pussy get you hard?"

"Frustrated," he yelled, and I jumped. "You talking about your pussy and Jace gets me frustrated because I made a promise to your father and to your mother. And I intend to keep my promise to protect you, so stop it. If you want us to keep our friendship, you'll stop. I mean it, Kay."

As much as his words pained me, over the past three years, Julian had become my best friend. On the weekends, we ate dinners at his parents'. Wilma and Fred had their hands full with a twelve-year-old daughter I loved like a sister, and they both worked full-time. So did Julian. Getting along with him was easy. I imagined I made his relationships difficult, but we were all family. Except it'd be easier if Julian admitted I wasn't his kid.

"Okay, I get it. We're friends, but it doesn't change the fact I'm horny, flustered, and emotional. I mean, how many wet dreams can a girl have?"

"I know it's difficult, but tone it down, please, because if you give me the chance, I'd love to take you out tomorrow night."

I stilled. "Like out on a date?"

"Not a date, but it will be just the two of us. We need to talk."

"It can't be to dump me, because you can't dump me."

"I would never dump you, but I hate to burst your bubble, Kay. My only goal tomorrow night will be to show you why Jace is wrong for you."

"Are you playing with me?"

He lowered his mouth to my ear. "I don't play around, Kay. I just don't want to see your heart broken, and so long as Jace is around, that's exactly what's going to happen."

"Your focus is on the wrong person, so we'll just have to agree to disagree." I smiled. "Don't let me hold you back. I'm going to Grace's for a wax. My friends say Jace probably likes his girls bare."

"Wait—you're still seeing the fuck turd? After all our talks?" Julian's face contorted into a painful twist.

"Tonight is the night, if you know what I mean."

He growled and muttered something about scoundrels before he left for the garage. The door slammed shut, and I jumped up. Julian had canceled his date last night and the night before. He fiddled with his motorcycle in the garage until I left for Grace's salon. Julian always cleaned his bike when he was stressed.

An hour later, I was soaking in a mud bath next to Cami with cucumber slices over my eyes. Tropical sounds played overhead, complementing the relaxing vibe. While the deep tissue massage nearly put me to sleep, the waxing tore through my every nerve, and my pussy burned. It was tender and swollen, and I was doubting I'd let Jace touch me tonight.

"Should there be anything else I do to get ready?" I asked. "Like, Kegel exercises?"

"That's for when you're old and loose. You're a virgin. You're as tight as you'll ever be."

"What if I'm too tight? What if he won't fit?"

"He'll fit, but he should finger your first—you know, give it a good stretch. But don't worry, we're made to fit them."

"How did you know who would be your first?" I asked her.

"Mine was easy. Kevin from high school."

"I don't know a Kevin."

"My point's made. It doesn't matter who it is as long as he knows what he's doing. You want a lot of lube and a lot of love."

"I'm pretty sure he knows what he's doing."

"Well, Jace is a lucky man."

I let out a shaky breath and removed the cucumbers from my eyes. Cami did the same as if she could read my mind.

"Jace is fun, but when I think about my first time, he's not the one on my mind."

The paste over her forehead cracked. "Who is?"

I wiggled my nose and glanced sideways to check the hallway, but Cami beat me to it.

"Oh, my God. It's the bodyguard."

"Shut up. You know how we all fantasized about him by the pool? I've been doing some fantasizing for a long time now. I mean, he's obviously hot and built to fuck. Jesus, Cami. You should see him fuck."

She sat up in the tub like a statue, with her mouth open and her eyes blinking repeatedly.

"Come on, Cami. Say something."

"You saw him fuck?"

I nodded.

"Tell me more."

I told Cami about Julian surprising me at home, then sequestering me to my room while he fucked the therapist. I'd throbbed that night so hard.

"Man, you've got it bad."

I slouched. "I know. I sleep with the man I love, except I'm not really sleeping with him." I sighed. "Every night I lie in his bed, and I dream about his cock. I've seen his wood so many times, Cami. It's big, thick, and beautiful. It's the kind of cock you'd see up for an award, and I've seen other ones because I've whacked Jace off. He's not as large when he gets hard… Way smaller than Julian. So my question is, what do I do? Get it over with pinky-winky, or wait until Julian gives into my temptations and I experience cataclysmic orgasms?"

"The cataclysms sound wonderful." She could barely speak.

"Jace would be easy. I'm sure I wouldn't feel any pain, but what if I want pain? A little pain would be nice, if it's at Julian's hands."

She blinked until I nudged her arm.

"Your life sounds like a nineties telenovela. You can't go wrong with either, so choose the one you want more. There. That's my advice."

"That's shitty advice."

"Well, you're sure you've done everything to persuade the

bodyguard? Like, slip your foot over his underneath a blanket while watching a movie? Tug his dick while he sleeps?"

I coughed. "That's got to be illegal. Assault or something? We respect each other."

"You sleep in the same bedroom. I'm sure you can slip inside his shower, at least." She wiggled her brows.

I'd already tried that, and it didn't go well.

"Julian's not like that. I don't want to do things the wrong way."

"You're overcomplicating what should be very simple; he's a man."

Cami wasn't helpful. I placed the cucumbers over my eyes and sank deeper into the mud. "There's nothing simple about Julian Silver."

The long afternoon of pampering left me hairless and as soft as a baby's bottom, but also very sore and swollen. Grace had done my makeup and hair, and now I twirled in a brand new, perfect little black dress. I stopped in front of the mirror when I heard Julian's voice from the staircase.

"Holy shit." He was standing on the third step from the bottom and slowly descended, keeping his focus on me. He coughed into his hand before clearing his throat. "You look incredible, Kay." The tight black dress with a plunging neckline and an overlay of lace complemented my every curve. A long zipper ran from the neck to the hem. Julian stepped closer.

"You think Jace will like it?" I asked.

"This is for the fuck turd?"

"Stop calling him that. It's getting pretty serious."

"I have one question. Who's driving?"

"I am, of course. I'm an independent woman now." I dangled the keys to my Jaguar: a gift from my deceased parents. Julian had made up these gifts every year to ease the pain. He was so full of it sometimes, but how could I reject a brand new car? The money I'd been putting away from my side hustle was adding up. Maybe one day, I'd have enough to go into business. I didn't know what kind of business, but a fantastic one, for sure.

"Good. And where are you taking the fuck turd?"

"I'm meeting Jace at his place, and he's taking me somewhere nice."

Julian wasn't happy with that answer, but it was the best I could tell him, because I didn't know where we were going either. If Jace got it right, hopefully, it rhymed with an expensive presidential suite.

"Look, I'll text you when we get there, okay?"

"Okay. Be careful, Kay."

"Julian?"

"Yeah?"

"I'll likely be late. If things go well, I may not be back till the morning, and I don't want you to worry."

He shut his eyes and grimaced like I'd made his worst dreams come true.

"You have plans for the night?" I asked.

He thought for a brief moment. "My plans just changed."

"What?"

"I mean, I remembered I have paperwork, so I'm staying in."

"Oh, all right. Well, good night." I waved.

I started the ignition with my shaky hand, barely able to control my breathing and the pounding in my chest. The nerves eased after the third turn, and I relaxed into the driver's seat. Tonight was a good night. Jace had promised to introduce me to a new client so I could sell everything I'd stashed. I'd been collecting all the pills he gave me and had a copious supply. The few rich parties I'd attended when Julian spent the night with Stefanie were drug havens. Rich people ate and shared pills like candy. I never rejected an offer, but never used myself. That was my rule after Jace had slipped me my first two mollies.

I hoped the meeting was in the same hotel he'd reserved for the night, because I was so ready to get this virginity crap over with.

He met me out on the front porch of his house, in boxer shorts and slippers.

"Jace? Why aren't you ready?" I asked. "Are you stoned?"

Jesus, was he ever stoned. But we were also meeting someone important, and I couldn't miss this opportunity.

"I'm not going anywhere unless you change." I pointed upstairs. He left, and I paced around the living room. Right there in the middle of the table, five pouches with at least fifty happy pills stared back at me. Three more were scattered over the couch and another few on the love seat. I stuffed as many as I could into my purse, then ran to the car and hid a few underneath the seats. When I returned, Jace was walking down the floating staircase in a suit and a bowtie. Jesus, he was fucking stoned.

"I'm driving," I told him. "Where to?"

"After Eve, Manhattan."

I'd never heard of the club, but quickly punched the name into the navigation.

"It's beside a strip club." I pointed to Club Forever.

"After Eve is a private invitation club only, for all the beautiful women who came after Eve." He smirked and removed a square plastic card from his back pocket with what looked like a crappy picture of my face.

"Sounds posh. Is that a fake ID, Jace?"

He twirled the card between his fingers. "It's the invitation. I'm about to make all your dreams come true, Kay."

He lifted his chin and stuck out his chest, beating it with his fists like a gorilla. It was a good thing he was cute. I pushed my foot on the pedal and steered for Manhattan.

♂♀

Jace held my hand, flashed his card, and the bouncer let him through the door to After Eve without checking my fake ID. Soft jazz played overhead as we walked down a softly lit hall lined with velvet tapestry. We took a turn left past a staircase, and headed for the bar, where Jace sat beside an older man in a hat and a trench coat. He looked nothing like the other suits, drinking their expensive whiskeys and smoking chocolate cigars.

The room was large enough to hold a crowd of a hundred, with tables and private booths. A woman with pasties over her nipples waltzed by, and I realized I was at a strip club. An apron tied around her hips covered her front, and a white bow tied at the small of her back decorated her ass.

"Is this a strip club, Jace?"

"It's more than a strip club, Blondie. You go downstairs and it's an à la carte menu for every man's fantasy."

A chill trickled down my spine. "Is this where we're meeting the buyer?" I asked. "Is that him?"

"Yeah, sure," he said, turning my way. The man beside him scanned my body, and a second wave of chills scattered over my skin.

"It's nice to meet you." I cleared my throat. "So, what are you looking to buy?"

"Here's the thing, Kay. I found a way to make much more, and we don't have to sell drugs. This is Mr. Martinez."

Mr. Martinez smelled like cigarettes and booze.

"So, how much for the blonde?" he asked. "It's a one night only thing with a virgin, so make it count."

"Jace? What is he talking about?"

"We're spending the night together, baby. Just a little different."

I might have been naïve, the way Julian said, but I didn't need to hear anything more from Jace's lying mouth to understand I'd found myself in deep trouble.

"That sounds good, babe. I'm game for whatever you're into. Just need to freshen up a little. Be back soon."

I slid off the seat and made a beeline for the washrooms, except I turned for the exit at the last minute. I rushed down the empty hall until I stalled at the security guard who blocked my way. He looked at me like he'd never seen a girl before.

"I'm seventeen, and my father's a cop. You can let me through or explain to him why you allowed an underage girl inside a brothel."

He stepped aside.

I hurried to my car, constantly glancing over my shoulder and tripping over my feet. By the time I made it to the parking lot, my hands were shaking and tears falling at their own will. I started the car and pulled out of the spot, trembling and sobbing. I drove behind a waterfall of tears until I parked in our driveway, but Julian didn't come out to greet me. He'd probably left to fuck Stefanie after all.

Why couldn't I be someone's Stefanie? I blew my nose into a tissue and removed a pill from a pouch. I placed it on my tongue and swallowed before I changed my mind. Half an hour later, Jace the fuck turd no longer mattered.

Chapter 9

Julian

I poured myself a glass of scotch and stretched out my legs to where Stefanie was supposed to be kneeling. The absence of her lips around my dick tortured me with thoughts of Kendra, who was on her way to see the fuck turd. I'd canceled my fourth date with Stefanie this month. She also had no clue I'd spied on Kendra and the flea dick when we sat five rows behind them at the movies. If she discovered the level of my obsession with keeping the two of them apart, she'd rethink our benefits-only relationship. But Kay's safety trumped all. I tilted the glass back for a good swig and opened the tracking app connected to Kendra's phone.

What had happened to the days when she loved spending evenings at home, watching re-runs? What had happened to the simple times when I could masturbate in the comfort of my bed without feeling like a pedophile? Kendra had grown out of her teenage shell within a couple of months, and dealing with the little woman who slept in my bed had challenges. She'd told me about the vibrator her friends bought for her last birthday and made me change the batteries three times in the last six months. I did the math, then found a relieving solution underneath my shower.

Point was, Kendra wasn't young anymore, and she was on a mission to get laid. The tracker showed her leaving Jace's. I plugged into the car's navigation. She was heading for After Eve.

Shit.

"I'm gonna kill Jace."

I slammed my glass on the counter hard enough that it cracked. The quick response settled as I gathered my thoughts. Maybe this wasn't such a bad thing after all. Kendra would run the moment she saw he'd taken her to an invitation-only strip club, and hopefully she wouldn't find herself in the basement before I got there. She had at least a half an hour's head start.

The car purred underneath my touch as I focused on the road, but my trouble started five minutes into my drive on the interstate when a collision blocked the way.

"Fuck!" I hit the steering wheel and gripped it until my hands hurt. The never-ending traffic line stood still. It felt like forever until they cleared the road, but Kendra's navigation changed, and she was heading home. I took the first exit off the interstate and turned around. By the time I arrived home, I found Kendra in our front driveway, passed out in her car.

I opened the door and shook her awake. "Kay? Wake up, Kay."

She inhaled a breath of air like she'd been holding it for the last two minutes. Her arms flew out, and she shot up. "I'm fine. Everything's fine."

"Is it? What's going on? What happened at After Eve? Please tell me you didn't go in."

She blinked three times and shuddered. Her gaze connected with mine. "The fuck turd can go fuck himself."

I gripped the seat's side. "Did he hurt you?"

Her head took a sharp slice left and right.

"What did Jace do?"

Her brows narrowed, and her eyes filled with tears. "I… I think he was trying to pimp me."

"I'm going to kill him."

She swayed in her seat, and I checked her puffy eyes again; then saw a pouch of pills on the passenger's seat. I had a bigger problem than the fuck turd right now.

"How many did you take?"

She lifted one finger in the air. Was she lying?

"Okay, let's get you inside."

"If you kiss me, I'll give you another pouch, Julian."

I stilled. She was high.

"What?"

"Kiss me like you kiss Stefanie, and I'll give you another pouch. There's fifty in each."

"Are you getting these from him?"

"I get them everywhere. So?"

"So?"

"Kiss?"

I lowered my lips to her ear and whispered, "If you think you can blackmail your way into what should be one of the most wonderful moments of your life, think again. Not with me, Kay. You should know I can find anything you're hiding."

"What if I'm hiding the pills in my panties?"

"Kay—"

"I'm warning you," she mocked. "Come on, Julian, it's just a kiss. It's not like I'm asking you to fuck me. Obviously Jace didn't want me, so I don't know why you would."

I bet other guardians and normal fathers didn't have these problems. Not that I ever imagined myself as a father. It was different with Kay.

I lifted her petite body out of the car. She wrapped her hands around my neck and settled in my hold.

"You know the best part about being a virgin, Kay?" I whispered.

She tilted her head and the lines of her neck moved as she swallowed. "What?"

"Anticipation. It's waiting for something you want so bad that it hurts. And when you get what you've been after, it doesn't seem so special anymore. Not unless—"

"Unless what?" Her lip trembled.

"Not unless you continue the moment: ensure the toes keep curling and the body keeps giving."

What the fuck was I doing? Why was I telling her this? If luck were on my side, she wouldn't remember the conversation.

"Come on. Let's get you better."

I carried her inside and upstairs, where I set her in front of the shower.

"Undress and shower. I'll wait here."

I twisted the knob and turned around, listening to her fumble with her clothes. I heard her step underneath the shower stream and shut my eyes. Unfortunately, imagination flowed clear in my mind, and I couldn't unsee the beautiful naked woman showering behind me.

The water turned off, and I passed her the towel.

"Okay, I'm decent, but I'm in a good place, Julian. Don't ruin it."

I followed her out of the bathroom.

"What do you mean, you're in a good place?"

"It's simple. When I'm high, I don't have to think. It's just *plain* in there." She pointed to her head. "It's nice."

I relaxed my shoulders and cranked my neck to the side. "Come on, let's go make you some tea and chill on the couch."

"We're not going to bed?"

"Whatever you took needs to wear off."

We went downstairs. Kendra curled up on the sofa, and I covered her with a blanket, then made us tea. We watched cartoons until she fell asleep on the couch. I checked her pulse and blood pressure over the next few hours. The pills would need lab analysis, as I doubted their contents.

I stretched out my legs on the couch and fell asleep in the early morning hours. By the time I opened my eyes, it was ten o'clock, and Kendra was sitting cross-legged on the couch with a cup of steaming coffee.

"Good morning," she said.

"Hey, how are you feeling?"

"Better. Thank you for last night, Julian."

I sat up and covered the wood in my joggers with a blanket. I braced my elbows on my knees and pulled my hands through my hair. She fumbled with the mug. Her arms and shoulders tensed and her lips pressed together.

"I'm sorry. I… I didn't know what to do, and, well, I don't have an excuse. I'm sorry."

I flicked both brows up and waited for a reply. I wanted to help her but wasn't sure what to do.

"I want to take you somewhere, Kay. I want to show you what a date should look like, so you never consider another fuck turd again."

Her eyes popped open. "So we're going on a date?"

"No, this is just an example of a date. An example, Kay. Dress well. We're taking my bike, and it will get nippy."

"Whatever. We're going on a date." She hopped off the couch and ran upstairs to change.

Half an hour later, wind whizzed by and the first sign of winter bit at exposed skin. Kendra wrapped her arms around me from behind and held on as I rode along the shoreline. She pressed hard into my back and held me firmly. The bike's vibration shook through our bodies. We leaned into the curves and she followed my body's lead like a pro-rider. Jake and Ash never told me she rode so well.

I rolled up to a park by the beach. The ocean's waves lapped at the shore. During winter months, the park was empty for the most part.

"Did you clear the place?" she asked.

"I had a guy cleverly position a few traffic cones. It's a quiet afternoon anyways, and I need quiet."

I removed my helmet, then hers, and set them on the seat.

"You're here because your parents used to study right over there." I pointed to a bench. "I walked around with your stroller while they quizzed one another on legislature and law."

"If you haven't noticed, I've grown since my stroller days." Joy shone in her smile. Sometimes I didn't understand why she was in such a hurry to grow up.

"I have noticed. Believe me, I've noticed—and that's the whole problem. I used to wipe ice cream off your face, and now… Now I picture wiping other things off your lips."

Her mouth fell open, bringing my attention to its plump curves.

"You've grown up to be a beautiful woman, Kay, and you deserve someone who can appreciate that. Not an old fart like me, and not Jace. Definitely not Jace."

"Will you stop calling yourself old?"

I lowered my head. "I cannot cross that line with you or we'll have to find you a new place to live. Your own place. You won't be sleeping in my room anymore, but across the street, or somewhere in the neighborhood."

"Wait—are you telling me there's an actual possibility you would cross the line with me?"

"Is that all you got from what I said?" I took her hand into mine and shook my head with disappointment, but couldn't hide the fact her mind kept dragging me to that one place I denied I wanted.

"I got everything you said." Mischief sparkled in her eyes.

"Come on. There's something else I want to show you." I grabbed her hand and pulled her off the bench. We walked down the sidewalk holding hands, more so because it was nippy—or at least that's what I told myself. We turned the corner to the park's center. The sound of carnival music blared from the carousel speakers as it slowed to a stop.

I helped her up to the circular platform and chose a horse carriage filled with blankets. The gentleman at the controls smiled and set the carousel in motion. She curled into my side, and I pulled up the covers.

"Did you set this up?" she asked.

"Possibly."

I'd tipped well for the carousel operator to show up with a basket of blankets and hot tea. A month's pay, at least. The lights flickered, music played, and the world spun around us. I glanced down and lifted her chin with my finger.

"This is what a date should feel like, Kay. Safe and secure. You should never worry about safety with the right man."

"It's easy for you to say when you're the right man."

Was I?

I cleared my throat. "Your parents used to come here. They would sit right here in this seat and talk about political campaigns. You slept right through the crap."

"They were smart."

"Very smart. Like, extra special smart. And they fought to save girls your age."

"From whom?" she asked.

"Is it cliché if I say the bad guys?"

She laughed. "Maybe. But I get it. There are plenty of bad guys in the world."

"Your parents hoped you'd follow their footsteps into politics."

"Politics? No way."

"Thank God."

"You're happy about that?"

"As long as you choose a low profile career, I'm game."

"I don't know what I want to do with my life. Sometimes I'm afraid the hypnosis switched something off in my brain."

"We can reverse it."

"No. We can't."

"You're so sure about that?"

"I mean, I know it's possible, but I wrote myself a note in a journal before my first appointment to never reverse it. I don't want to remember that life and the pain. I don't want to be sad anymore. This life, with you, is much better. " She took my hand and snuggled in closer. Somewhere deep inside I agreed. This life, with her, was much better.

"Since you'll be eighteen soon, I have a gift."

I removed a small box from my jacket pocket. "Your father left a safety deposit box key in our care. He said if anything happened to him, you were to open it after you were eighteen."

"So I'd heard."

"From whom?"

"Emma. Don't worry. I don't need the money."

I leaned back and arched my brows.

"I mean, why does everything good need to happen after I'm eighteen? And more importantly, does two weeks really make a difference?"

She scooted to the seat's centre.

"It does to me. And stop looking too far ahead or you'll miss the present."

"What would you do if I were older? Like eighteen. Could you love me if I were older?" she asked.

"You've got it all wrong, Kay. I already love you. I've loved you since the day you threw up green peas all over my Nintendo. But we live in two different worlds: adult and kid. Godfather, goddaughter. Old bachelor, forbidden virgin."

"You could change that story, you know." She looked up, and I looked down.

"What?"

"Easy. Just change the story. Your adult-kid analogy becomes man-woman." She pointed between us. "Same goes for godfather-goddaughter, and if you want to know the truth, Julian, I'm the only one whose permission you need. The only thing that's forbidding here is your will, because nobody's judging except you. That's all."

If she only knew what she did to me, and what I wanted to do to her. God, how I burned for her.

"The way I see it, Julian, we live in identical worlds, but you're not willing to accept the trouble that comes along with having me. You're afraid you'll actually like me and enjoy me, because I'm younger. I've imagined you taking me and kissing me the right way because you could show me things no boy can. You've said so yourself, yet you reject what I freely want to give. Why?"

I knew I'd enjoy her. I'd take her little body to love and cherish her every inch, but I so didn't imagine this conversation turning so quickly.

"You're too young, Kay. You're my best friend's daughter."

"All right. If you need a calendar, I'll play your game. I'm turning eighteen over Christmas in Colorado. If three weeks really makes that much of a difference for you, I can wait for you until then. But I promise, I'm not going to Colorado a virgin, with your help or without."

I shifted in discomfort, and the carousel came to a slow stop.

"Wait—you're not considering Jace again, are you? Because last night you said you were done with the fuck turd."

"I was high. And everyone deserves a second chance."

"He tried to pimp you. You can't give yourself to Jace, Kay."

"I'll make it my goal to have my cherry popped before Colorado. That way, if I meet someone new, I won't seem like a loser."

"I'll do it."

"What?"

"If you promise never to see or speak to the fuck turd again, I'll take you in Colorado."

"Are you being serious right now? Is this a pity offer?"

I swallowed hard. I didn't know where this was coming from, but the deep burn in my chest gave me a pretty good idea. "It's not a pity offer. As long as you stay away from Jace Donato, I promise you'll be mine in Colorado. And when we return home after the New Year, you'll remain mine, here."

Chapter 10

Kendra

The SUV drove along the snow-covered road with good traction. Thick flakes drifted to the ground and the full moon reflected off the white powder. I absolutely adored celebrating Christmas with the Silvers at their family resort, and this year would be no different. Jacob and Fred Silver, along with the Wagners, had bought the property in the late seventies. They'd renovated it ten times over to accommodate the growing families and friends. The enormous mountain lodge with a private ski lift had everything a billionaire could imagine, including a movie theater, a games room, and a spa, but it was the family atmosphere created by the owners that made it special.

My heart beat hard in my chest and my knees bounced until Julian lowered his hand to my leg. He glanced over from the driver's seat, and the tremble ceased. I'd kept my promise and avoided Jace like the plague while Julian's promise marinated at the back of my mind. Julian hadn't made us official to the family, but I was sure he would. Soon. They loved me anyway. My phone dinged with a top of the hour countdown notification to my birthday.

"Is that what I think it is?" he asked.

"A birthday countdown. I have an extra incentive to turn eighteen."

His focus returned to the road, and I watched as his mouth twisted into a sly smile.

"Teresa said they've updated the spruce suites." The beautiful rooms shared an interior passage. Indoor-outdoor pool, and all the privacy.

"When did you talk to my mother?" he asked.

"I talk to her every day."

"We're not staying in the spruce suites this year."

"Why? I love the spruce suites. They have the shared door between the bedrooms."

He coughed into his hand. "I booked the mountain cabin."

"The private one connected to the resort? With the outdoor hot spring? For us?"

"It has two bedrooms, Kay."

"And a king-sized bed where you'll fuck me silly for my birthday? Oops. Did I just say that?"

His expression hung on the border between pleasure and pain. "I'm not fucking you for your birthday, Kay."

I frowned, and he tightened his grip over my knee, leaning in to whisper, "But I'm also tired of wondering what it'd be like to sink inside you."

Arousal cruised through my bloodstream, and I stilled. He ran his hand over my thigh, the warmth relaxing me into the seat.

We arrived at the resort in the evening. Christmas music was playing overhead in the cozy lobby. Red, green, and silver decorations glittered, and warm lights twinkled. A twelve-foot pine stood in the middle of the foyer, overflowing with gifts underneath.

I removed my jacket, and Julian draped it over his arm.

"Why are you wearing that sash today?" he asked.

"It's my birthday sash."

"I see that. But your birthday is not until—"

"Two days, Julian. How do two days change anything when you could have me now? Today, in fact? I'll be waiting in that black negligée you liked, and we can consider this an early birthday gift."

He grinned, and my stomach fluttered with hope. He gently nudged me away from the family.

"You don't know this yet, but the good things are worth waiting for, and the bad things are worth fighting for. And you're worth absolutely everything."

My mouth dried and lips parted. When had he become a poet? I adjusted the sash over my shoulder and lifted my chin.

"I'd like to wear it until it's my birthday. If that's okay with you."

He grinned. "To remind me you're turning eighteen?"

I rolled my eyes. "Of course, it's to remind you I'm turning eighteen."

"Believe me, Kay. I won't forget."

My body heated, stirring the need between my thighs.

He leaned closer to my ear. "Does that turn you on?"

I nodded.

"Good."

I heated all over again, this promise never leaving my mind. This was actually going to happen.

Julian took our bags inside our cottage. The Silvers ran a skeleton staff over the holidays to give ninety percent of the workers some well-deserved time off.

I crossed the glass passageway connected to our new home, wheeling a smaller suitcase behind me. This spot had one of the most beautiful views of a winter waterfall, which split the stream into two. I looked below at the rushing waters.

"How safe is this bridge?" I asked, hopping on top of the glass.

"I'm pretty sure you're the first to jump on a glass bridge."

"This won't break, will it?"

I didn't wait for Julian's reply and hurried off the platform. The cabin glowed with cozy warmth. I lowered my suitcase and kicked off my boots. Wooden floors, walls, ceilings and furniture, with complementary cushions pillows, throws, and blankets added a touch of softness A wood-burning fireplace roared in the back. I removed my jacket, then my sweater.

"Someone turned up the heat in here." Julian opened a side window. The chilly breeze sucked some of the hot air outside. Then he closed the window again. "We better get used to this. It should cool as the wood burns down."

I doubted anything would stay cool in this cozy cabin. I strolled through the rooms. String lights were woven around the beams and hanging against the back wall. Beams ran across the ceiling, and the moon shone through the skylight. The open concept design, along with a wall of forest facing windows, brought the outdoors in. Warm blankets covered the couch and chairs and were scattered across the fluffy rug on the floor. I removed my socks and walked in front of the fireplace. The thick rug tickled my toes. I turned around and noticed that Julian was watching me the entire time.

"Do you like it?" he asked.

"I love it."

His head turned in slow motion, and I followed its path to the open barn door. Beyond, dozens of pillows were stacked on a king-sized bed. Canopy sheers hung around corner posts, draping over top. Julian held his head high and shoulders back. I found his confidence sexy because I'd lost mine somewhere between my third and fourth worry about tonight. He flicked on a switch, illuminating thousands of lights wound around the bedposts. My mouth fell open, and the corner of his lifted.

I ran to the king-size bed, jumped in the middle, and propped myself on my side, striking a pose.

"Okay, Julian. I'm ready. Take me!" I said dramatically, and he laughed.

"I have a meeting with my partners today."

"It's eight o'clock."

"I'll be awhile, Kay."

"Why are you working while on vacation?"

"We're always working. You know that."

I swung my legs over the bed's edge and sat up, pouting. "I've heard about this place, but I never thought I'd be here, and now you have to leave."

"I wanted our stay to be special, and we're here for over two weeks, Kay."

He strode to the bed where I was sitting. I parted my knees, and Julian stepped right up to the mattress. He tilted my chin and lowered his mouth to my ear. "If you didn't catch that, Kay, that's two weeks of me discovering every freckle on your skin, learning which touch makes you laugh, cry, and come. You think you want me, but you have no clue how much I desire you."

Goosebumps covered my skin as I trembled.

He rose and adjusted the erection behind his zipper. "Jesus, if you keep looking at me like this, I won't be able to walk."

I bit my lip and squirmed in my seat. He kissed the top of my head. The smell of his cologne launched my senses wildly and sent my head into a spin.

"Enjoy your stay, Kay. I'll see you later tonight."

"See you later."

I closed my eyes to get rid of the sound of awkwardness, but that didn't work. Julian left, and I explored the cozy mountain cabin.

I swam in the indoor pool near the sauna. A small door connected the area to an outdoor swimming spa underneath the sky. It was stunning and sad that I was here alone. I got out of the water just after midnight and decided on a warmer pair of shorts and a long-sleeved top for the night. I brushed my teeth, braided my hair, and Julian still wasn't back. What was the point of the cabin if the two of us wouldn't use it?

The clock shone three in the morning when he pulled my sheets aside and tried crawling over me to his side of the bed.

"Ouch. You're on the wrong side, Julian."

A faint scent of scotch lingered in the air. He braced his elbows on my sides and hovered above me, whisking my body with his. He was much warmer than the blanket. My nipples pebbled underneath his skin because, of course, Julian was wearing his boxer-briefs and nothing else. Boxer-briefs and muscles never looked better.

"It feels pretty right to me."

He breathed above me and lowered his weight further. He felt pretty damn good to me as well. His hard muscles, dominating thighs, and an erection that stroked over my pubic bone overwhelmed me, but the moment was gone just as fast.

"Shit, I'm sorry, Kay." He lifted and rolled to the other side.

"Are you drunk?" I asked.

"A little. I told my father about us, so he got drunk, and I had a few glasses with him. Then my brother came and… yeah. I think I may be drunk, a little."

A pungent smell wafted around the room. I jumped out of bed and opened the window a crack.

"Julian, your father's known about us for a while. He's been one of my biggest supporters." I went back to the bed and pulled on his hand.

"What are you doing?"

"Come on. You need a shower. I'm not sleeping with your stinky ass."

I twisted the shower knob, and when I turned back around, Julian was standing naked behind me, his boxer briefs dropped to the side. I stared at his stunning body, masterfully sculpted and glistening in the soft candle glow. He was hard and looking at me like this was it.

I slid open the glass door, and he walked past me and underneath the stream. I let go of my breath and went to the kitchen to put on some tea. Except I didn't know which tea to choose. There was a peppermint one and a chamomile, but maybe Julian would like hot cocoa? Since chocolate could make him nauseous, I opted for the ginger, chamomile, and honey option, but by the time I had it ready and returned to the bedroom, he was snoring.

I JOINED the family for breakfast and let Julian sleep in. He showed up fifteen minutes late, dazed and confused, sat next to Tristan and James, and waved to me at the other end of the table.

"You like my brother a lot, don't you?" Emma asked, and I nodded, sticking my fork into a pancake.

"I love him, Ems. It's as simple as that."

"But you're like my sister."

"Julian is not like my brother—"

"No. He's like your daddy."

I cringed and saw Wilma spit out the spiced eggnog she was sipping. She dabbed a napkin to her lips and tried to pretend she'd heard nothing.

"He's always been a friend, you know. He was there for me after my parents died, and he protects me. Julian's every girl's fantasy."

"Gross. I prefer horses and cowboys."

"The thing is, Ems, in a few years you won't think it's gross."

"I think James has someone new." She sighed. "Whatever happened to independence?"

I held back the chuckle. Emma was the best family gossip vault. "Tiffany didn't come?"

"No, they broke up a while ago. That girl over there—that's James's girl. She's gonna be a cop."

"James brought her? She looks young."

"Her name is Laura, and she was part of the festive welcome decorations Hunter organized."

"Who put him in charge of that?" Hunter and decorating never married well.

"He volunteered." She slumped in her seat.

"I think you should take over the decorations next year, Ems."

"Really?" She perked up again. "You think I could do it?"

"I know you can. You're eleven already."

"Almost twelve."

"See? And I can always help you as well."

"You're the best sister I never had." She hugged me from the side.

"Ditto."

Wilma's eyes welled, and Fred pulled in a sniffle. I loved Christmas.

Julian disappeared to another meeting right after breakfast. I took Emma to the spa, where we enjoyed the jets and gave one another a quick massage. The skeleton staff meant there was no full-time masseuse. Grace Wagner joined us in the salts baths and helped us apply face masks. It was a splendid afternoon.

In the evening, the common room with the central fireplace filled with family. Music played, laughter bubbled, and I snuck in a glass of spiced eggnog. Suspended overhead, sparkling snowflakes twirled. Lights were wrapped around the windows and beams, while evergreen branches, ornaments, and ribbons decorated the mantel.

Hunter entertained his ascot twins by the bar, and I still

couldn't find Julian. Jenga and Scrabble took us to the early afternoon and then the buffet-style dinner until James came out dressed as Santa and started listening to wishes.

My wish was sitting near the tree. Julian looked at me from across the room, like he was ready to pounce. I checked my notification app, and we still had a few hours until my birthday. I yawned and went to the coffee station for a double espresso.

"Planning to stay up all night?" I heard from behind me, and turned around to face Julian. He stood close enough that his thick thighs brushed against mine.

"If you play your cards right." I wiggled my brows, and his lifted in amusement.

He removed the steaming cup from my hand and took a sip. "Pretty sure I'll be up all night as well. Santa hour is over. What did you wish for?"

I lowered a fresh cup underneath the espresso machine and pressed the auto button. The machine ground beans behind me, and I waited until it finished.

"If I tell you my wish, it won't come true."

"I don't think Santa works like a birthday."

"It does in my mind."

The espresso dripped, and I shot him a narrow look. "You're up to something."

"Do you know what time it is, Kay?"

I checked my watch and the notification countdown to my birthday.

"Sixteen hours until my birthday."

But Julian shook his head. The right side of his mouth lifted into a slow smile. A spark ignited in my chest. He set his espresso on the counter and I lowered mine.

"No, it's not." The bottomless depth of his gaze shook me awake more than the coffee could. "Have you forgotten you were born in Auckland? The time difference means you're already eighteen. Happy birthday, Kay."

He lifted my chin with his finger and lowered his mouth to mine. I closed my eyes. It was just like in the movies: my lips hid within his as his tongue slid between them. He kissed me hard and deep, guiding my senses to ecstasy. Sounds faded, the world spun around us, and my knees buckled. Julian caught my limp body and held it against his.

When he pulled away, I wasn't sure whether to stare at his lovely mouth, the sparking need in his eyes, or the impatient grip of his fingers which remained on my skin. I looked up at the ceiling to where he was pointing.

"You kissed me because of the mistletoe?" I asked.

"No, Kay. I kissed you because I wanted to, and now I'll kiss you because of the mistletoe."

His arms wound tighter, and his lips took my mouth again, tongue sweeping all the illicit promises that had been made between us.

I trembled, and he lifted me into his arms. I wound my hands around Julian's neck as he carried me across the lobby with his head held high. Someone whistled, but Julian gave no flying fuck who saw us.

Julian continued down the long hallway, then cradled me in his arms across the glass bridge to our cabin. He kicked the door back to lock it, and its echo brought out the shivers on my arms. My heels slipped off of my feet and hit the floor with a thump, thump. I listened to his heavy breaths, waiting for his next move.

His sultry gaze held all the answers to my questions.

"How would you like to start your birthday celebration with my dick inside you?"

I whimpered and dripped down my inner thigh. The sheer panties I was wearing were completely useless.

Chapter 11

Julian

I stepped inside our bedroom with Kendra in my arms. Passing the threshold like this felt different today. She'd happily settled in my hold as I'd carried her across the resort to our cabin. Wonderment swam in her eyes, and it was driving me crazy. If she knew the things I wanted to do to her, she'd rethink her quest to lose her virginity. But I was better than Jace and better than any other man. I knew her and cared for her, and I'd never harm her.

She played with my hair, scraping her nails over my scalp and putting me off balance. I brushed my nose against her curls and inhaled. Her scent was sharper, and for the first time in my life, it finally felt right to hold her like this, to touch her like she was the only woman I wanted to touch and to show her how fucking desperate I was to have her. I could finally tell her I burned for her.

I kissed her hard and slow, meandering through her willing mouth the way I imagined she'dwant to be kissed. She slid down my body without letting go of my mouth and rested on her tiptoes. I held her tiny ass in my hands and swallowed her soft moans. My dick became extremely uncomfortable in the confinement of my slacks. She gripped my arms and pressed herself against my body until she pulled away, breathing hard and looking up.

"You need to pinch me. Is this really happening, Julian?"

Her eyes were soft as a whisper and reminded me to be gentle. Question was, could I be? I lowered my lips to her ear. "I'll do better than pinch you, my sweet Kay. I'll fuck you instead."

She backed away into the bed and I stepped forward, giving her one way out. "I've imagined this moment, and I've dreamed about it."

Her eyes grew wide, and she covered her mouth with her hand. "So have I," she whispered.

"Nothing can stop me from feasting on your pussy tonight. Now get up on that bed."

She shuddered, and her skin flushed with a beautiful shade. I wanted to see more of that shade, and so I lifted her. She squealed in my hold but calmed as soon as I set her on the edge of the bed. I leaned into the mattress and brushed her hair aside, exposing her neck. I chose the spot behind her ear as the perfect place to begin, but she stopped me.

"You want my pussy, but I want you too."

She parted her knees and lifted her dress, drawing my attention to the barely-there panties and soaked lips while her little fingers played over my shirt's buttons. She popped them all the way down, distracting me, and slid down to remove the shirt from my shoulders. Her fingers danced through the sprinkle of my chest hair, and I closed my eyes. No woman's hand had ever felt this good on my skin.

"I've known you half my life, Kay," I breathed, and her hand slid down my abs and over my happy trail, teasing me before her hands made the journey back to my hair, smoothing it over.

"I've known you my entire life." She stood up on the bed and brushed my hair back, bringing my chin to her belly. I slid my hands up her legs, underneath her dress, and right up to her ass, cupping both cheeks, and felt her out around the G-string. Her body yielded to my touch.

"I want to make love to you, Kay," I whispered.

"Then make love to me, Julian. I've wanted to make love to you for a long time, and I've thought about this moment for a long time, but I don't really know what to do, so you need to tell me what you like...because I don't know." Her breath finished, and she drew in more air. "Teach me, so I can please you right the first time, and every time."

God, she was so fucking cute. "It's okay to be nervous." I couldn't wait to teach her everything.

"I'm not nervous. I just want you so bad. All of you."

The fact I'd resisted this woman for so long was a miracle, but it had also left me proud. I'd asked my parents' blessing before tonight, and now, I could date Kendra freely. Except we were well past the dating stage. I gripped her ankles and pulled her feet from underneath her. She flew down to the bedding, screaming in laughter, the sound bouncing through the room and lifting the mood. I traced my fingers up her thighs and climbed up on the bed above her, scrunching her dress on the way. She bit her lip, and I pushed her dress further up, exposing her sheer black triangle at the front of her G-string. She was shaved underneath, or waxed, at least. I swept my finger over her mound and snuck my hand inside the panties, sweeping over her soaked pussy.

Her knees pushed further out, relaxed, pussy throbbing and eyes closed.

"Is that for me?" I asked, and she gripped my hand.

"You don't get to ask me questions right now. Of course, it's for you. I need you, Julian. I need you to take me like a woman."

"I will do nothing less, Kay, that I promise you. What I don't promise is fast." I pulled a slow smile. "So lie back and relax. We have time."

She removed her grip from my hand, and I yanked at her panties. The fabric snapped over her hip and she let out a loud gasp. A naughty smile stretched across her face. She liked that, and I enjoyed discovering what she enjoyed. Another smile followed, so I knew I was on the right track.

I kissed my way back up her body and to her ear, grasping the zipper underneath her armpit and pulled it to the hem. I liked the easy access dress even more. "Take the dress off, Kay. I want you naked."

The fabric opened, revealing her white flesh, perky breasts, and very pink nipples. She shimmied out of the fabric while I slipped out of my slacks and socks. I freed my straining cock from underneath the boxer briefs. Kendra gaped as it sprang to its ready position.

She pointed. "How is that ever going to fit inside me?"The better question was, how soon before I could be inside her?

I gripped my cock and stroked it twice, eyeing her much smaller body. "It will fit, but we'll have some fun before we get there."

I let go of my dick and lowered to her earlobe from where I kissed my way over her mouth, grazed her lips, and lingered to the other ear. "I will taste and kiss every inch of your skin before I'm inside you, Kay."

"Oh, my God…. You…you're going to torture me."

"No, Kay. I will please you, and then I'll obliterate you until you think about my cock every time you sit, walk, run, or ski."

I stroked my tongue along her neck and over to her chest. Her whimper echoed with desire. My hand played with each breast, brushing over her erect nipples. Kay pushed her chest to my mouth and her pussy hard against my thigh. I closed my lips around her nub, pulling on the flesh. Her body coiled underneath me. It was beautiful. She parted her knees, and my hand slid down to her soaked pussy.

I kissed my way down her body, eager to taste her. She writhed underneath me, stroking her foot along my throbbing dick while I dove between her legs and kissed over her pink lips and heated flesh. She gripped the sheets and held on. I looked up from between her legs, down her belly, and through the valley between her breasts. Jesus, she looked so beautiful.

She lifted her head. "What's wrong?"

"Nothing. Just taking in the moment. You're fucking delicious and irresistible."

She smiled and a dimple appeared in her cheek, and I returned to her glistening flesh. She shuddered and closed her eyes. I pulled my finger down the slit and rimmed her opening, sliding it in. I knew she used tampons and this wouldn't hurt, so I added another finger, stretching her. Kay slid further down, begging for more until I closed my mouth around her. She gave into my touch, and my tongue. I swept around her clit, flicking back and forth. Her legs straightened and her swollen pussy pulsed in my mouth as she screamed, "Oh, my God! Julian!"

She spasmed in my hold. I licked through her orgasm, clasping my mouth hard over her clit. The bud pulsed between my lips as arousal shook through her body. She tensed and relaxed repeatedly, and when she thought she was done, I hooked my fingers inside her and rubbed on her spot, sucking harder. Her pussy tightened around my fingers as I revived her orgasm. This time I held firm and swept my tongue over her clit until she fell limp to the bed.

I looked up between her thighs and kissed my way up to her body and to her mouth. She parted her lips, changing the kiss into an erotic moment as I realized she wanted to taste the feast I'd had. My cock prodded at her entrance, and she opened her eyes.

I brushed the hair back over her forehead. "Are you ready, Kay?"

Her lips pressed into a smile.

"Tell me what you want me to do, Kay. Tell me if it's too much."

"Make love to me, Julian. Make me a woman."

I braced my arms over the bed and hovered above her, pushing forward until the head of my cock settled at the rim of her opening. Her mouth opened in awe as she watched me enter her an inch.

"Wait." She gripped the sheet, and I stilled. "You don't need a condom? I mean, after all the talks we've had about safe sex?"

"I haven't slept with another woman in months and I've been tested, Kay, so I know I'm clean. And you're a virgin. Also, you ovulated already, and you're getting your period in three days, so I can come inside you until my semen drips out of your pussy."

"Holy crap."

"If that's alright with you."

She swallowed hard and blew out a long breath while holding my gaze. She bit back a grin and slid further onto my cock. I was two inches in when her lips parted and eyes closed, and there was no way I could pull out now, so I pushed further in. She tightened around my cock, and her eyes flew open. Jesus, it would be more difficult not to fuck her than I thought. I watched her watching me sink deeper inside her, her eyes growing wide. She gripped the sheets and held still until I reached her depth and stayed there. I lowered my mouth to hers and kissed her. "Did that hurt?"

"A little. It's very…filling, But I like it. I like you inside of me."

I enjoyed being inside her, too. How could I fucking not enjoy it? She kissed me and rolled her hips up and down my cock at an agonizingly slow pace. Her open mouth and pouty lips forced an image of my cock there. I thrust harder at the thought, and she flew higher on the bed.

"Yes, like that, Julian."

Her legs fell apart again, opening for my hips. I knelt in front of her and gripped her waist while deep inside her, holding her steady. My next thrust pushed her against the headboard. "Like that?"

"Yes," she panted.

"You give yourself to me like this and we won't leave this cabin for days, Kay."

"We'll starve." She laughed.

"All I need is your pussy."

I pushed forward again and again, finding the perfect rhythm to her willing body, bouncing breasts, and singing moans. I sank inside her warmth like I belonged there. Sheets crumpled, pillows fell to the floor, and I thought I'd last much longer…until Kay lifted her legs and rested her feet on my chest. She grasped her breasts, pinched her nipples, and my balls tightened.

I braced my arms at her sides. Her tight pussy gripped my cock as I retracted, forcing me back inside. I stretched her and watched her watch me as I took her virginity. She was glistening with sweat and need as I slid in and out. I followed her twirling fingers over her breasts and pure ecstasy zapped through my lower spine, then into my balls. I pulled out, spilling over her stomach and waxed pussy.

She was finally mine, and it was only nine in the evening.

I lowered her legs to the bed. Her flushed skin, wild hair and dreamy eyes, along with that light smile, were a picture worth painting.

I made a square border with my fingers, outlining her shape. "If I had a portrait I wanted to hang, you would be it."

She grinned from ear to ear. "I knew it would be good, but I didn't expect amazing."

"Amazing? I guess that's a good start."

"Start? That was just a start?"

I scratched at my jaw. "You do not know what's coming your way, do you?"

She lifted to her elbows. "So show me. I want to do everything with you, Julian. Teach me everything."

My dick had barely settled, and it was already getting hard again.

"Hold all that eagerness for later. Let's go wash you up." I wiggled my brows, but she remained still, looking at my dick like it was the golden prize.

As much as I would've liked to fill that open gap between her lips, I shed the image of my golden dick and concentrated on the necessities. We'd get to her mouth later. "If I wasn't clear, Kay, come with me so that I can wash you. I will be very thorough."

I scooped her in my arms, and she squealed in delight as I carried her to the oversized shower. I set her down, ran the warm water, and soaped a sponge. The suds lathered over her arms and chest. I stepped around her and washed her back, all the way down to her ass and through her sensitive crack. She set her feet apart and glanced back over her shoulder. "You want my ass?"

Her willingness for anything was one of the many reasons my dick rarely had a break.

"I want everything, darling, but in due time."

I stepped back to her front and circled the sponge over her chest and down her stained belly.

"Why are you smiling like that?" she asked.

"Like how?"

"You're gloating."

I couldn't deny the pleasure of seeing my cum on her skin.

I dropped the sponge to the bench and lowered my hand down her stomach and to her pussy, cupping it—"I just slept with a woman half my age. A man's gotta be a little proud of that."

I pulled my fingers between her folds, and she winced.

"Are you hurt?"

"Sore. In a good way. You should definitely be proud of that."

My brows furrowed.

"And not sore enough that I can't sit on your cock. Because I'm ready to go again. I promise."

That eagerness didn't help my dick, either.

"We have time. And I'm all about making your wishes come true."

Her tiny frown disappeared as soon as I resumed washing her. Her bare pussy felt a little swollen, but definitely not swollen enough. She closed her eyes and lifted her face to the shower. The night was young, and our fun in this private cabin had only begun.

"Do you think my parents would let me date you?" she said out of nowhere.

"Never thought about it."

"Why not?"

"Because I never thought about dating you when they were alive, and now it's a moot point."

"You mean a moo point," she corrected.

My brows narrowed. "I didn't know you were into *Friends*. That's Joey's line. Joey says moo."

She giggled. "That's cute."

"What?"

"You mooing." She tilted her head. "Why are you so surprised I watch *Friends*?" She twisted her hair into a knot and wrung out the water before stepping out of the shower. "It's a classic. I obviously love everything older... Things... Men included."

"Man," I corrected her. "You're only into one older man."

She stepped out of the shower and sauntered out of the bathroom. I watched her round ass sway back and forth and realized I was living out every man's wet dream. Except I wanted this dream to last much longer than a few nights. I wanted this forever.

Chapter 12

Kendra

I stepped out of our bedroom into the open area. Tea was steaming in the pot on the table, and Julian had prepared something in the kitchen across the family room. I stared at the stack of perfectly sculpted muscles on his back, down to his boxer briefs, and smiled. I secured the tie on my robe and tiptoed behind him, snaking my hands around his torso.

"I changed the sheets." I kissed him on his back. "We made quite the mess."

He turned around and placed a strawberry between my lips. "Hungry?"

I glanced at the fruit platter on the kitchen counter and pushed my thigh into his semi-hard dick. "No eggplant?"

"I'm assuming that's supposed to be a joke, because all I have is dick." He set the knife aside and grasped me by my hips. I squealed in his hold. We spun in a semi-circle, and he lifted me to the table's edge. "But I won't refuse your pussy or your peach."

He kissed me hard on the lips and held me until I couldn't breathe and pulled away.

"Julian, this is where we eat."

"Exactly." He was grinning from ear to ear, kissing me every few breaths. His lips tasted like watermelon and mint. "I'm ready to move on to the main course."

His hand drew along my inner thigh and I parted my legs, giving him full access at the table's ledge. He reached for a piece of watermelon and placed it between our lips. I sucked on the fruit, then on his tongue, and pulled apart with reluctance.

"I've been thinking—"

"You know, that usually ends with me warning you."

"I like it when you warn me, so that's not really a threat, but I've been thinking about how you put your finger in Stef's ass that night."

"Oh, Kay. Do we need to mention other women when I kiss you?"

"I want that from you. I want you to take me in every way, Julian. I want to experience all of you. Your dick and finger inside me. I want you on this table, on the floor, in the pool, on the staircase—"

"There's no staircase in this cabin."

"We can add it to our bucket list."

"We have a bucket list?"

I showed him a full rack of teeth and wiggled my behind. "Of course, we do. The kitchen counter's on the list too."

He lowered his hand to between my legs. "And the table?"

I inched my fingers toward his erection. "Everything's on the list."

"You're swollen, and need a break."

"Is your old heart threatening to give out?"

I curled my hair around my finger, the move I used to work his need like a charm.

"So table, it is?" His smile turned crooked, and I rubbed my hand over his straining dick.

"Slide back." His chest rumbled.

I backed up onto the wooden table. He gripped my ankles, bending me at the knees and forcing me to lie back. The robe parted to the sides, exposing me. He kissed from my toe and up, past my knee and along my inner thigh. His mouth left a searing trail all the way to my sex. He looked up from between my legs.

I lifted to my elbows. I'd frame the picture of his head between my legs if I could.

"I've dreamed about your mouth there. I rubbed a few out too, thinking—ahh..."

His tongue swept along my folds, magically drawing out hot arousal. He closed his mouth around my clit and cut off my senses. The gentle strokes wound me up in waves until the ice cube along my flesh made me jump. He held it between his lips and pulled it along my heat, adding fuel to my desire. My pussy pulsed with impatience, and I trembled in his hold. I pushed on his head, forcing his mouth harder against me. He licked around the spot where I needed him to suck me.

"Julian, please."

His lips closed over my swollen clit.

"Ahh..." I closed my eyes. His tongue flicked over the nub with sweet promises. He slid his fingers inside me and pumped in a delectable rhythm. I pressed on his head, and his tender strokes registered stronger. I lost control sometime between the eighth and ninth finger fuck. This orgasm was stronger and longer, and left me panting on top of the table.

A pleased smile stretched across his face. "You look fucking beautiful, Kay."

I wiggled my brows and focused on his standing dick as he rose. "The view's not so bad from here either."

He pushed back his shoulders and set his jaw, fighting back mischief. "I want to keep you to myself for a while."

"What?"

"How about we make it official with the family after New Year?"

"I'm pretty sure our family already knows, Julian."

"We have this cabin until after New Year. There's enough food here until then."

I counted in my mind. "That gives us ten secret days to ourselves—"

"Making love in this cabin."

He pulled on my knees, bringing my ass to the table's edge, and bent down, kissing me. "Just you and me," he murmured into the crook of my neck. His lips vibrated over my skin.

"I don't want to make love, Julian. I want you to fuck me."

"Kay—"

I flattened my palm against his chest. "I won't take no for an answer until you fuck me. I want to know what it feels like when Julian Silver loses control."

"If you don't stop talking like that, I will lose control."

"Oh yeah? And what would you do if—"

He closed his mouth over mine so quickly, I had no time to catch my breath. His tongue maneuvered between my lips with inviting strokes, and my body went limp. He definitely had experience working on his side.

"I want you inside me again, Julian. I… I can't wait."

"Patience has never been your strength, has it?"

He gripped me by my hips and slid me off the table, kissing me. The robe slid off my shoulders, leaving me naked. He turned me around and bent me over the table, stroking my ass cheek with his hand. A breeze blew between my legs, cooling my heat. Julian lined himself up behind me and pushed forward, filling me.

I smiled and looked back over my shoulder. He was standing at the table's edge. His eyes were closed as he held his dick inside me, savoring the moment. He looked incredible. The broad shoulders, hard chest, stacked abs, and a tantalizing v-line with a sprinkled happy trail were a picture worth pure gold.

"I won't last if you keep looking at me like that."

I giggled. "I shall make that my challenge. How fast can Julian come inside my pussy?"

"The answer to that is very fast."

But how could I not look at him when he was pumping so beautifully from behind? I gripped the table and braced myself. The sound of slapping skin and heavy breaths carried through the cabin. The smell of burning wood, us, and sex blended into euphoria. The pressure below my belt neared another climax. I sucked in short breaths as Julian gripped my hips and pressed to my lower back, tilting my ass.

"Jesus, you look so beautiful. Perfect."

I watched him watching his dick slide in and out of my pussy, and arousal flooded my veins. His hands slid to my ass cheeks, and he spread them apart. The tip of his finger rimmed my remaining virgin hole, and I stilled. The sensitive skin around my ass tingled with pleasure, but he pulled away.

"More," I begged. Instead, he drew his hand underneath and to my pussy. His fingers and my skin sparked the fuse, throwing me into a frenzy. I lost it at the first touch. Julian pushed in once more and found his release as he rubbed me to the finish line.

I lay spent on the table, my chest and cheeks pressed flat against the surface, until Julian withdrew and helped me up.

"You all right?" he asked.

"Never been better." My breath eased out on a wave of satisfaction.

Julian squatted to his ankles and pulled up his boxer-briefs. He picked my robe up off of the floor and draped it over my shoulders. "I'm starving. Time to eat."

"I have to wash up. You're dripping down my thighs."

"Perfect." He contained to gloat behind his lips. "Food should be ready when you're done. I'll use the other bathroom."

I kissed him once more and showered in haste. By the time I finished, a delicious aroma of fried veggies and meat was wafting into the bathroom. I put on my bathing suit and joined Julian in the kitchen.

"Are those fajitas?" I pointed to the platter of fried veggies and beef.

"They are."

"I didn't know you could cook so well."

"Because you've only seen me order take out?"

"No, because Olivier stuffs your fridge full of prepped meals."

"Right. Well, as you can see, my talents extend beyond fucking."

I giggled. We ate the fajitas and washed them down with sparkling, non-alcoholic wine.

"Don't you find it odd that I can't buy alcohol, but I can have sex?"

"Never really thought about it. But just because you can buy something doesn't mean you should have it."

He set the plates in the dishwasher and cleaned up the table.

I frowned. "I'm not into drugs anymore."

"Kay, I didn't mean to imply you were. I didn't mean to upset you."

"No, it's okay. I'm not upset."

"I'd argue that."

"I promise I'm not. Julian?"

"Yes?"

"What will happen when we go home?"

"I'm going to take you to our bedroom and finally christen the bed we've been sleeping in, then every single room in that house."

"So we're going to be a couple? Together?"

"I don't see another way. You're stuck with me, whether you like it or not."

I bit my lip. "That's good."

He refilled my glass and joined me on the rug in front of the fireplace. I pushed the pillows to the side and lay my head on his lap. The wood crackled and flames flickered with orange spit.

"But I have a few rules, Kay."

I looked up. "I want to hear them."

"Why are you so keen to hear them?"

"So I know exactly which ones to break."

"If you break a rule, I'll... Punish you?"

"Was that a question or a promise, Julian? Because if it was a question, then my answer is, yes, please. Same goes if it was a promise."

"I'm serious about this, Kay, and I won't stand for these rules to be broken."

My face sobered. "All right. What are these rules?"

"No Jace."

"Done. Next?"

"No drugs."

My heart gunned into overdrive. "Done again. See, we're doing great with rules so far. I don't need to break any rules. Definitely not the drug one."

His brows furrowed. Julian might have promised me Colorado, but since I wasn't sure he'd go through with it, I'd brought a back-up pouch. But I'd throw it out as soon as I had the chance.

"Kay—"

"You don't have to warn me, Julian. The only drug I need right now is you."

He pounced on me, taking me down to the couch and then the floor. I rolled in his secure hold, and we made love by the fireplace. I lost count of how many times he took me that night. All I knew was that I was sore, and I loved every moment.

I woke up to the sun streaming down my face. Julian lay beside me, tangled in the sheets. His mouth was partially open, curving up. The best part of falling asleep in the same bed was falling asleep in his arms. I eyeballed his sculpted body. He lay naked underneath the thin sheets like a picture of perfection. I watched him sleep and didn't want to move until I saw the tenting fabric. My mouth watered.

I shimmied lower and snaked my hand underneath the sheets and down to his morning wood. I wrapped my fingers around his length, brushing my thumb along the thick vein in his cock. Jesus, was he ever beautiful! No wonder I could still feel him on the inside from last night. He'd claimed me like I was his, and I was ready to claim what was mine. I lowered my mouth to his crown.

"Ahh." His sigh synched with his flexed dick in my mouth. "Good morning," he murmured. "That feels amazing."

I released him with a quiet *pop*. "Morning."

"Please, don't stop."

He focused on my lips like they were the key to the heavens. I lowered my mouth and pulled my tongue around his crown, watching him grip the sheets. He finally closed his eyes, and I slid down his cock, pushing my lips against the heated skin and tightening my grip. My pussy throbbed as I stroked him. His veins thickened underneath my lips, and I increased the momentum. The urge to touch him and play with him quickly turned to a need to satisfy him. I wanted to please him the way he'd pleased me.

He reached for me, and I shifted so he could touch me, but as I concentrated on his dick, he swung my leg over his chest and brought my knees near his shoulders, lining my crotch up above his face. I embraced the new position, tightened my lips around him and took him to the back of my throat. His mouth covered my pussy, tasting me and teasing until I settled in the perfect spot. I reached for his balls. His immediate response, to inflict torturous tongue strokes, was very welcome but very distracting to my blowjob, because I wanted more. More of him in my mouth and of me in his. He slid in and out of my mouth while excitement swelled in my nether region. My knees wobbled, and the bed rocked.

"Julian, the ground is shaking."

He sucked harder, and I pumped quicker, until I erupted like a volcano. Julian spilled into my mouth as I shook through my climax. By then, the atmosphere was rumbling, the ground was shaking, and dishes clattered to the floor. I shot off Julian as soon as he finished. He grabbed me in his arms and pulled me into his body as the rolling boomed, until it stopped.

"Is it over? Was that an earthquake?"

He removed his phone from the nightstand and checked his messages.

"Avalanche. It fell all the way to the resort. I have to go, Kay. There's a rescue underway. Scar was out in the helicopter, and they're afraid the avalanche swept him and his girl away."

Julian jumped out of bed and dressed in a hurry. I slipped into a pair of warm tights and a sweater. "You should join the family in the common room. I don't want you here alone," he said.

"I will as soon as I clean up. Be careful. I'll see you soon."

Outside, the clear skies and sunny day gave a perfect view of the mountain and the avalanche aftermath which had touched the resort. I made our bed, cleared the dishes, and went to the main building, where I spent the day with the Silvers as they organized a search party. Emma ran to the window and back with any progress she thought she could see up on the mountain. When she nudged me in the early afternoon, I thought the rescue was done.

"Who's that?" She pointed to the front door, and I turned with Wilma at the same time.

A woman in a full-length fur coat removed her sunglasses. The man with her walked over to Fred Silver and shook his hand.

"Oh, my God," I whispered.

"Oh, my God," Wilma repeated.

"It's my parents." I said, and my knees buckled.

Chapter 13

Julian

"Honey, I'm home!" I called out and locked the door behind me. "You won't believe the day I had. Scar and Jules are safe, the main road is cleared, and I can't fucking wait to sink inside you again."

I removed my jacket and stepped further inside the cabin, where Kendra was standing in the middle of the room with her eyes wide and mouth open.

I froze. "Is everything all right?"

"No. It's not." The male voice from the side came with a powerful right hook to my jaw.

"Daddy!"

"Jake!"

"What the fuck?" I turned, only to receive a punch from the left and closer to my nose.

I shook off the pain and backed behind the kitchen counter, from where I stared openmouthed at the two people I'd never expected to see again. Ashley was covering her mouth with her hand. Dark circles underlined her eyes. She was thinner and more frail than I remembered. The new wrinkles paired well with the worry in her eyes. Jake's nostrils flared, and anger dripped down his forehead with sweat.

"What the fuck are you doing with my daughter?" His face turned red, and his eyes popped like a psycho's. He stepped forward, trying to get at me again, but I backed up into the dining area and made sure there was a table between us.

What the fuck was going on?

"You're…you're here."

"You didn't know?" Kendra's grape-sized eyes were going to pop as well. This was worse than a nightmare. It was reality. Ashley and Jake were alive, which was good—but also pretty fucking bad timing.

"Of course, I didn't know," I said.

"What the hell is going on, Katherine? You said Julian took good care of you. You…you had separate bedrooms."

"Mom, it's Kendra now." She left her mother's side and came to stand beside me, taking my hand. I weaved my fingers through her open ones.

"I tried to cover up," she whispered.

"I see."

"What is this?" Ashley's heels clicked over the floor. "What is going on here?"

"We're together." Kendra squared her shoulders and lifted her chin.

I tightened my grip on her hand, partially to stop her trembling but also to stabilize mine. I couldn't have even imagined this moment if I tried. How the fuck were Ashley and Jake alive? I mean, I was happy to see them, and completely stunned as well. I pinched the bridge of my nose. A sickening regret loomed in my chest, because right at this fucking moment I couldn't deny I'd be feeling much better if I hadn't fucked my best friend's daughter.

"You're off the case." Jake threw his hands up in the air. He paced the length of the room, back and forth, pulling his fingers through his hair.

"What fucking case?"

I let go of Kendra's hand and stepped around the table, but as soon as Jake's gaze connected with mine, I retreated.

"My daughter's, asshole."

"Daddy!"

"Jake!"

"You have some fucking balls….touching her. We…we trusted you. You were supposed to take care of her, and you… Oh, my God, I can't even picture what you've done."

"Then stop picturing, Daddy."

Sweat dripped profusely down Jake's forehead and face. His shirt was stained over the chest and underarms. His grip remained on the chair in front of him, eyes cold and lips tight.

"How are you here?"

Ashley linked her arms in a stubborn fold. "We missed Kath… Kendra. We need her back."

"After three years? You waited three years? Donaldson's still going strong, and the Hartleys—"

"We had no choice back then—"

"She's your daughter. She should have never been a choice." Silence.

I removed my jacket and set it on a chair. A patch of snow crumbled off the roof and fell to the ground.

Ashley turned to her daughter. "Baby, we made a mistake. A big mistake, and I can never tell you just how sorry we are for that. But we want to make things better."

"You can't. She needs protection, she needs—"

"Her parents."

"Where were you when she sobbed after we told her you were dead? Where were you when she lay curled up in bed after countless nightmares?"

I slammed my fist on the table, and Ashley jumped back.

"I'm sorry." I lifted my hands in the air. "This is just a lot."

Kendra's gaze darted from me to her parents and back to me again. I needed to think, and I couldn't do it here.

"You have no clue what we gave up for the cause."

I lifted my gaze. "I do. You gave up your daughter."

Jake let go of the chair and advanced toward me, but Ashley physically stopped him.

"No, Jake. No violence."

He removed the tie from around his neck and straightened his ironed shirt. He pulled his fingers through his hair and cranked his neck to the side.

"We're here now, and we're not leaving without Kendra."

"She's coming home with us."

Over my dead body.

"No, I'm not." Kendra let go of my hand. The sudden loss of her touch unnerved me. "I already have a home," she said.

My head pounded with pain. How did this happen? How could they have kept themselves from us? This wasn't right.

"Kendra remains under my protection." I lifted my chin.

"We know Donaldson better than anyone. She's safest with us."

"Who's Donaldson?" Kendra asked, and I turned her way.

"You don't remember?" Ashley touched her lips.

I hunched forward, and my chest caved in.

"Kendra underwent hypnosis after the accident to stop her nightmares."

"Oh, honey—"

"I'm fine, Mom. Really. Julian's been amazing."

"I'll bet." Jake's nostrils flared. "You took advantage of my daughter."

"It's not like that, you hypocrite. You've been alive all this time and never had the fucking decency to trust and call the same company you hired to take care of your daughter?"

"You call fucking her *taking care* of her?"

"All right, stop it, you two." Ashley's voice bounced off the wall. She stepped midway between us. "We're all adults here. I'm sure we can figure this out. Jake, sit." She pointed to the couch, and he listened like a dog. Her confidence and authority reminded me of Kendra's.

We paced around the table to the family room, where we sat on the half-moon cushioned couch. The square ottoman in the middle provided no barrier. I focused on Jake, and he focused on me.

"I will not sit here and discuss how he ruined my daughter." He lifted his hand to stop our protest. "We're taking Kendra home where she belongs, and we'll find another security company to take care of our needs."

Why did he make this feel like a business transaction? And Silver Securities were best in the business. No one could protect her better than me. Besides, Kay wasn't a piece of chattel. I knew she didn't want this.

"So what? Now you're back, and you want her because you know what's best for her?" I stood up. "Well, you can't have her."

Kay's happy yelp tickled at my ears. She was worth more than her father could ever respect. Yet the dread I would be the one to break her heart almost cut off my breath.

"I always thought of you both as amazing parents, but after what you've pulled, I no longer give a shit. I've been more of a parent to her than either of you. A parent doesn't abandon their child."

"A parent doesn't fuck them either, you pedophile."

I cringed. The accusation tore through my very middle and hit a nerve. I lunged forward and over the ottoman. The perfect aim connected my knuckles with Jake's nose. The bone cracked and vibrated through my hand.

"Jake!"

"Julian!"

Jake's hands flew to the area where blood fountained. Kendra and her mother rushed between us, both pulling me off of him. I rose, and Jake flew into my side. Unfortunately, my

Congressman ex-friend lived up to his ironed slacks and shirt and tie ensemble, and fought like a five-year-old girl. I kneed him gently enough so he'd lose his breath, and all the air wheezed out of his lungs. He bent over in half, fell to the couch, and pulled his knees to his chest.

The room fell quiet. Jake gathered himself with a groan and stood up. The new angle of his nose made me cringe. He was the second person whose nose I'd broken. He straightened his shirt, cranked his neck to the side, and approached me, keeping a three-foot distance.

"I'm done with the bullshit, Julian. If you want Silver Securities to survive, don't ever fucking touch my daughter again."

"But Dad—"

"He seduced you, honey, and this isn't your fault." Jake's gaze remained on my face, with a solid promise of retaliation in his eyes.

"He didn't seduce me. I seduced him."

"I read about this, honey." Kay flinched at her mother's touch. "It's the Stockholm Syndrome, but we can help, baby."

"It's not Stockholm Syndrome." Kay's eyes filled with tears. She gripped my arm, holding on as if her life depended on mine.

"I don't care what the fuck you call it. She's coming home with us. You're no longer on the case, Silver."

Since when was I just a Silver?

"I am not a *case*," Kendra cried out.

I blocked Kendra before she stepped too close. I didn't trust Jake. The profuse sweating and uncontrollable anger were new. While I saw the predicament I'd created, we'd eventually move past this. Wouldn't we?

"If you want my professional opinion, I can keep Kay safe," I said.

"Are you talking as a professional or as a man who's had his dick in my daughter?"

"Jake!"

"It's true, Ash."

Kay sobbed while her mother looked inward and blinked more rapidly. She watched her husband from the corner of her eye, as if afraid for him to catch her in the act. I could feel Jake's heated stare on me. His cheeks were glowing beet red, and if I were to picture Satan, Jake's hellish face would come to mind first.

"That's all he wants, Ash. He wants a woman half his age to fuck so he can brag about it to his friends. And I won't allow it. I won't allow him to disgrace my daughter like that."

Oh, it so wasn't like that, but I couldn't retaliate against an emotionally unstable man and had to stop him before he said or did something stupid.

His lips thinned, and his jaw clenched. "Touch her again and I pull the plug on everything I know about Silver Securities."

Something exactly like that.

Ashley gasped, "Jake—"

"I have never bluffed in my life." His chin lifted and focus clung to solely me. "I will tie you in a legal battle that will bankrupt you and your family. If you don't believe me, read the fucking contract Silver Securities signed."

I might not have broken the law, but I'd broken a promise to Jake Moore, and that was enough. I slowly removed Kendra's stiff fingers from my arm. She watched as I released each finger, her mouth opening wider and eyes filling. I swallowed hard before I let go of Kendra's hand. Her tiny gasp shredded my heart into pieces and turned me into a complete coward. But Jake wouldn't have become a Congressman if he made empty threats. This was no longer about what either of us wanted.

"Kay—"

"I'm warning you, Julian. Don't do this." Tears streamed down her face like a river. The unstoppable and never-ending flow accompanied the shrieking sound she made with each breath, turning my shredded heart into mush.

I lowered my head. "I don't have a choice."

"But you do have a choice. Choose me. Pick me, because I'm yours."

"See the madness you've put in her head?" Jake shouted. "She's infatuated with you."

"I'm not infatuated with him. I'm in love with him. I love Julian, and I know he loves me, too."

I couldn't think. Neither choice at this point was the right one, and I had to consider all the lives Jake's threat would ruin.

I turned toward her and lifted her hands into mine. "Maybe this is the chance you've been waiting for to get your life back, Kay—"

"No," she cried. "Julian, please."

"This will be good for you. You're young, and you need your family. Your parents want what's best for you."

"I thought *we* were family." Her shoulders curled forward and her chest caved in, but then she looked up, sniffled, and wrapped her arms around me so quickly I barely stopped her.

"Please, Julian." she begged.

Jake stiffened while Ashley looked away. His unyielding Congressional stare bore through my core, and I slowly unwrapped Kendra's arms from around me.

"I'm sorry, Kay. It's for the best."

"No, please," she cried, and Ashley took her daughter into her arms.

"It's okay, honey. We've got you, and I have some Xanax if you need—"

"No drugs," I growled. "She can't have any Xanax."

I retreated and Kay shuddered in her mother's hold. Kendra looked me dead in the eyes before I left, and my insides twisted. Half an hour later, I drove home on my own, feeling like the biggest fucking coward who'd ever breathed.

Chapter 14

Kendra

I moved to my parents' new house in a secure neighborhood, which ironically, was near Jace's. We drove by the angular structure every morning on our way out to the coffee shop. Six months had passed since Jake and Ashley Moore decided to play family. Six painfully lonely months.

My mother's new love of wigs bordered on an obsession. She changed them daily and never repeated a look. The combination of sunglasses, scarves, and her stupid hats drew more attention than she would have had without them. It seemed that the paranoia someone would find them and retaliate had grown faster than inflation. Meanwhile, my father paced the halls with a drink and a cigar in his hand, making phone calls to secret people no one knew. Gabriel Silver probably knew. As the newly appointed Silver to my case, Julian's cousin was the one in touch with my father. Julian's cousin now led the team to fight a battle I couldn't even remember.

I was curled up on a window seat with a book when my mother came into the room. "It's a beautiful day today, honey. Why don't you go for a swim?"

My mother was right. It was a perfect day for a swim, but

the pool reminded me of Julian's hot body dripping with cold water.

"Aren't we going to the Silvers' barbecue?" I asked.

She shifted from one foot to another. "Your father was saying you should probably stay home."

"Haven't you two done enough?" I lowered my feet off the seat and onto the floor. "The Silvers are like family to me, and I miss them. I'm going to the barbecue whether Father likes it, or not. And I'm bringing a date."

"A date?"

"Don't worry, mom, he's my age."

I'd called Julian for weeks and left countless messages. He'd replied a few times, but cut our communication soon after. Weeks passed and my shattered heart turned into mush and left me broken until one morning at the coffee shop, I ran into my lovely therapist, Stefanie. She stopped by my table and emphasized how she couldn't wait to see me at the family barbecue. Clearly, Julian was fucking her again, and the time to reconnect was more urgent than ever. I'd been waiting for the opportunity to speak with him, but my parents wouldn't allow me to come within feet of the man. I'd pondered a way to get his attention, and thus planned to kill two birds with one enormous stone: Jace.

"A boy your age?" My mother asked.

"He's three years older. That's it. And he's in business."

My mother's brow lifted.

"His name is Jace, and he's very cute. He's into business and international politics." I made that second part up and left out the type of business Jace ran. "But I'm not sure Father will like him."

"I believe at this point, anyone other than Julian would make your father happy." She sighed.

Truth was, pleasing my father was the least of my concerns, but raining misery over his priorities pumped my heart with pure determination. I had to remind Julian of what we were, and if anyone could rain misery and happiness at the same time, it was Jace.

My parents had missed out on so much over three years. Three years sounded short, but it was long enough for me to morph into a new woman. Their ignorance was my best weapon against them. My mother hadn't asked whether I graduated, and since their return six months ago, my father had spent two point five hours in my presence. I didn't remember this selfish side of them, and sometimes I wished they had never come back.

Silver Securities continued leading my case because they were, in fact, the best, which meant spending time with Julian in some near future was inevitable. As more time passed, the urge to recall all the trouble I'd caused grew. I nearly asked Stefanie to undo my hypnosis more than once. I was ready to make peace with my old life, so it could stay in the past, but she mentioned her date with Julian, and I chickened out.

"So, this Jace boy. Tell me more about him," my mother asked, and the right side of my mouth crept up.

If they only knew, they'd give me a set of keys to Julian's and be grateful. Julian may have been older, but he was safer. The constant reminder of how he'd changed my life kept me going, the moments we shared burned into my memory. He'd made me a woman, and I could never stop loving him.

I missed him. I missed him with my body and heart, and today, if I played my cards right, he'd take me away from here for good.

⚭

WILMA GREETED me with a giant embrace. Her motherly hug overpowered any I'd received from my mother. I didn't want to let go.

"How are you doing, sweetheart?" she cooed in my ear.

"I've been better. Is Julian here?" I asked, and Wilma eyed me. "I have a date for today, I just wanted to—"

"Backyard, Kay. He's in the back. I'll keep your father occupied for a few minutes."

"Thanks, Wilma." I kissed her cheek.

I hurried out the back door, where a delicious barbecue aroma filled the yard. I made a beeline to the couches, where Julian was sitting cross-legged. He set the orange liquor and ice cubes aside and stood up. An uncomfortable moment passed between us as I felt the world stare at us both. I stepped closer and so did he, until we finally came in for a slow and achingly soft embrace. He not only looked good, he also smelled good. I took a longer whiff before pulling away. The skin-hugging t-shirt and capri shorts advertised sinful adventures. His beard was freshly trimmed, and his hair had extra product and puff. God, he looked real good. I took another whiff of him. The immediate pounding in my chest turned the world around me like a carousel.

I took a deep breath and steadied myself. "I've missed you."

"You're here," he said. "I didn't know you were coming."

"Have you missed me?"

"Yes, of course I've missed you, but I didn't know you were coming," he repeated, and I felt my forehead crease.

"Neither did I, and I don't know how much time I have because my father is anal and he would flip if he saw me talking to you."

"Kay, I'm not alone."

"What?" My head whipped to the side seats to check if I'd missed anyone. I'd been so focused on him since crossing the threshold, I hadn't noticed a couple of his lawyer friends by the fire pit.

"I invited Stefanie," he said.

Oh, right.

"My therapist?"

"She's no longer your therapist."

"But she remains your fuck buddy?"

His gaze drifted over my shoulder, and he cleared his throat. The smell of pungent lilac wafted from behind me. I turned around to meet Stephanie's pasted smile and realized the chance she didn't hear me calling her a fuck buddy was nil.

"Hello, Kendra. How are you doing?"

"Great. Perfect. In fact, I just found out my ex-boyfriend is screwing my therapist again."

Julian shifted in discomfort.

"Kendra—"

"It's all right. No need to warn me, Julian. I can see I don't fit in your picture, but you no longer fit in mine either, so all is good."

His head tilted, giving me the what-are-you-doing-look, and Stephanie asked, "Are you doing all right, Kay? How is the new therapist?"

Sometimes, I was convinced Stef only looked smart because she gave him ass.

"All is good. She told me best way to overcome my fears is to get right back up on that horse." I punched through the air. "So, I have a new boyfriend and a new life, and I've been thinking about reverse hypnosis."

Julian's focus flew from me to Stef and back, but then when neither one of us spoke, he didn't know where to look.

"You're ready to face your past. That's great," she finally said. "I'm sure I could help with that."

"She's not ready," Julian grunted, and Stefanie sat down on the couch, pulling him down beside her. She lowered her hand over his knee, rubbing it up and down his leg. The sight made me sick to my stomach.

"You're not my doctor, Julian."

Now it was Stefanie who looked awkwardly between me and Julian.

"What about your nightmares?" he asked.

"No more nightmares. My new boyfriend is very tender and caring."

"What boyfriend?" Julian barked out. Watching his anger gain steam sent adrenaline rushing through my veins.

"He should be here soon. I better go. My parents still don't like you that much, Julian. No offense, Stef, but I should call you soon. To reverse my hypnosis."

It felt good to make him squirm in his seat. I doubted he'd told Stef about us, but she wasn't stupid either. She wouldn't stand for being Julian's second choice for long.

I hurried back to the house and went to the powder room, where I made a call. Half an hour later, Jace showed up at the front porch. I introduced him to Wilma and Fred, then to my parents, and assured them Jace had been screened. Except he hadn't been, because I'd showed him a back way around the security. He'd slicked his hair into a bun, and the overgrowth on his face added to his age. But he was still younger than Julian, and that's what mattered to my mother the most.

I peeked out the window to where Julian was explaining something to Stefanie by the grapevines. She had crossed her arms over her chest and was tapping her foot.

"Kendra? Aren't you going to introduce us?" My mother asked.

My father crossed the room, keeping a keen eye on Jace. It wouldn't even matter in the end, because my father would always think of Jace as a better man than Julian. He was so wrong.

"Yes. Sorry. Mom, Dad, this is a friend of mine, Jace."

Jace kissed my mother's hand, and her cheeks turned bright red. The firm shake of my father's hand gained Jace's immediate approval.

"What is it that you do, Jace?"

"Trade management, sir."

Thankfully, Jace had prepared.

"Trade management," my father repeated, like he knew everything about Jace's profession, when he had no clue what my drug dealer friend did. Connectedness had made my father an excellent Congressman and a self-righteous, ignorant asshole at the same time.

"You can grill him later, Dad. We're starving." I pulled Jace out the door and led him across the deck to the back garden. Julian's heated stare followed us, but I was sure Jace's new beard and the tight bun of hair bought us a few minutes.

"Trade management?" I snickered.

"I didn't think they would like me if I said drugs."

"Good call. I've been wondering what happened to you."

That was a lie because I hadn't thought of Jace since I'd made the promise to Julian; but tonight, I needed Jace for a greater cause.

"Family business. What have you been up to? Still into Molly?"

"She's my best girl," he winked. "But I'm also scouting real estate for a nightclub."

"Wait—you're opening up a nightclub?"

"Yeah, if I can get an investor. Gotta wash the money. Hey, you would be a perfect waitress."

Waitressing wasn't exactly what I had in mind when I thought about work, but Jace didn't need to know that. Also, I had no interest in washing money. Tonight, he was here for only one reason: to make Julian Silver jealous.

"Sure, I'd love to. Come on, let's get some burgers outside."

I took his hand and led him down the patio steps, fully aware of Julian's heated stare following us. He must not have recognized Jace right away, but when he did, his footsteps thundered across the deck. He jumped down to the lawn and Jace scurried behind me.

"What the hell is he doing here? Who cleared him?" Julian towered over us both.

I lifted my chin. "He's my guest."

"Like hell he is."

I crossed my arms over my chest. "My father approves."

"I. Don't." His stare bore through mine in a showdown and something else. His jaw locked and his shoulders tensed.

"It doesn't matter. He's cleared—"

Julian grabbed my arm and guided me down the steps out into the backyard.

"I'll be right back," I called out to Jace, and ripped my arm out of Julian's grip. "What do you think you're doing?"

"Making sure you stop seeing the fuck turd."

We turned a corner near the garden, where the fruit orchard concealed us from the party.

"What? You can bring Stefanie and I can't invite Jace?"

His nostrils flared, and I backed up into an apple tree. Julian stood a foot away, steaming with heat and anger. His desire rolled through my body, reviving the memories I held from Colorado. Painful lust followed. He must have noticed, because the contours of his mouth softened. He skimmed the back of his hand over my cheek. "This has nothing to do with Stefanie. Kay—"

"I'm warning you, Julian. You better accept Jace if you want—"

"If I want what?"

He stepped closer, and his erection pressed into my stomach. His scent hit me like a drug, and my longing for him skyrocketed.

"You know exactly what you want." I took in a shuddery breath and guided his hand up my dress, along my inner thighs, and over my soaked pussy.

"Where are your panties, Kay?"

"At home," I whispered.

"Figures," he grumbled. "Why do you act like a brat half the time and the other half, I want to spank you, and the other half I want to give you everything you're asking for? Everything you need."

"That's three halves."

"What?"

"You can't have three halves to make a full."

"Why are you doing math when I'm trying to tell you I've fucking missed you?" His raspy breath drew goosebumps along my arms. He braced himself with his free hand against the bark, and I opened my legs so his middle finger could pull over my opening as he withdrew between my folds. God, how I'd missed him as well.

"You missed me?"

He lowered his forehead to mine.

"Of course I missed you."

"Like you haven't been tracking me?" I asked.

I'd bought a burner phone for when I snuck out of the house, so I knew he didn't know about Jace.

"Tracking isn't the same as fucking. I miss you, Kay." His hand paused at my inner thigh. I quickly lowered my hand to his and guided him higher. His lips pressed hard against my forehead, as if he feared to take my mouth.

"What are you doing, Kay?" His ragged voice vibrated against my skin.

"I want you."

"Your father will find us."

"So? Stop me if you can, but I propose we don't waste the little time we have."

His finger slipped inside me. I tightened around him and I went for his zipper, freeing his hard cock in one point three seconds. My desire soared as I wrapped my fingers around him and stroked twice. The idea was to turn around so he could fuck me, but I couldn't resist his dick. I let his finger slip out of me and I dropped to my knees. My lips covered his heated crown with delicate kisses and tongue sweeps. I dragged the tip underneath his rim before I licked down his length, then back up, taking him all the way in.

"Fuck, Kay." His knees trembled.

I looked up. He must have liked me going down so far he hit the back of my throat, because he touched his full palm to the side of my head and held me steady. I felt him grow in my mouth and lifted his balls in my other hand, stroking my finger over his scrotum.

"Shit, Kay…"

I tightened my grip and urged my strokes until his thrusts stilled and he spilled in my mouth, letting go of a strained breath.

"Kendra? Are you here with him?" We heard my father's voice.

My eyes flew wide open, and I pulled away. Julian popped out of my mouth and hurried to gather himself while I sealed my lips. My father turned the corner just as I swallowed.

"What are you two doing here?"

The wide grin of satisfaction on Julian's face was everything my father needed.

"I'm breaking Julian's heart," I blurted.

"You're what?"

"I'm breaking his heart."

My father's forehead wrinkled as he pointed to my legs.

"You have grass stains on your knees. Are you fucking her again? What do I have to do to stop this?"

"Truth is, Dad, I love Julian."

"And I don't give a flying fuck." He turned to Julian. "I warned you once not to touch her, and I won't do it again."

"Don't worry, Jake. You've made yourself perfectly clear. I

won't touch her as long as the case remains open, and I'll make sure it closes soon."

At that moment, more than ever, I wanted to know details about my case. I wanted to remember. Why were they protecting me, and from whom?

"I need you to call me, Julian. We need to talk. "

"I can't. I'm under an agreement, and…"

"Is that all I am to you? An agreement?" He shut his eyes at my whimper.

"Please, stay away from Jace." He kissed the top of my head, gathered himself, and walked away, past my father, leaving me once again. I stared after him until he stopped, turned around, and said, "Don't worry, Jake. I haven't made you a grandpa. Not today." He then pointed right at me. "Wipe your mouth, Kay. I'm dripping down your chin."

Chapter 15

Julian

The phone's never-ending ring woke me at ten in the morning. I groaned and pulled my hand across my eyes. The last three sleepless nights without Kendra, as I planned how to get away from here, had been torturous. The night after the barbecue, I'd snuck into her room and watched her sleep. An urge to climb underneath the covers and fuck her silly right underneath Jake's roof drew all my blood south, but I didn't. Instead, I watched her toss and turn, then left before the sun came up.

Jake met with my father, Gabe, and Julian on Monday, and I'd heard nothing since.

"Morning. What's up?"

"What the fuck happened between you and Jake last weekend?"

I pinched the bridge of my nose. "He walked in on Kay giving me a blow job."

"Fuck, Julian. He compromised the entire operation."

"What?"

"He was snooping around After Eve, and surveillance cameras picked him up at Scar's strip-club talking to Martinez. If he fucks this up for us, Kay won't be the only one in trouble."

"I know, I know. Is Gabe making a move today?"

My cousin had undertaken the case against Martinez and Donaldson along with his wife, Joanne. From what I'd been told, Martinez was recruiting women with a sex-trafficking intent, and Donaldson, along with Hartley, were paying him the big bucks. Gabe had secured a warrant for Martinez's arrest.

"They're out in the field already. They finally found a cell. Thirty women."

"You guys need my help?"

"No, you're too involved."

"I know. I know."

"Julian, Jake also fired Silver Securities."

I'd expected Jake's retaliation, but I never thought he would compromise his daughter's safety. If he'd stoop this low, he'd go after my family next, which meant I couldn't afford to see Kendra again.

"Did you double up the files?" I asked.

"You know I did."

"Good. I want to keep up the surveillance on her. And make sure she doesn't get with Jace."

"He's the one who led us to the cell."

"What?"

"He came to talk to me after the barbecue. He's not a bad guy, but he hangs with the wrong crowd."

"Which is exactly why Kendra shouldn't be around him."

"We'll do our best. Are you still going to New Zealand?"

"Flying out this afternoon." I glanced over at my suitcase. "I don't have another choice. Staying here, with her so close and not being able to touch her, is too hard. And I have a fresh case, so New Zealand will keep me busy."

"We'll miss you."

The only person I worried about missing me was Kay.

"Thanks. Maybe Jake and Ash are right. She needs a normal

life. We'll get Martinez, and once Donaldson goes behind bars, she'll be free."

"We're still looking for Wright. He'll testify for Kendra and against Donaldson. We just need to find him."

"How do you lose a witness?"

"Jake spooked him, and he's gone incognito."

"Isn't he supposed to stay under the radar? What the fuck is he doing?"

"I don't know, but that's why I called. You need to talk to him before you leave. He can't keep blabbing about Silver Securities."

"I'll stop by their house before I leave. Talk to you soon."

"Later."

We hung up. I showered, gathered my passport and documents, packed the car, and drove to Jake and Ashley's house. They buzzed me in and waited on the front porch, standing firm.

"What the fuck are you doing here?" Jake asked.

"I'm here to ask you to stop your investigation."

"I'm gathering information for my daughter's case."

"Information we already have."

"You should have thought about that before—"

"I already said I wouldn't touch her."

"Yet you did."

"Look, this shouldn't be about me. It should be about Kay and the fact that she's vulnerable without proper security—and so are you guys."

"Kay is not your problem any longer, and neither are we."

"Ashley, you know I want what's best."

She glanced from me to Jake and back to me again, but remained silent. She didn't look like she'd had a good night of sleep, either.

I shook my head just as Kendra popped her head from inside the door. "Julian?"

Jake turned around, "Go back inside, Kay."

She ignored her father and ran into my arms, throwing her body at me. "Please, take me with you."

Jake gave me a deadly stare, and I unwrapped her arms from around my neck. Her eyes welled in an instant as I passed her from my hold to Ashley's.

"I'm sorry," I whispered, and looked back at Jake again. "Make sure she has a bodyguard with her wherever she goes. Jace cannot be trusted."

"Julian, no!" Kendra cried.

My phone rang with Tristan's number. "Excuse me."

I stepped away, but I was not ready for the news on the other end of the call. I watched Jake's smug face as my brother told me how Jake had met up with Martinez last night and made a deal with the criminal for Kendra's safety in exchange for information. Except the information he gave him had spooked Martinez. Gabe and Joanne's operation had failed, and my cousin's wife was dead.

"You fucking caused this."

I lunged at Jake. Kay and Ashley screamed while I brought him to the ground and punched until my fists and his nose bled.

"Julian, stop!" Kendra pulled on my arm, but I couldn't stop.

"You're going to kill him," Ashley cried out.

"He fucking killed Joanne! You killed my cousin's wife."

I got off him and stepped back. My blood was boiling and my hands were shaking. I pulled my hands through my hair.

"What are you talking about?" Kendra asked.

"Your father made a deal with a devil who doesn't make deals. He told Martinez about the operation. He killed Joanne."

"I don't know what you're talking about." Jake mumbled, gathering himself off the ground.

"You tried to make a fucking deal for Kendra's safety."

"As you should have done a long time ago. I did what was right to protect her."

"You killed her!" I lunged forward again, but Ashley and Kendra stopped me. "You're going to pay for this, Jake. If I were you, I'd move, because now Donaldson will find out you're alive."

I threw my hands up in the air and left. I postponed my trip for a week and took the flight to New Zealand with Gabe and Joanne's casket. They'd met there during training, and he was taking her body back home. After the funeral, he locked himself up while I took over his surveillance work on the island.

Kendra called me daily for three weeks straight, but I didn't pick up. The family was once again in hiding, but I couldn't run the risk Jake would retaliate again, so I cut off all contact.

They moved to a different location in Oyster Bay Cove. The new security firm Jake hired gave them new names and identities and, as much as I worried about Kendra's wellbeing, the situation was out of my hands.

I did call her for her nineteenth birthday, but she never picked up. Four months later, I flew to Austria, where winter passed in a flash, along with spring and summer. The first news of Kendra's troubles with Jace reached me last week. Then came a growing feud between Donaldson's puppet, Martinez and Jake's new bodyguard. Jake's security company dropped them, and he came crawling back like a dog. Silver Securities continued its pursuit of information for Kendra's case, and Martinez screwed everything up along the way, forcing my return.

I'd landed two hours ago and now stood in my hallway, looking at a wrapped painting propped against my wall. I walked along its length, eyeing its eight to nine feet in height.

"What is it?" Stefanie asked, reminding me she was there, supposedly welcoming me back home. She'd attached herself to my side like an octopus the moment I landed. Breaking up with a woman had never been an issue because, before Stefanie, I never slept with the same woman more than once. Kendra was an exception, of course. Kendra was also exceptional. When Stefanie became Kendra's therapist, the constant appointments gave us both an excuse to fulfill a mutual need. It was easier than dating when I had a troubled teenager at home, but now I lived on my own. Neither one of us found a need to commit, so the benefit part of our friendship worked. The clingy part, where she showed up for lunch at work or stopped by to drop off my shirt, not so much.

I fucking missed Kendra. I missed her spirit and the comfort of her body in my bed. My troubled Kay was in trouble, and I couldn't stop thinking about her. And as of now, I couldn't stop thinking about that painting, either.

I crossed the hall and pulled on the cover. The fabric dropped off the canvas and revealed paint-brushed strokes of a woman's back view. I recognized the beautiful body in an instant, and it wasn't the therapist's. My dick hardened. The sheer black fabric over skin as she walked away in a black negligée, her beautiful ass in a G-string, made me hard. The fact she'd been able to pull this gift off for my return was only part of the perfect puzzle that was Kendra. The painting was a painful reminder of everything I'd lost and now missed. It was perfection, and I couldn't believe she'd let Scar fucking Wagner paint her like that live.

Stefanie's audible gasp brought me back to the room, and I cleared my throat. "This is Scar Wagner's work."

"Scar Wagner? He's that lawyer friend of yours, isn't he?"

I nodded. The one and only, and I couldn't believe the detail of the painting. I lifted the cover and draped it back over the frame, imagining which of my bedroom walls would do the art justice.

I turned around. "Listen, Stef. I'm tired, and I have an early morning meeting."

She sauntered toward me and tugged at my pants. "It's been months, Julian. You can't tell me you haven't thought about me."

She drew her hand along my erection. Of course I'd thought about her. I'd also thought about the intern at work, who reminded me of Kendra, the ski-lift operator in Austria, and the tour guide in New Zealand. They all reminded me of Kendra and how much I missed her, not Stef. I thought about my troubled girl from the moment I opened my eyes all the way through the sleepless nights. She was with me in the morning when I showered, and at night when I lay alone underneath my sheets. God, how I missed her!

"What would you like me to do, Julian? Beg? I can beg—"

"No, please, Stef. Don't beg."

My phone rang with a private number, temporarily saving my sanity and dick. I couldn't fuck Stef and think about Kendra at the same time. It didn't feel right.

"Julian Silver."

"Julian, this is Julia Blakely. Dr. Blakely. I'm calling from the hospital about Kendra because you're listed as the contact in her file."

"Is she all right?"

"I'm not sure. We administered Naloxone."

"What? She was using?" I walked to the staircase and sat on the bottom step.

"I called her parents, but no one answered. I thought you should come because this isn't her first visit here, and I like your family. This girl's been through a lot."

Not the first time?

I jumped to my feet and grabbed my car keys off the table, along with my jacket. "How is she doing now?"

I was out the door and in my car within seconds. I put Julia on the speaker and turned the car's ignition.

"She's better than she was before, but she keeps repeating your name. There's a young man with her as well, Jace, and he's not in good shape."

"Have you called anyone else?"

"No. I'm aware Silver Securities enjoys keeping a low profile, but I'm also only an intern, so I'm not sure how long I can keep it under wraps."

I pulled out of the driveway and headed straight for the hospital. "Don't worry about it. I'll have one of our doctors take over. Thank you. I appreciate it. You're the one who was trapped in the avalanche, aren't you?"

"That's correct. Can you come soon?"

"I'll be there in fifteen minutes, Jules. Thank you."

"You're welcome."

I hung up.

"Shit… Stefanie." I'd forgotten I'd left her at my house and dialed her number as I merged on the highway. It went straight to voicemail. I didn't leave voicemails, so I didn't dial again.

She called me right back.

"I'm so sorry, Stef. It was an emergency."

"It's all right. I wanted to let you know I let myself out. Is everything okay?"

"Looks like Kendra overdosed, so I'm on my way to the hospital."

"Let me know how she's doing. And Julian?"

"Yes?"

"There's a note at the back of the painting with the model's name."

Fuck.

I'd deck Scar Wagner for that one.

"I should go, Stef. I'll call you back when I can."

My chance of getting laid faded with the click of her phone.

But the thing was, I didn't want to get laid. At least, not with Stef. Snow collected along the windshield wipers, and I turned them on, breaking all speed limits. I parked the car in the front and hurried to the emergency room.

"She's sleeping now." Julia pulled me away from the nurse's station. "Julian, the people she's dealing with... They're not good."

"How do you know?"

Her face paled, and her jaw locked shut before she composed herself. "I work at a hospital. I see a lot and I hear a lot."

"What did you hear?"

"Donaldson and the Hartleys? They're behind the drugs... and...the sex-trafficking. Keep her away from them or they'll get her in trouble."

"And Jace linked her to the group?"

She nodded and pointed to the other gurney where Jace was lying unconscious, hooked up to monitors and fluids.

"No one's come to visit him?" I asked.

"He has no listed family."

I wasn't sure whether that was good or bad, because when you had no family, you made one—and I had yet to meet Jace's.

"Thanks, Jules." I sat down in the corner chair in Kendra's room. The time change was getting to me, and I dozed off until someone tapped on my shoulder. I startled and shot up to my feet.

"Jake, Ash, it's good to see you." I pulled my hand across my eyes. "I wish it were under better circumstances."

"What the hell are you doing here?"

"They had me listed as Kendra's contact. They called you first, but you didn't pick up."

The couple exchanged a knowing look.

"How is she doing?" Ashley asked. Dark circles shadowed her eyes, and her hair roots had grown out. She wore no makeup and looked like she just returned from hell. We stepped outside and found a quiet corner.

"They pumped her stomach, and she's stable. The doctor said they can release her today, so you can take her home."

Ashley took a deep breath and composed herself. "We can't afford the trouble she brings."

"What are you talking about?"

"Jace said he could help when she came home unwell the first time, but then it happened more often—"

"You two let her hang out with a drug dealer? This is the result. This is exactly what I worried about." I pointed to Kay's room.

Jake shifted in discomfort. "Jace was in trade management—"

"Is that what you call drug dealing these days? Did you fucking know he deals for Donaldson's people? We linked Jace to Martinez. Fucking remember him?"

"All the more reason we should separate."

"What do you mean by separate?" That blank stare in their eyes was too familiar. "You mean abandon her again?"

When the hell did they lose their priorities?

"She's not the same Kendra we left under your care. She's into drugs and trouble."

"And why the fuck do you think that is?"

"You have no right, and no fucking clue what's been happening." Jake's nostrils flared.

"Gabe filled me in, and I can give you the short version: you fucked up big time, and now when your daughter needs you, you decide she's not worth the trouble anymore?"

Jake's profuse sweat collected in patches under his armpits. "She needs to be on her own and learn how to live with the trouble she sows. We can no longer afford the attention she attracts. If we don't let go now, our fight against the money laundering and sex-trafficking will be for nothing. You should focus on fighting the right battles instead of getting inside my daughter's panties."

"I've got news for you, Jake. I already got inside her panties. Countless times. And not that it's any of your business, but Kendra prefers commando."

Ashley held him back. It was enough to stop his lunge, because that was how little he truly cared about his daughter. Or maybe he didn't want his nose broken again.

"Just make sure she's okay, and we'll see her soon."

"Wait a moment. Who's going to care for her?"

"Kendra's twenty, with a wealthy bank account. She can live on her own."

I stepped forward. "Money won't save her from Martinez. You leave her now, and I'll make sure you never see her again."

Jake scoffed and held his stance. "Whatever. Come on, Ash. We're leaving."

Ashley whispered, "Please take care of her, Julian."

Kendra's parents turned around and left. I sat by her bedside, remaining on guard until the doctor discharged her that afternoon. I took her to my house and lay her in our bed, covering her with blankets. She shivered, and I found the fluffy throw she liked.

She stirred. "Julian?"

"I'm here, Kay. I'm here, and I've got you." She settled into my body after I spooned her from behind. My nerves eased. She was finally where she belonged.

Chapter 16

Kendra

I found Julian at the library. He was sleeping in a chair with both feet up on an ottoman. An empty glass and a half-empty bottle of whiskey stood in the middle of his mahogany desk. I picked a random book off a shelf and sat on an empty chair sideways. My legs swung back and forth as I flipped the pages, pretending to read. The man I'd cried after for the past eighteen months was back, and I was at his house. I'd been sitting here for an hour, staring at him while crossing my fingers and toes that he wouldn't be upset.

He stirred and rubbed his eyes, focusing on me.

"Hey," I said. "I didn't want to wake you."

He lowered his feet to the ground and sat up in the chair, shifting his morning wood. God, how I'd missed that, too.

"Morning." He checked his watch. The sun shone through the library window and over his legs.

"You came to get me at the hospital," I said.

He stilled before returning my smile. "The hospital had me listed as an emergency contact." He rubbed his eyes again. "Sorry, I'm jet-lagged."

"They left me, didn't they?"

His head flew up, and he nodded with reluctance. My heart sank. I'd lost my parents again.

"I'm sorry." His voice broke all the way across the room.

"They left because they don't care. Moms and Pops want to save their asses because, somehow, their troubles became mine. Not that I helped." My shoulder twitched. So much had gone wrong since my parents returned from the dead, I could barely keep count, and my faith in a hopeful future had dwindled. "They said they loved me, but you don't abandon those you love."

"No. You don't. They'll be back, Kay, and I'll always be here. We will figure this out."

"Why didn't you stay in bed with me this morning?" I slumped in the chair.

"I stayed. Right up to the point when your tiny ass found a parking spot over my dick."

I curled my lower lip inward. "Sorry."

"You needed rest, and I had no strength to fight the temptation. I've missed you."

There it was. The glimmer of hope I needed shone in his eyes.

"I've missed you too. Wish you'd stayed in bed. It's a beautiful morning, and I didn't want to get up."

He removed his feet from the footrest and patted the seat.

I set the book aside and swung my legs off the armrest so fast it almost flipped. I composed myself and walked across the room, taking a seat in front of him. His three-day stubble was new but the worry in his eyes was the same as always. The smell of him hit me next, awakening my senses. As I stared at him from two feet away, my suppressed desires stirred. I regretted all the months we'd lost, but now that he was here, the idea of taking him in was more appetizing than a fresh pack of bubblegum.

"Why didn't you want to get up?" The corner of his mouth curved, softening his chiseled cheeks and rough edges.

"I was afraid if I woke up, this beautiful day would disappear. I need this morning to last longer; you know, so maybe you'll forget you're pissed at me for overdosing." My nose tingled as I pouted.

"Right. That." He sighed and scratched his chin. "What happened, Kay? How did you end up at the hospital?"

I reached for his hand. The touch electrified my skin, but he didn't let go. I came forward and slid his palm underneath the t-shirt and up to my breast.

"What are you doing, Kay?" His ragged breath betrayed him.

"Distracting you, obviously."

He sucked in a sharp breath, then let it out. My nipple found its spot between his fingers. The pinch zapped down to where I needed him the most.

"Is it working?"

"Possibly. I can't deny I want to tear off your panties and have you sit on my cock."

I bit my lip. "I can make that wish come true."

"But I can't, Kay." He removed his hand from under my shirt. "Not after the way I found you last night."

I shot off his lap and walked over to the window. Last night wasn't my fault, and how could I make him understand we were simply better as one? "Don't you get it? Didn't the past eighteen months teach you we belong together? After you left—"

"I'm sorry, Kay, but your father stayed true to his word. He went against my family because I touched you. I had to leave before more people died. You may feel like I left you, but it was the only way to stop him from causing further damage."

He walked up behind me and I spun to face him. We stood by the window, face to face. He lifted my hands to his mouth and kissed them.

"I don't blame you, and I'm sorry about Joanne."

"Thank you."

"Are you staying here?" I asked.

He nodded.

"Good."

"Under one condition."

I shut my eyes.

"You go to rehab."

"I'm not an addict, Julian."

"The hospital report says otherwise."

Regret tightened around my throat. "That was a mistake."

"It's always a mistake. It's never you, Kay, but if you continue hanging out with Jace, that same mistake will kill you one day. Just like a mistake killed Joanne."

I'd gone to therapy after I found out about her kidnapping and brutal death. It didn't help. His pained expression hit me in the chest. I no longer had an excuse for the trouble I'd caused.

"I didn't mean for her to die. I don't think my father knew what he was doing."

"No, he didn't, but it's too late for anything else."

"But I don't do drugs, Julian, I swear to you on"—I looked up—"I swear to you on us. I went to a party with Jace, and… I really don't remember what happened."

I lowered my head, and he pushed my chin back up with his finger.

"I believe you."

My eyes welled. "Really?"

Nobody had ever believed me before.

He reached forward and brought me to his front. I wrapped my arms around him, closed my eyes, and savored the moment my body remembered his every muscle. I curled into his hold and lowered my head over his chest while he smoothed my hair back and kissed my temple.

"Yeah, really. We'll figure it all out, babe. We'll make sure these assholes stay far away from you. I want you to stay here with me."

"No." I let go and retreated a few steps. "I don't think I should."

"Kay—"

"It's not you, Julian. It's my life. I think I'm ready to take the reins." I pulled away and walked over to the sleek mahogany desk, leaning my backside against it. "This time around, I want to start the right way."

His forehead creased.

"I bought a condo three blocks from here with a bay view. I want to try life on my own; without my parents, obviously. I want to date you like a normal woman. Have you pick me up at home and take me to the movies or to a restaurant."

"How did you buy a condo?"

"My inheritance. I used half the money from the safe deposit box for the condo and half for my business."

"Why don't you stay here with me?" he offered, but I stayed firm. I had to do this my way.

"There's nothing I'd like more, but I have to figure out my life, just like you have yours figured out. Besides, I'm trouble."

"That's a far cry from the truth." He chuckled and stepped closer, his fingers skimming over my hips. "And I like a little trouble. Keeps me young and fresh. Keeps me on the edge."

I smoothed my palm over his chest. "I want to try independence, but I'm open to revisiting the subject in a few months."

"You sound like a different person." He smiled, running his hand down my hip and exposed thigh. My skin tingled everywhere. Jesus, I'd missed his touch.

"I don't want to be your trouble, either. One day, I just want to be yours."

"You've been mine for a long time, Kay, and that will never change." He bent down to kiss me, but stopped mid-way. "Wait —did you just say you bought a business?"

I pulled a slow smile. "I did."

"You're serious?"

I dipped my chin.

"When? How?"

"Not too long ago. There was a market opportunity, and I couldn't pass up the deal. Real estate is an excellent investment."

"Real estate? I'd like to look over the purchase agreement."

"Sure, but before you do, you should know, Jace is on the title."

"What?"

Julian's hands fell off my hips, and he stepped back.

"It was a quick decision, and we had to act before the market shifted and the opportunity vanished."

"Is that how he sucked you into this?"

"He didn't suck me into anything." I rolled my eyes.

"Jace is not a suitable partner. You need to stay away from him. What is this business you bought? Where's the property?"

"It's an old building we're renovating into a club."

"Where's the property?"

Here it was. The moment of truth. Would he truly have my back?

"Across the street from Club Forever." At the look on his face, I said, "What?"

"You know exactly what. I'm sure neither one of us is worried about Club Forever across the street as much as After Eve."

"This will be totally different. My plan is to get those women from After Eve working for me. Maybe they'll stop being sex slaves."

"How do you know what goes on down there?"

"It's where Jace tried to pawn me."

"And you still think it's a good idea to open up there? Not to mention going into business with him?"

I shimmied closer. "It's a great idea. It will help get women off these streets, because everyone needs a chance, and it would mean the world to me if I had your support."

His forehead creased again. He was doing that a lot this morning.

"And you got this idea from Jace?"

"We both worked on the idea, and we're both invested financially. We're partners now, and I can't change that."

"I can. And the drugs? How long have you been using?"

"I already swore to you, I don't use. Last night…something went wrong. Someone doped my drink. Nurses told me Jace brought me to the hospital unconscious before he passed out."

"And before then? This wasn't your first trip to the hospital, Kay"

"It happened once before, and Jace wasn't there. I was selling, but I don't sell anymore… What I'm trying to say, Julian, is that I need a new life, and I need you in it. Badly. Help me make my life right."

He scratched his chin. "I'm tired of running away from you as well, so I'll make you an offer."

Yes!

"Drop Jace, and I'm willing to try this dating thing."

He reached to his crotch, removed his cock, and stroked himself. I watched him with my mouth open as all the butterflies in the world fluttered in my stomach.

"I will drop Jace personally, but he sort of comes with the club."

"Let me worry about the club."

He leaned forward and took my chin between his fingers, guiding his mouth to mine. His needy lips and commanding tongue drew a moan out of my lungs and threw me off balance, as did the clear arousal beneath his pants. He walked backward to the chair and brought me to his lap, kissing my mouth like a madman, but the chair tilted backward underneath our weight, and I fell into his arms in laughter.

"I've missed you, Kay." He kissed the tip of my nose. "And we'll figure everything out."

"I've missed you too."

He secured me within his giant arms, and we rolled on the floor, kissing. It was the best feeling in the world. For the first time in months, my heart finally felt full.

"I'll have paperwork drafted for the club's sole ownership before the end of the day. If you agree, you'll hire Silver Securities to help with the club's surveillance and security."

"You'd do that for me?"

"I'd die for you, Kay."

This couldn't be happening, could it? "I want to make a change, Julian. A genuine change. I don't like Jace's friends, so I'll compromise."

He lay on the ground, and I lifted to straddle him. His dick throbbed against my heat.

"Compromise?"

"You'll date me and court me. I want the perfect beginning we never had."

He shifted underneath me. "Courting like that stipulates no sex."

I lowered, cupped his face with my hand, and whispered, "I'm sure we can upgrade the stipulations a little."

He pulled on my shirt and dragged the hem upward. I lifted my arms as he stripped me. He dragged his gaze down my body, leaving a scorching trail over my skin.

"No panties?"

The trail burst into flames, burning through my veins.

"Perfect." His chest rumbled. "And if you ever let Scar Wagner paint you like that again, I will kill him."

He lowered his mouth to my pebbled nipple and his hand pushed in between my inner thighs, settling at my opening. He slid his fingers through my folds before fingering my pussy. I closed around him. God, how I'd missed his fingers!

My head lolled back. "Do you like the portrait?"

"I fucking love it." He pumped slowly, in a rhythmic motion, working me so well.

"Did you jerk off to it yet?" I asked.

"No. I like the original much better."

He withdrew his fingers, aimed his cock, and moved forward. I took him to my depth, and as delight and relief rolled through my body, for the first time in months, I felt complete.

Chapter 11

Julian

My office intercom buzzed.

"Mr. Silver, Ms. Shepherd is here to see you."

Stefanie had arrived ten minutes before our scheduled lunch.

"Send her in."

I closed my laptop and stood up from behind my desk, walking around. She strolled in, her high heels tapping, with the takeout in her hand. She set the food aside and side-stepped in front of me.

"Hello, Julian." Seduction slithered along her tongue, pulling my attention to her talented mouth.

"It's nice to see you, Stefanie. Thank you for meeting me here."

"I'd been wondering when you'd call." She curved her hand to the left of my zipper and I wished I had more restraint.

"I called you for your professional services."

"I always stay professional."

I removed her hand from my zipper and showed her to the sitting area. I removed the two cartons of shrimp pad thai on the table and passed her a set of chopsticks.

"Dig in."

"I was hoping it would be your mouth on mine that would shut me up today, but so be it." She smiled like she already knew my intentions. "Aren't you going to offer me a drink?"

"Would you like a drink?"

"Champagne would be nice."

"What are we celebrating?" I stood up, walked to the corner bar, and popped a bottle.

"You, finally realizing you should have never left her? I'm assuming you called regarding Kendra."

I sighed. She was a smart woman.

"I respect you too much not to admit we've rekindled our friendship."

She coughed into her hand.

"All right, more than a friendship."

"I'll drink to that." She clinked her glass against mine and took a sip. "Thanks, Julian. She's definitely chosen one of a kind."

I sipped on the champagne and set the glass aside.

"What can I help you with?" she asked.

I lowered my elbows to my knees and cracked my knuckles.

"I want to know if there's a way to help Kendra overcome her past. She's moved out on her own and has worked hard, but she has no clue what or who she's hiding from. I believe she's matured enough to deal with everything she wanted to forget, and if the time ever comes to face one of those bastards, I'd rather she were ready."

"You've thought this through."

"I have."

"If there's one thing I learned over the past few years, it's that you can't ask Kendra to do what she doesn't want to do."

I lowered my head.

"But I agree with you. She would be safer if she knew the enemy she might face."

"How do I do that?"

She shrugged. "Take her to a gun range and see what happens."

"I can tell you exactly what happens. She'll hit every mark."

"No, I mean—see whether she remembers. She trained for the Olympics, and she's completely blocked her passion from her life. If she remembers her talents, there's a chance she'll recall the murder."

"How do I know whether she's ready?"

She waved her hand. "You're never ready for that shit. Trust your gut. Make sure she stays clean and out of trouble, but prepare her."

I sat up straight. "All right. Gun range it is."

"You're lucky she trusts you enough to have agreed to couples therapy beforehand."

"What are you talking about?"

"She listed you as more than her guardian a long time ago, Julian. She's talked about you like you're her partner, and she gave me permission to speak about this openly."

"So you've known for a while?"

Her shoulders lifted with a nonchalant shrug. "I've suspected for some time. You made it obvious enough."

I grunted a laugh. My heart was beating so hard I feared it would rip out of my chest. There was so much I had to fix, and I didn't know where to start. But taking Kendra out on a date sounded like the right thing to do. I'd take this relationship at her pace—well, despite all the sex we'd already had.

"Thanks, Stef. I appreciate it."

We finished our lunch, and she went back to work. I loosened my tie, sat down at Kendra's file, and flipped through the pages. Tristan had found a witness for Kendra and against Donaldson. For the first time in a long time, I got the sense of a hopeful outcome.

Kendra's ringtone chimed: the sound of popping bubblegum. I slid my finger across the screen.

"Julian? My father's here, and he's drunk."

"He's at your apartment?"

"No, he's at your house. I was dropping off your shirt, and he came in, and… Julian, I don't know what's going on, but he's in terrible shape. He's all soaked, and he's talking about taking me out of the country because there's a threat from Donaldson. It's that Congressman, right?"

I checked my laptop for notifications, but there were none. I'd thought Jake and Ashley had already left the state, but it seemed Kendra wasn't the only one haunted by their past. My chest inflated and my hands shook.

"Leave the house through the back door and go to my parents'. Do it now."

"No, it's okay. He's not asking me to pack."

I heard the clinking of glasses on the other end.

"He's pouring himself one of your whiskeys," she whispered. Why wasn't she listening to me?

"Can you just please do me a big favor and leave the house to a safer place? I don't trust Jake right now."

Her five-second pause felt like the longest moment of my life.

"Okay, I will. Ahem, I'll turn on a football game or something, and he'll be fine." The worry in her voice worried me.

"Leave the television alone. He'll be fine. Just get out of there, Kay. Please." I pulled out of the Silver Securities garage with tires screeching. "Keep your phone on. I'm coming."

I heard her hurry across the yard, her breaths as hard as mine, and my heart likely pounding as hard as hers. If Jake had disclosed Kay's location or done anything to jeopardize her safety, I would fucking kill him. And how the hell did he get onto the property?

I listened over the phone as Kendra ran home. My father

called Tristan, who was closer, and when the two of them went to check on Jake, he was having seizures and foaming out of his mouth. It felt like forever before I arrived. The ambulance got there much quicker and took the unresponsive Jake to the hospital.

I made sure Kendra was out of earshot and approached a paramedic. "How long was he out?"

"About ten minutes from the time we got here. We found him pretty blue."

"Thanks. Make sure we get the toxicology results."

"Yes, sir."

Tristan came outside with his hands on his hips. He rolled his sleeves up to the elbows, and his shirt was stained with sweat.

"What do you think?" I asked.

"I suspect he was poisoned."

"Kay mentioned Donaldson on the phone. We should double-check our security; run a few health checks on the company."

"I'm already on it with Gabe. He'll be working from Austria for a few months."

"As he should."

"Grief can be a bitch." My brother lowered his head. It felt like yesterday that his fiancée had died in a car wreck while he came out of the accident alive.

"Thanks for your help."

"No problem."

I gave my brother a stronger hug than usual, keeping the tight grip longer. It was good to have a brother who was one of your best friends. Tristan and my father left soon after. I found Kay curled up in our bed. She barely stirred when I pulled the covers aside. Her eyes were puffy and swollen and lips lightly parted. I removed her leggings, sweater, and bra, and dragged one of my t-shirts over her head, the way she liked.

She stirred and wiped her eyes before opening them. "Julian?"

"Yes?"

"Is he dead?"

I smoothed my hand over her arm. "Yes, he is, babe. I'm sorry."

She shut her eyes and swept her hand over her forehead. "You'd think it would be easier this time around, but it's not."

"What?"

"This will be his second funeral for me. The second time grieving when I don't really feel like grieving."

"You felt the same way the first time?"

"No, this time is different. This time, I don't think I care as much. Nothing good has happened since their return."

"I'm sorry."

"Why couldn't it just have been the train?"

"You still remember the train?"

"I do. It's all the stuff before that's fuzzy."

She yawned and turned on her side, her hip jutting upward.

"Would you ever reconsider remembering what happened before then? A lot has changed since the train crash."

"I don't know what to do at this point. I thought life would get easier, but it keeps getting harder with every passing year."

"I know exactly what you mean." I bent down and traced a column of kisses from her forehead down her nose to her lips.

She rose to a sitting position, holding the kiss, and I pulled away. "You should sleep, Kay."

She shook her head. "I should go home."

"I'm not saying you shouldn't, but not today. Today you stay here, with me."

"Does my mother know?"

"Not yet. We're trying to locate her."

"You'll let me know when you do?"

"Of course I will. Tomorrow morning, you'll sign for sole

ownership on your property, then Jace will sign it, and you'll distance yourself from him and the club. I've talked to Scar's legal team, and we'll orchestrate a sale and hide the true business ownership. Any work you do will be from home, and if you need to see the interior, we'll get you inside, in disguise and with security."

"You can do all that?" she asked.

She closed her eyes with relief after I nodded. I tucked her in and waited until she fell asleep before I went downstairs to the office. I opened the computer and started working on a plan to keep Kendra safe.

SHE JOINED me in the kitchen at eight in the morning. Her tiny feet flapped against the wooden floor, and she sported a white towel wrapped around her freshly washed hair. Her lavender scent hit me like an aphrodisiac.

"Good morning," she said as she rose up on her toes.

I grasped her chin between my fingers and guided her mouth to mine. Life would be so much easier if she could stay here, but Kendra needed normalcy. I had to side-step my crazy need to have her live with me again—for now.

"Good morning," I murmured against her lips. "How are you feeling?"

"Better. I slept like a rock."

She lowered herself, and I pulled out a stool by the counter. "Sit and eat. We're going for a drive after breakfast."

"Where are we going?"

"It's a surprise."

She squealed. "I like surprises."

"I know."

She reached over to her plate and picked up the blindfold I'd set there. "What's this for?"

"Not for what you think." I winked, and her bottom lip curled in disappointment. "But we can keep it for later."

"I like both options. Are you trying to help me forget my father died yesterday?"

"I don't think I'm that talented, but I am hoping to take your mind off everything today."

"Sounds perfect."

She chowed down on the pancakes and sunny-side-up eggs with appetite, blow dried her hair, and we were out the door minutes later. I helped her with the blindfold in the car. She squealed as soon as we left, but it only took us a few minutes to arrive at the destination.

I parked in the private spot, turned off the ignition, and walked around to open Kay's door.

"Where are we?"

I took her hand and helped her out. "Patience."

She popped her bubblegum, then snickered. "Do you not know who you're talking to?"

"I promise it will be worth it." I guided her to the elevator and the penthouse apartment, and I keyed in her private code. We stepped inside, and I locked the door.

"Julian, you're making me nervous. Where are we?"

"Take off your blindfold."

She stepped from one foot to another before removing her blindfold. Her beautiful brown eyes popped open with a spark.

"Did you buy a new condo?"

"I did."

She stepped forward. "Wait a minute. Is that my table?" She hurried further in again. "And these are my couches. Julian, what's my furniture doing here?"

"This condo is yours."

She spun on her heel. "What?"

"We'll put your old one up for sale. That one's not secure enough."

"I can't afford this."

"But I can, and I want you safe. It's closer to my house and, unlike your old apartment, this one has top-notch security. You won't be far from me, and you'll have your independence, so I can pick you up for dates, visit you on movie-nights, and takeout Thursday. And…" I stepped closer, took her by her hips, and brought her against my body.

"And?"

Her sweet breath curled around my face. It was enough to drive my need all the way south to my dick.

"And christen every corner of this apartment."

I lowered my mouth to hers and tightened my hold. Her tender lips opened, and her hands snaked around my neck, her fingers dragging along my hairline. I lifted her into my arms and carried her to the nearest counter.

She opened her eyes and pulled away. Her purring lips slid down my jawline. "There's a staircase. It's a two-story penthouse?"

I took her mouth again and pulled away too fast. "Aha, and a king-sized bed beyond that railing." I pointed to the second floor.

"You got me a larger bed?"

"It's only fair, since I'll be staying here often."

Her abdomen pulsed with a hint of laughter. "I like that."

"I'm glad you do. I'm hoping this home will give you at least a sliver of the normalcy you seek. I just don't want you afraid, Kay. We'll make this work."

"We'll make this work," she whispered.

Her head tilted back, and I lowered my mouth to hers.

"What are the files for?" she murmured, abusing my lips, and I pulled away.

"Sole ownership paperwork for your new club, Kissed. Scar dropped it off earlier."

She picked a tissue from a box and spat out her bubblegum. "We'll need to find Jace to sign it."

I was sure the fuck turd would show sooner than later, and my people would find him before he did. I, on the other hand, had a king-sized bed and a beautiful woman in my arms.

"How do you kiss me with bubblegum in your mouth, and aside from the sweet taste, I never feel any?" I lowered my hands to her hips and brought her closer.

"It's a talent." She shrugged.

"Don't worry about Jace. I'll find him, but right now, I have more important things to do. Want to join me?"

"The staircase is tempting, but that king-sized bed should be the perfect spot to throw me around like a rag doll."

Her seductive whisper slithered through my mind, and I lost myself in touching her, kissing her, and fondling her until she came in my mouth, around my cock, and most importantly, in her bed.

Chapter 18

Kendra

I pulled the drapes apart, and the sun shone through my penthouse apartment. The harbor view of Oyster Bay was worth every penny Julian had spent. With a suitable set of binoculars, I'd be able to see Julian's house from here, so maybe it was a good thing I didn't have a set. It was a beautiful morning, and I dreaded calling the funeral home about last-minute arrangements. My father had died a week ago, and they'd held his body in the morgue as we waited to find my mother.

I brushed my teeth and changed into jean shorts. The terrace thermometer pointed to a beautiful eighty-eight degrees, and it was only nine in the morning. I used to spend my lazy mornings and sunny days watching Julian swim laps in the pool, but living on my own gave me the confidence and independence I'd lacked my entire life. It also gave me the comfort of security, but even so, Julian rarely left me alone, which was nice.

Our new relationship, without spoken rules or strings, eased my constant ache for the man. He'd surprised me with beautiful sex twice, without warning. Once at night in my bedroom, I woke up in the middle of the night with his mouth over mine and his hand down my panties. As I realized it was Julian restraining me, the panic over someone in my bed turned into lust and arousal. He fucked me silly in my bed that night until I couldn't move, and then left without saying a word.

My second surprise came while I was showering. I couldn't walk for days after that one, and retaliated when we went out for dinner at the Marina. I climbed underneath the table and under the tablecloth; I sucked him off in the middle of dinner. He spanked me afterward, as punishment, but his cock inside my pussy while he did so certainly felt more like a reward.

I poured myself a cup of coffee and removed a shoe box from the top shelf in my closet. I lifted the lid and eyed the bundles of cash. Two hundred thousand took a lot less physical space than I'd expected. The money from my parents' safe deposit box had come in handy when I'd bribed Jace to add me to the deal. Apparently, property purchases in Manhattan came with a heap of favors from everyone, and a year from now, I'd be running my own nightclub, Kissed. If Jace had really signed the ownership documents. I called him daily, but he returned none of my calls.

The sun rose higher, along with the temperature, and by early afternoon, I had the urge to visit Fred and Wilma for a dip in the pool. I grabbed my bathing suit, and as I passed by the front door, a note slipped underneath the frame.

I picked up the white paper and turned it over.

Meet me at the carousel park in thirty minutes. Jace.

I sent a quick good morning text to Julian, threw my phone in my purse, and rushed out the door.

I clutched my purse under my arm and hurried through the park. An uncomfortable chill trickled down my spine. Jace didn't answer when I called, and as I searched around the park and couldn't find him, dread filled my gut. A soft whistle sounded from my right and I turned. Martinez was leaning against a mature chestnut tree with Jace beside him. Dark circles underlined my friend's eyes. He was sweating profusely while shivering, and could barely hold himself up. His messy hair, torn shirt, and soiled jeans didn't help his cause.

"Jace? Are you all right? I've been trying to reach you for days."

He looked up, and his blank stare shook me.

"Why didn't you return my call, Jace?"

Jace lost his balance, and Martinez grabbed his arm to steady him.

"What's wrong with him?" I asked.

"Nothing. Is it true what he says about you? Your father thinks you're something special." Martinez hacked up spit and aimed it at the ground.

"I have no contact with my parents." Hindsight twenty-twenty, I should have kept my mouth shut because the look of satisfaction on the asshole's face sucked the breath out of my lungs.

"What's it to you?"

Martinez let go of Jace, and my friend fell to the ground. I ran to Jace and dropped to my knees.as Martinez growled from above me. "I always collect."

Jace's muscles contracted and his limbs contorted as he convulsed.

"Oh, my God. Oh, my God." I grabbed my phone, dialing for an ambulance while rolling Jace on his side. I propped my purse underneath his head and held him still.

"Yes, I need help at Oyster Cove Park. Hold on, Jace. Help is on the way."

His mouth foamed, and he stopped breathing.

"Shit."

I rolled him flat on his back and administered CPR, waiting for the ambulance to arrive. The passing minutes felt like hours. The paramedics took over his revival and asked me to follow them to the hospital, but by the time we arrived, Jace was cold, blue, and dead. I stood and watched as they removed his corpse from the ambulance, unable to move.

I shuffled my feet into the hospital café and sat slouched at a table. My hands were dirty, my knees ached, and my fingers itched. I had no clue why my fingers itched. At least I wasn't dead, like Jace. I stood up again and went to the bathroom. Dirty water ran off my skin. I added soap and washed them again, picking at my nails, when a tiny sob echoed from the stall behind me.

The toilet flushed, and an elegant, middle-aged woman stepped out. Her eyes were puffy as she blew her nose, shuffling her feet to the sink. She threw the tissue into the garbage and started sobbing again. She looked up in the mirror.

"I'm sorry. This is not something I usually do. I'm usually calm and composed, but how do you stay composed when your father dies?"

"I'm sorry for your loss. I wish I knew what that felt like." I pointed my finger her way, then quickly realized how stupid that looked and hid my hand behind my back.

"You wish you knew what it felt like to lose a father? You don't know what you're wishing for."

"I mean no disrespect. My father died a week ago, actually, and because we didn't have a close relationship, I don't grieve and mourn him like you do. I wish I could, though. I wish I could feel what I lost. You must have been close to your father."

"He was my role model, and I was his world."

"Wow."

She pointed to my knees. "What happened there?"

"I was trying to save a friend's life. But he died. Today. I'm Kendra."

She shook my hand. "Mila. Jesus. A father and a friend in such a short time? That's some streak. I'm so sorry."

She blew her nose once again, composed herself, splashed some water over her cheeks, and pointed to the door. "Do you want to grab a coffee or tea out there?"

"Sure. That sounds nice. And I'm truly sorry about your loss."

We walked to the food court, and I sat at a round table. She pulled out a chair and sat beside me. I drew my finger along a penned scribble while my new friend ordered two cappuccinos.

"Are you gonna be okay to go home?" she asked.

"I'll be fine. I'm fine."

"'I'm fine' is exactly what someone says when they're not. Is anyone here with you?"

"I'll be fine as long as I don't die like my friend."

She leaned in. "May I ask how he died?"

"Poisoned."

She drew back.

"What makes you think that?"

"It's speculation, but I'm sure the toxicology report will be wild."

"And why aren't you talking to the police?"

I knew Martinez had killed Jace, but I had no proof, and I couldn't afford any attention.

"The police can't help me. My friend got himself in more trouble than he was ready for." I swallowed hard. "He must have crossed someone."

"Sounds complicated," the woman said. "My advice would be to take this opportunity to simplify your life."

I pulled a tissue out of my pocket and blew my nose. "You're asking me to make wine out of water. I'd give anything to go back in time and be simple again. I thought I was getting there this morning, but then Jace died and, well... Now I'm here."

I moved out to start over. I left my old life, and I wanted a simple boyfriend, Julian, but I got a dead Jace as well. Was this a warning from Martinez?

The woman checked the time on her phone, removed a business card from her purse, and set it on the table. "Looks like I have paperwork to sign in administration. I have to run, but you sound just like me when I was your age."

"How so?"

She jutted her hip sideways. "You ever feel like trouble follows you and Karma gives you the finger?"

I tilted my head in a yes.

"That's why I make sure Karma gets it right. Thank you for your kind words in the bathroom, Kendra. Hope we can get together for another coffee soon. "

"That would be nice."

I waved her off as she walked away, and sank in my seat. The hospital intercom announced a code blue. Maybe I was the Grim Reaper? I certainly felt like it. I stood up to leave and bumped into a smelly man. The cigar stench hit me deep in the lungs before I saw him.

"Our friend didn't make it?"

Martinez pushed me down to the chair and sat where the Honorable Judge Mila Curtis had been sitting a moment ago. I slid her business card inside my purse and ignored the incoming message notification.

This asshole was responsible for Jace's death, and likely my father's, and I wouldn't waste an opportunity to get my answers.

A car honked outside, and I jumped up. Martinez smirked.

"What did you give Jace?" I asked.

"Nothing he hasn't taken himself."

"But definitely something you knew could have killed him."

Martinez leaned in, his stinky breath overpowering my air, and I backed into my chair.

"I'm not here to talk about Jace's fuck up with fentanyl. I'm here because Jace owes me."

"You mean owed. He doesn't owe you anymore because he's dead."

Martinez closed in, his brows drawing together. Rows of unforgiving frown lines stretched across his forehead. "You heard me right, sweetheart. Jace owes me, and since you were partners, his debts become yours."

I wished someone would put a bullet through this man, and a memory of me pulling a trigger flashed through my mind. I shook off the image.

"How much are we talking about here? How much does he owe you? Because I have some money."

"I know you have money, but our deal wasn't for money. When I got him the property deal from Hartley, he promised to bring me a girl, barely legal. Someone like you. So when the time comes to collect, I will collect."

"What are you after?" Hindsight twenty-twenty. It was a stupid question.

"The payment comes due when you begin operations."

"Who the fuck are you? A fairy godmother foretelling a pointless future? You must be fucking crazy if you think I owe on a sick promise Jace made."

"And you must be naïve if you think I won't collect. I always collect and it's not the first time I've taken something from the Silvers. You must remember, sweetheart—people who deny me vanish."

He was talking about Joanne. Shivers covered my arms. He stood up, towering above me, and my muscles lost their will. Fortunately, Martinez turned on his heel and left. I watched the long trench coat disappear out the door and finally breathed again. The extra air eased the pressure behind my eyes and I let go, sobbing without restraint. People were looking at me, probably assuming I had lost someone. And that was true. A friend had died in front of me. But what made me cry even harder was the knowledge I'd received a threat I had no clue how to fight. Maybe my parents knew what they were doing when they left me after all. Maybe I could never truly escape trouble.

I trembled until familiar arms helped me up from the seat. I cuddled against Julian's chest, and he sat down on a chair, cooing into my ear.

"Everything is going to be okay, Kay. I promise." His tone lowered to a comforting level.

"You'll be happy to know Jace is dead."

"There's nothing happy about death when it comes too early or unjustly. So no, Kay, I'm not happy about his death."

I pulled back a little and looked into his eyes. What was he trying to tell me? My nose dripped, and I wiped it on his shirt.

"Jace made his bed," he grumbled, and I recoiled.

"I think Martinez laced his drugs. He was there when Jace OD'd, and he just left us. Then, he came here, to the hospital, to threaten me. I keep seeing him everywhere." I couldn't stop the shakes.

"Martinez was here?" Julian shot up to his feet, set me on the floor, and gripped my hand firmly.

I pulled in my sniffles, blew my nose, and wiped my tears. "I shouldn't cry, I should fight, but I don't want to. Martinez drugged Jace, so he could get what Jace didn't want to give him."

"What's that?"

I shuddered. "Me."

"We're leaving." He led me out of the hospital and to his illegally parked car.

"Jace was protecting me, Julian, and now he's dead. Martinez won't stop. If I don't go of my own free will, he'll take me by force."

Julian stopped in front of his car and removed the parking

ticket from underneath the windshield wiper. "Well, he can't have you. No one can."

I slid into the passenger's seat, and Julian took the wheel.

"How did you find me?" I turned to look at him.

"I tracked your phone. I've been trying to reach you all day."

"You have? What's so important that you had to track me?"

His lips thinned. "I was hoping to tell you when we get home, because I'm not even sure how to say this."

"Just say it, Julian. My life can't get much worse."

But it would get worse. I just didn't know it.

⌒⌒

"GOOD MORNING."

I was lying on my side near Julian's feet, taking him in from the bottom. The view of his healthy erection obstructed his face. He lifted to his elbows and smiled.

"Good morning."

"Certainly looks good from here." I wiggled my brows. I thought I'd fallen asleep in his arms, but I must have moved. "When are we going to stop sleeping this way?"

He frowned. "We've always slept this way."

"What if I want to be on that side of the bed?" I pointed. "In your arms… Or on your dick?"

He burst out in laughter, and I rose up on my elbows, as well.

"Come hither." He winked, but I stayed in my spot.

"What if I want you forever, Julian? Because… What exactly are we?"

"Were you overthinking life last night?"

"A little."

"I get it. You need a commitment." He reached out to the side and patted the pillow beside him. "Come up here, my love."

Goosebumps scattered over my skin. I climbed out from

underneath the covers in my usual Julian t-shirt and panties nightie, crossed the bed, and slid under the covers again, snuggling into his side. He wrapped his arm around me, and I laid my head in the nook between his shoulder and chest.

"I'm not asking for a ring, I just… I want to be more than your fuck buddy. I want to be more than another Stefanie."

He kissed my temple.

"You're right, Kay. You deserve better than what I've offered. I should have said this back in Colorado, when I made love to you, and I'm so sorry I didn't. You've never been a fuck buddy to me because I love you. I've loved you for a very long time."

"I know that, silly. I love you too."

"No. I mean, I love you like a man loves a woman, and I want to share my life with you."

I stilled. What did that mean?

"I love you just as hard, Julian," I whispered. "And I'll never stop loving you."

He tightened his hold around me and caressed my arm.

"You had a nightmare last night. You mentioned Martinez."

The conversation I'd had with the extortionist at the hospital flashed in my memory, and I shivered. He'd made it clear he was after me.

"He killed Jace."

"Jace made his own bed."

His words hit me deep in the chest and I shut my eyes. "I made my bed too. I trusted the wrong person." I lowered my head. "If Jace was a true friend he'd want me nowhere near Martinez, so I deserve whatever's coming my way."

He kissed the top of my head. "You can't compare yourself to Jace. They took advantage of you. Simple as that. And I'm sorry about your father."

"They died the same way, Julian."

"If it makes you feel better, we tipped off the police about

Martinez. They should keep him busy and away from you. If we're lucky, they'll arrest him."

"But they're gone. It still doesn't feel real."

"Grief hits everyone differently."

I inhaled a stuttering breath. "Is it bad if I feel relieved they're gone? You know, like I don't have to worry about them anymore, and maybe I can have my life back?"

"It's not bad."

"Should I even plan a funeral? I mean, do I even want my father to have a proper funeral? And what if we don't find my mother before then?"

"We can always request a private ceremony and have his ashes placed where they supposedly lay before."

I didn't know what to do and whether it would be what he would've wanted, and I was worried about my mother. Julian reached for my hand and weaved his fingers through mine.

"You know what? You don't have to decide now. We have time. I have a few calls to make today, and as of now, we have plans for tonight as well. You'll need to dress for a ride."

"On your bike?"

He shifted and reached down into my panties, his fingers meandering between my folds and over my opening.

"Feels like we should start with riding my dick," he whispered.

Instant arousal rushed through my veins. I climbed over his body, shimmied out of my panties, removed my t-shirt, and straddled him.

"Sounds like the perfect place to start." I smiled.

"Slide lower." The request rumbled through his chest with a promise. I held my legs around him and slid down his body and onto his cock. The glorious slow entry quickly turned into a rolling frenzy. I rose and rode his girth at an unforgiving pace, bringing him to a fast climax. I lowered myself to his chest and stayed there until Julian's phone drew his attention back to reality. He kissed me hard before he left to work in his office, and I pulled the covers around my body into a cocoon. While Jace's passing and my father's murder felt a little like freedom, I couldn't shake the feeling the target on my back was still flashing bright red.

Chapter 19

Julian

I turned the ignition, and the sound of the bike's motor rolled through the garage. I played with the gas under my right hand. The engine's power purred with my wrist twists until I turned the key. I'd spent most of the day making phone calls and arranging the private funeral for Kendra's father. This evening couldn't come any sooner. She'd spent the day in the backyard, curled up on a seat and staring out into space. The news of her father's death had leaked, and the newfound interest in the Moore family spiked. Silver Securities dove deep into damage control.

Outside, the sun had set and the sky glowed in orange and pink tones. I set the bike helmets aside and wiped the water marks off the fuel tank. Kendra walked into the garage in her tight leggings, boots, and a sweatshirt. I removed her helmet from the stacked column of spare tires and passed it her way.

"Ready?" I asked.

She stepped up on her toes and brushed her lips over mine. "Did you go for a ride without me?"

"I had an errand to run before our date." I lowered to the ground and reached for the large box behind the bike. "Thought you might like this one better than the old one."

Her eyes grew wide, and she beamed. "For me?"

She pulled on the black bow tied around the package and lifted the lid. My chest drummed with impatience as she removed the leather riding jacket and matching gloves.

"Oh, my God, Julian. It's beautiful. Thank you." She jumped up into my arms and puckered for a drawn-out kiss.

"Thought you could use a new one."

"I love it," she said against my mouth, then slid down my body.

"Put it on. We're going for a ride."

She put on her jacket, helmet, and gloves, and climbed on the bike behind me. Her arms wrapped around my torso.

"Like a pro." I glanced over my shoulder and turned on the ignition. The engine's vibrations traveled up my spine. Kendra tightened her grip, and I pulled out of the garage.

We rode along the shoreline, the force of the passing wind curling around us. On our left, a handful of boats bopped on the black ocean. The salty air receded as we pulled away from the shore and I turned into the city. She pressed her chest to my back and leaned into each turn, following the bike's sway. In front of us, the city's seductive glow lit up the sky. I turned left and drove past the city limits, to a gun range. I'd practiced here often with my brothers.

I parked the bike, and we removed our helmets. I secured them on the bike and took her hand. Cameron, the owner, met us in the hall and locked the door behind us.

"It's all yours." He showed me to the door, and I led Kendra through.

We walked into a room with a wall stacked with guns and rifles. Kendra paced along the wall and stopped at a Glock 19 mid-range. She chose the gun she'd once asked me for, gripped its handle, and checked the magazine.

"It's empty."

"Bullets are on that side." I pointed across the room.

"I feel like I've seen this gun before."

"You have."

She walked along the counter until she found the right bullet and loaded the gun.

"Holy shit. How do I know all this?"

"You tell me."

She flexed her fingers, cranked her neck sideways, and grinned. "I want to shoot."

"I was hoping you'd say that."

I grabbed a couple of pairs of noise-canceling headphones and stuck one over her ears, pointing to the door behind her. I followed her into the shooting area. "You can choose any target."

Kendra stepped up to the line like she'd done this hundreds of times. In fact, she *had* done this hundreds of times. She was a pro.

She took a firm stance, lifted the gun, and aimed. She pulled the trigger three seconds later, hitting the bull's eye three times at the end of the hall.

She spun around to face me. "Holy shit." Her ribs rose in a steady rhythm.

"I know. Keep going."

She recovered her breath, turned around, and emptied the magazine, one shot after another, hitting the target every time.

She lowered her gun and turned my way. "I'm pretty sure I can shoot the other ones, too."

"Then do it." The corner of her mouth twitched as I pulled on the string to pull back the targets. "Let's see if you can get this one." I pointed in the direction.

She loaded the gun, aimed and finished the round, each bullet hitting the bullseye.

She stuck out her forefinger like it was a barrel and blew a breath of air over the top. "Like a pro."

"You enjoyed that?"

"It was easy." Her nose crinkled. "Like second nature."

"I thought it would be."

"Okay, now I'm very ready for you to tell me what I just did."

"You sure?"

"Yes, I'm sure. How do I know so much about guns?"

She returned the piece to Cameron, I took her hand, and we walked back to the parking lot.

"You were an Olympic candidate, and you trained in biathlon. Shooting was your thing."

"An Olympic candidate?"

"Yup. You're an excellent skier, too."

"Wow."

"I know. Does it spark any memories?"

Her body frame shrank inward.

"It's okay. It may take some time to remember."

I brought her in for a long hug. We stood at the end of the parking lot underneath the streetlight as a vendor approached with a small, rolling hot dog cart. I watched as her eyes grew wide, and the moment was worth every penny I'd spent to hire him.

She tugged at my arm. "We should get one."

"We definitely should."

We hurried to the man and the row of perfectly grilled hot dogs.

"Look, there's sauerkraut."

"Yes, there is."

"Oh, no." She paused half-way while reaching to the container. "I should probably wait for the dog."

"You probably should."

"Wait—did you plan all this?"

I shrugged. "I might have."

I lifted my hand to the man and showed him two fingers. He set two long buns on the grill to toast.

Kendra's smile spread. "I love it. Thank you for taking my mind off… Well, everything, actually."

"You're welcome. I'm glad you enjoyed our evening."

"What's not to enjoy? Bike ride, shooting, hotdog, and dick. It's the perfect date."

"When did you have dick?"

"I'm still looking forward to it." She winked, and the man behind the cart chuckled. He passed us the hot dogs, and we topped them with condiments, scooping more sauerkraut than should be legal.

"I'm a fucking great shooter," she said, before taking her bite.

"Yes, you are. We can come back here anytime."

"Will the hot dogs be here?" she mumbled while chewing.

"I'm sure that can be arranged."

She tilted her head. "You would do anything for me, wouldn't you?"

"I believe we established that a long time ago."

She stuffed the rest of her foot-long into her mouth when I wasn't even half-way done with mine. The move impressed and scared me at the same time. That mouth was fucking irresistible.

We washed down the food with root beer, hopped back on the bike, and returned home. I parked in the garage and slid off while Kendra stayed in her spot.

I removed a small box off a shelf and held it out in front of her, her eyes wide and hair wild.

"What are you doing?"

I laughed. "Open it."

She cautiously lifted the cover, revealing a set of car keys. She dangled them between her fingers.

"You got me a Beamer?"

"Heard you crashed the Jaguar while I was away. I'm sure you'll want to get back into the swing of normalcy with something dependable. I wanted to get you a Bentley, but I know you like these more. It's in the garage by the guest house."

"Julian, this is too much." She placed the keys in my palm.

"Why?"

"I can buy my own car, you know—once I get the club going. Also, I have my own money."

"Drugs?"

"No. From the safety deposit box my father left me the first time they died."

"All right, but can you just accept the gift? This model has a GPS tracker, so I'll know where you are at all times."

"That sounds creepy and comforting at the same time. Thank you for the car. I appreciate it."

She gripped my shirt and pulled me in for a kiss.

"Did you remember anything else from the gun range?" I asked, but she kissed me again. She tasted like ocean and wind, and I couldn't get enough.

"I might not remember everything—she kissed my upper lip, then the lower one, skimming her lips over mine with temptation—"but I remember how much I want you. I've always wanted you."

She hopped off the bike, lifted her leg over the back, and straddled the seat, facing me. I stood behind the bike and held her gaze. Her eyes darkened with lust and her hands slithered up my chest. She lowered the jacket zipper in a slow pull. I removed the leather from my shoulders and withdrew my arms. The jacket flopped to the floor. Kendra disposed of hers, mischief sparkling in her eyes. She leaned forward, gripped my neck, and brought me to her mouth. Her tongue caught mine, swirling with a surprising promise. She was like a hurricane, calm on the inside but tearing through the world on the outside. She tasted like trouble, and I pulled away.

"What are you doing, Kay?"

"Hopefully, you."

"This will end only one way if you tease me like this."

She kissed me again while I gripped her sweater and pulled it upward. She lifted her arms, helping me.

"That's the idea."

I walked around to the front, set the garments over the odometer between the handles where she could rest her head, and went back for her mouth, but she pulled away. "Julian?"

"Yes?"

Her smile beamed from ear to ear, and need curled on her heated breath.

"If I forget, thank you for everything you've done for me. I don't deserve—"

I stole her mouth again and leaned forward, forcing her to lie back on the fuselage and taking her control. I didn't want or need to be thanked. If I'd done my job right the first time, Kendra would have suffered less. She had the right to live in peace, walk down the street without fear, and answer for her own mistakes, not her parents'. She deserved much better than her parents, but I'd kept that to myself.

I pulled my fingers along the hollow of her neck before sliding down her chest. Her breasts rose and fell with each breath, and her nipples poked from underneath her bra. I skimmed over the pebbled peaks, and she shuddered.

"I can't make it to the bedroom without having you, Kay." The possessive voice was not my own. I lowered my mouth to her breast and clasped my teeth around the stone-hard nipple, gently rolling my tongue over the tip before pulling up and letting go. She pushed her chest higher. The helmet hanging on the bike's handle dropped to the floor, startling her.

"Easy baby." My fingers played over her waistband and then slowly lowered the stretchy leggings off her hips. I removed her boots and slipped the fabric down her legs. The bike wobbled with the shift.

"Better keep your balance, Silver, or we'll tip over."

"No, we won't." I scanned over her body from above. She looked like an absolute goddess in her lacy bra and panties. To me, she was a goddess.

A gust of wind swept through the garage, peppering her skin. Moonlight filtered through the door window, lighting the space in gray and white tones.

I lifted her hips and gently pulled her body forward so that her back rested flat on the motorcycle. I crouched behind the bike to where her ass was balanced at the edge, and one foot dangled on the side. I lifted that foot to my mouth and skimmed my lips along her toes, slowly trailing upward past her calf to her inner thigh. I rested her leg over my shoulder and pulled my nose along her panties, inhaling her need.

Her soft moan made my dick hard. I swept my finger along the drenched fabric and grabbed a pair of box cutters from nearby. The fabric surrendered to the blade's first pull.

I dragged my fingers down her slit. "You're so fucking wet, Kay."

She lifted her hips, and my thumb strummed her throbbing clit. I slid two fingers inside her while rubbing the sensitive area. She tightened around me, her body rocking with my rhythmic pumps. I fingered harder and faster until my fingers weren't enough for her, nor for me. I hooked the middle finger and rubbed against her inner wall. She squeezed around my digit, and her hands flew to her breasts, fingers molding the flesh and gripping nipples. I lowered my mouth to her pussy and licked around where I'd pumped.

"Oh, my God." Her moans echoed through the garage and fueled my hunger.

I removed my fingers and gripped her ass, setting her in one spot. I licked through her pussy, swirling close to her need. She tasted like trouble and pleasure. I skimmed my tongue over her throbbing clit several times before closing over the sensitive spot. The alternating sucks and flicks coerced her arousal. She swelled between my lips, gripped my head, and pushed my mouth to the pulsing flesh.

"Please, Julian. Make me come," she begged, and let go of my hair. Eight tongue strokes later, she trembled in my hold and erupted in my mouth. She screamed as I sucked on her release and watched the jitters flow along her skin. I licked through her settling orgasm until her legs lowered and her arms flopped to the sides.

I trailed soft kisses along her belly, through the valley between her breasts, over her neck and to her mouth. She tasted hot and sweet. I swirled my tongue along her gums the same way I had between her legs. The quiet yelp from the back of her throat alerted me to my hard cock. I pulled away and stood at the bike's side. She reached for my jeans and curved her hand over the strain underneath my zipper. The corner of her mouth rose as she met my gaze.

She sat up and took hold of my jeans. But with an erection of this size, it would be a challenge to remove them. She tugged at the jeans twice, working them down with more patience. I sucked in my stomach, which didn't help much. The zipper, then the waistband slid past the bulge without damaging the goods.

"You couldn't find any underwear this morning?" she asked.

"Are you complaining?"

"Nah-ah." She shook her head, and my jeans dropped to my ankles.

I watched her stare at the glistening pre-cum and passed her a condom.

"You don't like condoms." She looked up.

"You're ovulating, and I'm not waiting until you're not. Want to do the honors?"

But she didn't wait. Instead, she wrapped her fingers around my cock and stroked from the base up, looking right into my eyes. I sucked in a sharp breath and my abs sank in.

The first hit of pleasure came with the first touch of her warm hand. But it was her pussy's warmth that I sought.

She lowered the condom over my cock and rolled the latex to my base.

"Stand up, Kay. And turn around." I helped her off the bike, and she braced her arms over the seat, wiggling her ready ass.

"So beautiful," I reached between her legs, spreading the dampness and positioning my cock. I pushed my hips forward and slid inside her slowly, then almost withdrew before filling her again, deeper an harder.

"You're so perfect, baby."

I rocked back and forth before picking up the momentum. Her hips held steady in my hands as she braced against the bike. The sound of our slapping skin echoed through the garage. The smell of our sweat mixed with the faint scent of gasoline and leather. I pulled more of her weight against me, and she screamed out.

She leaked down her pussy, and I pushed harder, reviving her need with my fingers over her throbbing clit. I let out a loud groan, pushing harder, and she lost her control.

"Oh, fuck!"

I pushed right back inside her, forcing another scream until she closed around me, shaking. As her orgasm settled, I pushed three more times and found my release. Her knees buckled as I filled that condom inside her. I withdrew, removed the latex, tied a knot around the top, and threw it into the corner garbage can. I made the shot, turned Kendra around, and scooped her into my arms. She fell asleep in the comfort of my body after I carried her to our bedroom. That night, while I cradled her in my arms, I contemplated how to tell her about the text I had received—that they'd found her mother with a bullet in her head.

Chapter 20

Kendra

My phone battery dinged with a two-percent warning.

"Crap."

I slowed my jog, turned off the apps, and removed the earbuds from my ears when I noticed a dark-haired man standing across the street and staring. He resembled Martinez, but I couldn't be sure from this far. A bitter taste filled my mouth.

It had been a week since the police found my mother with a bullet in her head. Now, both of my parents had reclaimed their grave spots, and I didn't want to be next. Today would be my first night in the condo on my own since the news. Julian was away on business, but the condo was supposedly safe.

Martinez hadn't threatened me since the hospital, but he was always lurking nearby. At least, I felt him lurking, and my tense muscles reminded me I felt like I was under constant threat. I side-stepped into the street leading to the marina and Oyster Bay Port, where the street buzzed with weekend visitors. I swerved through the crowd, passing cafes and restaurants, but the man was following me. This time I recognized Martinez's bushy brows. The harbor was filled with tourists, but as I tried to get lost in the afternoon commotion, he picked up his pace. I was heading for the marina, hoping to catch my breath at Olivier's, but he was getting closer, so I pushed open the first door on my right.

People with name tags and sashes filled the foyer. They were exchanging folders and photographs. Some cried in a reunion by the food court. Boards with family trees lined the wall.

"Ancestry conference? What the hell is that?"

I made a beeline for the ladies' room and snuck inside as Martinez entered the building, but I was pretty sure he didn't see me. I turned on the tap water and washed my face. Sweat dripped down my back and my heart was pounding.

I fumbled with the phone in my pocket, but when I swept my finger, the battery was dead, and I couldn't call Julian.

"Are you all right?" I whipped my head up to the woman's reflection in the mirror. Her blonde hair, pristine makeup, jeans, and sweater with the name *Samantha* scribbled in neat handwriting on a tag gave me hope I'd run into someone nice for a change.

"I think I'm being followed," I blurted, and her gaze skidded to the door. "By a man. I don't think he saw me walk in here, but I'm not sure how to get out, either."

Her limbs stiffened and her neck tensed. "Should we call the police?"

"No. The police can't help with this asshole. I... I need to change into something."

My current sports top and running leggings didn't offer many options to blend in with the crowd.

"You can have my sweater, but if he's following you—"

"A sweater won't help." I turned to the air dryer and bumped into a maintenance cart. My gaze connected with Samantha's. "But this will."

Her eyes grew wide.

"I need a huge favor," I whispered.

She hurried to open the supply door underneath the cart and removed the toilet paper rolls and soap from underneath, passing them to me. I stacked them all on the counter by the sink. She peeled off her nametag, shed her sweater, straightened her crispy white blouse, and tied her hair up in a bun.

"Will this do?" she asked, and I grinned.

"You think it will work?"

"I'll scream if it's not working. Get in."

It had been some time since I'd placed my life in a stranger's hands, but right now, I had no choice, and Samantha oozed with trustworthy vibes.

"Take me to the second floor." I climbed inside, and she shut the door.

The cart wobbled as Samantha pushed. I listened to the humming crowd outside. We took the elevator, and moments later, as the music drifted by, the elevator opened, and by the disgusting smell I figured we were in a different bathroom. She finally let me out.

"Hi." She grinned. "I think we're out of the woods. I didn't see anyone on this floor, and no one followed me."

I scrambled out and checked the empty hall.

"Who are you hiding from?" she asked.

"An obsessive ex," I lied. "Can I use your phone?"

"I'm embarrassed to say I don't have one on me. I dropped it a couple of days ago, and I'm waiting for a replacement."

"Crap."

"If you want to get out of here, I have my car in the parking lot."

I did want to get out of there, and I wanted to do it fast. After Julian changed the club's ownership, I'd hoped Martinez would abandon his belief that I was responsible for his deal with Jace, but my gut told me Martinez would never give up. He'd force me to hide for the rest of my life.

"As long as we can leave unseen, I'd like that very much."

"There's a staircase at the back of the building."

We exchanged identical looks and took off at the same time. Samantha was right. There was a back staircase, and thankfully, it was empty. We hurried to the back parking lot, got inside her Honda Civic, and I crouched in the foot well as we left the port.

"My name's Kendra. Thank you for your help."

"Samantha. My friends call me Sam, but I don't have many friends. I just started a new job in the city, and my work friends are still new."

"You're not from around here?"

She gripped the steering wheel and checked her mirrors every few seconds. "No, the city's new to me. We lived out in the country; sort of secluded, I guess."

"You and your husband?"

She shook her head.

"Boyfriend?" I asked as she made a left turn to merge on the parkway.

"No, I lived with my parents before they died. I just moved to Long Island recently."

"I'm sorry about your parents." My brows lifted, and she side-glanced from her seat. "The city's probably more chaotic than where you're from."

"Oh, don't make that face. There was plenty to do out in the middle of nowhere."

"Listen, you don't need to sell it to me."

"I was adopted as a baby, and I went to the conference, hoping to find a trace of my birth parents."

"Any luck?"

"Nope. Looks like I don't exist in any system, anywhere."

"You should do that ancestry DNA thingy. That should do it."

"I was going to get the pamphlets, but then got sidetracked in the bathroom."

"Sorry about that."

"It's all right. I'm sure I can find the info online. I can't believe you run away from bad guys."

"This ain't the movies, Sam."

"Right. Sorry. It's just that I don't go out that often, and my adrenaline is still pumping."

"Keep your eyes on the road. I promise you, my adventures aren't worth the danger."

She switched lanes and took the third exit, slowing down. "Wanna know what the best part of today is?" She grinned from her side. "I get to have a new friend. Like I said, I don't have many friends."

"Believe it or not, neither do I."

"That's impossible. You sound like you're from around here. And you're beautiful."

"I've lived in Oyster Bay Cove my entire life, but…" I shuddered. "My life is complicated."

"Sounds like I'm not the only one who got the finger from Destiny. I'm glad I ran into you, Kendra."

"My friends call me Kay, and I'm glad I ran into you as well."

And I was. After all, Sam had saved my life. She focused on the road, and twenty minutes later, we pulled up to a row of wall-to-wall homes. White drapes covered the front windows of one. The set of stairs and potted plants on each step were cute and inviting.

Sam cleared her throat. "This is my place. You're welcome to stay as long as you'd like. I'll try to find a charger for your phone, but I have an Android, so we'll have to see if we can borrow one from my cute neighbor. Then, you can call whoever you want to come get you because I don't think you should be alone out there."

She pointed to the street from the top of the steps. The

thing was, I didn't feel that alone with her at all. Sam turned the lock, and I followed her inside.

"I don't think anyone could mistake you for coming from the city," I said.

"No?"

"Nobody from the city is ever this nice. Thank you for the offer."

"My pleasure. You can pass it forward."

I chuckled.

"Oh, come on. Are you laughing at my expense? I'm trying to fit into the city now."

"Trying is the operative word."

We burst out in laugher, and that's how I knew our genuine friendship was for life. Actually, I knew the moment she volunteered to help me out of trouble. I clicked with Sam from the moment we met. She made tea, plated a slice of apple pie with a scoop of vanilla ice cream, and borrowed a charger from her cute neighbor. Her adventurous nature, and even her face and mannerisms, reminded me of Joanne. It would be bad to tell Gabe that Sam reminded me of Joanne, so I kept my mouth shut. But damn, was she ever a doppelgänger.

We sat cross-legged on two giant bean bags and ate ice cream. Gosh, this girl knew how to soothe a soul.

"Kay? Are you in trouble?"

"More than I'd like to admit."

"Who was following you?"

"An asshole. He's one of those people you don't want to be in a room with, one on one. But now that I lost him, don't worry about it. I'm sorry I pulled you out of the conference."

"No worries. It was a loss anyway."

"So you moved from the country to the city to find your biological parents?"

"I moved for work. I'm an insurance underwriter. Corporate, mostly."

"Let me guess—you went to NYU and fell in love with the city life."

She giggled. "Something like that."

"Do you insure night clubs? Like one smack in the middle of Manhattan?"

"The company's just north of the financial district, and yes, we do. A deal like that would put me on the map."

I squealed and made jazz hands, which Sam grabbed.

"Why are you so happy?"

"Because I found an insurer for Kissed."

"What's Kissed?" she laughed.

"The nightclub I'm opening late this summer. It's going to be posh and sexy and, most importantly, safe. Very safe, because I hired the best security company in the state."

"Sounds like a great opportunity. I can't believe this, Kay. Are you sure? You barely know me."

"You saved my life today. And for what it's worth, that means I owe you my life. I'm also thrilled to have someone I can trust with my business." I squeezed my arms hard around her small frame.

"Thanks." She leaned in, returning my embrace.

"You're welcome."

"Do you have a family?" she asked.

"Here comes the complicated part I'm not sure you're ready for."

"Try me. My father died in a shark attack, and I saw the whole thing."

"What?"

"We went diving in a shark cage, but a shark got inside."

"A shark broke through a cage?"

She nodded.

"So I can definitely handle shit, you know."

That was definitely good news, because a lot of shit often

happened around me, and I could use someone who could also handle that shit.

My phone charged, and Sam drove me home late in the evening. I should have left sooner, but her company and conversation kept my mind off the threat on my life. My parents had already died, and so had Jace. Was I next?

"Wow," Samantha said, as she walked around my penthouse. "You live here?"

"A gift from my boyfriend."

"Is he a sugar daddy?"

"No, it's nothing like that."

"Wait—is he like, keeping you a prisoner?"

I rolled my eyes. "Not even close. We don't live together because he respects me."

Her brows rose, and she leaned in. "Sometimes it's nice to be disrespected, especially by someone who looks like that." Sam pointed to Julian's photograph on a shelf.

"I have to admit, he *is* good looking."

"Good looking? Girl, you hit the jackpot."

She wasn't wrong. I gave Sam a tour of the apartment. We spent forever on the balcony, spying through the binoculars. I ordered pizza and wings and made virgin margaritas.

"You're not a good influence on me." She checked her watch before midnight. "If I don't go home now, I'll be dead tired in the morning."

"You'll be dead tired anyway. Why don't you stay over?"

Truth was, I didn't want to be alone. Not when Martinez could get so close to me.

"I can't, Kay. Not tonight. I have an early meeting in the morning."

A shiver ran down my spine. "Thank you for your help today."

"That's what friends do, and we're friends now. Maybe next weekend?"

My spirits lifted, but I wasn't thrilled that after today's ordeal, I'd be spending the night alone. "Sounds good. And let's meet up for that insurance quote. "

She smiled. "I'd love to walk through once the club is ready. Stay safe, Kay."

"You too."

She hugged me in that old-fashioned way, warm and cuddly, but the security blanket disappeared as soon as I shut the door.

The empty apartment soon turned into a hollow space. I grabbed a few blankets and climbed into the closet with my phone. I texted Julian.

Kay: Come over, please.

He didn't reply, of course. He was mid flight, coming home. If he had no delays, he'd get my message in a couple of hours. It would be an extra thirty minutes to speed home.

Kay: I'm in my closet.

I crawled out of the closed on all fours and made it to my nightstand. I removed a pouch taped underneath my bed frame, took one tiny pill, and crawled back inside the closet. It didn't take long for the Molly to kick in, and when it did, Martinez no longer existed. I closed my eyes, pulled the blanket to my chest, and pressed my back into the corner, lost in the drug's powerful grip on my reality. By the time Julian arrived, I wasn't responding. It turned out that Molly had tricked me. I thought I had taken one; when in fact, I'd overdosed.

Chapter 21

Julian

I found Kendra having convulsions in the closet. Her mouth was foaming and her lips had turned purple. I removed her body from the corner, lay her on her side, and dialed for the ambulance. I never should have left. Time slowed to a ticking nightmare until the paramedics arrived. Time slowed again on our way there, and I needed answers. I watched them work on her and prayed she didn't slip away. How many times would I have to watch her fall prey to trouble?

How did this happen? It couldn't have been Jace, because they'd poisoned him, and he was dead. At first, I thought Martinez had poisoned Kendra as well, but that wasn't it. She was using again. While many pills were missing from the pouch on her nightstand, many were left.

Twelve hours after we'd arrived at the hospital, the heart monitor was beeping steadily and an IV dripped fluids into her arm. Emma sat on a chair against the wall and was taking a stab at knitting. It wasn't coming out so well.

I sat beside Kendra's bed, stretched my legs out front, and sipped on the coffee Emma had brought as soon as I'd informed my family of the situation. There was nothing pleasant about drinking coffee ten or twelve times in a row, but it was all I could take right now.

"What are you making?" I pulled my hand over my eyes.

"I think I'll be better out in the field," she said. "This looks nothing like a blanket. A square frickin' blanket. It shouldn't be this hard."

"You're too young for the field, Ems." I grunted. "But I'll keep it in mind. Maybe we could do a trial run?"

"As long as I get to solve crimes and do everything that you guys do, I'm in. And horses. I'll need to find time for horses."

I gave her a serious look. "I'm proud of you."

She set the needles aside and crossed her arms over her chest. "A good agent never reveals her secrets. I think keeping secrets is my best quality. I should add that to my marriage profile."

"You have a marriage profile?"

"As every responsible bride-to-be should. It keeps my plans on track. I'm not ready to get married, but Grace told me she had a profile, too."

"You've been hanging out with Grace Wagner? Isn't she like, twice your age?"

"Kendra's half your age." She tilted her head, and I shook mine.

"Grace will be my best friend forever."

"Why is that?"

"You wouldn't understand."

I sighed and leaned forward, lowering my elbows to my knees. "Does it have anything to do with Eric Waters?"

She shook her head so quickly I knew it did. I made a mental note to speak with Grace about Emma's intentions when Kendra stirred.

She groaned, and I pressed the nurse's call button, backing away from the bed. They removed the breathing tube from her throat and checked her vitals. She coughed until her lungs settled and she breathed on her own. They took a blood sample, and left. I rolled my chair next to her bed.

"How are you feeling?"

She blinked three times. "Like I died and something brought me back."

I brushed my hand over her forehead. "That's pretty much how it went. You scared the shit out of me, Kay."

"I'm sorry. I didn't know how to make it stop. He was about to find me. He would get to me. I knew he would."

"What are you afraid of?"

Her gaze drifted to Emma, who remained in her chair by the wall, listening to our conversation.

"She means Martinez."

"Ems—"

"It's okay, Julian. I've read the file."

"What? Ems, I don't think I have the patience for this right now."

"It's okay. She's the best secret keeper in the family."

I turned Kendra's way.

"Has he threatened you?"

"Not directly. He followed me earlier in the day, but I think I'm overreacting. I didn't mean to overreact, but I guess I did. I was scared, Julian. I was afraid he would find me, and I didn't want to be afraid."

I cracked my neck sideways. Hopefully, the handgun I'd bought her would never need to be used, but if there were a need, she could protect herself. She was one of the best shooters in the country, and from what I'd witnessed at the gun range, her muscle memory had never died. But if Martinez was around, she needed protection. I lifted my hand to hers and smoothed my thumb over her skin.

"Once you're better, you'll come back home with me. At least for a little while, until we can figure out what's going on.

I'll be working from home for the next little while. What do you say?"

She held my gaze. The fear swam in her eyes like a deceiving rip current.

"Say yes, Kay."

"Yes. I'd like that."

"Good. Now, why don't you tell me about the email I received this morning from a Samantha Connor confirming walk-through appointments for an insurance quote?"

"I want her as my agent."

"I've never even heard of her."

"She saved me from Martinez when he followed me to the Marina."

"What?"

"She's awesome. Sam is the kind of friend who'd bury an ex's body with me in the middle of the night and wouldn't ask me a question."

"How many exes do you have?"

"Zero, Julian. You know that. And Jace doesn't count. You need to stop asking me all these questions and trust me. I must have given Sam your information. I… I don't remember, but she's a good friend. She's solid."

I was certain Silver Securities would call Kendra's solid assessment a solid risk. After clearing my throat, I stopped the conversation in front of my sister. "I'll sign the documents, and I'll forward the paper to legal with a note to fast-track."

"Thank you."

I took my hand off of hers and added the note to my phone.

"You're welcome. It's nice what you're accomplishing for women. Your staff is mostly female."

"And most of them will be able to afford a home once they start work," Emma added.

"Women work harder than most men. That's scientifically proven. Most deserve much more help than they receive."

"You're making a change. Your parents would be proud." Someone passed by the hospital door, and she shivered. I placed my hand over hers."It's okay, Kay. He's not coming here. No one knows you're here."

"You're under an alias." Emma set the knitting aside, hopped off her chair, and strolled to the door. "I'll be back in a moment. The nurse's station has popsicles. They said you might want one when you wake up."

"Thanks, Ems."

Emma closed the door behind her, and I turned Kendra's way. "We should think about rehab again. I talked to the staff, and we can have a nurse come over."

She shook her head and pulled up her cover. "I don't need rehab. I need Martinez off my back."

"You resort to pills when the paranoia sets in."

"It's not paranoia. He *was* following me. If it weren't for Sam, he would have caught me. I don't think he's given up on Jace's promise."

"I'll arrange for your things to be moved back. It feels empty without you, and I'd like to be nearby."

"I love the condo."

"The condo was a mistake. Once Martinez is out of the way, we can think about going back, but right now, I'm more concerned about your safety."

She frowned as if I weren't getting the fact she was afraid. I got it, and I'd always prioritize her safety.

After a long day at the hospital, I met up with my cousin Gabe for a drink in a bar across the street. He'd spent the months since Joanne's death in her homeland, New Zealand, and was ready to return to work.

"Welcome back."

"Thank you. It's nice to be back, but it feels like Joanne is far away."

"Are you thinking of getting your head back in the game?"

"Sure, but I'd prefer to stick with surveillance. I obviously failed as a bodyguard."

I lifted the whiskey glass to my mouth. The alcohol burned along my tongue.

"I have a unique offer for you that may require your surveillance and bodyguard skills. Honestly, I need your help."

"What can I do for you?"

"You better drink before I tell you."

He swung back his beer and let out a soft belch.

"Martinez is after Kendra," I blurted.

"How sure are you?"

"Jace made a deal for her. He lured her to After Eve and promised her to the organization. She snuck out before they snatched her. Martinez and Hartley don't take well to rejection, and they'll come back for her."

"What do you suggest?"

"I need you to be on standby for New Zealand. The more distance between Kendra and Martinez, the better, and I'll work better if I know she's safe."

Gabe tilted his beer back, emptied the bottle, and lowered it to the bar. "I'll do what's necessary, but if I have the chance to take him out, I'll take him out."

My cousin's grief needed an outlet, and Martinez was the perfect target.

"You'd be a hero if you did. The Hartleys have been pushing boundaries and my gut tells me she's next on their list. She's paranoid as it is, and if we don't catch him, she'll go crazy. Worse yet, he'll get to her again. Kay needs more help with this case. She needs safety."

"This case became more than a case when he took Joanne. It's personal now."

I nodded. "Once the club opens, she'll draw the wrong attention. Every time I leave her on her own, something new happens. I'm tired of running, Gabe. I think I'm ready to put a bullet in his head, and I wanted to know whether you'd help me."

"I'm game for anything that rhymes with a bullet in that bastard's head."

"I'll secure the club for the opening and prepare Kendra. She'll be with a friend at the bar, and you make sure she doesn't leave."

"Wait—you want me to bartend?"

"You'll have a three-sixty view from that location," I explained.

"And if something goes wrong?"

"We put Kendra on the first plane to New Zealand."

"Sounds like a plan."

"Thanks, Gabe."

He gave me a brotherly hug and left. I finished my drink and walked across the street to the hospital. The door squeaked, and Kendra opened her eyes.

"Hey, didn't mean to wake you."

"I wasn't sleeping. Sam was here. I called her."

"Your friend?"

"My only friend. She invited me to a girls' night with her work friends, but I don't think I'd make very good company in this condition."

"When am I finally going to meet her?"

"I dunno."

I pulled my chair closer to her bed. I'd seen this face before. Guilt was finally getting to my Kay.

"Wanna talk about why you took so many pills?"

"I believe the answer is obvious, so I'd prefer to skip to the good part where you make me feel better." She batted her eyelashes.

I sighed and took her hand in mine. "You have a problem, Kay. I found two more stashes in your nightstand."

"It was only one pill. Besides, it's just a one-time thing, Julian. I promise. But I don't do well when you're not there."

She lowered her head, and my heart turned to mush.

I lowered the bed rail and climbed into her hospital bed. "We'll get you a nurse. We'll get you better."

She snuggled into my body and dozed off.

The doctor discharged Kay into my care that afternoon. I took her home, helped her shower, and made her comfortable in the middle of a pile of pillows, blankets, and throws. She sank into the cushions with a smile.

"I missed being here."

"I missed having you here. Dating is overrated."

"That's because you've been dating your entire life."

"Technically, so have you."

"Not the same." She pouted, but she was right. It wasn't the same because I'd never dated anyone as unique as this girl. A need to fulfill all of her heart's desires meandered in my chest. That smile, when she was happy, was worth every sacrifice and obstacle. And if Kendra wanted a nightclub, I would give that to her, and much more, because I lived to make all of her dreams come true.

"WE HAVE the staffing ready for the club, Kay. We're all set to go."

She crossed the back room, biting her nails.

"Don't be so nervous. You're ready."

"And everyone's screened?"

"Every employee and every guest. No one's getting in who shouldn't be there. There's additional security in the alleys and parking lots. Gabe will stay at the bar. Your entire family is here today, Kay. Nobody's gonna be stupid enough to come near you."

"Okay."

She lowered her hands to her thighs. Her heavy breaths worried me. Her jugular pumped visibly; her heart rate must have spiked.

"Kay? Did you take anything tonight? Molly or anything else?"

She looked up, then stood. "No. I'm clean. Just nervous. This is my baby, you know. But if the club's successful, I'd like to sell it."

"What?" I chuckled. "You haven't opened it yet, and you're already thinking of selling?"

"It's only brought trouble, and I'm tired of trouble. I'm sure I can invest the money into a better venture. Also, I think I want to go back to school…maybe get a degree?"

"A degree in what?" I leaned back against a counter.

"Business. So I actually know how to run one." She shook her hands and tiptoed in place like she was trying to shed the nerves.

"You won't get a better experience than the one you've had, Kay. You're the one who got this place ready. Come on. Let's go open the front door."

She took my hand and gave it a little squeeze. "Me and Silver Securities. I couldn't have asked for better partners, Julian. Let's do this."

I circled the club's perimeter with a bodyguard attached to my side. The crowd buzzed with energy, lights flickered, steam rose, and Kissed, my nightclub, was finally open. My skin prickled with excitement, and blood rushed through my veins, cruising on waves of Molly. On what should have been the best day of my life, Martinez haunted me the same way he had since Jace's murder. I hid my fear of Martinez from Julian the same way I hid my new addiction. Julian had searched my apartment and my stash was gone, but I had more than one hiding spot. I was certain one of the fundamental business principles revolved around not putting all of your eggs in one basket, at which I excelled when hiding my pills. Functioning without them, at this point, was a struggle.

I bumped into a brawny guy, and the personal bodyguard Julian hired nearly ripped the man's head off. He growled before composing himself.

"Hey, easy, big guy. No harm done." I hooked my hand over his large arm, wishing Julian could be here.

"Where's Julian?"

My legs wobbled, and I stumbled forward. I'd thrown Julian off with that school and degree bullshit, but I needed him to see me in a good light. I wanted my move back to his house to be my last, even if he found my Molly; which he wouldn't.

"Ma'am? Are you okay?"

No one had ever called me *ma'am* before.

"Yes, yes. I'm fine. I need to use the washroom. Help me find the washroom, please." I turned to my brawny guard. He supported me underneath my elbow and guided me to the ladies' room.

"I'll wait out here."

"I think that's a good idea." I tapped my hand over his hard chest.

Inside the stall, I removed a small white pill from within my bra pocket... swallowed, and waited for my heart to stop pounding. Minutes later, a loud banging sounded at the door, and I jolted awake, not realizing I had passed out against the wall after washing my face.

"I'm coming!"

Outside, the broad dude was standing with a frown on his face. The rows of wrinkles ran from his forehead all the way up and over his bald head.

"Sorry about that. Let's go to the bar. I'm meeting a friend there, and judging by that look, you could use a shot."

I scanned the crowd until I found Sam's familiar shape at the bar. She was sitting in a new corset top and a pair of skin tight pleather jeans and looked absolutely stunning. Tonight would be a good night. I sauntered to the bar and greeted her with a kiss on each cheek. She smelled like peaches and cream, and from the way Gabe was eyeing her from behind the bar, it looked like someone would get some peaches, and someone else would get some cream.

"Kendra! You're here!" She threw her arms around my neck.

"You're early," I said.

"I couldn't miss your opening night."

I scanned the nightclub. Lights flickered, music blasted, and alcohol flowed. My bodyguard stood nearby, but out of view, and Gabe was a few feet away, but I couldn't shake the feeling Martinez would slip through the crowd.

"I can't believe it's your opening night."

I scanned over her Barbie body. The pleather pants and corset top we'd picked were the perfect choice.

"You approve?" she asked.

"Much better than your pencil skirt suit."

"I wouldn't wear office clothes to a club."

I laughed, and I wasn't sure why I did, but it felt so good to laugh.

"Did I not tell you I have an awesome sense of style?" I tapped her nose with my finger. She swiveled on her seat and fanned herself.

"So? Anyone yet?" I scanned the bar, but I wasn't looking for a hookup, like my friend. I was looking for a threat.

"Anyone what?" she asked.

"Anyone you fancy? I'm making sure you get laid before the sun's up," I told her. The girl deserved it. Sam worked insane hours and rarely went out to have fun.

"Shh. Lower your voice. Everyone can hear you."

I laughed again. "So? That's the point. If you advertise what you want, you get what you want."

"Don't you have more important things to worry about tonight? It's your opening night."

No, because I was a planner. I had stayed off drugs because the planning kept me busy, but now that the workload had returned to normal and Martinez was lurking nearby, I needed to take the edge off.

"This club has been a success since its inception. Besides, I have people for that."

"You look great!" Sam's lifted voice drew attention as the music lowered in tone.

"Thanks! What are we drinking?"

"A Virgin Mary."

"Virgins are fine, but not in a drink."

I motioned for Gabe to pour us a couple of orgasms. He'd had his eye on Sam, but I couldn't blame him. Her uncanny resemblance to his dead wife threw me off too, but maybe that was why we could be good friends. Maybe that was why the two of them met? Her cheerful personality sealed the deal for me, but every time Gabe winked, she stiffened. I needed her to relax and have fun. More importantly, I wanted us both to disappear.

"This place is amazing. I still don't get how you managed the investment." She brought my attention back to the bar.

"I found a silent partner. Gabe, two orgasms!" I waved him down, leaned into my friend, and whispered, "You need to relax, Sam. Here, take this. I'm prescribing fun for tonight. Nothing else." I took her mouth and left a delicate kiss, along with a little pill on her tongue. Her eyes grew wide, but once she reached my euphoria, we'd party without fear. After all, this venture could not have happened without her.

"Now swallow." I winked.

The room faded in and out of focus, keeping my vibe with the music's beat. The voices blurred, and my euphoric safety cocoon insulated me from the outside.

Sam flirted with Gabe, and he flirted back. The wise move would be to leave them alone, but that would mean I'd have to be alone, and according to my brawny bodyguard, Julian hadn't returned yet.

I lifted my shot, and Sam lifted hers. "Cheers! To Kissed!"

"To Kissed," she said.

Sam was talking to me, but her words no longer registered in my head. I scanned the bar in search of shaggy brows and a mustache, and remembered Julian's promise the asshole wouldn't slip through. But how would he know? He wasn't even here. My conversation with Sam floated on a cloud of relaxation. I watched as her pupils dilated. Once my gift hit her, I took her hand and helped her slip off the stool.

"Come on, Sam. It's time for some fun."

I led her across the dance floor, past the horny bodies and gyrating couples. Her grip on my hand tightened. Sam's face glistened with sweat, and she blinked like she wanted to clear her vision.

I pulled on her hand, guiding her to the staircase where she'd find more room to breathe. The first hint of regret for slipping her that pill hit me. Another reason Julian had every right to call me Trouble. I should have kept her out of my mess, and now she looked like a mess too.

"Look up." I pointed to the glass ceiling, but I couldn't focus on the reflection. Ecstasy rushed through my veins and I joined the crowd in the dance, swinging my arms in the air. By the time we reached the staircase, Sam was pale and on the floor. Gabe hovered above her, and Julian was gripping my wrist.

Where did he come from?

"What happened, Kay?" he asked, but I couldn't answer. The disappointment drifting in his eyes as he examined my state hit me deep in my chest. It almost killed me when I figured out he saw through me.

But I wasn't quick enough. He lifted me up and draped me over his shoulder.

"Wait, Julian. Wait. I think I see Martinez."

He froze.

"That way." I pointed in a random direction. He slowly set me down, and, as he focused on where I was pointing, I used the opportunity to slip away. Before he realized, I was gone in the crowd.

I could run, or I could hide, and hiding in the place they thought I would flee made sense to me. I hurried to the storeroom and hid behind the boxes filled with decorations. I stayed hidden until the search at the club ended and everyone left..

I turned off my phone. Minutes slowly ticked into hours, and hours into nights and days. When the club closed down for the week, I moved upstairs to the terrace, still closed off to the crowd, and lived on the rooftop couches, washed in the bubbling Jacuzzi. The kitchen at night to eat. In between, I devoured the pills like candy, drifting in and out of this world.On my third night I slid into a negligee which reminded me of Julian.

He found me days later in the cabana on the club's rooftop terrace.

"Martinez is looking for you." He removed his hands from his pockets. "He already attacked Sam at work. We think it would be best if you left with her and Gabe both for New Zealand."

The island of my birth brought back all the nostalgia. Julian had definitely practiced this conversation ahead of time.

"That's great. You, me, Gabe, and Sam. A perfect combination. When are we flying out?"

"I'm not coming."

"Julian—"

"I can't come, Kay. When I worry about you, I can't look for this bastard. I mean, look at you." He motioned his hand my way. "You're a mess. Get yourself together. Gabe will be here shortly."

"I can't go without you. You can't do this to me. You can't abandon me again." I pulled away. "I already found my safe place."

I shut the door to the rooftop lounge and hurried down the stairs and back into the kitchen, passing the chef and his team as they unloaded the fruit delivery in the back. I slipped on the floor near my cupboard and twisted my ankle. My pills spilled to the floor, and I fell to my knees to collect them. The desperate attempt, in my negligée, must have looked awful. What was happening to me?

"Are you all right, ma'am?" the chef asked.

"I'm fine! Just leave me alone."

My survival instincts kicked in, along with desperation. I depended on a five-millimeter drug, and I could no longer deny the soothing effect it had on my soul. The tiny thing had stolen my will before I'd realized what was happening. I lay on the club's kitchen floor until Gabe found me. He ignored my objections and stabbed me with a sedative.

I REMEMBERED LITTLE until we landed in New Zealand. I was thirsty and groggy, but at least, we were far from Martinez. Gabe left me and Sam on our own in his beautiful mansion, but I couldn't wait to get home to Auckland. I drank a full glass of water and went outside to show Sam the backyard.

I glanced out at the ocean, where a yacht's outline appeared and disappeared between the waves in the distance. Gabe's's boat was docked on the beach.

"Come on, Sam! Let's go!"

I ran down the twinkling path, excited to take Gabe's boat home to Auckland. I boarded, sat in the skipper's chair, turned the ignition, and the engine roared.

Sam ran down the beach swinging her arms high in the air. "Turn the engine off!"

I waved for her to come aboard. She was screaming from the dock, but I couldn't hear her.

"You comin' or stayin'?" I cheered into the night. Sam finally joined me and hopped aboard. I pushed the throttle forward, and she fell back into a seat. I sped into the dark ocean and quickly realized Gabe's dinghy had little fuel, so I turned to the shore just around the cove and pulled up to the dock where Joanne used to live.

Jace had once showed me how to syphon motorcycle fuel, so I took a canister and set it by the boat. A pack of cigarettes in the seat's side compartment had drawn my attention, and I hadn't hesitated to grab one. I lit a cigarette, and everything went dark.

Chapter 23

Julian

Gabe's call from New Zealand came at two in the morning. I turned on the night light and slid my finger across my phone.

"Hello? Gabe? Yo, slow down. What's going on?"

"She blew up a boat on our first night here."

"What?!"

"I don't know if this is going to work if I can't keep a low profile, Julian."

"Fuck. Is she off Molly?"

"She took another one on the plane. I don't know where she hides this stuff. She made a move on Sam, too. Kendra tried to steal my woman."

"I'm sorry for the trouble, man. We need to move in on Donaldson as soon as possible. I'll be out on the next flight, I promise. Put an anklet on her and pray she doesn't cause any further trouble."

"Already did. I'll see you soon."

"See you soon."

Three days later, I flew to New Zealand, helped Gabe set up his yacht, and went to get my troublemaker. I pulled up to the beach mansion and walked around to the back patio, where Sam and Kendra were floating in the pool.

"Julian?" She lowered the sunglasses and jumped off her float. "What the—"

"Before you start, let me explain. I'm taking you for a few days to get things…sorted."

Kendra hurried through the water and up the steps. "Okay."

"Okay?" I asked at the same time as Sam, who was sitting at the pool's edge.

"Yeah, okay. I'll come with you, but you have to get this off." She wiggled her foot with the security anklet.

I removed the key from my pocket, knelt in front of her, and turned the lock on the clasp, freeing Kendra.

"Next time you put a ring around me, I hope it's the right kind." She winked.

I ignored Kendra's comment and turned to Sam. "I'm Julian Silver. Gabe's fixing a couple of things for me." I pointed toward the yacht where I'd left Gabe, but I couldn't take my eyes off Samantha. Her uncanny resemblance to Joanne was remarkable.

"It's nice to meet you. Samantha Connor."

"Yeah, you're definitely her."

Her brows narrowed. She rubbed her elbow the way Joanne used to.

"I gave Clara a few days off," I said. "We can hang around here until Gabe gets here, or—"

"You guys go." She waved me away. "I'll be fine. Gabe should be back soon. Besides, I'll turn on the alarm and the property is secure. Right?"

"Of course it is. Have a great day."

I opened the convertible's passenger door, and Kendra hopped inside. She secured her seatbelt and turned around, waving to Sam. "Don't forget to get out of the sun. There's wonderful shade underneath the gazebo. See you in a few days, Sam!"

I pulled away, locked the front gate, and drove along the coastline to the rental house.

"I heard you had a heck of a trip," I said.

"Gabe tranquilized me like a horse," she groaned.

"You were right, though. Martinez was looking for you. But he found Sam."

"He's looking to cash in on his deal with Jace. He won't stop until he gets me. I know he won't."

"That's absurd, because I'm here now, and I'm not leaving your side. The club's running fine, Kay, and I'm gonna make sure you're safe and drug free."

Her knees bopped up and down as I pulled up the driveway.

"Are you drug free, Kay?"

She threw her hands up indignantly and nodded. "Did Martinez show up on the island?"

"Not yet."

"You don't sound happy about that."

"I'd rather know the enemy's location. It just means he has something up his sleeve, and that's never good. He's after Sam now."

"If he hurts her—"

"Gabe won't let that happen."

I parked the car, turned off the ignition, and walked around to the passenger door. "Come on, Kay. Time to see how well you do without the Molly."

She followed me inside, through the hall, and out to the infinity pool in the back. I removed my flip flops, and she removed her sandals. We sat on the pool's edge and dipped our legs inside.

"I'm sorry about blowing up Gabe's boat," she said.

"Where did you learn how to syphon fuel?"

"Jace taught me. Not successfully, obviously."

"Fuel and cigarettes are never a good combination."

"No shit."

"And what's going on with the drugs?"

She bit her lip. "I'm trying, Julian. I'm trying hard, but when I think the man who murdered my parents and Jace is after me, and now Sam, I… I don't know how to deal with that fear, and I do stupid things. I'm trouble. I've always been trouble."

I sighed. "You're not trouble, and I need you to trust me, Kay, so I can protect you."

Her legs swayed back and forth. I stood up and opened the umbrella, moving the shade over her body. "Don't want you getting sunstroke. I'm gonna make dinner. Your clothes are in the master closet upstairs. Make yourself comfortable. We'll talk about going back to the States after dinner."

"Thanks."

She remained sitting on the ledge, watching the ocean for over an hour. I barbecued prawns and salmon, along with heirloom potatoes and vegetables, and set the food on the outdoor patio. Kay opened a bottle of wine and poured us each a glass.

"What's gonna happen now?" she asked.

"We'll fly home and put Martinez behind bars, so we can live our happily ever after."

She sighed. "Sounds like too good to be true; and when things sound too good to be true, it's because they are."

I pulled out her chair when my phone rang with its bubblegum pop.

"I bet that's bad news." She pointed.

"How do you figure?"

"Instinct. Trouble follows me." She shrugged, and I slid my finger across the screen.

"Gabe?"

"Guess what? Kendra tried to pay off Martinez today by using Sam."

I glanced over to the lounge chair, where Kendra was making herself comfortable.

"What?"

Her eyes popped open.

"Tristan set a trap for Kendra, but she sent Sam on the mission, placing her in danger because fucking Martinez is on the island. And he found her."

"Fuck. And Sam?"

"She's fine. Shaken, but fine. Marge helped me. She's ready to have her daughter back."

"So tell her the truth. It's not something you can ignore forever."

"I'm trying, but this Martinez shit is getting in the way. Bottom line is that he's in town. Keep the doors locked. We should think about returning home."

"Will do. And I'm sorry for all the trouble."

I turned off the phone, set my hands on my hips, and faced Kendra. She blinked repeatedly and bit her lip, shuffling her feet in one spot, like she knew she'd screwed up.

"You took the bait today?" I asked.

"What bait?"

"Tristan sent you a message to make a payment to Martinez."

"Tristan did that?"

I nodded.

"I thought it was Martinez. I… I thought I paid my debts, and he'd leave me alone."

"Instead, he found Sam."

"What? Is she okay?"

"She's fine, but you should know better than that, Kay. Martinez won't take money for what Jace promised him. And where did you get the money, anyway?"

"I have a bank account, Julian. And it was only ten grand."

"Ten grand? And that didn't throw you off?"

I covered my face with my hands and lowered them, walking up to the lounge.

"When is the last time you used, Kay?"

"Before I blew up the boat. I haven't used since, Julian. I promise. The nurse has been great." She sat on the lounge with her knees curled to her body.

"Martinez is in town. He got too close to Sam."

"What did you want me to do? Not pay him off? Anyone in my shoes would have made the same decision."

I knelt on the oversized lounge in front of her. I lowered my hands to her shoulders, pulling her closer in.

"You let Gabe sedate me and kidnap me," she whispered.

"Gabe had to intervene. I couldn't find you after you left the terrace, and we had to get you out of there quickly."

"With a sedative? I… I thought you'd abandoned me."

I pulled her into my hold. "I would never abandon you, Kay. You should know better than that."

"I'm sorry. I never meant to—"

"I need you clean and alert from now on. I mean it. No mistakes. These fuckers are brave, and they're stepping too close."

"I'll never touch another drug again. I promise."

I stroked her hair and lay back on the lounge. She bent down on her side, her soft body molding to mine.

"I'll see how soon the jet can be ready."

"I wish we could stay in this paradise longer."

I leaned over and stroked her arm. "We'll come back soon."

She skimmed her fingers along my abdomen, laying her hand flat once she reached the chest. "So, you forgive me?"

"I forgive you, Kay, but you have some healing to do before we can think about a future."

She frowned. "That sounds like you're saying no to sex. Please tell me that's not true."

"That's not what I'm saying, but I would like to focus on your wellbeing over having sex."

"Are you about to give me the line where you tell me we should be friends first?"

I took a deep breath. My work would quadruple if Kendra agreed to my stipulations, but I couldn't fix us until I fixed her. It was time to reverse her hypnosis. I wanted her in control of her life.

"No, I'm not. I don't play games, Kay. You belong with me, and that won't change."

"No?"

I shook my head.

She clutched her fists to her chest and squeezed her body tightly, then released before climbing up my body.

"I have something special ready for you when we return home."

She hovered over me, her tempting kisses overpowering my control. Mischief sparkled in her eyes. "Does it rhyme with sex on the beach?"

"How would you feel about seeing Stefanie again?" I asked.

"So it doesn't rhyme with sex on the beach?"

I sat up and crossed my legs. She did the same. We sat across from one another, staring forever. She tilted her head, and her face fell serious. I swallowed hard, and she waited with patience as I took her hands in mine.

"When we return to the US and they're all behind bars, I'd like you to return to therapy and consider facing the past."

"Sooo…no sex until then?"

"I didn't say that, but I can see I've neglected you." My fingers skimmed up her inner thigh. I outlined her silhouette and came to rest on her mouth. I traced her beautiful lips with my finger. "And I'm going to change that."

"How?" Her voice trembled and her lips quivered, waiting. I closed in, my mouth a breath away from hers.

"I really like the sex on the beach option, but you, here and now, sounds much better."

I took her mouth and manipulated her lips, guiding her to lie back. It had been too long since she'd been mine, and too long since she'd been safe, living her life. She deserved better.

I pulled away just enough to feel her breath curl around my face. "I want to take you somewhere."

She kissed me. "Where?"

I kissed her back. "Come. You'll love it." I stood up and reached my hand out.

"Now?"

"No, tomorrow. Yes, now. Come on, Kay."

Her mouth slowly stretched into a smile, and she jumped off the lounge. "I love surprises."

I led her down the stone path and to the private beach. Kendra removed her sandals, and her heels sank into the powdery sand. The warm wind blew, shuffling the palm trees and grasses.

"It's deserted."

"It's part of the property. This is actually Axel Wagner's house."

"Your lawyer friend," she said.

"The Wagners will merge with Silver Securities. We need a team of good lawyers, and they're the best."

"I heard otherwise."

I rolled back my shoulders. "What have you heard?"

"Did you know Scar Wagner went to school with Brad and Chad Hartley?"

"I did."

"Oh."

"How did you know?"

"I eavesdropped. I don't remember when, though."

"Scar is doing what he does best, Kay. His espionage skills match James'."

"James Bond's?" Her forehead creased.

"No, silly. James Silver, my cousin. How has this conversation turned away from the fact we're on a beautiful beach, about to go on a yacht?"

"What?" She spun around to face the ocean and pointed. "That one?"

I nodded. "Come on— We have a few hours before the sunset. We can still turn this day around."

We took a single-engine boat out to the yacht, exchanged the boat with the two-man crew, and they left for the shore. I lifted the anchor.

"Wait—you're sailing on your own? I didn't know you could do that."

"Learned when I came here after your parents came back. When I couldn't see you. There are two more crewmen below deck. Have a seat and relax. The forecast is perfect."

She had barely made herself comfortable when the sound of a single engine boat drew my attention out to the ocean. I lifted the binoculars to my eyes. "It's Gabe. What the hell is he doing?"

I caught up, bringing our family yacht behind his dinghy. "What are you doing with that?"

"Shut up and get closer," he called out.

Gabe boarded the yacht while one of my crewmen took Marge's boat back home. Gabe ripped into Kendra as soon as she sat down, accusing her of knowing Sam's true identity and dragging her into trouble. Sam had found out the truth, panicked, and took a boat out into the ocean.

A deafening boom thundered from the ocean, interrupting his angry tirade. A plume of fire and smoke lifted into the sky.

Gabe checked the monitor. "That's Sam's location!"

I pushed on the throttle, but by the time we arrived, all we could find was debris—and no sign of Sam.

I anchored the yacht, and Gabe dove underwater with an

oxygen tank. We watched from above as he searched the bottom. He surfaced and removed his mask, holding up something that sparkled in his hand. "She's not here. She must have lost the bracelet in the explosion."

Gabe had gifted Sam with a tracking bracelet, just in case, but it didn't seem the jewelry would help now.

"When a body explodes, there's nothing left," Kendra cried out, gasping for air. She was hysterical and shaking.

"She's not dead!" Gabe insisted as he climbed aboard.

I crouched in front of Kendra and took her hands into mine. "Sam's a survivor, just like you are. We'll find her."

Pearl-sized tears dripped down her cheeks; she didn't move for the next ten hours it took us to find Sam drifting out in the Ocean. Gabe dove into the darkness, and Kendra sat up from her curled position.

"Is it her? Is she alive?" She hurried up the stairs to the bridge.

"Binoculars right there." I pointed.

She lifted them to her eyes, and I waited for confirmation.

"It's her, and she's alive. Barely alive."

"Lift that bench. It has warming blankets. Take them down."

Kendra hurried with the blankets. The crewman took over the controls, and I helped Gabe board with Sam. He wrapped her in a cocoon and held her shivering body while Kendra gave Sam water. She met me out at the bow as we sailed back to Marge's.

"I think she's gonna be okay," she whispered before the tears came rolling again. "I'm so sorry for getting her into this trouble. This is all my fault."

"Shh," I turned her way and brought her closer, giving her the security she sought. I didn't let go until Gabe left with Sam. I cruised back home across the dark ocean and Kendra lay back on a bench. She watched the night sky and the stars and I motioned to the control deck to park it. The yacht slowed to a gentle stop by the dock, the crewmen left, and joined her on the bench, lying on my back, head to head.

"Do you know anything about stars?" I asked her.

"They're beautiful," she said. "And they're everlasting, though I made three wishes already tonight."

"Oh, yeah? What wishes?"

"My first one already came true because we found Sam. The second one..." her voice cracked. "That wish will help me put my past behind me."

"Anything I can do to make it come true?" I asked her, very aware she wanted me to ask.

"Maybe," she whispered. "Maybe, yes."

"Good. What's the third one?"

"I can't tell you all of my wishes. I have to leave something to Will and Fate."

"Will and Fate? Wait, those aren't children's names, are they?"

She laughed out loud into the night.

Exhausted, we went back home, showered, and climbed into bed. I could barely move a muscle.. But Gabe's panicked phone call in the morning jolted us both out of bed.

Chapter 24

Kendra

Gabe sent Julian a text with an update that a medic had administered Sam an IV. She was barely alive, but the doctor said she'd make it. I lay in Julian's arms this morning, thinking about how much trouble I'd brought on my friends. One of them died, and the other one nearly died, and thank God, Julian had been there for me, for his cousin, and for my friend. The morning sun streamed through the window, and I stretched in Julian's hold.

"Penny for your thoughts," he said.

"You're a superhero." I twisted in the bedsheets.

"I get a superhero and we haven't even had sex. That is a good start to the day."

"I think you're right."

"Words I've been waiting to hear since the day I met you." He tickled under my ribcage. I settled in his hold, and he rubbed the side of my arm.

"Julian, this shit with Martinez and Donaldson won't end for me unless I remember."

"Now that Donaldson knows you're alive and psycho Martinez wants to collect, it's better we keep on guard."

"I may not be ready for the trial, but I want to reverse the hypnosis. It's time I remember what I did, Julian. I'm tired of running away."

He rose and hovered above me, his morning wood awakening a morning need between my legs.

"I'm tired of you running, Kay." He placed a gentle kiss on my lips. His mouth followed a slow trail along my jawline and down my neck. He cupped my breast in his hand, skimming over my nipple, when his phone chimed.

"No, no. Don't get that."

Julian pulled away. "I have to. It's Gabe."

He sat on the bed and answered the call. "Gabe? Slow down, Gabe. What's going on?"

I waited as he listened, but his expression didn't bode well.

"I'll be there soon." He hung up his phone, and we jumped in the car wearing our bathing suits. Sam had been kidnapped at night from underneath Gabe's nose. Julian drove to Gabe's house like a madman. I bit my nails and shivered despite it being a hot summer morning. "What if we don't find her?"

"She's a rebellious one, isn't she? Maybe she learned from a friend?" His grip eased on the steering wheel. "It's going to be okay, Kay. We'll find Sam. But you stay close to me, all right?"

I twisted in my seat, turning his way. "Aren't you worried Gabe's gonna kill me? This is all my fault."

We passed the last tree line separating our properties, and he eased his foot off the gas.

"This is not your fault. None of it is—but Gabe loves Sam, so he'll be upset. I'll help with the search, so it's best you stay with Marge."

I threw my hands up in the air. "Great! Another person who wants to kill me."

"And how do you come up with that?" I asked.

"I put her daughter in danger, Julian. The woman hates my guts. I can feel the negative energy and death vibes already. I guess I'd be pissed if someone endangered my daughter's life."

"None of this is your fault, Kay. He pulled into the driveway and parked the car. Despite the scorching morning, I shivered in my seat. "You running a fever?"

"No, it's the vibes."

We heard loud arguing from Gabe's back yard.

Julian paused, his hands still on the steering wheel. "Something tells me we should listen to your vibes."

We went to the backyard, where Gabe and Marge were running around frantically. I sat on a chair in the corner while Gabe and Julian exchanged information about Sam's kidnapping last night. The next thing I knew, Julian and Gabe had packed a couple of shovels into the Jeep's trunk and left.

Why would they need shovels?

I remained motionless in the chair until Marge came out with two cups of coffee. She set them on the table and sat down. "I put something a little extra in there."

"I don't know how you can be calm about this." Her calmness was soothing, and I couldn't understand the coping mechanism.

"I'm not calm, Kay. That's why there's Bailey's in the coffee."

I took a sip. The rush of sweet heat definitely took my mind off our troubles, but not for long.

"I'm sorry about Joanne, and I'm sorry for all the trouble I dragged your family into. They would have never connected me with Sam if she hadn't underwritten the club, but then she became a friend, and… It's all my fault."

Marge covered my hand with hers. "It's not your fault. The boys will find her. I can't lose another daughter."

I couldn't lose another friend. I didn't have many in the first place.

"Marge?"

"Yes?"

"Why did they need shovels?"

She took a deep breath in and let it go. "Joanne died buried alive."

My stomach twisted into a knot. It was a good thing I hadn't had breakfast, because I would have thrown up.

Two hours passed before Julian called and told Marge that Sam was safe and at the hospital with Gabe. Marge insisted we immediately drive there, and since I couldn't let her go alone, I went with her. I watched through the door window as Marge sat by Sam's bedside and held her daughter's hand. Sam's eyes had sunken deeply into her face, and her body was covered with scrapes.

"She's in an induced coma," Julian whispered.

"But she'll be okay?" My heart pounded harder and my chest tightened.

Gabe gave a brief nod. "Yes, she'll be okay."

I let go of the tension, and my knees buckled.

Julian caught my fall. "Hey, hey. It's okay. You heard him. She's going to be okay."

"I know…but what she went through… I'm so sorry, Gabe."

"I appreciate your apology, Kay. But don't fucking ever slip her a pill again, you hear me?"

Julian cleared his throat.

"I'll make this up to her. I promise."

"You should. You're her best friend." He took me in for a surprising hug and held me like the brother I never had. Gabe was softening on me, and maybe one day he could forgive me.

"You take good care of her, and call me as soon as she's well." I squeezed my arms hard around him for emphasis.

"I will."

We let go, and the cousins said their goodbyes with a handshake and a single shoulder bump. Julian took me under his arm and we left the hospital.

That afternoon, I slipped into my bathing suit and sat at the edge of the pool. Julian came out with a giant glass of lemonade with two straws, and a banana split with two spoons.

"Dinner looks great."

He sat down, dipped his feet in the pool, and set the drink between us. "You should see the dessert." He winked. "I forecast peaches and cream."

I took ownership of a spoon, and he grabbed his. I scooped the chocolate ice cream, and he dug into the vanilla. Julian cut into the banana and added strawberry ice cream with whipped cream. He aimed the spoon straight into my mouth..

He reached for my chin and drew his finger up, sweeping the dripping cream. It was even sexier when he licked it off with a grin.

I finished a quarter of the float, and Julian devoured the rest.

"You'll get a sugar rush."

"I'm hoping for a different kind of rush. Let's go to the beach."

We walked down the path to the secluded beach with a hammock hanging over the water near the shore.

"Is that where we're going?" I pulled my hand to cover my mouth. The green palm trees and mangroves, white beach, and turquoise water were like a fairy tale.

Julian's phone dinged. He checked his messages, turned on his heel, and connected his gaze with mine.

"What is it?"

"It's actually good news. Our team spotted Martinez landing in the US. He's far away from you, for now."

His news was great, but we would have to return home within days, if not less. The pressure of his finger on my chin brought my gaze back to his.

"And when we go back home, we'll implement extra security measures before the arrest and all the way through trial and conviction. We'll lock them up, and you'll be free."

His plan sounded too good to be true, but I'd take it, for now.

I curled in his hold as our hammock swayed back and forth. My bottom swept over the ocean's surface. I lay on Julian's broad chest, inhaling the salty air. A seagull flew above, where the ocean's horizon met the orange and pink skyline. The setting sun was absolutely breathtaking.

"Julian?" I looked up.

"Yes, my love?"

"Why do I drift between heaven and hell so often?"

He kissed my temple and sighed. "Your control over the life you were given was stolen. You'll stop drifting when you regain that control."

"Does Martinez know I own the club yet? Does he know where I live?"

"I suspect the answer is *yes* to both, but I don't think it's about the property anymore."

My shoulders sank. "That's what I was afraid of."

"You can still get out of it, Kay. Just keep a low profile until the trial, and I'll be right by your side, all the way."

The tension in my chest eased, and my heart vaulted. "I like your plan, but I *should* try to remember what I did and what happened. I want to know everything Silver Securities has been protecting me from."

"What about the nightmares?"

"I'm not fifteen anymore, Julian. I think I'm ready to handle this."

The wind swayed us both over the ocean. It was the perfect moment, and all I needed was his perfect answer.

"I'm glad we feel the same way. We'll get in touch with a professional when we return home. But right now, there's something else I want."

He lowered his mouth to mine and kissed me hard. The kiss deepened as he stroked his tongue over mine. His hand dropped to the cup of my bathing suit and he swept the fabric aside. He strummed his thumb over my erect nipple. The electrifying touch rolled through me and I pushed my chest further into his hand, prompting a delightful pinch. He swallowed my moans while mangling my breast. A stronger gust of wind blew by and swayed us in the hammock. A swollen wave crashed against our side, cooling my heat.

We pulled apart in laughter. The ocean calmed, and I return to rest over his chest. I listened as his thumping heart beat slowed, the rhythm nearly matching the lazy water waves.

"We're flying back home tomorrow," he whispered.

I groaned in his hold, stretching lazily. "I want to stay here forever."

"Sam is flying out to Austria with Gabe. She'll stay there, at least, until we catch Martinez. Her mom is coming along, and I was thinking that maybe you should go with them."

"What?" I pulled back. "Don't even say that. I go where you go. I'm not causing anymore trouble for anyone until I figure out my shit."

He flattened my palm over his heart. "The great thing about that is you're my trouble, and you're not alone."

Water splashed against our bodies from a larger incoming wave.

"I'm happy Marge has at least one of her daughters back. I can't imagine what it was like to lose one, then the other."

"Do you ever think about having kids?" I asked him.

He lifted his arm and rubbed his chin. "I've never had time to think about it. You gave me a heck of a lesson about teenagers, though."

I shifted in the hammock, higher up his body. I tried tickling his ribcage, but he didn't budge.

"I'm afraid to ask what you've learned."

"I've learned that age is just a number, and that there's no one I'd rather age with than you."

He lowered his lips to mine, and I melted. The sensual kiss heated when his knee found my crotch. I rubbed myself over his knee. My hands roamed across his wide chest and hard abs. I'd longed for this comfort and commitment with my heart and soul. I'd spent too many lonely days without him. His chest rose higher and fell deeper until another wave splashed, and I screamed.

"I'm getting the feeling you chose this place to make seduction impossible."

"You don't need to seduce me, Kay. I'm already yours. And by the way, it doesn't have to be Stefanie to help you remember. It shouldn't be."

"I'll do whatever's necessary to get my life back."

He secured his hold around me and I made myself comfortable for the sunset, not realizing this would be the one of the last sunsets I'd see for a long time.

Chapter 25

Julian

The plane's engine slowed to a stop. I took Kendra's hand and our passports, and we cleared the US border. Kendra was wearing a wig and bubble sunglasses she bought in New Zealand. As she walked across the tarmac, the oversized hat shadowed her face. The muggy day matched her grayish mood, yet she still thrilled me. I couldn't wait to have her back in our home. Wind blew across the airport, sweeping her hat off, and the guard chased after the thing.

"What's wrong with this weather?" she whined.

"They're forecasting rain for a week."

"This is not summer at all." She pulled the throw over her shoulders. "We should have stayed in paradise."

"How about we make our own paradise?" I opened the Bentley's passenger door as the private jet concierge packed our suitcases in the trunk. Kendra climbed inside and secured her seatbelt.

I hopped in on the driver's side and turned the ignition.

"I'll go anywhere with you." Her hand covered mine over the gearshift.

"The only place I want to be right now is our home."

She wiggled in her seat.

"We'll spend a quiet evening by the fireplace."

Her eyes grew wider, and her mouth crept into a grin.

"I'll have you sit in my hold, ideally on my dick."

She burst out in laughter. "Words every woman wants to hear."

Kendra closed in, her mouth hovering above mine. Her floral scent fused in my lungs and sang to my blood's southern flow, hardening my dick. If she kept this up, I'd have a hard time driving.

Hard dick, hard drive.

Everything would be hard if she didn't stop twirling the hair around her finger.

"I can't wait to come home," she whispered, kissed me deeply, and pulled away, turning up the car's heat.

I took the shortest route home, unpacked the car, and showered. Kendra hung her clothes in the closet and showered right after me. I went downstairs, set the fireplace bright, turned on soft jazz, and popped coconut shrimp in the oven. It would pair well with the Prosecco chilling in the fridge. By the time I ordered the groceries and Kendra watered the plants, the food was ready. She ran upstairs to change while I poured two glasses of wine and set them by the fireplace. Kendra sauntered around the corner in the same black negligée I'd once forbidden her to wear.

The sheer fabric exposed her skin, and my hand itched for a touch. Her natural hair, flushed skin, pink nipples, and barely-there panties taunted my will and my straining dick.

"Do you remember what you once said about this outfit?" Her hips swayed back and forth as she walked closer.

Stunning.

I gulped through a dry patch of words. "Only a man worthy should see you in this."

"So, here I am, Julian. New Zealand was nice, and I appreciate the heavy petting and pussy eating, but I'm ready for more. I need you back."

She stopped in front of me. I moved forward in the chair, lining her perky breasts up with my face. I lowered my mouth to her poking pink nipple and bit through the fabric as my hands cupped her small ass. Her whimper awakened my deep desire. She raked her fingers through my hair, scraping along the scalp.

I closed my eyes and inhaled her floral scent while licking around her perfectly ripened bud. My erection strained in my pants as her body yielded to my touch. I slid my hands up her back and then lowered them to her ass, digging my fingers into her soft flesh. She quivered in my hold, and I lost control. I let go of her nipple and it sprang from my mouth.

Her tiny gasps lengthened as I turned her body over the couch's comfortable end, guiding her forward. She stood in front of me, bent over, and parted her legs. Her beautiful ass tilted up, and she opened her cheeks for me. I tugged the thread slicing into her crack and snapped it between my fingers. I blew a breath, and her puckered hole tightened and eased. It was beautiful.

"Don't move." I lowered my pants and stepped out. My dick sprang up, and I walked around the couch to the bookshelves. Kendra watched me bring over a black box with a red bow. She eyed me from her bent position as I set the gift in front of her.

"It's for you, but I believe we'll both benefit from this."

She wiggled her brows and lifted the cover, unveiling a row of butt plugs within.

Her mouth opened wide. "How are you benefiting from this? Am I sticking that up your—"

"No, no. You won't be doing any sticking."

Her eyes enslaved my movements as I extracted the classic silicone toy, walked around to her ass, and poured lube over the toy. She wiggled her behind and locked her gaze on mine.

"Impatient?"

I slammed my throbbing cock inside her, launching her forward.

"Oh, my God."

"The name is Julian." I gently slapped her ass and held my hand over the ass cheek, keeping her steady to my rhythm. She propped her arms on the cushion and swayed back and forth underneath me. I lined up the plug and began working her other hole. She stiffened at first, then relaxed as I pulled back. I pushed deeper, and her ass accepted the plug. Her lips parted and moans turned into desperate wails for more. My arousal increased along with hers as I studied her beautifully bent-over form.

The glowing fire cast an orange tone over her pale skin. She looked so delicate, yet begged for more.

I worked the short, thin plug all the way in, then exchanged it for a thicker size. Her ass pulled the toy in and held it there, the diamond plug shining in her butt. It matched her shiny personality. Her pussy tightened around me and I nearly lost it, so I pulled out. It was too early to spill, and I needed more of her and me, together.

"What's wrong?" she asked.

"You turn me on too much. Relax and hold still." I gently removed the plug and set it aside.

I reached for her hand and guided her to the soft blankets and pillows by the fireplace. We sat facing one another. I passed her two champagne flutes and filled them to the top, then took my glass and clinked it with hers.

"As delicious as you look tonight, I don't want to fuck you, Kay."

She shifted her hip sideways and tilted her head. "Why not?"

"Because tonight, I'm making love to you."

"I'll drink to that," she whispered through a smile. "Because I love you just as hard."

We each took a sip and set our glasses aside. I covered her mouth with mine, tasting her slowly until my tongue slipped in between her lips and her body went limp.

She lay back on the cushions and parted her legs. I held our kiss, hovering above her until her knees fell further apart and I lined up my dick and slid in. Our kiss deepened the further I pushed. Her engorged breasts rubbed against my chest, their hard peaks tender to touch. I kissed her swollen lips and pushed into her soaked pussy. She clenched around me, throwing me into a frenzy. I pulled my mouth away, and she heaved in air.

I lifted to my knees and brought her legs over my thighs, thrusting hard. Her eyes rolled back. I watched her delicate body yield to mine, completely vulnerable and beautiful. My balls tightened in response to her tiny gasps and moans. She dragged the black negligée up her body and pinched her nipples, driving me crazy. Her hand slid down her belly and lower, to where we connected, her fingers feeling me pushing inside her. The sight from above was hot as hell until her fingers danced up to her clit and I watched her rub herself. The move shot spasms through my balls.

Her building pleasure grew along with mine, body thrusting and pussy contracting around my cock. She screamed out, and I released the pressure. She closed around me and milked my release through her orgasm, shaking underneath me. I waited until she settled and kissed her forehead. Sated, I withdrew and lowered myself to the ground. She immediately rolled over to my chest and folded her hands underneath her chin.

"You come inside me and you're never afraid I'll get pregnant?" she asked.

"Afraid? No, because I know you won't."

"How are you so sure?"

"You ovulated in New Zealand, baby."

"Is that why you didn't want to touch me then?"

"No. We were exhausted, and… Well, a lot happened."

"So we only have sex when I can't get pregnant?" She squinted.

"Kay, don't make anything out of this, because one day, when we're both ready, there's nothing I'd like more than to sink and come inside you, fully aware you're ovulating and we're making a baby."

She smiled. "So you're not opposed to having kids? With me? The troublemaker?"

"I already told you once—you may be trouble, but you're *my* trouble." I lifted my head to kiss her. "One day, you're going to make a wonderful mother."

"And you're going to make a hot daddy. I can't wait until my stupid case is closed, and Martinez is behind bars."

"Your lawyers are almost ready to move forward with the charges against Donaldson and the Hartleys. Tristan found the guy who will testify against the Congressman, so we should be good to go."

She looked out into the distance.

"What happened before the train accident? What did I do?"

I squeezed her hand. "You were in the wrong place at the wrong time. Someone tried to hurt you, and you protected yourself."

"I killed someone, didn't I?"

"You shouldn't worry about this. You defended yourself against a predator with power."

"A Donaldson," she whispered. "I don't know whether the name sounds familiar because I've heard it so many times or because I actually remember it."

"You remember, Kay," I confirmed, as I reached back and passed her the champagne glass from the table. "We might have had five shitty years, but it will be over soon."

"I can't wait." She took a sip and lowered her sweet lips to mine. The grandfather clock chimed from my office ten times. We had hours of each other until the morning, and I would use every minute of the night to show her how much I loved her.

BIRDS CHIRPED AND BEES BUZZED. I swept my hand over the pillow beside mine and shot up when I found the cabana spot empty.

A faint splash of water drew my attention to Kay, swimming naked in our pool. It was the fucking best investment I could have made. Last night, she'd won some sort of bet between us I was willing to lose, and we went swimming in the middle of the night. I obeyed her every wish, including the one where she wanted to sleep in the cabana until morning. I fucked her on the pool steps, made love to her underneath the stars, and feasted on her body like a starved man.

The sound of her laps made me feel like the luckiest bastard in the world. I began dozing off when I heard her feet flapping against the concrete, closer to the cabana. I waited for her to climb back onto the mattress, but I must have fallen asleep before she reached me. A passing cloud's shadow stirred me awake.

"Kay?" I sat up, but I couldn't spot her.

"Kay?" I called out louder and hurried inside and to the kitchen, where she'd left a note on the counter.

Couldn't resist the beautiful morning and went for a jog. I'll be back soon.

I pulled my hand across my eyes, a little surprised at the clear skies. Kay had won the bet we made last night that if the sun came up before breakfast, I'd be responsible for the food. I showered and made pancakes, but Kay wasn't back. I cut up more fruit, made a fresh pot of coffee, and called my parents, but she hadn't stopped by there at all. She always stopped by on her jogs. I pinched the bridge of my nose, turned on my app, and found her location ping disconnected from my phone. The last update had been sent from down the street. I ran across the lawn in the direction, calling out her name. A bright red reflection caught my eye, and I picked up Kay's broken phone along with her earbuds.

"Fuck. No."

I dropped to my knees. My hands shook as I sent a quick message out to the family, writing words I didn't want to believe but knew to be true. Kendra was missing, and my gut twisted into knots. I should have known better. I should have kept better guard in the morning.

Why the fuck did she leave the house?

Tristan picked me up by the road and took over the search because I couldn't. Instead, I sat in my home office pulling out my hair, helpless. I stayed there for six hours, then searched the streets for another eight. Rain poured and thunder rolled across the black skies. I searched the streets in the downpour for three long days before my cousin James returned from Magnet, an exclusive billionaire's club, with confirmation from a source that Jeffrey Hartley had enslaved Kendra. The notorious sex trafficker was Tristan's former future father-in-law.

"I'm gonna rip Hartley's throat out." I shoved the papers across my desk.

"You're not the only one with that dream, my brother." Tristan gripped my arm. "We might have something else, but you won't like what you hear."

"At this point, I'm willing to take anything."

"James is going to infiltrate the group this weekend. There are rumors of an auction, and there's a chance Kendra will be there."

"An auction? They're gonna sell her? When is this happening?"

"It could be next week, and it could be a couple of months from now."

"What? We can't let her wait that long."

"It's just an option. We're looking into more options…"

I couldn't hear him after that because we were clearly out of options, and I collapsed. The exhaustion kicked my ass and brought me to my knees. I couldn't breathe, and I couldn't swallow, but I would have done anything to trade places with the woman I loved.

Chapter 26

Kendra

My wrists ached and my ankles stung from the rope burns. They'd chained me to a bed frame with a stained mattress and left me to wait for my turn. A girl's desperate screams tore through the hall, and I pressed my hands to my ears, shutting out her agony. The tone varied with every encounter as masked gents took their turns with the imprisoned girls.

For many women, death quickly became the only way to escape sex-trafficking. The Grim Reaper was always standing nearby, waiting for the next victim to slash her wrists, give into hypothermia, or overdose from the concoction of drugs they snuck in with the little food we received. I shivered in my cell. Last night had been colder than the previous one, and evening was approached.

They fed drugs to the girls like candy. Bruised patches all the needles had left stained my arms, and some of the oval spots were turning green. Their changing shades confirmed passing time and reaffirmed the hope someone was looking for me. The deep purple ones looked the worst, like my skin had bled from the inside.

The cries and wails of torture rang in my ears. But once the narcotics made their rounds to each cell, the skin-cringing sobs stopped. The prisoners passed out on the floor or were too stoned for their voices to be heard. I stayed in my corner, quiet, pretending to sleep; praying they wouldn't pry my mouth open to feed me the drugs. They had snuck enough into my body with the little food I ate.

Once the basement fell silent, the faint hum of flowing water on the outside reminded me there was an outside. We had to be close to a river, but the knowledge did nothing to help my cause. I fought against sleep, afraid to be touched. Sleeping on guard and in short bursts came at the price of dark shadows underneath my eyes.

A man's footsteps echoed through the dungeon, bouncing off the walls. I lifted my last glass of water to the light. A powdered substance drifted near the bottom, and I realized why it was difficult to move.

The yellow light faded in and out of focus, transforming into torches. The hallucinogens turned the gray prison into a medieval dungeon where men ruined my body. I wouldn't remember the abuse because the drugs took me to a fantasy land.

I should have known better; I should have stayed in the cabana that morning with Julian. Instead I went for a stupid run. The white van came out of nowhere. The side door slid open, and two men dragged me inside. They placed a chloroformed cloth over my mouth, and then I woke up in this place.

Two nights ago, they stripped me and hosed me down. A guard tied my hands to a bar over my head and my feet to one below. Ropes burned at my ankles. My raw wrists bled as I yanked them. Hartley lowered a vibrating prod against my flesh. I tensed my thighs, trying to move away at first, but the more he touched the metal tip against me, the less I could resist. I cried, fighting the pleasure. I didn't want it; not like that. But after a while, my body forced my hips forward, pressing into the pulsating equipment, giving into the titillation. They brought me to a near climax, only to remove the glistening dildo and watch me twist in pain.

Please!

As the agony eased, they revived it, repeating the torture for hours. I lost track of time and ached for a release they denied me. My body shivered, my muscles strained, and a pounding pain throbbed from between my legs. I was embarrassed at first, but all that shame quickly turned into disgust, and I threw up near the end. They laughed, and I lost consciousness.

Fucking Martinez and Hartley. I wished they were dead at least a thousand times.

I woke up naked on the stained mattress with a single sheet to wrap around my body. I curled into a corner when the sound of clattering keys broke through the cell.

Jeffrey Hartley crossed the room, examining me from afar.

"Stand up," he ordered.

I obeyed, because I'd quickly learned that when I didn't, the torture would start again.

"Drop the sheet and turn around." He twirled his finger, and I did as he asked.

When I came to a stop, he shook his head. "You look nothing like your mother."

My head flew up.

"We spent a few fun nights together—you know, before the police found her with a bullet in her head."

My insides twisted. "You bastard."

He slapped me so hard that my cheek split open. He lowered his zipper.

"On your knees, bitch. Let's see if you're worth buying."

I did nothing to make myself worth buying. I zoned out as I knelt in front of him with my mouth open, and threw up after he left. My will to live faded with time, and my confidence someone would find me evaporated with that will. I didn't know where to pick up the pieces of my soul, because I was convinced the task was impossible. How could I ever forget this? Death was the clearest answer to stop it all.

Days of torture passed until I found out Hartley had decided and agreed to buy me. The asshole visited me every day for weeks. I shut my eyes and pretended to be elsewhere as he had his way with my body. It was easier to pretend and engage than cry and shake. I had a feeling the crying and shaking would come later. Martinez told me Hartley would take me to his private island. The more times the sun set, the more I doubted I'd ever see Julian again.

I backed into a corner at the sound of approaching men. The keys turned, and my stomach tightened. It must have been late at night, because I yawned. Martinez lowered a bag over my head and took me under my elbow. Someone dressed me and someone else tied a rope around my wrist. They threw me in the back of a car and didn't remove the bag until the car stopped. Martinez walked me into a bar connected to a hotel and pushed me into a booth.

"Open your mouth," he said, and I obeyed. He placed a pill on my tongue and pushed my chin up to close my mouth. "Now swallow."

Fuck.

I snuck the pill underneath my tongue and pretended to swallow.

"Open again." I repeated the process, hiding the pill under my tongue. They'd drugged me enough as it was.

A younger woman was sitting at the bar. She drew his attention like a lamp drew a moth, or cheese drew a mouse. I would die for some cheese right now. He stared her way, and I removed the pill from my mouth and threw it under the table. The bitter aftertaste spread like fire along my tongue. What the fuck did he give me?

It didn't take long before the woman made a fatal mistake

and joined us. She slipped into the seat beside mine, and they started drinking tequila. What the hell was she doing? Why was she making conversation with a man who wanted me caged? There was no way this beautiful woman would be attracted to this scum—he had to see that—yet she flirted with him like he was the best thing since sliced bread.

"Bathroom," I whispered.

"Hold it. We're almost done," Martinez growled. His alcohol breath hit me, and I fought to hold back the gag.

"I can take your puma on a walk to the washroom. Unless you're afraid she'll bite?"

Why was she calling me by animal names, and why was the room spinning? The acidic taste in my mouth reminded me the pill I spat out had dissolved a bit before I did so. At least Hartley wasn't here yet.

They made more small talk, and he gripped her wrist before we left for the bathroom. "Drink first."

She reached out her hand for the rope he held, saying, "Let's go pee-pee."

My eyes grew wide as I tried to warn her not to drink the spiked shot, but she did.

"You have three minutes," he warned.

She led me in first, closed the door, then made a sprint for the toilet and shoved her fingers down her throat.

I could barely breathe as my heart raced. She was my only opportunity to escape, but we needed a plan. My brain fogged. It would be hard to come up with a plan in this state.

"Run. You should run while you can." I told her my best plan. I knew it wasn't too good, but if I did nothing, we'd both serve Hartley for the rest of my life.

My knees were shaking, and so were my hands. She shuffled her feet to the sink, rinsed her mouth, and braced herself. She quickly typed something into her phone.

"Who are you?" I asked.

"I'm Tristan's friend, and I'm not leaving without you. What did he slip me?" She started untying my wrists. They burned, but I held steady as she focused on the knots. I could barely see past the fear in my eyes, but she wasn't doing too well.

"A tranquilizer. It was a lot. He'll kill us both for this."

"If that's the case, we'll get rid of him. It's two against one. I know you're strong enough, Kendra. Please tell me you want out of this. I need you on my side."

The drugs must have gotten to her because she was talking crazy, but her plan was definitely better than mine. She was talking so fast, I barely followed until she asked, "Are you with me?"

"I'm with you," I whispered.

"Don't get too excited."

She stood up and wobbled on her feet, turning in a circle until she focused on a small window at the end of the room. She stood on her tiptoes, unlocked it, and slid the frame up enough for a squeeze.

A chilly breeze blew through the room, and I shivered.

"Do you know who he's waiting for? Who's your buyer?" she asked.

"Hartley. Hartley's always behind shit, but he's untouchable."

Martinez knocked on the door. "Hurry."

"Almost done," she replied, and checked her phone. "Is Martinez alone?"

"I don't think so. And they're always armed."

"I figured." She shoved her phone down my bra. "Julian and Tristan's numbers are there. They're in this hotel. Run and find them."

He was here? Julian was here? Looking for me? The last jolt of energy I'd saved for an escape shot through my body.

I touched her arm. "What about you?"

"I'll be right behind you."

Martinez pounded on the door, but we both ignored him. She locked her hands together. "Hop up."

I secured my foot in her grip, which got me to the window ledge. I reached my hand out for her.

"Go! Jump. Now!"

She grabbed the ledge and pulled herself up just as I jumped down. I spun in a circle, trying to get my bearings.

"Do not turn back," she said.

I hurried down the alley, toward a light shining from the corner, turned left, and ran. Disoriented, I ran into another alley. When I backed up and turned around, a man punched me in my face.

"Ahh!" My hands flew to my nose.

"You thought you could get away from me, bitch?" Martinez marched forward, and I stumbled backward, seeking an entrance I knew wasn't there.

I tripped over something, probably my feet, because I no longer had control over my body and was shaking with pure fear. My ass planted in a puddle. My knees gave out as I lifted and I crouched to all fours, at an asshole's mercy, underneath a patch of moonlight. He removed a gun from behind his back and aimed it my way.

This was it. My life would end in an alley at the hands of a predator.

A scream tore through the alley, and Martinez turned on his heel to the alley's entrance The woman from the bar who'd tried to save me was standing there. My vision blurred and my ears rang as two gunshots echoed. I screamed, curled in a corner by a garbage container, and covered my ears, shaking. When I opened my eyes, Martinez was down, but so was the woman.

Julian ran into view. Tristan ran in right behind him and hurried to the woman.

"Shit!" Tristan dropped to his knees and ripped the sleeve

off his shirt, which he stuffed underneath her. He ripped the other one off and stuffed her front.

"I didn't do this. He shot her." I pointed to Martinez.

"I know, K. Come on, Julian. Get a grip. Call an ambulance."

"I was late."

"You're not late, Julian. Get a grip and get over here."

"I shot him," he said. "It's over. It's all over."

Julian dropped the gun and ran my way. He lifted me off the ground and carried me in his arms. "We're gonna get you to the hospital, Kay, but I need to help Allie."

He set me down close to where Tristan was doing chest compressions.

"Hold here." Tristan guided Julian's hand and pressed it into Allie's belly. "Don't let go."

We didn't wait for the ambulance. Julian helped me into the car and slid into the back seat with Allie, where he took over Tristan's compressions and CPR. The ride was a haze, and the world began falling in and out of focus, but as I faded into unconsciousness, the last memory of Julian running through the hospital door with me in his arms felt like the first right moment in a long time.

Chapter 21

Julian

The sound of the hospital monitor beeped in my ears. Kendra had been at the hospital for three days and she'd slept through most of them. She'd open her eyes, waking periodically in a panic, and I'd soothe her back to sleep. She'd lost at least twenty pounds since her kidnapping. The night we found her was a fluke, and I didn't dare imagine what would have happened if it hadn't been for Allie, who was recovering in a room across the hall. Kendra wasn't at the auction, the way we'd thought she might be, but Allie had found her at the bar, tied to a rope like an animal.

I shuddered and opened my eyes. She was sleeping, and I'd keep guard on my girl for the rest of our lives. If she'd have me, that is. Truth was, I'd failed her. I was a fucking bodyguard with years of experience and security in my blood, and I had failed the only woman I've ever loved. While I couldn't wait for her to wake up, I wasn't sure whether I truly deserved her love. Kay had barely survived, and months would pass before she healed from the trauma. The ring in my pocket would have to wait.

Her sunken cheeks cut into a V at the chin. She was beautiful and broken, and I wasn't sure whether I could fix every-thing. Why couldn't I get to her sooner?

She stirred with a groan, and I shot off the makeshift bed to a chair by her bedside.

"Hey, hey. It's okay. I'm here. You're safe now."

Her eyes flew wide open as she searched the room like she didn't believe me. The heart monitor spiked.

"It's all right, Kay. You're in a hospital, and Martinez and Hartley are dead. They're both dead. You're in a hospital."

She finally focused on me, but dragged her hand away from mine and brought it closer to her body.

"Allie's in the hospital as well. She'll make it. You can see her if you'd like, when you're ready."

She shook her head with a quick *no*, and shifted sideways with a wince. This place wasn't good for her. She'd heal faster at home.

"Stay still. You have a broken rib and a dislocated shoulder." I reached for her, but she turned away. My heart deflated. She settled back against the pillow just as her doctor and nurse knocked on the door and opened it gently.

"Can we come in?"

"Yes, please. She just woke up." I shot off my chair. "I'd like to take her home as soon as possible."

"Mr. Silver—"

"I can hire a permanent nurse who will stay by her side day and night. I'll hire a naturopath and a nutrition consultant as well. I'll make sure she's well taken care of."

"Mr. Silver, I know your level of care for Ms. Moore would be exceptional, but I respect you enough to ask you to please step aside so we can examine our patient. We can discuss all the safe treatment options afterward."

I stepped out of the way and waited against the wall as they examined her. It was taking a while, so I sent out a group message that Kay was awake.

"She's stable and will need constant monitoring. You mentioned a nutrition consultant, and I highly recommend one as well. There's definitely severe PTSD present. The treatment plan will be extensive, but if you think Kendra would benefit from healing at home, I'm confident she can overcome the trauma. I'll leave it up to Kendra to decide." He turned her way. "Ms. Moore?"

She glanced from the doctor to me. Our eyes met, and I hoped she saw the desperation in mine. Her tiny nod lit a spark in my chest, and they discharged her that night.

But my Trouble came with trouble.

She screamed through her first night here, waking every five minutes. She barely slept through the day either, but I figured she felt safer in daylight, so I stayed by her side, ensuring she remained hydrated and ate. But she barely ate. The nurse tended to her wounds in the morning, at noon, and in the evening. She changed Kendra's dressings, checked her vitals, gave her meds, and helped her bathe. Kay didn't enjoy swallowing the pills; she cried and shook every time. I instructed the nutritionist to find liquid and injectable alternatives because all the carefully chosen meals weren't working.

She had nightmares the second night, and we both barely slept. The forecasted freak snowstorm arrived as a surprise at the beginning of November. I watched the falling flakes through the window while Kendra lay curled on the sofa. A stack of medications and vitamin replacements stood at a nearby table. The fireplace crackled, and I sipped on my first whiskey since her return.

Exhaustion pulled on my eyelids. I dreamed of her tortures, misery, and pain. She hadn't told me what she'd gone through, but she didn't need to. I'd heard enough from other victims, and if Martinez and Hartley weren't dead, I'd rip out their hearts. I'd dreamed about that too, but just as I reached inside a warm chest and gripped the beating heart, a chilling breeze swept through the house and I woke up.

"Holy shit." I jumped to my feet and to the backyard door.

"Kay? Kay, where are you?"

I bolted through the back door and followed her footprint path, slowing when I spotted the first snow angel print, then the second and the third: there must have been over a dozen, in between her footprints. And there was Kay, splayed out in the snow, mesmerized at the heavens, and completely frozen. She was wearing nothing but one of my t-shirts and her panties. Her bare feet were blue, and she wasn't moving. I ran through the snow, dropped to my knees, and scooped her into my arms.

"Jesus, Kay. What are you doing? How long have you been out here?"

But she didn't reply. She hadn't said a word since her rescue.

Her frail body shivered in my arms as I carried her inside and upstairs. I tried to lower her to a chair, but she clasped her hands tightly around my neck, so I just held her.

I turned on the cold faucet in the shower and stepped inside. The stream hit my clothes and skin like ice, but Kendra didn't react. I set her on the bench and aimed the stream over her body.

"Let me know when it gets too cold, and we'll warm it up."

I should have gone into the bathtub, but this was quicker.

"Kay, I need to take off your shirt. Is that okay?"

She gave a brief nod.

I turned up the water temperature by a notch and peeled off her frozen t-shirt. Her bra straps hung loose and her breasts barely filled the cups. Her gaunt body, with visible signs of torture, made me sick to my stomach. My insides twisted, but I held back the hurl. You could fucking count her ribs.

I wasn't a religious man, but if God was out there, I hoped he heard my desperate prayers at night to heal Kendra. And in return, I promised to make the world a million times better. I just needed a chance with her. Our team had found the dungeon where Martinez tortured and trafficked women, and we'd freed them, but a lot more work remained, and I could only continue if Kay lived.

Please God, let her live.

I helped her up, twisting the hot water knob again, and held her underneath the stream. Her boney body dug into mine as I wished I could turn back the time to Colorado, when we were free and happy, and never let her go.

The color of her skin slowly changed from grayish to pink. The purple faded from her lips, and her toes wiggled as her feet regained circulation. I took her hands into mine and lifted them up to kiss them. "You're going to be okay, you hear me?"

She bopped her head.

I missed the sound of her voice. She'd cry out at night, but she hadn't spoken since the rescue. She would pick at her dinner before we fell asleep on the couch, but sometimes I doubted she swallowed a bite. The doctor attributed the lack of speech to trauma and prescribed patience. I took a deep breath, shut my eyes, and held her close. I waited a few more minutes until the hot water penetrated through our bones, stepped out of the shower, and grabbed our towels. I wrapped one around her, shed my soaked clothes, wrapped a towel around my hips, and reached underneath the cabinet.

"I'm gonna brush and dry your hair, Kay. We're going out."

Her eyes opened wide with fear.

"I promise you'll love it."

A glimpse of life shone across her face.

"Good." I pulled a chair out in front of a mirror. "Sit back and relax."

I finished with the hair, brought her comfortable clothes, and left the bathroom so I could change as well. The leather jacket I'd gifted her hung loosely on her body, and I definitely needed to fix that.

"I wish we could take the bike, but it's too dangerous in the snow." I opened her door and motioned to the Bentley's passenger seat.

She took her seat, and I secured her seatbelt. She rolled her eyes, and I felt hope spark in my chest. Kay was showing emotions, which I preferred more than the fearful stone face. There was much less of her than I remembered, but I'd take this over nothing any day, and I'd nurture her back to health in no time.

I pulled the Bentley out of the garage. Heavy flakes fell from the sky as I drove along the shoreline. It was the middle of the night, and the freak storm had emptied the streets and the park. I pulled into a spot near the main entrance. Fairy lights were strung along the paths and around the trees, twinkling through the falling snow. The white powder caught the surrounding lights, shining. Kendra stepped out of the car and kicked the powder. She stopped in the middle of a sidewalk, tilted back her head and turned in a circle, taking in the early winter. Her arms stretched out and palms faced flat to the sky, catching giant snowflakes. Her turn stopped at me. She lowered her head and, for the first time since her rescue, she smiled.

My heart kicked up its beat and the tension in my jaw eased.

"Unfortunately, the carousel is off," I said to her. "I didn't want to drag the operator out in this weather, but I have something else you'll like."

She stepped closer with interest. I popped open the trunk and removed a picnic basket. I set it on the hood and removed a steaming hot dog from a container. Her eyes and mouth dropped open. It was exactly the reaction I'd been hoping for. She brought the dog to her mouth, but I stopped her.

"Hold on." I opened another container. The faint scent of brine and pickled cabbage lifted in the air. Kendra grinned from ear to ear.

"You didn't think I'd forget sauerkraut, did you?"

She stepped from one foot to another, holding the hot dog in a paper towel and mittens. Her eyes followed my spoon as I topped the foot-long with sauerkraut. She stuffed it in her mouth, and I swear, it was one of the most beautiful sights I'd seen in a long time.

I pulled out two cans of root beer and popped hers open. A spark of the old Kay flashed in her eyes.

"I know you're recovering, but there is something I need to tell you about."

She swallowed her last bite and set the napkin aside.

"Sam and Gabe are getting married, and Sam asked whether you're strong enough to be her maid of honor. You have every right to say no, Kay. It would be over Christmas in Austria. The whole family will be there. I'd like us to go. It would be good for you, but you decide."

A tear rolled down her cheek. It didn't match the grin stretching over her face until I realized it was a happy tear.

"Is that a yes?" I asked. "Blink once for yes, and hold your eyes open without blinking for a no."

She laughed, and my heart jumped. The beautiful sound gave me hope. The sauerkraut hot dog had worked.

"Yes," she said, and snuggled into my side. "Thank you for everything, Julian. Thank you for saving my life."

Although scratchy and faint from disuse, the sound of her voice threw my heart into high gear. I wrapped my arms around her and pulled her to my body. "You're going to be okay. We're going to be okay."

Chapter 28

Kendra

My body jerked every time I thought about the dungeon. Fear snaked along my skin like poison, intensifying at night. Darkness reminded me of the dungeon where they'd imprisoned me. I twisted my arms into pretzels, searching for pain, because the aches in my joints dulled the horrific memories. My jaw clenched, pressure built in my lungs and behind my eyes, and yet I couldn't release it. I ran my fingers through my hair, gripped it, and pulled hard. My ever-itching scalp and constant throbbing kept me focused on the present, not the past.

I concentrated on the slushy puddle where I was sitting. Three nights ago, Julian had found me in the yard, soaked and half frozen, but at least I felt no pain. The snow angels I'd traced with my body were beautiful, and I couldn't stop making beautiful things. I had lain on the powder-covered ground and watched the flakes fall through moonlight. Snow had caught on my face and melted. The night had been one of the most beautiful ones I'd experienced since Julian had brought me home. But the snowstorm had passed, and the rain came with full fury, drowning all my snow angels.

I turned around at the sound of Julian's sloshing footsteps.

"Kay, you can't keep doing this." His voice was gentle, but he didn't need to be. The scowls in the dungeon had been much worse.

Shivers nipped at my spine, and I traded a glance with Julian. "The cold helps."

Julian blew out his cheeks. "You said before it's the pain that helps."

"That too. Pain helps me forget, and cold stimulates that pain."

"I see hypothermia hasn't hit your brain. Not yet, at least."

If he was trying to be funny, it wasn't working. Pain was the only way.

He approached from behind, dropped to his bottom, and wrapped himself around me, nuzzling his nose into the nook of my neck. His hands drew up my arms, fingers working hard over my skin. It felt...nice, even a little better than the pain. My back rested against his chest. It was still dark outside. Heavy rain soaked us both and melted the last of the snow.

I closed my eyes. Julian's comforting hold eased my ache. He brushed his cheek against mine, gripping my hair in his fists. He pressed his warm lips to my temple and forehead, cooing into my ear. "What happened to you is not your fault."

The smell of him pulled me deeper into his safe hold.

"What they did to you, Kay, it's unforgivable. They deserved more than death," he whispered through the rain.

"I just don't want to feel, because it's...it's overwhelming when I feel. I'm glad it's over."

He stiffened behind me.

"It is over, isn't it?"

His frame firmed. "Why don't you want to feel?"

Feeling would mean giving into their psychotic manipulations. Feeling would mean giving them what they wanted, and I wasn't ready to feel. I dipped my head forward. Raindrops splattered in the puddle at my feet.

"All right. It's time to come inside or you'll catch pneumonia."

He helped me to my feet. Rain poured down my face, plastering my hair to my skin. We crossed the drenched yard and went inside. I shuffled my feet along the floor upstairs to the bathroom.

My fingers were stiff and my toes bright red, barely moving. I reached for the bubble mix, and it slipped from my clasp, spilling onto the floor and dripping down the sides of the tub.

"I'm sorry. I'm so sorry." I crouched to clean up the mess, fumbling with the purplish goo.

"It's all right, Kay. It's no big deal." He lowered to his knees and took my hands into his.

His soothing tone calmed the tremors, and his comforting hold brought me back to the present. He tightened his arms around me, and forced my darting gaze back to his, calming me with his eyes. He poured the remaining mix into the running water, and the smell of lilac sailed through the bathroom.

"It spilled." I pointed to the floor.

"Don't worry about it. I'll clean it up."

White bubbles foamed on the water's surface, and Julian dipped his hand in. "Feels perfect. You can go in now. I'll be right there in that chair." He pointed to the corner of the room, but I held onto his hand.

He was mine now, and he kept me grounded in the present. The chair was too far away.

"All right. I'll stay with you."

He removed my soaked t-shirt and dropped it to the floor. As soon as I stepped into the tub, I sank under the bubbles. I didn't want Julian seeing my flat chest, sunken stomach, and protruding ribs. I no longer recognized the woman in the mirror.

I slid lower in the bathtub and let out a long, exhausted

breath. When Allie found me, I was on the brink of death—starving, drugged and ill. Not long ago, I'd thought I'd never feel warm water again.

"Emma dropped off a new pair of fluffy socks while you were sleeping. They're by the bedside." Julian said. He sat on a corner chair and scrolled through his phone.

"Thank you." I cracked a smile. Warm socks were a necessity to pull me through the night's shivers and terrors.

"That smile really suits you. You're looking better every day, Kay."

My body melted underneath his adoring stare. I'd missed him. I'd missed his touch and freedom. I savored the warm water and pulled a sponge along my arms. Julian came to the bath's side, soaked a washcloth, and pulled the suds down my back. I recoiled instinctively.

"I won't hurt you," he whispered.

My shoulders relaxed, and I leaned my head forward onto my folded knees. His clean strokes over my spine drew goosebumps over my arms. I didn't think I'd want him to touch me, but this felt nice.

"Kendra, you need to eat when you finish bathing," he said. "Otherwise, they'll stick tubes up your nose when the doctor comes in for your weekly exam. If you don't gain weight, the doctor won't clear you for Sam and Gabe's wedding."

The trip to Austria was inching closer, but I didn't want to see a doctor. In fact, I didn't want to see anyone other than Julian. Tristan had visited, and so had Wilma and Emma. They'd brought fresh pastries and breads, all the things I wanted to eat, but couldn't.

"How about a hot dog?" he asked, and my stomach grumbled. I'd been on a sauerkraut and hot dog diet for days, but at least I'd kept them in.

"I think I may be ready for something new."

"Great! I can do grilled chicken, salmon, steak, baked

potato… Wait, I'll just make everything and you tell me what you like best."

I laughed. "Slow down, and one protein will be fine. You choose."

Julian stood up, happily opened his arms wide, and held out a towel. I stepped out of the tub and he wrapped me in the soft cotton. Back in our bedroom, I changed into a fresh set of clothes while Julian lingered in the bathroom, cleaning up the spilled detergent. The clean scent brought back comfort.

"Julian?" I whispered, and he hurried to my side.

"You said something?"

"Thank you. I mean that sincerely."

"You're welcome."

We went to the kitchen, where I sat on the stool. He spun me around and, without thinking, stole an unexpected kiss. I froze in my spot. His smile faded and his eyes filled with worry. I couldn't move.

"I'm sorry," he said. "It just happened."

Time stood still until I pinched myself. This wasn't a dream, and I wasn't caged.

"It's okay, Julian. I just…" I rubbed my hands over my arms. "I need time, and…"

He waited with all the patience I didn't realize I needed.

"I'll tell you when I'm ready. I promise." The tension around his neck lessened as I squeezed his hand with reassurance.

"I can give you all the time you need, Kay. All of it."

"Thank you," I whispered, fearing I'd need more time than existed. As much as I wanted to, I couldn't erase the past, and as the hours ticked by, the urge to face the crimes I'd erased from my memory grew.

Julian turned on soft jazz and cooked filet mignon with mushroom sauce, grilled asparagus, and a purple cauliflower puree. I watched him move around the kitchen like a professional chef and realized I'd never seen him this comfortable in the kitchen before.

"When did you learn how to cook like that?"

"After your parents returned, I had more time on my hands." He shrugged. "You should see me make kangaroo."

"What?"

"I can do alligator meat, too. Tastes like chicken."

He set a filled plate in front of me and passed me a fork. A single nasturtium decorated the plate side. It looked stunning.

"Dig in. It's best while it's hot."

I stared at the steak like it was about to moo its way off my plate. I wiggled my nose at the delicious aroma.

"The hunger's passed," I whispered, but my stomach disagreed with a loud growl.

Julian's eyebrows met in the middle, and he set his fork aside.

"But the steak does look delicious," I said.

His eyebrows shot up. "It tastes even better."

"Maybe later?" I sank down in my seat.

A long stream of air leaked from his lungs. He walked over to the window and stared for a long time, lost in his thoughts, likely pondering ways to stuff that filet mignon down my throat.

"You know what? I may have something that will trigger your appetite."

My head flew up.

"It's time to remember who you are, Kay. Get dressed and put on your rain boots. We're going outside."

"Backyard?" I asked.

"That's right."

Moments later, Julian took my hand, and we headed toward the wooded area at the Silvers' fence line. There was a path along the shore that connected the two Silver properties. His brother Tristan was in escrow for the house on the other side of his parents' home. Emma had told me all the secrets when she'd thought I was sleeping at the hospital.

Afternoon fog hovered over the bay, slowly drifting upward. We headed toward the half dozen rows of trees on the property line between the Silvers, the soaked lawn swishing underneath our galoshes. The harder my heart beat, the harder I squeezed Julian's hand. We stopped past the first few trees. Wilma and Fred's house, as well as the backyard next door, were visible from the shoreline. Julian tugged at my arm and pointed to a storage box by the tree. The lock on its front caught my attention.

"Ready?" Julian asked.

"What is it?" I couldn't keep my eyes off the lock.

He unfastened the chain with a few clicks and lifted the lid. A set of a long-range rifles and their separate components filled the inside. The smell of metal and gunpowder drifted around me.

"Assemble it," he instructed.

I automatically took hold of the gun, attached the sound suppressor, adjusted the handle to my arm's reach, and loaded the ammunition. I left the bipod in the storage box. Julian stood with his arms crossed over his chest.

"You're not surprised I can do this?" I asked.

"You were an unbeatable Olympian candidate. Let's see if this brings back some memories." He pointed in between the trees, about one hundred yards north. "There's a target with a red bull's eye. Shoot it down."

"Creative." I wiggled my brow, and he bellowed out a laugh.

I spread my legs apart, stood sideways, pushed the rifle's butt against the pit of my arm, and focused. My breath steadied as I aimed. A swoosh of adrenaline rushed through my body. The wind stilled, and the birds stopped singing. On my fifth breath, I shot without hesitation and hit the target in the center. The world around me ceased to exist. I shut my eyes and saw a man's body lying in a pool of blood. A red stream flowed from underneath him. A patch of red stained the shirt over his chest, where the bullet hit. I lowered the rifle and let go of an easy breath.

"Kay? Kay?" Julian's voice sounded from a far distance away. "Kay, are you all right?"

I shook out of the trance and passed the rifle back to Julian. "I'm not ready to remember."

"But you remembered something?"

I whipped my body around and away from him. The space in my lungs tightened, and I crouched to the ground.

"Kay?"

"I'm okay. I'm okay." I let out a shaky breath and stood up. "But I think I want to shoot again."

"You're sure?"

I bowed my head by a fraction.

I emptied all the bullets and hit the target every time. The same bloody mess flashed through my mind with each shot. This wasn't working. I gave the rifle to Julian, turned on my heel, and went home.

We flew to Austria with Allie's friend and her little boy, Foxy. Laura slept in the back of the private jet while Kendra kept Foxy busy with coloring books. From my conversation with Emma, Laura was on her way to Austria to see whether she could work things out with my cousin James.

I sat back in the leather chair. The sound of Disney cartoons played on the television. Foxy laughed at something Kendra said, and she giggled. I hadn't realized Kay had a natural ability to connect with a three-year-old. If we ever had a kid, motherhood would suit her.

I didn't know where the sudden thought had come from, but now that it had, I could envision a future with her and a bunch of little Silvers running around in our backyard.

"Penny for your thoughts," she asked, sitting across from me. "Foxy finally fell asleep."

She pointed to Foxy on the seat where he was sleeping, covered with a blanket and a stuffed bear underneath his arm.

"I was thinking about how good you are with him."

"He's a happy kid. It's nice to see the world's problems haven't touched him." Her face beamed with love.

"Laura's a wonderful mom. You'd be a good mom, too."

Her eyes softened and crinkled with a smile. "Possibly. Would you want kids, Julian? With me?"

I hadn't seen hope on her face in weeks.

"There's no one else I imagine my life with, Kay, so my answer is possibly, as long as you're ready and well."

She rolled her lips to contain a smile. "I'm glad we're on the same page."

"Me too. We should get some sleep. The time change will kick our asses."

"Shh." She pressed her finger to her lips. "No swearing."

"Sorry."

She covered herself with a blanket, but opened her eyes as soon as I lowered the cabin lights.

"Julian? You think Sam will be happy I'm coming? Maybe we should have told her?"

"She wouldn't have asked you to be her maid of honor if she wasn't happy, Kay."

"I look like a stick figure."

"You've gained fifty percent of what you've lost. That's progress, Kay and you look beautiful. The entire family can't wait to see you."

"Okay." She closed her eyes.

I WAITED until she dozed off, adjusted her slipping blanket, and stretched out my legs.

Eight hours later, we were standing at Sam and Gabe's front door. I pushed it open and screamed out, "Surprise!"

Emma jumped up to her feet, getting everyone's attention as Foxy ran past me and into his grandmother's arms, then to the twelve-foot Christmas tree in the foyer. James stared at Laura from beyond the second floor railing. His expression totally matched the icy winter wonderland theme.

Kendra and Sam spotted one another and ran into each other's arms, crying. Kendra sobbed softly, and Sam comforted her. Sam drew Kay's attention to her growing belly. After a few tears and many hugs, Kay settled in with Allie and Sam, and I met up with my brother and cousins by the fireplace.

I swirled the iced whiskey in my glass.

"So, you're ready to get married?" I asked Gabe.

"There's not a doubt in my mind. What's happening with Kay's case?"

"The Wagner brothers are closing in on all the Hartleys and Donaldson."

"And Simone's still a fucking psycho," Tristan blurted.

"We'll get her too, and once everyone's behind bars, Kendra will be free. You ready to be the best man, James?"

"I'm not the one saying 'I do,' am I?"

"Maybe you should be. Laura's an exceptional woman. Don't fuck it up."

"I never said she wasn't. And I won't. But we have some shit to work through first." James took a long sip and cleared his throat. "But who doesn't, right?"

"Cheers." We lifted our glasses high and clinked them together. There was nothing better than the feeling of family closeness at Christmas.

The winter wonderland wedding was beautiful. Aunt Teresa cried, and so did Sam's mother. Kendra kept her soft-as-silk gaze on the couple, and I imagined her there in Sam's place and me in Gabe's, and I could see it. I could see myself marrying Kendra and placing the ring I was carrying in my suitcase on her finger.

Sam and Gabe left for their honeymoon the day after their vows. The rest of us went skiing, soaked in the hot tub, and swam in the heated pool at night. As days passed, the smile on Kendra's face grew wider. Christmas Eve at Gabe and Sam's chalet, with our closest family and friends, brought back feelings of nostalgia. Days of games, hot chocolate, and snowball fights passed quickly. Every time I looked at Kendra, it was like looking at a new woman—a woman I'd missed and wanted more every day. Her bellowing laughter cruised down my spine. Her skin-tight leggings and breast-hugging turtlenecks were driving me crazy.

Allie and Tristan's surprise wedding on New Year's Eve was the perfect excuse to steal Kendra away from the family and reignite what we once had.

We left the family in town for New Year's fireworks and returned to the house before midnight. I switched on the bedroom fireplace and lit all the candles I could find in the house. I spread rose petals on the floor in a path leading to the bed, and scattered more over the sheets. My heart pattered in a nervous rhythm. I checked my tie and the chilling champagne at the bed's side. Everything was perfect for our first night together. I'd organized the evening without expectation, but if my instinct was right, Kay was ready. My left shoelace came undone, and I knelt on the floor to tie it up when she walked into the bedroom.

"Julian? Are you here?" She stopped two feet in, visibly inhaling.

I finished the knot, and my head flew up. She covered her mouth with her hand and whispered, "What is this?"

I took in the situation of me kneeling on one knee, in a candlelit room littered with red roses.

No, no, no. She wasn't ready for a proposal. Neither was I. Not today.

"I…ahh…"

Her lashes flipped fully open. "Yes—the answer is yes."

I stood up. "Kay, I wasn't proposing. This isn't what you think."

Her eyes doubled in size and filled with tears. She turned on her heel and ran downstairs.

"Kay, wait."

My desperate voice echoed through the house. I reached the top of the staircase as she opened the front door and ran out.

"Kay, please stay. You misunderstood,"

She slammed the door behind her. I jumped the stairs every

third step, grabbed a jacket off a hook, and stumbled outside into the snow.

Thick flakes were drifting lazily to the ground. Kay was standing in the shelter of an enormous pine. The snowy ground reflected the moonlight, illuminating her deep footsteps. The village lights shimmered in the distance.

I removed my jacket and came up behind her, draping it over her shoulders.

"Thank you." Her breath puffed white from between her beautiful lips. How had this night gone so wrong, and more importantly, how could I turn it around? I gave the sides of her arms a gentle squeeze and pivoted her to face me.

"I'm sorry about upstairs. I didn't mean to upset you. Come inside. Let's talk about it."

She shook her head in a swift arc. "I don't want to talk about anything. I'm tired of talking. I'm ready to feel, and when I try to feel, I… I don't know whether I'm feeling the right things because you were on your knee—"

"Tying a shoelace when you walked in," I explained.

Her eyes flashed wide open. "A shoelace?"

"Yeah. And these tie-on shoes aren't winter friendly, so we should get back inside."

She lifted her hands to her face and covered her eyes. "Argh… I'm such a fool."

"That's a far stretch, Kay. Besides, you're not the only one who's been having thoughts of marriage. It's crossed my mind as well."

"It has?"

"A lot."

Her mouth pulled into a slow smile. I gripped her by the hips and brought her closer.

"Just because I didn't plan a proposal tonight doesn't mean I don't want one in the future." She anchored her gaze to mine.

"But for tonight, I hoped to reconnect physically. Hence the candles and roses."

"I stand firm: I'm a fool."

"If that's so, then you're *my* fool. But honestly, the only fool here is me, because I'm so madly in love with you, it hurts." I brought my fist to my chest. "I will never let you go, Kay. I've got you."

She stepped back and lowered her head. "You still want me? After…after what Hartley and his goons did to me?"

Her whispered words were like a stab into the middle of my heart. I cupped her face between both of my hands and slowly brought her mouth to my lips, settling them there. I held the connection until her body's heat blended into my skin. Her inhibitions slipped away as her hands drew along my waistline and up my back, her touch stirring my senses. But what if she wasn't ready? I pulled away from her mouth.

"Do you want to make snow angels?" I asked.

"No." She chuckled.

"What do you want to do?"

Her chest rose and fell with heavy breaths. She sucked her lower lip between her teeth, gripped the shirt on my chest with her fists, and nudged me with her gaze. "I want to make love to you. I need you, Julian, and I want you. I want all of you, but…"

She swallowed the nerves and met my questioning look. "But I'm not sure if you want me."

My brows furrowed, and I tilted my head sideways.

"What I'm saying is that I want you to touch me. But you're asking me to make snow angels? So I'm confused."

"You want me to touch you?" I asked.

"I do. Badly." She met my gaze directly, desire swimming in her eyes.

"Then I don't know why we're standing out in the cold."

I lifted her into my arms, and she squealed. She wound her legs around my waist and held onto my neck, pressing her mouth hard to mine. Linked to her lips, I carried her back home. I set her down, peeled off her jacket, and her body immediately glued back to mine. Her hands searched over my chest, pulling on the last strings of my control.

"Slow down, baby," I said against her lips. "We have time."

She yanked the shirt out of my pants, loosened the tie around my neck, and fumbled with the buttons, her icy fingers quivering. She gave up on the shirt and unfastened my buckle and zipper. The fabric around my hips loosened, and I seized her mouth with a crushing kiss. Her sweet taste sailed through me on the winds of lust.

The sound of her white jeans popping open echoed in my ears. We pulled away, breathing hard. Her soft eyes held mine. Seconds ticked by, and I couldn't stop looking at her until she allowed a crinkle of a smile.

"Penny for your thoughts," she whispered.

"I'm sure you know exactly what I'm thinking."

I stole a quick kiss and stepped out of my slacks. Her cute snicker as she lowered her pants left a tightening sensation in my balls. She stood in front of me, her long turtleneck draping over her naked legs and her nipples poking through the fabric. She was the most beautiful thing I'd ever seen in my life.

I stepped on the front of my sock with one foot and pulled it off, then the other. Kendra lowered her nude panties, her long turtleneck hiding the heat between her legs. We moved across the foyer toward the staircase, leaving a meandering path of clothing in the hall.

She licked her lips and skewered me with her ardent gaze. My blood rushed south, and I backed into the staircase. We both looked at the bottom step, and I arched my brows.

"I believe this has been on our bucket list for a while," I said.

Her pearly teeth showed as she grinned. She gripped my shirt with her hands and tore it open. The three buttons she'd left fastened tore off and scattered over the hardwood floor. God, how I'd missed her!

I peeled off her turtleneck and lowered my mouth to hers, swallowing her whimper. She surrendered her lips to my mouth, and I captured her breath. Her tiny body bent underneath mine. I gripped her sides, pleased she had more meat on her bones. As her hands spread fire over my chest, I skimmed down her beautiful curves. I flicked open her bra clasp and pulled away.

Her breasts spilled out, her erect nipples tinted with a lustful shade.

Puffs of air fluttered through her nostrils. Her swollen lips parted, her rosy cheeks reddened, and her brown eyes widened with vulnerability.

She slid her palm up my chest to my neck, drawing me closer. Her body pressed to mine, her soft curves bending underneath my muscles. I snapped out of my daze at her faint yelp and lowered my lips to her jawline. I scattered kisses from there to her neck. She tilted her head back, and the swell of her breasts rose. I cupped her full breast and licked around the other sensitive nipple, tugging it away from her chest. It slipped from my mouth and bounced back.

She squirmed in my hold, forcing my erection hard against her stomach. Her hands took hold of my boxer briefs and she lowered them, agonizingly slowly, her breath coasting over my abs and dick. I was ready to blow right there.

"Sit." I pointed to the third step.

Her crooked smile stopped my heart as she sat on the step and leaned back on her elbows. She spread her legs wide open, showing off her glistening pussy.

I stepped forward, bent to my knees, and reached between her thighs. I skimmed my fingers over her heat, and she quivered. She pulled my weight to her body and my mouth to hers as I slid two fingers inside.

"I need you inside me." Her needy trembles matched her erratic breaths, swollen lips, and hooded eyes. I pulled away and brushed my cock down between her folds and over her soaked opening. Her mouth parted.

"Turn around, Kay."

She switched her position on the staircase, anchoring her ass high in the air. I sucked in a stuttered breath, gripped my cock, and aligned myself behind her. Her look of approval over her shoulder was all I needed to plunge deep into her tight pussy.

"Ahh!"

She braced her arms on the stairs and tilted her ass. I thrust again, hitting her depth, my dick snug inside her warmth. I splayed my hands over her tiny ass, squeezing the flesh while rolling my hips back and forth. She tightened around every inch of my cock.

"Fuck." I blew out my cheeks, keeping her steady, but lost my focus to her pleasurable moans. She sang to my arousal like a mermaid. Her body swayed to my advance as I drove harder and deeper. Drenched in sweat, I drew my hand underneath her and circled my fingers over her swollen clit.

She tensed at the first touch, then pushed against my rubbing fingers. Fireworks blew in the distance, joining the loud echo of our slapping bodies. Her whimpers drove me crazy until she lost control and came in my hand with my dick still inside her.

I counted her monthly cycle days in my head and kept coming up with a number, which told me she was ovulating. Then again, she suffered physical and emotional trauma. No amount of counting could help me. The thought somehow fucking made it that much more difficult to pull back. I wanted little Silvers running on the backyard lawn. The feel of her pulsing flesh in my palm, as her orgasm settled, pushed me over the edge. I emptied myself inside her, losing my mind and losing count.

I withdrew and lifted her off the stairs, but we both fell back to the staircase, laughing. I brought her body to mine and held her in a twisted and uncomfortable position on the steps, but it was the best feeling in the world. She was hot, flustered, beautiful, and finally mine again.

The fireworks lit the sky outside. We watched them through the window for the next five minutes as they detonated far in the distance.

"We should tidy up the clothes and go upstairs before the family returns." I kissed the top of her head.

"It's New Years." She brushed her fingers over my thigh. "I doubt they'll be back too soon."

She was right. It was the New Year, and we'd certainly started with a bang.

Chapter 30

Kendra

I turned up the television volume and plopped on the couch beside Julian. The announcement scrolling across the bottom of the screen was like an early Christmas gift.

"After a long delay, the district attorney's office has taken into custody this morning the Hartley brothers. The sex trafficking and corruption allegations have been growing against the Hartley family for years. Both parties have declined to comment on the case. Leaked information received by the network about the parties responsible for Jeff Hartley's death has been sent for confirmation."

I opened the window. Spring air blew through the house, and spring birds chirped outside.

"Does that mean it's over?" I asked him.

"No, baby. But it means we're one step closer to having your case dismissed. We still have Simone to worry about. Hartley's daughter is traumatizing Allie."

"Why is that bitch still alive?"

"We're working on an arrest, which is exactly what I need to talk to you about."

He turned sideways and bit his lip. Julian never bit his lip.

I squeezed his hand. "What's the matter?"

"We're luring Simone to the casino during Allie's bachelorette party, and you may see her."

My throat lurched with a hard swallow. "I'm not afraid of Simone."

"I fear seeing her may bring back your trauma. She knew what her father did—"

"I won't let that man control my life, Julian. He's dead. Case closed."

"Not your case."

"Because Donaldson is alive? Yeah, I know." I rolled my eyes.

"We believe Simone may use Dave Wright's body double to get to Allie."

"But he's dead."

"It's not enough to stop Simone's tortures. This guy held evidence against Donaldson to clear your name."

He scrolled through his phone and showed me a picture of a scummy man. I'd overheard Tristan telling Julian about how the guy had raped Allie's mother, causing her to miscarry.

"So, if I remember what I did, there's no evidence to back me up?"

"Donaldson will be jailed before that happens."

I hoped he was right and gulped down a steadying breath. I squeezed his hand with more reassurance. It was more so for me than him. The rapid-fire heartbeats tore through my chest as I wished I could help more.

"I need to remember what I did and why my parents ran."

"What?"

"Why don't you tell me?" My eyes were stationed on him.

"I'm not messing with hypnosis, and I'm not sure I want to call Stefanie. But if you'd really like me to—"

"Julian, I don't want to see any woman you've fucked ever again."

The lie burned in my throat, as I'd already made plans to see Stefanie today. I had to take control of my life. I wanted to be me again so I could laugh and cry for all the right reasons. I needed to return to my club, Kissed, and thrive.

"You're right. I'm sorry. So, are you okay with Simone at the casino?"

"I'm not missing Allie's bachelorette party. She saved my life. And she's family."

His teeth flashed white. "All right. I have a good feeling about this. We leave at six."

I checked my watch and jumped to my feet. "And my hair appointment at Grace's is in an hour. I've gotta go."

Truth is, my appointment was in a couple of hours, but I'd called Stefanie ahead of time and asked her to meet me for a coffee near Grace's.

An hour later, she walked through the café door. Her Louboutin heels clicked on the floor. The pasted smile on her bright red lips kept me on guard. She set two coffee orders on the table and removed her sunglasses. "You like a latte, if I remember correctly?"

"Yes, thank you." I reached for the cup marked with my name and she took a seat across the table. "Thank you for agreeing to see me."

"I can't say I expected the call. If you're worried about Julian, don't be. I'm seeing someone new, and it's serious. We're engaged." She wiggled her ring finger with an emerald-cut diamond. It was the biggest jewel I'd seen in my life.

"Congratulations, but this isn't about Julian. It's about reversing my hypnosis."

She pulled her hand back, sipped on her coffee, and after a long dramatic pause, gave me a resigned stare.

"I'm sorry, but I can't help you."

"Why not?" I perked up in my seat.

"We fucked the same guy. It feels weird to be your therapist."

I leaned in over the table. "But you hypnotized me."

"Your hypnosis should have waned long ago. I set many triggers and none of them helped; which means it's you who's suppressing the past."

I sat back. "What does that mean?"

"You're the only one who can stimulate your memories."

"How?"

"Has anything ever clicked? Like, have you ever closed your eyes and seen moments from your life you didn't think you remembered?"

Like splattered brain and blood? Like the one where I was holding a gun and standing over a dead body?

"Yes." My voice came out raspy. "But how do I remember more? How do I remember in sequence and…everything?"

"Think back to when the memories came. What were you doing?"

Shooting.

I sat at that table like a statue and didn't hear another word she said. I think she talked about her fiancé, an oil tycoon, but she left without me truly noticing. I took my cold coffee and arrived at Grace's five minutes late. As she did my hair and makeup, Grace gossiped with her friends about Hunter, Julian's younger cousin. A mutual prank went wrong, and Grace proclaimed she'd never fall for a younger man again. Trouble was, she had no clue she still loved him.

My trouble was, I was more sure every day that I was a murderer.

THE CASINO FLOOR buzzed with chatter, laughter, and beeping slot machines. I sat at the roulette table beside Laura and joined her obnoxious cheer. What could I say? The woman's enthusiasm was contagious, and it had been a long time since I'd enjoyed an evening out. Allie was standing at the side of the table with her large pregnant belly, and we watched the ball roll around the roulette wheel. Laura was on a hot streak, and the stack of chips in front of her grew taller with each spin. I couldn't stop cheering, but with the constant drink in my hand, my bladder filled fast. I didn't want to miss a minute of tonight, especially since Laura had promised we'd continue the party after they cuffed Simone.

Finally Allie gave me a knowing nod that Simone had arrived, and I hopped off the stool.

"And this is where my adventure ends. I'm out, and I need to use the washroom."

I hugged them both and made a beeline for the bathroom.

I locked the stall door and had just squatted when a woman passed a piece of paper underneath the stall wall.

"This is for you."

I automatically took the note from her hand. The adjacent door opened, and I heard her footsteps rushing out of the bathroom. I opened the paper mid-squat and nearly peed myself reading the chicken-scratched warning: *We're coming for you.*

I dropped the paper to the floor, wiped myself, forgot to wash my hands, and stumbled out of the bathroom and into Julian's hard chest.

"What happened to you? You were supposed to meet me by the cashiers."

I stared off into the distance.

"Kay? What's the matter?"

"Bathroom. Paper." My finger shook as I pointed behind me.

Time passed at lightning speed, sounds blurred, and the surrounding haze didn't lift until that night when I overheard Julian talking to his cousin, James.

"The woman said someone gave her a picture of Kendra along with a thousand bucks ahead of the deal. All she had to do was give the note to Kay. The woman doesn't know who it was."

Wonderful.

"And all cameras have been checked?"

"Her story pans out."

I didn't sleep that night, nor the night after, but on my third morning, I dressed in a camo outfit and went out to the storage box by the tree line where Julian kept the rifles. I opened the box, added the silencer, loaded the Glock, and emptied the magazine, one bullet after another.

Nothing came to mind.

I put the gun back inside the chest and locked it, but returned the next morning to try the rifle. This time, as I shot, oozing blood flashed behind my eyelids.

"It's working." My heart kicked up its heels.

The sporadic memories jumped between the train accident, which I'd thought took my parent's lives, and a dead man. I knew I'd killed him, but I had no idea who it was nor why. My daily shooting ritual must have caught Julian's attention because three weeks later on a foggy morning, amusement danced in his eyes.

"What are you so happy about?" I asked.

"I have a surprise for you in the gun chest. Let me know what you think."

My brow lifted into a slow arch. "You want to come and shoot with me?"

"So I can witness the level of my inaccuracy? No, thank you. Besides, I promised Tristan to go fishing."

"Since when do you fish?"

"Allie insisted Tristan take a break before the twins arrive, but I'll see you later for breakfast?"

"Sounds perfect." I stepped up on my toes and left a lingering smooch.

I crossed the yard to the tree line and unlocked the coded box. My mouth opened wide when I saw the new long-range biathlon rifle with an extra guide and suppressor. I didn't know how I knew this stuff, but so far, I'd named every single firearm Julian surprised me with. The flashbacks of brain matter and spilling blood returned every morning when I shot, but brought me no closer to answers about my crime. I strapped the rifle over my shoulder and crossed our yard to Wilma and Fred's. I jumped over the meandering stream of water in the ditch and found a hill between the willow trees. Morning fog hovered further out in the ocean, dissipating at its lazy pace. Julian and Tristan were sitting in their camping chairs on Tristan's dock with steaming coffee cups. I'd never seen the brothers fish before, but there they were: fishing. Julian set his mug on the dock and walked to the ledge. Tristan joined him there. I drew my lower lip in between my teeth and was aiming the rifle at the mug, hoping to startle them, when a delicious batter aroma wafted from Allie's kitchen window. I focused through the lens to where she was standing by the patio door, bracing a bowl against her eight-month belly. She was mixing what I assumed was a second batch of waffle batter.

Allie disappeared from the kitchen view and I shifted my focus back to the steaming cup of coffee. I let out a snicker when just then the smell of burning batter quickly drew my attention back to Allie's house. She stood frozen, with her mouth open. A man came into view, and I pulled in a sharp breath.

That's impossible.

I drew my hand across my eyes and cleared the sweat. A chilling breeze carried the burned scent my way; the brothers were unaware of Allie's danger. I checked through the lens again and knew my eyes weren't deceiving me. Wright stood behind Allie with a gun pointed against her belly. Puffing smoke drifted from the window and blew south. I let out the shaky breath and inhaled courage, setting my finger on the trigger. I steadied the rifle over a branch for support. Allie braced her arms on the counter as he pinned her and lowered his pants to his knees.

I held back the hurl and turned on the laser light, focusing on his temple. He jutted the gun against her belly again. It took me three seconds longer to assess the situation because the past flashed in my mind: my teacher, Peter Donaldson, trying to take advantage of me. I zoned back into the present and zoomed in on the target, waiting for Wright to lower his gun. Allie stepped out of view and moved closer to the kitchen window.

Steady... nice and easy. I regulated my breathing, and let out a slow swoosh of air.

"I've got you, Allie," I pulled the trigger just as Tristan yelled out from the shore.

"Kendra, no!"

The patio glass shattered, and Allie screamed.

I looped the rifle over my shoulder and sped toward the house. I hopped the five steps up to the deck and stopped just outside the door. Allie was sobbing from somewhere inside, but she was safe. The brain matter splattered over the white floors confirmed it.

I had just killed Wright.

My stomach twisted, and the world spun around me. Old memories flashed in my mind: the school, Donaldson's blood, and my hands on the gun that killed him. My fingers wrapped tightly around the handle. I sat back against the railing at the same time Julian and Tristan caught up.

Julian crouched beside me and removed the rifle from my grip. "You're all right, Kay. You're all right." I got lost in his arms. "Don't look that way. Will you be okay by yourself for a moment?"

"Yes," I whispered.

"I'm just gonna check on Allie, and I'll be right back. Don't move."

During the few seconds Julian was gone, I lived through both murders all over again.

"Allie's all right. She's safe. God, Kay, we thought you were aiming at Allie."

My gaze rose to meet his. "Why would I aim at Allie?"

"I don't know. I'm sorry. How did you know she was in danger?"

"I saw him through my rifle lens. He had a gun pointed at her belly. You said he was dead."

"We were wrong."

He planted his hands on his hips and stepped from one foot to another. My chest compressed, and I lowered my head between my knees, counting to ten, desperate to find my anchor.

"Are you all right?"

"He was gonna rape her." Air left my nostrils in rapid jets.

The bloody memory returned to my mind, and I clenched my hands. I remembered my life—or Katherine's life—and all the trouble that came along with it.

"Julian, call the ambulance. Allie's water just broke!" Tristan yelled from inside.

Julian reached into his pocket and dialed the number. Time passed in a haze. I sat back against the patio railing, with my knees curled underneath me. Julian draped a sweatshirt over my shoulders and went to speak with a police officer. The surrounding commotion blended into a low hum. The ambulance took Allie to the hospital, and a swarm of agents and detectives began their work. I kept repeating my story of what had happened until Julian stepped in.

"I think that's enough for today." The detective gave him a nod and left. "Let's get you home, Kay."

"The place is a mess. I should clean it up."

"I'll take care of the cleanup. We're going home." His eyes darted from me to the house.

"Julian, I just killed someone. Why aren't they arresting me?"

He crouched in front of me and took my hands in his. "You killed a man on the FBI's most wanted list, Kay. A man who attempted to rape and kill my sister-in-law."

I cleared the thickening lump my throat. "But that's not who I'm talking about."

"Kay—"

"Mr. Silver?" one worker called out. "What do you want us to do with the cabinets?"

He looked back over his shoulder. "Replace them."

"Any word from Allie?" I asked.

"She's in active labor. Tristan's with her."

He tightened his hold around my arm. "You did amazing today, Kay. You saved Allie's life and the baby's. If it weren't for you… I can't even fathom the thought."

I shut my eyes and saw Allie in a casket with her swollen tummy. Julian was right: the thought was unfathomable. My stomach flipped upside-down and I jumped to my feet, bending over the patio railing. My muscles tensed, and I threw up. Julian gently caressed my back. "Let's go home, Kay."

With Julian's support, we slowly treaded across the green lawn, leaving the chaos, along with a cleaning crew, behind us. My life flashed through my mind as I lay in my bed that night. The chase had exhausted me, and I didn't want to run any longer. I wanted to live, and the only way to get over my past was to face my crimes.

The day I killed my teacher, Peter Donaldson, was clearer in my mind than ever. I'd gone back to my physics class before the end of school, but hadn't expected one of my classmates to be standing with a gun pointed at Mr. Donaldson.

I stopped in the doorway. "Olivia? What are you doing?"

Mr. Donaldson and Olivia turned their heads my way. She kept her aim steady on the teacher.

"I will not let this asshole touch another girl again."

Her words hit me hard in the chest as I realized I wasn't the only one who'd caught my teacher's interest. Despite Peter Donaldson's horrid school reputation, the board allowed him to teach. Girls accused him of inappropriate behavior, but the administration did nothing. I should have stopped him.

"Put the gun down, Olivia," he said.

I stepped further inside the classroom and reached out. "Olivia? Give me the gun."

"You don't know what he's done."

"I do know what he's done, Olivia. You're not alone in this, and killing solves nothing," I whispered.

"It will stop him from hurting anyone else," she said.

"Lower the gun. My parents will make sure this bastard ends up behind bars."

"How?"

"They make sure people like him go behind bars. They can help. I promise."

"Listen to Katherine, Olivia."

"Shut the fuck up." She wiggled the gun at Donaldson, and he lifted his arms in the air again. "Don't you get it? He won't go to jail. His brother's a scummy Congressman who's kept this asshole's ass protected. Do you know how many girls he's raped?"

I didn't know, but one rape was one too many. I stepped further into the classroom and shook my head. "You're right. I don't know, but I know this isn't the way. You have your whole life ahead of you, Olivia. Don't let him ruin that, too."

I inched forward with every word until I was standing in

front of her. Donaldson kept his hands in the air until she lowered the gun. I slowly removed the weapon from her hand.

"Give me that!"

He grabbed me from behind, reaching for the gun in my hand, but Olivia jumped in between us. The three of us struggled over the weapon. It went off twice. The first shot burst through Olivia's belly and the second one hit Donaldson's brain. They were both dead.

I ran home that afternoon faster than I'd ever run before.

THE CLOCK TURNED to four in the morning. Julian was lying peacefully beside me. I slipped out of bed, dressed, and snuck out of the house. Fifteen minutes later, I sat on the small bench in front of my parent's graves.

"Hi, Mom. Hi, Dad."

I laced my fingers together and whispered, "You were trying to protect me. I get that now."

No one replied. I wasn't sure why I wished they did. "I'm sorry I dragged you into this mess." I lowered my head. "But I'm tired of running and hiding. I'm going to do this the right way."

Morning fog hovered above the graveyard, holding the powerful smell of earth, mold, and moisture. I rubbed my wrists where the memory of ropes still burned to build courage, but cold chills scattered over my body.

I sat at the cemetery for another fifteen minutes, then drove to the police station and turned myself in for murder.

Chapter 31

Julian

Allie gave birth to the twins, and Kendra made bail. Tristan recovered evidence of the Congressman's crimes. Although Donaldson was stuck in jail, Kay's case rested in the intricately prepared statement by the Wagner team. But as prepared as we were, her future would be determined by the judge.

We sat in the courtroom with a team of lawyers, waiting for the judge. Kendra turned around in her seat, fear clouding her eyes.

"Wright could have testified in my defense?"

"Peter Donaldson was a friend of his. Donaldson bragged about his conquests, and Wright agreed to testify for leniency."

"Are you mad at me for going to the police?"

"No, baby. I'm not. You reached a breaking point. I get it."

"I don't want to go to jail," she blurted. "If I go back to a cold cell… If they cuff me… I'm not feeling well, Julian."

Her eyes welled and her face turned ashen. I passed her the tissue I had ready.

"It was self-defense, Kay. The only place you're going from here is home. I promise."

"Congressman Donaldson still has pull in the courts."

"And you have a team of the best lawyers in the country working on your side. The Wagners have never lost a case."

"I hope you're right." She hunched her shoulders up.

I prayed I was right.

"Will the people in the courtroom please stand? The Honorable Judge Mila Curtis."

"Oh, my God."

I tapped on Kendra's shoulder, and she turned around, her eyes snapping open. They lit with a burst of hope.

"You know her?"

Kendra's cheeks sank in.

"Shh," Scar threw me a dirty look.

Judge Curtis walked up behind the judge's bench. "Please resume your seats."

I sat on the bench as the judge's gaze locked onto Kendra's. She lowered her glasses, set them back on her nose, and flipped through the papers.

"Kendra?" she said out loud and checked the papers in front of her again. "I have a Katherine Moore here."

Kendra lifted her hand. "That's me."

"Approach the bench."

Scar stood up.

"The defendant only," the judge said.

Kendra pushed back her chair and walked to the judge. The two of them whispered for a couple of minutes before Kendra turned on her heel and walked back to her seat. Her stone face told me nothing. My throat lurched with a hard swallow.

The next few minutes felt like luck raining down from the heavens. Judge Curtis dismissed the case, and Kendra was a free woman. She jumped into my arms and cried happy tears while I spun her around.

This day had started on the right foot, and I'd make sure it ended the same way. We picked up a new outfit on our way home. Kendra twirled in front of the mirror. The flowing dress clung to her figure. She fixed her plunging neckline and checked her hair. Tonight we were celebrating her freedom.

"Are you finally gonna tell me what you said to the judge?"

She spun around to face me. Her teeth shone pearly through her grin. It was so good to see the spark back in her eyes. She strolled toward me with a bounce in her step.

"I met Judge Curtis at the hospital after my father and Jace died. She was grief-stricken, and we talked for a few minutes. I told her about the poisonings, and I guess we connected. She asked me in court for details about Peter Donaldson's death. I told her what happened, and she believed me. That's the gist of it. Now, are you finally gonna tell me where we're going tonight?"

She hooked her fingers through the belt loops in my pants and brought me to her body. I kissed her luscious lips and whispered against her mouth. "I'm not ruining the surprise."

She pressed her lips to mine again, taking longer to pull away. "It's okay. Nothing will make me feel better than freedom."

While I could list at least a dozen ways to disprove her, I held back, because she was right. For now.

An hour later, I opened the passenger door and reached for Kendra's hand. The silky scarf tied around her eyes matched the shade of her dress. The aroma of New York's French fries and spices filled the air.

"We're in Manhattan?" she asked.

"Will you please just let me surprise you?" I begged.

The first wave of summer's wind blew through the crowded street as we crossed the sidewalk. I pulled open the club's front door and guided her inside. The sounds from the street dissolved as the door shut behind us. I guided her to the dance floor center and steadied her stance. "All right. We're here. Are you ready?"

She nodded, and I walked behind her, loosening the blind-fold knot. The silk scarf slid down her face.

"Surprise!" Everyone cheered, and Kendra jumped up.

"Easy, Kay. I've got you."

The staff from her Kissed nightclub lined the bar. Their classy black outfits with the logo of pink lips on the shirt fronts looked posh. Our closest family and friends huddled in front, waving pom-poms and lighting sparklers. A spanning *Welcome Back* sign hung overhead.

"I mean, *we've* got you," I whispered into her ear as Sam and Gabe stepped from behind the group. Kendra ran to her friend with open arms.

"Sam!"

The girls jumped as if they were twelve, screaming. Champagne bottles popped, and upbeat music blasted. We toasted to family, friends, and second chances before I stole Kendra into my arms.

"How're you doing?"

"I feel like I'm dreaming."

"Come to the rooftop with me."

I took her hand and turned away, concealing the smile behind my lips and the nerves in my neck. We walked up the staircase and I pushed the rooftop door open. Fairy lights twin-kled around the perimeter. Below, a warm Manhattan night hummed with excitement.

I spun Kendra in a circle to the subtle jazz playing overhead, then lowered my lips to her ear. "Let's dance together at our wedding."

She pulled back, stunned. "What?"

I stopped the spin, removed the small box from my pocket, and bent to my knee. Kendra covered her mouth with her hands. I opened the box with the cushion-cut diamond and her eyes grew wide.

"Kay, this story of our love is only beginning, and if you'd do me the honor of marrying me, I'll make sure to write our happy ending, every night and every day. Kendra Moore, will you be my wife?"

She pushed her hand forward and splayed her shaking fingers, saying the single best word I'd heard in my life.

"Yes."

I rose to my feet, lifted her into my arms, and spun her in the air.

"Set me down, set me down." She tapped on my arm.

I lowered her to the ground and steadied her stance. "What's the matter?"

"Morning sickness."

"At night?"

"Yeah, at night."

"Wait—did you just say *morning sickness?*"

The hint of a smile touched her lips.

"You're pregnant?"

Her smile doubled in size. "I believe you counted my cycle wrong." Her chin descended in a nod.

I took my fiancée into my arms, and we swayed to the romantic music. I kissed her temple, bent to her ear, and whispered, "No, baby. I believe I counted just right."

Chapter 1

Laura

I searched through the colorful rack of costumes for the perfect Halloween dinosaur outfit. Not for me. For my son. Three years ago, motherhood hadn't been near my radar, but neither was James Silver, the man who knocked me up. Three years later, with a badge on my chest and a best friend for a partner, I was rocking single parenting like Mary Poppins.

"I found it." Allie removed a furry brown onesie with a white-tipped tail. "It's perfect for Foxy."

"No more foxes. He's got a fox toothbrush, PJ, slippers, and bed sheets. It's enough. Foxy needs to get into normal things, like dinosaurs."

"Because dinosaurs are missing from his life."

That tone.

Allie's judgment carried far, but we'd gone through this before. Foxy's father could never be in his life. I dropped my arms to the sides and swiveled on my foot, facing my best friend. The stink-eye she gave me fueled an urge to rescind her godmother title.

"Your mother called—checking to see if you're alive. She hasn't heard from you in six months."

Maybe it wasn't about Foxy's father after all.

"Did you tell her I'm alive?"

"No, I told her she can find you at Evergreen Memorial. Of course I told her you're alive, and I told her Foxy's doing great too."

She wouldn't.

My throat seized. "You didn't."

"No, I didn't, but it's about time you told her she's a grandmother. Your father would be happy as well."

"Not happening. I'm not giving my son a grandmother who sends a hundred bucks for his birthday instead of hugging him. No thanks."

"Laura…" She touched my shoulder. "They say a grandmother's love is unlike any other. And since you're a mother now, you have more in common."

"You think that because your mother is great. She gives you love, and you give her…safety and tequila. All I ever gave my parents were gray hairs."

"My mother's a mess just like yours. Maybe a different kind of a mess, but still a mess. Point is, she should know. Maybe she'd surprise you."

I sighed. "I'll think about it, but that's all I can promise. Now, help me find a costume. Our morning break is almost over."

Allie scanned the remaining rack of Halloween costumes. Who was I kidding? I could never rescind her godmother title. She was the best, and she was correct. As screwed up as our family dynamics were, they were still my family, and I missed them. Except, my parents had expectations I couldn't meet. Their disappointment carried all the way from Manhattan and their home in the Hamptons. Avoiding the doctor duo was a challenge, but easier accomplished from further away.

So, I'd kept my pregnancy to myself and now thrived as a single mother. Changing things up wasn't on the calendar, and

Allie confirmed I was alive whenever she answered my mother's calls.

She picked a dinosaur costume, dangling the monstrosity in the air. "A T-Rex with plastic claws. You could poke a kid's eye out."

"Clearly, the fox one wins. It's safe, perfect, and cute." I checked my watch. "And our break is over."

I paid for the costume and threw the bag inside the cruiser. I secured my seatbelt and took a sip of my cooling latte when the dispatch call came through.

"Two armed suspects seen entering the Cameo building near Fifth and Park. All units respond."

I spat out my coffee and fumbled with the cup holder, "Allie, that's us."

My streak of welfare checks and no arrests had earned me the longest time without a bust at the precinct. The snickers behind my back were getting annoying, but today, I would prove them all wrong.

My partner reached for the receiver. "Ten-four. Unit twelve-oh-one in the vicinity responding."

We shot out of the cruiser like two rookies and ran a quarter block to the Cameo building, where we stopped at the corner and assessed the area. A businessman lit a cigarette outside the door. A couple passed a homeless man sleeping on a bench, then entered the building. We watched for clues, but there were none.

"No visible chaos," I said.

"No sign of commotion."

"Seems quiet for an armed entry."

"Maybe they're professionals."

"I'd love to cuff a pro more than I'd like to scratch that two-year-and-nine-month itch."

This was my day. I could feel it in my bones.

"You've had no sex in two years?"

"Two years and nine months. Foxy's conception was my last. This bust is better than an orange in your Christmas stocking."

She looked at me like I was crazy. "Fuck, Laura. That's bad. I bet you forgot how to orgasm."

"Nonsense. I flicked one off under the shower this morning."

"Argh, Laura. I didn't need to know that."

"Shouldn't have asked then. Let's be cautious in there."

I fixed my shoulders back, and we walked to the revolving door. Inside, business carried on as usual. A handful of office workers were waiting for the elevator, and a security guard was sitting at the information desk.

"You think it was a prank call?" I asked her.

"Or whoever ran in here is already upstairs. Let's take the stairs."

"No, wait. Look at the stiff guard."

We approached the desk, and I lowered my voice. "Sir, did you call in an armed entry?"

"Yes—third floor. He's on the third floor. Black hoodie and a patch of silver hair."

My best friend's forehead creased.

"How many exits?"

"He took the south stairwell. North is closed off for renovations."

I scanned the area. Two suits were standing by the elevator, along with a stressed woman who seemed in dire need of a vacation. More entered the front, followed by the homeless man in a black hoodie.

"Clear the area and stand at the front. Don't let anyone else inside until they're all out. Back up will be here soon," I said, and followed Allie's lead up the stairs.

We took the stairs two at a time all the way to the third floor. My chest compressed, my heart hammering and ears drumming with the sound of ticking time. Sweat dripped down my back. The nerves were new; they'd started when I returned to work after my short maternity leave, forcing me to leave my baby with Mrs. Brewers across the street. With motherhood came the additional need to survive for my son. While I was lucky to have a wonderful nanny, she was getting more kids, and Foxy was getting sick more often.

Allie grabbed my arm before I opened the stairwell door. "Laura, please be careful. My godson needs his mom home tonight."

"Fifty percent more police officers died in the line of duty this year than last." The worry coasting over her eyes turned into fearlessness, but I continued anyway. "And since we're not ready to be a statistic, you be careful as well."

She punched me playfully on my arm, and I swallowed past the lump in my throat. "This could be your first bust."

"Not if we keep standing here."

Using her body, she pushed me aside and opened the stairwell door. I followed her down the hallway. After the second turn, a man entered an office. The door shut behind him, and Allie ran forward while I stood in the middle of the hall.

The black hoodie he was wearing was the same one as the homeless man's.

"That's his partner," I said under my breath, but Allie had already burst through the office door. By the time I arrived, she had someone on the ground.

I turned on my heel and ran back to the stairwell. Downstairs, the foyer filled as security ushered everyone outside. I scanned the area, my eyes stopping on the homeless man leaning against a tree. He was watching the exits. I left through the side door and ran around the corner so I could come up behind him. The stretched hoodie over his wide shoulders was the same one as the attacker's upstairs. I removed my gun and aimed at the man's back.

"Hands up!"

His shoulders jerked as he startled.

"NYPD. Step away from the tree and put your hands up."

He lifted his hands in slow motion, palms flat to the front and stance wide.

"Hurry up."

"You've got the wrong man, officer." His deep voice stirred fuzzy memories, but I pushed past the tingling at the back of my mind. I was going to cuff this co-conspirator, no matter what.

"Don't fucking move." I stepped closer. As his arms rose, his hoodie lifted above his belt, exposing a weapon. "Is that gun behind your back registered?"

I removed the gun from behind his belt, noting his tight ass.

"You're under arrest for breaking and entering. Anything you say can and will be used against you in a court of law."

"Breaking and entering? At least make up something believable. I didn't break in."

The cuffs clicked, the final piece of my memory slotting into place.

Oh, my God. That voice.

The dread that someone wanted to complicate my life ran through my veins.

"Fox." His name slipped from my tongue.

"Laura? Laura, is that you?"

His head turned with a snap of the neck, and my body went limp. The one man I'd been avoiding for two years was now standing less than a breath away from me. And the best plan my brain could come up with was to take him to the station. If they locked him away for possession, I could kill two birds with one stone: score my bust and disappear. The plan flew through my mind like a stray bullet, until the smell of him invaded my lungs, and the bullet settled near my heart.

"Fox?" His name curled along my tongue. I hadn't spoken

his real name ever, but I certainly held it close to my heart. "I mean, James? Is that you? What the fuck?"

He stood still, as if he shared my shock.

"You're reading my mind. Uncuff me." He twisted sideways.

"I can't. I already read you your rights."

"You mean, you mumbled my rights."

"Shut up. You're under arrest. What are you doing here?" I asked him.

"If I'm under arrest, I believe I get a phone call before I answer your questions, officer."

He was right. And I already knew what he was doing here. My two-way radio confirmed that backup had arrived for Allie. She was getting a ride with a colleague.

"Looks like we're ready to go."

"Laura, take off the cuffs. I'm not the guy you're looking for."

"I beg to differ." He caught onto my hushed breath, and I realized my mistake. The spark in his eyes lit my blood on fire, and I swallowed to clear the rushing heat. It didn't work. I doubted anything would work when his smoldering eyes did their magic. Although the crazy morning we'd spent in Colorado seemed long ago, every minute had stayed fresh in my mind.

"If you run the number on the gun, it's registered to Fox Silver. Take the damn cuffs off, Laura."

His tone drew me out of my daze.

"Ninety-eight percent of criminals try to persuade an officer to remove their cuffs. That's criminal. You're under arrest, and you're coming with me to the station."

"You're making a mistake. I'll be out of the station before you fill out the paperwork."

Backup arrived for Allie, and I directed them inside before I turned back to James.

"Wonderful. Then you won't mind coming along, after all."

"I don't have time for this, Laura. I'm a busy father with obligations who's trying to catch a criminal."

His fatherhood was why I'd left without saying goodbye—and the woman who'd interrupted our stay with her pregnant belly. I wasn't about to compete with the mother of his child, and I wouldn't let my son be second, either. My only other choice was disappearing.

"Laura? Are you even listening to me? There's somewhere I need to be, and if I don't leave right now, I'll miss the appointment."

"All right. We can leave right now. In my cruiser."

"Oh, great. I would really appreciate a ride—"

"I meant *you* in the back of my cruiser."

"You're really gonna do this?" He closed his eyes and took in a calming breath.

A pinch of regret loomed in my chest. "I'm just doing my job."

"Your job?' Anger flamed in his bright eyes. "For fuck's sake, Laura. You were a nutcracker three years ago."

Fury steamed out of my ears.

"Well, then, I guess this nutcracker just got her bust."

I opened the back door and pushed against his heavy body, but he resisted, turning my way. The corner of his mouth lifted, and a dimple sank into his cheek.

Damn.

"Will you not embarrass me and let me ride shotgun?"

My heart hammered in my chest, constricting my lungs. A tingling sensation scattered over my skin, reacting to his dangerously sexy tone.

"Rules are rules, Mr. Silver. Suspects ride from the back. I mean, in the back."

Fuck, neither one sounded innocent.

He smirked.

"Get in." I gripped his bulging arm and nudged his mass of

muscles inside. Jesus, was he ever strong. I gathered my wits and pulled away from the curb.

"So, what happened to you in Colorado?" he asked.

A better question was, why was the sky blue and his girlfriend pregnant? Why did he seduce me when he had a family, and why did I let him?

Play dumb.

"What do you mean, what happened in Colorado?"

I pushed on the gas, throwing him against the back seat. He groaned, and I checked the rearview mirror as he sat closer to the partition between us.

"I mean, why did you leave?" The deep tone rumbled through his chest, and a memory of his beautiful torso flashed through my mind. I cranked the window open for some air.

"There was an avalanche. The mountains got dangerous, and…" I stopped along with the car, waiting for the pedestrians to pass. "And I went to see my sick friend."

I started rolling again.

"And you didn't call?"

I pushed on the brake, and his face pressed against the wired divider. At this pace, we'd never get to the station, but I wasn't about to explain how I despised love triangles and players.

"Look, I had a good time in Colorado, but as you can see, I'm more than a nutcracker now."

"Right—you're a cop who's busting a guy for nothing. Significant improvement."

Was that sarcasm in his voice? I checked the rearview mirror as he rolled his eyes.

"You know nothing about me, Silver. I'm great at my job."

Eighty percent of relationships started with lies; except we had no relationship. I had been good at my job until Mrs. Brewers took another child to babysit. Foxy caught one bug after another, forcing me to cut back on my hours.

"You're definitely great at running," he mumbled and sat back in his seat. I was not about to get into this with him while on the job. Any woman in my shoes would have done the same. I said nothing else until we arrived at the precinct and I put him in a room for booking. I had just signed off on the paperwork when Sargent Dwight called me over to his desk.

"The gun is registered. Mr. Silver's lawyer says you should have checked before booking him for possession."

"He got a lawyer?"

"The Silvers always lawyer up. You would have known that if you followed protocol, which you didn't. I don't want to demote you, Young, but—"

"Demote me? Sir, I know I've been off my game the past couple of months, but I can do my job."

He loosened the tie around his neck.

"You're a good cop, Laura, and I need you here, but you will need to apologize to Mr. Silver."

"So he's walking?"

"Your bust is a no-bust. What do you want me to hold him on?"

Good genes, bright blue eyes, and a body to die for? I shrugged instead.

"I haven't seen you slip like this before. Is something going on at home?"

Did three stacks of laundry, a sink full of dishes, and a sick two-year-old count?

"Foxy's puking again. He's getting all kinds of germs when Mrs. Brewers brings on new kids, so I'm looking for a new sitter, and I'm… I'm sorry about the gun. I won't slip again, sir."

"All right. Go pay your dues and make sure the lawyers are off our back."

"Yes, sir."

I turned and saw him standing by the main desk. He was leaning forward, resting his elbow on the counter, charming the secretary. The overgrown beard was new, but it matched his long lashes. If it weren't for the darker circles underneath his eyes, I'd argue he looked hotter than the night we met. His gaze lifted and caught my stare.

I fixed my shoulders back, lifted my head, mustered my confidence, and straightened my spine, taking calculated steps to the front.

"Hey," I said. "I'm sorry about the power trip. I shouldn't have arrested you."

"Don't worry. I won't press charges if you have dinner with me."

"What?"

"I thought we could catch up."

"Dinner?"

"That's what I said."

"I don't think my boyfriend would appreciate that."

"So you're not single? You're seeing someone?"

"Yes."

Sometimes my lies came out so beautifully. How could I deny the talent? Besides, didn't he have a family to worry about?

The disappointment in his eyes stopped my next breath. I didn't expect the sudden clench around my heart, either. The precinct door opened, and I thanked the lord for some air.

We turned to the entry at the same time. A blonde bombshell was pacing down the hall like it was a catwalk.

It was her. The woman from Colorado.

Her long, flowing dress clung to her delicate curves, and her hair fluttered in the draft. Her earrings matched the diamond tips in her long nails, and her purse matched her shoes. I rarely noticed such details, but it was hard not to notice hers.

"There you are, Fox. I can't believe they impounded your Bentley. We're running late, and I have the car running. I'm going to sue whoever is responsible for this."

That would be me. Normally, I didn't stoop to begging, but I would if it meant I'd keep this job.

She hooked her arm underneath his, but he peeled her clingy fingers off one by one. What was her name again?

"Thanks for coming, Tiffany."

Right. Tiffany.

"Ms. Tiffany, I'm sorry for keeping Mr. Silver so long—"

"You're the one who did this?" She eyed my badge. "Officer Young?"

"Yes," I turned to James. I'd rather swallow my pride here than have Tiffany sue me. "I should have never arrested you. I'm sorry."

His chin lifted, and he winked. "My offer stands, Officer Young. We have a lot to talk about. Have dinner with me."

Tiffany took hold of his hand and pulled him toward the door. "Come on, Fox. We don't want to be late."

He stopped, retreated a few steps, and pointed with his finger like he was giving a lecture. "The gun is not the only thing you were wrong about, Laura."

Sergeant Dwight came up from behind me. "I left my wife's homemade cough drops on your desk. I hope your little boy feels better soon, Laura."

My lashes flipped fully open while James's eyes tightened at the corners.

"Ahem, thank you. I've got to go."

I darted to the back room and waited until James Silver, aka Fox Silver, aka my son's secret father, had left with his baby mama.

☙

Silver Fox, Book 6 in the *Silver Brothers Securities Family Saga*, should be read after *Silver Santa*.

Silver
SANTA
USA TODAY BESTSELLING AUTHOR
LACEY SILKS

Silver
FOX
USA TODAY BESTSELLING AUTHOR
LACEY SILKS

ALSO BY LACEY SILKS

Silver Brothers Securities

Silver Santa

Silver's Rebel

Silver's Pawn

Silver's Secret

Silver's Trouble

Silver Fox

Silver Hunter

Dirty Deeds Series

Dirty Cowboy

Dirty Mechanic

Dirty Con

Be the first to know!

Visit www.laceysilks.com

ABOUT THE AUTHOR

USA Today Bestselling Author Lacey Silks crafts riveting romantic suspense filled with heat, spice, and pulse-pounding tension. Many of her endearing characters are inspired by her own life, and her loved ones often find themselves playfully woven into her tales. Her two children and her dog, Kygo, keep her days lively with homework queries and affectionate slobbery kisses (courtesy of Kygo, of course).

Outside of penning intense love stories, Lacey is an avid camper and skier. Naturally an early riser, she often finds herself reaching for coffee over water, crediting her billionaire heroes for her packed schedule.

Lacey's characters, replete with flaws and quirks, evoke laughter, sass, and emotion on every page. She cheekily measures men by their foot size, has a penchant for sultry lingerie, and harbors dreams of exploring the nation in a motorhome.

ACKNOWLEDGMENTS

Writing Silver's Trouble was a challenge. I wrote this book during deep grief and I would not have been able to complete the work if my best friend's last words didn't ring true: "Don't waste the time crying. Life is too short and you have to keep going." So I did. And he was right. Writing about love and sex and heartwarming moments helped with the grief.

I couldn't have done the work without my reader support or the ever-inspiring indie author community filled with a wealth of knowledge. The continued encouragement and faith in my work, along with the outpouring of love, replenished my muse.

To my amazing editor who always finds the time for me, thank you for making my life easy and my writing understandable.

To my beta readers, thank you for your keen eyes! Once I read a story twenty times (or more), the details aren't easy to spot. Your feedback is invaluable and makes the novel what it should be.

To my family, the past few years have tested us in more ways than we would have liked, and I could not do what I love without you. Thank you for your support, faith and encouragement.

Maya, thank you for your artistic eye and cover design. I'm honoured to watch you grow and develop as an artist. Alex, your loving heart and sense of humour are a constant inspiration.

To my parents, this book would not have happened without you. Thank you for believing in my dreams.

www.ingramcontent.com/pod-product-compliance
Lightning Source LLC
Chambersburg PA
CBHW021702220726
48290CB00020B/1542